Cibola's Revenge

Erin Lausten

Drago Fortuna Publishing

For information on permissions to reproduce selections from this book contact - ElizaDFP@gmail.com
Drago Fortuna Publishing
Phoenix

For Bryan
My Love, My Life, My Everything

Prologue

Rage and flames leapt into the sky as a mass of harlots huddled in the relative safety of the boardwalk. A burst of glass shattered from the second story window as the immense heat raked its hazardous claws through his establishment. Zhao Jin narrowed his eyes, pulled a palm-sized tin from his vest and removed a pinch of snuff. Several women screamed and jumped back into the shadows as another series of windows erupted into a shower of shards.

He snapped the tin shut and sneezed, allowing the prickly sensation to ride down his scalp and into his spine. Sliding his hand into his vest, he returned the tin to its place within the folds and beckoned his man Martin to his side.

The bulk-shouldered man lumbered toward him, ducking his head to hear his master. "I want them found."

"But Mister Zhao, we don't got no notion which direction they went."

Zhao Jin spat into the street then kicked dust across Martin's worn boots. "Then I suggest you find a notion and soon. No one takes what is mine."

The burly man fumbled for words, but when it became clear he would never find them, he turned and shuffled across the street, motioning for his compatriot to join him. They would lose time retrieving their mounts from the stables. By the time they were on the trail, the pock-marked man would be long gone with his prize. Zhao Jin must make preparations for a long campaign.

A satchel hung from his shoulder, three scrolls rolled tight and hidden within the fabric. It was the only thing he'd been able to save from his bordello before the flames engulfed the clapboard building. Zhao Jin flared his nose as the locals heaved water onto the fire, local businessmen beside miners, intent on saving the town from the pestilence of fire. Prescott lived in daily fear of a fiery outbreak. They would eagerly blame a Chinaman's bordello for the tragedy.

Zhao Jin's ladies trembled beside him, unsure of where to go. Haunted eyes stared at him, their emaciated bodies translucent in the smoky darkness. He turned his back and strode into the shadows. The girls would have to find their way to the cribs like the rest of the useless chattel in the god-forsaken town. Perhaps some would survive until he was able to rebuild. Anything, after all, was possible.

Coin jingled within his pocket, enough to get him through several weeks on the road. More could be retrieved from the bank in Phoenix. With luck he would not need to travel so far. The insurance would replace most of his loss; he would want to begin the rebuilding process as soon as possible.

But first he must catch a serpent.

1

The cards slid across the table and a hush settled over the room. Slim leaned back in his chair, linked his hands behind his head and flashed a wide grin. There was enough cash sitting in the pot to keep him for months.

"Impossible," the young man across the way growled. Slim hadn't bothered to remember his name. With wire-rimmed glasses settled on a pinched nose, the boy had a sense of easy living about him. Pressed clothes wrinkled in the sweat of nerves throughout the evening, and now the fancy seemed to be all wrung out of him. Slim had seen it before.

"Sometimes the cards just don't fall the way you want 'em," Slim said.

A shadow crossed the boy's brow and Slim pulled his hands down and leaned forward, casting a quick look at the crowd around them. Something buzzed in the air. Something dangerous. The boy stood, pushing against the table and slamming the chair into the wall behind him. Slim flexed his hand beside his hip, but did not stand. He wouldn't be too quick to draw. Not this time.

"You can't have won! That was the best hand I ever had." The boy's lips trembled and his hand moved toward his hip.

Slim held up a hand. "Now, I understand. That there is a mighty good hand. Mine just happened to be better. That's why it's a game of chance."

The boy snapped his eyes to the table, shooting his gaze from his own full house to Slim's royal flush. He stuttered, "It just isn't possible. It just…"

"Course it is. When a man's a cheat."

A shadow crossed over the cards and Slim turned his head to a man standing to his side. Candle light glinted off the edges of a brass star. A black coat hung loosely on the man's shoulders, showing the easy access to the pistols beneath the fabric. Slim slid his eyes up to the man's face. Hard planes and stark recognition glared back at him.

"Marshal Parker," Slim drawled. "It's been a while."

"Cheat? He's been cheating?" The young man across the table, reached for his gun. Slim had his peacemaker out before he could pull his own weapon.

"Don't you draw, Jimmy." Marshal Parker had his gun pointed at Slim's chest, but had an eye on the nervous boy across the way. "I got this handled."

"But sir!"

"Leave. Take you money and go. This game's done for the night."

"That money ain't his, Marshal," Slim growled as he reholstered his pistol. The night had been so promising. And once again, he'd be leaving empty handed. A champion with no winnings.

"You won't be needing the money. You'll have your meals courtesy of the State." Parker stepped back and motioned for Slim to stand.

"You ever tire of chasin' innocent men, Parker?"

The crowd around them huddled close, intent on hearing it all. Dirty men with too much dust in their skin brushed shoulders with primped up ladies trained to take a man's hard-earned money with a smile and a drink. Wide-eyed, they didn't bother to hide their interest. One couldn't pay for entertainment like this.

Slim had faced his share of dangerous men, Parker not being the top of the list. But the man had a dogged focus which proved effective more than once. The last time the two men met, Slim retreated out the window of a particularly lovely lady of ill repute's establishment. He glanced to the back of the room. The exits in the saloon weren't nearly as convenient. He wasn't usually this careless.

"You're wanted for murder. You've been running for a long time."

"It was self-defense and you know it." Slim flexed his hands as Parker removed the peacemaker from the holster at his hip. The loss of his weapon felt heavy in Slim's heart as it lightened his belt. Damn, a man felt naked without his pistol.

"I don't care nothin' about you being guilty or innocent. That is for the judge to decide," Parker answered with direct confidence, but his eyes scanned the crowd with careful unease. Slim bit back his retort. There was no way he'd get a fair trial. Not since the man that'd died had been the Governor's boy. There wasn't a territory in the Union that wouldn't find him guilty.

Parker grabbed him by the arm and turned them to the door. "Come on. The sheriff said he'd have coffee waiting for us."

"Ain't that nice and proper of him."

The marshal pushed him through the crowd. The night hung like a hangman's hood behind the swinging saloon doors and the people resettled as their source of entertainment made for the exit. There seemed little recourse for him at the moment, but hopefully with time, he'd find himself a way out. Though it seemed his winning streak may have just come to an end.

Lady would never forgive him for this. The thought brought a smile to his lips.

"Marshal!"

Heads turned toward the stairs, where a figure shrouded in silk stood, a green and purple haze dancing at their feet.

"Fire!" A voice shouted.

"Fire ain't purple you idiot," another responded.

The figure lifted a hand, as the iridescent smoke billowed between the balusters and oozed toward the ceiling. "You may want to reconsider your intentionzz thizz night, Marshal."

Parker bristled beside him, hovering his hand over his hip. "What are you..."

"Tizz a warning, sir." Several pops echoed through the saloon, followed by a loud hiss. Suddenly, smoke rose from all corners of the room, filling the air, the colors merging in a rainbow of ethereal mystery. The figure lifted their hands and removed the silk about the face. Green eyes glowed and she said, "There are monsterzz about tonight."

Silence hit the room like the space between a dust storm and monsoon. All eyes stared at the creature who stood before them, majestic with elegant features and full, perfectly formed lips, with skin the texture of serpent scales. Horror filled the faces and a whimper sounded from across the room.

Slim whooped, and looked to Parker. "She's a beaut

ain't she?"

The marshal turned shocked eyes toward him in time for Slim to grab his arm, bend it back and grab his pistol. Slim looked to the crowded room and shouted, "Run!"

The rush of bodies pushed Slim toward the door and Parker was lost in the melee. Before he entered the night, Slim glanced toward the stairs and sent a salute to the figure disappearing into one of the rooms that lined the second story. A gust of wind pushed at his hat as his feet hit the dirt in the lane. Grinning, he attempted to restrain his euphoria. Sybil. What a lovely, miraculously clever lady.

Just as he moved to free himself from the confines of the crowd, the mass of bodies stopped. They stood stark and still, shoulders tensed and fear coalescing in a fog about them. And then he noticed the orange glow that filled the night.

Peeking over the heads and hats standing before him, he watched flames sputter and hiss.

"What is it?"

"The eyes! Oh Lord in heaven! Do you see the eyes?"

Slim ducked between two men and sidled to the edge of the crowd, keeping one eye out for Parker and the other on the fire that had captured the audience. As he slid toward the side-alley beside the saloon, a whinny was cut short by a curt command. His eyes snapped to a shadowed figure waiting in the dark. She hissed, "What are you waiting for?"

"Lady. I thought you'd have gone and left me all to myself by now."

"Next time I will. Now get your skinny, disreputable self over here before they discover our game."

Slim covered the distance to Lady in half a stride and took hold of the reins. Sharp, brown eyes glared down a long, elegant nose. Her lips thinned and nearly disappeared in the shadows. His smile grew wider. Lord, the woman was astounding when he got her all riled up. He swung up behind her just as a voice shouted, "Look, the fire. It's burning out!"

A rumble of confusion and then sudden outrage flowed through the crowd standing just outside the saloon. From the height upon the horse, Slim could make out the last of the flames, drawn like a serpent in the dust, green smoke eyes petering out with the wind. Slim said, "Quite a show, but I think the magic may be gone."

Lady snapped the reins and the horse reared, a piercing whinny drawing attention their direction. Then they were off, hooves pounding into the packed dirt lane. The sudden speed was just enough to tamp the pleasure he took in wrapping his arms about her waist. The corset created the perfect shape, but he had the notion that it was no illusion. The woman was just about as perfect a shape as they came. Prickly as a cactus field-- but perfect in all the ways that counted.

Shouts filled the streets behind them, but as the distance grew, Slim relaxed. Parker wasn't a chasing kind of man. He much preferred the slow and steady approach. It was doggone frustrating having the man pop up every few months on his trail, but if he made an escape, Slim was pretty certain he'd gained just a little more time.

The last of the town of Socorro passed by as Lady pushed the horse in a hard gallop, her chestnut-colored hair slapping against his cheek like tiny whips. Another mile and Slim would urge her to slow down. He turned back to look at the town receding into the distance then shouted, "Where's Sybil?"

"She is fine."

"How do you know that?"

"Because, you idiot, she's right beside us."

Slim jerked his head to scan the area. Sure enough, another horse thundered along beside them, ten feet to their right. Silks flowed like flags on a windy day, the corners snapping with violent precision. Delicate, slippered feet barely reached the stirrups. The head turned and green eyes glinted with an eerie, yellow glow. There wasn't enough moonlight to create such an effect. He shook his head then looked back. Sybil's face was once again facing forward. Lithe, and elegant on her seat, Sybil looked as she always did. Unmoved and capable of anything. Pushing the image of what he thought he'd seen into the back of his mind, he returned his attention to where they were headed and what they hoped to find.

***

Fury was too mild a word. Absolute, tempestuous antipathy would be closer. But still not quite right. Lady had more important things to do than rescue a two-bit gambler from himself. The MacHurdyGurdys already had several weeks ahead on the chase and Lady could feel her prize slipping further from her grasp. What insanity compelled her to take up with the infuriating man? She should have left him in the hands of the law. He quite obviously belonged with them.

"That was some performance. Did you see the looks on their faces when you pulled back your pretties to show them your face? Hot dang, I would pay to see that again. And that smoke? Where the devil did you find smoke that color? I ain't seen nothing like it," Slim said, as he strode beside the fire. Sybil looked up at him, her back against a boulder which hid them from the old wagon road, the fire painting shadows against its face. Slim stopped his pace and threw up his arms. "And what was it you said? There be monsters out tonight? Brilliant! I bet you'll have those miners crying like babies in their beds tonight. Where'd you learn something like that?"

Sybil tipped her head to the side, her voice hushed. "One can learn quite a bit from the deviouzz Mordecai MacHurdyGurdy."

Slim dropped his hands. "Man, what a trick. Makes me almost wish I had a face like that." He put his hand to his pock-marked cheek. "Well now, I sorta do. But it don't get the reaction you do. She's something, don't you think, Lady?"

Lady crossed her arms and glared at him. Sybil had ducked her head to stare into the fire as he waxed on about the evening's event. The man had the tact of a four-year old. "I'm certain she would prefer not to be reminded of her affliction. Don't you agree?"

"Her what?" Slim asked, his brows pulled together in confusion. Understanding came a moment later and he dropped to a knee, putting his hand out to Sybil's chin. Her scars and scales were eerie in the night's shadow, the reptilian skin a blight that was difficult to overlook--even by friends that loved her dearly. Slim said, "Ah now, little darling. You ain't got nothing to worry about. You got a face of an angel. My avengin angel. And you sure as all hell saved me tonight."

Sybil's head snapped up and she pierced him with her mossy-green eyes. Lady took a step back at the intensity shining from the woman's expression. Sybil said, "I wazz merely the player. It wazz Lady that orchestrated your rescue. Perhapzz you should beg her forgivenezz for your trespazz."

Uncomfortable, Lady turned from the scene. Sybil had an uncanny way of reading her reactions. Kind and generous with a beautiful heart, the woman could still run streaks of unease down a person's spine. Slim murmured, "Well, now, I don't think Lady is in any mood to be forgivin me just yet."

The man might be ordinarily obtuse, but in this instance he was correct. Lady said, "Get some rest. We must leave before dawn. Who knows who will be on our trail, and the MacHurdyGurdys are still quite far away."

Neither of her companions replied as she strode into the darkness. All she would find this night was anger and frustration. Perhaps the daylight would bring peace to their group. Perhaps they could finally focus on the task at hand. Finding Mordecai MacHurdyGurdy

.

2

Nothing moved. Not even a breeze touched the brush and trees that sprinkled the area surrounding the old Zuni village. Mordecai MacHurdyGurdy dropped the thin, brass telescope from his eye and concealed it within the leather satchel hung from his shoulder. It seemed the rumors were true. According to the local lore, the Zuni abandoned their villages hundreds of years ago in the wake of the Spanish explorers and their lust for treasure. The people had sought refuge in the centralized Pueblo of Zuni, leaving behind their homes and their secrets.

For Mordecai, it left the ancient villages open to his purposes.

"Well?" Beatrice asked, her forehead creased and frown surly. "What now?"

"We go in. The village is empty," Mordecai said to his sister-in-law as he turned to the carts. His brother, Bernard, sat on the bench, his fingers loosely gripping the reins to the mule team, his eyes shallow and unseeing. As the weeks progressed, Mordecai continued to witness his brother's fall into a dejected melancholy.

The man's wife had only grown more irritable. "What do you expect to find in a deserted village? The savages are gone. Do you honestly believe they would have left you gold to find?" Beatrice yanked the reins from her husband's hands and glared at Mordecai.

He ignored her and vaulted onto his own cart, jostling the two women waiting on the bench. His assistants, Isabel and Charlotte, had been lovely once. Now, they clung to each other, their hair knotted and frazzled, eyes sunken and lips parched. The road to the village had been a hard one, but something else infected his companions. Something he could not understand.

The chase had provided him a new vitality, a purpose, and hope. They were fools to not see it. He snapped the reins, and the mules began the slow trudge toward the village. On the very edges of the Arizona and New Mexico Territories, the land was conveniently devoid of humanity, but for the few struggling individuals searching for gold and copper in the great southwestern desert mountains.

Copper and gold were the great yellow fortunes. But they were fortunes hard won through the grasp of nature's monolithic prisons. A miner could go a century and find barely a strain of the majestic metals. And when they did, the hands of the elite business men from the east would descend like a biblical pestilence, stealing the work of honest men, draining their souls beneath the earth in hard labor. Mordecai had no intention of wasting his life, only to have it stolen by the copper and gold barons. His triumph would be complete and undeniable. His fortune firmly within his control.

A delicate chain hung from the pocket of his vest, diligently maintained despite weeks on the trail. Within the pocket, lying heavy against his belly was the key to his success. Two lockets were attached to the same chain. Cast in copper, the intricate design was a mask of gold. The coral carvings set in the very center of the locket were the only thing to distinguish the two. One carved as a screaming eagle, its talons spread wide as it dove toward its prey. The second, a coiled rattlesnake, its head ready to strike and fangs extended.

The lockets had not left his person. Not since he had very nearly lost one to a lovely young lady in Tucson. Her interest in his prize still had him baffled. A woman out of place in the west, she held a solid determination within her continence that Mordecai had only witnessed on rare occasions. Women were not usually of such resilient fortitude. But this would not have been the type to be fooled twice--a suitable adversary.

He shook away his thoughts. The woman was no matter. The chestnut-haired beauty had been dealt with and his curiosity would remain unfulfilled. A shame though, very little intrigued him anymore.

The first multistory building came into view as they rode over a slight rise. The grasses surrounding the village lay bent and still, the birds suddenly quiet. Mordecai shaded his eyes to the sunlight, watching as the shadows cast geometric anomalies of shape across the landscape. Three pueblos stood, their walls pitted by the wind, the round, wood beams rotted from time and neglect.

Isabel let out a held breath, her eyes wide and unusually bright. When Mordecai looked to her, she quickly looked away. Quite strange.

Beatrice pulled her buckboard to a halt beside one of the entrances, hopping down and calling to the girls. "Go see if you can find water. A village this big had to have water somewhere about."

Charlotte grabbed Isabel's hand to steady herself as they

struggled from the cart. The women teetered as they hit the ground, but shuffled off toward the surrounding lands, their obvious first choice a stand of trees behind the second Pueblo. Mordecai jumped from the bench and secured the horses. When he turned Beatrice stood beside him. "How long since you last gave them the elixir?"

"They do not need it." He moved to pass her, but she grabbed his arm.

"Yes they do, look at them," she hissed.

"They passed the time of withdrawal a week ago. It is more likely the lack of drink that has them unsteady," he said and wrenched his arm from her grasp. Stalking past, he scanned the buildings. There had to be a clue to why they were led here.

Mordecai pulled the lockets from his vest and snapped open the lid which held the serpent. Within the locket was the first half of the map, two images, drawn by Cabeza de Vaca himself nearly three hundred years ago. This map had been the piece Coronado held when he'd advanced on the Zuni, only to be thwarted when the natives refused to admit him entrance to the fabled cities. His fury saw to the burning of those villages.

Mordecai ducked his head into one of the pueblos to find the entire room blackened by an ancient fire. Even this village had not escaped Coronado's wrath.

Mordecai perched a pair of spectacles on his long nose and peered at the miniscule drawing. This was indeed the right place. The next stop on the map that led to Cibola. But how could that be? There was nothing here. Just three burned-out pueblos and fields of nothingness.

He spat into the dust and returned to his cart. There would be time to explore. No detail would slide beyond his notice. Too many years led to this moment and he would have his prize, no matter the cost. Throwing open the door to his cart, he ducked into the darkness. His tables lay empty, his bottles of elixir packed securely within the stacks of boxes that filled the room.

Lighting a lantern, he pulled a stool toward one of his work tables. With short, efficient movements he unrolled a large piece of paper and secured it with weights. His own handwriting lay before him with lines carefully drawn to exacting dimensions. It was a perfect scale version of the map within the serpent locket. The land, as the Spanish had known it, was depicted exactly. But it required years of study before Mordecai could decipher its meaning.

Many believed it to be a hoax; that the maps de Vaca had drawn were only the tales of a man made mad by the years spent in the wilderness, wandering among the savages. This belief had only been compounded when even the great Coronado returned a failure. His only glory the deaths of thousands of natives.

But Mordecai knew something that Coronado did not. He had found a journal, tucked deep within the corners of an ancient Spanish Mission abandoned nearly as long as the village he now visited. The servant Esteban left the journal with his own accounts of the remarkable journey the castaway men endured in the hauntingly unfamiliar lands of America long before other white men tread on those shores.

The stories were true. The seven cities of gold held a promise which could tempt even the most pious of men. De Vaca had known this, had seen the danger of such a secret being discovered. And so he altered the maps drawn for Coronado. Those had brought Coronado to this village and every other village within the Zuni homeland. But the trail ended there. Frustrated and arrogant, Coronado had no other clues to lead him forward. He tortured and coerced the peoples of the land, but they refused him.

Mordecai looked up from his map. What a treasure it must be for them to prefer to die than give in to the threat of the Spanish. But Mordecai did not need to torture Indians to discover the way. No. De Vaca had been a loyal Spaniard to his death. He drew clues into the maps within the lockets and sent them to his Queen.

However, they never made it to Spain. And now they were in the hands of Mordecai MacHurdyGurdy. Only fate could have brought such promise. And only a great and clever man could solve this mystery.

The map did indeed end in this village. But Mordecai viewed a copy of the map given to Coronado. And there was a single difference between the two. That difference lay in the center of this village. A small circle with a cross within was drawn beside miniscule square boxes. The boxes must represent the three Pueblo buildings. But what did the circle mean? He had not seen a circular building. There was something missing. Or could it have disappeared with time and he was too late?

A scream careened through the air and Mordecai flew from the cart and into the sunlight. Beatrice looked to him as she too came running, then they both turned as a second scream came from the copse of trees behind the pueblo. Beatrice grabbed her skirts and ran toward the sound, Mordecai only steps behind her.

Another scream encouraged their pace to quicken. As they reached the copse of trees, Charlotte emerged, her eyes wide with panic, her hands held out toward Mordecai and Beatrice. Tears streamed down her cheeks and she cried, "I can't make her stop! She won't stop. She just keeps screamin' and screamin' and she won't stop!"

Charlotte grabbed at his vest, tearing at the fabric and babbling. He pushed her away, into the arms of Beatrice and strode into the trees. The temperature lowered to an unnatural level. Still and quiet as the rest of the land, the air felt as stale as a cabin frozen beneath the deepest winter snows. To his right, a scream pierced the silence, this one weaker than the rest, guttural and anguished.

Pushing aside a branch he peered into a clearing. A pool of clear water shimmered within a red rock basin, a column of light creating a glow which tricked the mind and appeared to shine from below. He shook his head as the image shifted and lost its surreal quality. A whimper drew his attention to a huddled mass beside the water.

"Isabel, what are you going on about?" He took a step toward her and she screamed again. With a frustrated breath he said, "That is quite enough. Stand up woman and let me see you."

She did not answer him, beginning to rock, her shoulders shivering. Two steps took him to her side and he grabbed her arm. Like a strike, she reacted, snapping her head up, her body suddenly rigid. Mordecai dropped his hand and nearly fell to the earth. Blood flowed from her eyes, her lips ripped in giant gashes, hands caked in blood and hair pulled from her scalp.

"Good God woman, what have you done?"

With a flicker of recognition hit her expression and she spoke, her voice scratched and strained, "The shadows. The shadows. A snake in the shadows."

"A snake? You have seen snakes before." Her scream interrupted him as she began to rock again.

"Mordecai?" His brother rushed to his side. "What has happened? What—my God, Isabel." Bernard reached for her, but Mordecai put a hand to his elbow.

"Do not touch her."

"But what has happened? She is ill, we must help her."

"Ill? No, I do not think she is ill." Mordecai straightened his vest and leaned over the pool to gaze into the water. Shallow and devoid of life, it smelt of sweet promise. "We will want to find another source of water."

"The water? Is that what did this to her? Is it poisoned?"

Mordecai looked at his brother and frowned. The man had the brilliance of a thousand mechanical fabricators, but when it came to the mysteries of life, he was unredeemable obtuse. "No not poisoned. Look at her."

Isabel let forth a keening wail that could have challenged the banshee of the Irishmen. She looked to the sky and held her hands up, the blood coagulating in sickening globules. Bernard gasped, and stepped back. "I don't understand."

Mordecai said, "She is quite clearly terrified. As terrified as is humanly possible."

3

Lady balanced on her knees, letting the warmth of the fire seep into her bones. The days were warm, but the moment the sun sank behind the distant mountains, the creep of the cold night threaded into the body and took away everything the sun had given. Sybil sat beside her, arms wrapped about her knees, her head tilted to the side as though she could read a story within the flames. Lady remained still, waiting for the rest of the tale.

"My mother wazz a talented dancer. The best that had ever performed in Dodge City. Sometimezz, I can remember other stagezz. Faraway stagezz where the men were clean and ladiezz dressed in the finest clothing. I think she wazz well loved there. But I wazz so young, I can hardly remember."

"But you remember Dodge City," Lady prompted.

"Yezz," Sybil said, her expression suddenly clouded. "It izz a place I can never forget."

"If you do not wish to speak of it--"

"Do you know," Sybil interrupted, "That if a man hazz a dark heart and containzz all the evilzz of the earth, he izz well-loved when his face izz unmarked and pretty?"

"I hadn't ever thought of it to be honest,"Lady said.

"But if a woman, sweet and innocent, hazz a mark of

the serpent, she is hated, despised, and disregarded? What doezz that tell uzz of mankind?" Sybil looked away, back into the torrent of flame as it turned the wood to coals and lifted its smoky essence to the sky. "What doezz it say of me?"

Lady leaned back on her heels. "It says nothing of you. If a man calls a dove a swine, it says nothing of the dove and everything about the idiocy of the man."

Sybil snickered and released a subtle smile. "You are quite remarkable, Lady. The name fitzz you."

The words caught Lady off-guard. The name. It wasn't really hers. Of course, anyone could figure that out, certainly one as clever as Sybil. But it wasn't a secret she was ready to reveal. Not now, perhaps not ever. There was a life before, when she was a silly young girl, innocent, naïve--an idiot. What person would wish to remember that childhood? Despite her infirmity, Sybil could never have been anything but beautiful and intelligent. If only Lady could have an ounce of the young woman's composure, what amazing things she could accomplish.

Lady stood, brushing the detritus from her divided skirt. As it was, all she had was a stubbornness granted from generations of elitism and privilege. It would have to be enough.

A series of curses came from the direction of the horses. Slim's lanky frame appeared out of the shadows as he bent over to retrieve his bag, the contents strewn across the ground beneath the feet of his mount. Lady's nose flared and she turned away from him. Crossing her arms against her chest, she said, "What has compelled us to keep him around? The man has been far more trouble than he is worth."

"He izz worth more than you give him credit."

Lady snorted, but immediately blushed. If her mother could hear her now. Years of study in deportment were evaporating away by the day. What a mess this western influence was making of her.

"What are you fighting against, Lady? How many enemiezz do you see in the shadowzz?"

"I do not know what you mean. I have no enemies. None beyond MacHurdyGurdy, of course."

Sybil tipped her head up. "Of course. Perhapzz if thizz izz true, you should cease fighting the false enemiezz that fill your mind."

A shot rang out and Lady turned toward its origin. The horses strained against their bonds, their shrill screams hard against the ears. Slim raised his hands as he ducked between the slicing hooves, his hat askew as he attempted to soothe them. He shouted as Lady approached, "Get back! I got it. It's fine."

Lady didn't believe him, but the moment's distraction gave Slim the time to reach a hand along the horse's neck, his other grabbing the reins. The horse brought his hooves back to earth, and danced with irritation as Slim spoke into his ear. Lady's own steed followed suit, calming beneath the words of the irascible gambler.

With the horses managed, Lady moved to scout the area. The shot which set them off had been very near. It sounded practically within the camp. Pulling her most recent acquisition from her bag, she engaged the condensed steam wand, letting it warm beneath her touch. It was not much of a deterrent for the distant assailant, but the wand could deliver an agonizing burn within close quarters. Let them come to her. She had a surprise.

"Lady? What are you doin? There ain't nothing out there," Slim said.

"You would have me believe the shot was a figment of my imagination? Oh no sir, I have not lost my faculties in such a way. Not yet, at least." She stalked the night beyond the fire. Where were they, the bastards who sought to terrorize them? Only a man of devious intent would stalk them in the darkness. But they would not haunt them tonight, not here. She'd had quite enough of stagecoach villains and cowardly thieves.

"Lady."

She jumped as Slim's hand wrapped about her elbow. She said, "Are you mad? Do you even know what this is?" She brandished her steam wand, the red, bulbous tip sizzled from the contact with the cool air.

"Well, now that you bring it up. No. Didn't even know you had somethin like that. What else do you got in that bag of yours?" Slim pulled at her satchel and she wrenched it from his grasp.

"You idiot. We have enemies at the gate and you haven't a mind to focus?"

Slim laughed and Lady felt the overwhelming urge to place the wand against his nose. But, she rather liked his nose, so perhaps another time. Slim tugged her toward the fire. "Darlin, there ain't no enemy out there. Just an idiot man in here."

"What?"

"You're not going to make me confess my mistake, are you?"

"What?"

He stopped and looked down at her. His shoulders slightly hunched in a way she assumed meant to make him seem less imposing. It only made him appear to loom like a giant vulture. Even with her unusual height for a woman, he towered over her. The dark brooding stare only intensified the experience, making her wish for distance. He seemed such a harmless man when he bumbled around in his confident gaiety, but now, she feared again that she'd made another terrible mistake.

"I dropped my gun," he said.

"What?" she said, his words not registering.

He released her arm and threw his into the air. "Is that the only word you know? What?? I did it. I was the one that shot that bullet. Me. My gun. I dropped my gun and it went off." He stormed off toward the fire and reached for his bedroll. Lady pulled herself together just as he disappeared into the darkness.

Sybil stood to the side, veil pulled across her face, but her green eyes reflected like fairy fire from the flames. "Perhapzz you should follow him."

"Follow him? Are you mad?"

"You seem particularly concerned for our sanity. But no, I am not mad. Go to him. Have your wordzz. It izz time the two of you spoke that which cloudzz your mindzz."

Lady pursed her lips and stared stubbornly at the slight woman. Sybil turned and walked back to the fire. Lady grumbled beneath her breath. What nonsense. She had nothing to say to that man. Not after all the trouble he'd caused. But for the point that he'd saved her life, she kept him around. Then again, had she not saved his life several times since? This recent rescue from the marshal's grasp was only the last in a line of incidents spanning several weeks. Slim had a weakness for gambling and a warrant for his arrest. It seemed every town knew this man and none wanted him around. What did that say about him? Perhaps it was time she paid attention to logic and stopped listening to her pitifully useless heart.

Stomping toward the spot where he'd disappeared beyond the firelight, she made enough noise to frighten mountain lions for the next thirty miles. She had no intention of sneaking up on a man that quite obviously had no control of his gun.

In the glow of the moonlight, Slim lay with his back against a tree, his bedroll tucked at his lower back and hat pushed down over his face. Lady took a breath to prevent the shriek of frustration at the tip of her lips from escaping.

"What has you all bothered now? Come to read me another list of my failins?"he said.

"This partnership is not working."

"Partnership? This ain't no partnership. Your control's wound so tight, you can't walk without lookin like you got a stick--"

"Really, Slim! I may not look like a proper lady out here in this wilderness. But, you will treat me as such." He tipped his hat up to stare at her and she huffed. "And I will have you know, I walk straight because of the corset. A proper lady's corset."

"Then take it off."

"Take it off?"

Slim pushed away from the tree and braced his weight on one arm, leaning toward her as he said, "What do you got to be proper for out here?"

Lady crossed her arms and withheld the urge to turn and walk away from the man. But, it was time to have their words, as Sybil so eloquently phrased it. She could make it through this one conversation with the insufferable ingrate.

If only he'd stop looking at her with those bright, round eyes. How those eyes made her want to stop the bickering and that slight smile made her want to return the expression.

No. He was unconscionable and was getting in the way of her purpose. "Slim, you saved my life. I can never repay that. And we have the same mission. But you simply cannot work with me. Do you not remember why we are doing this? What the MacHurdyGurdys did to us?"

Pulling off his hat, he laid it to his side and leaned back against the tree. "I remember."

"Can you not see? Neither of us will find vengeance against them if we continue as we are." She took a breath and continued, "And I simply cannot see how we solve the issue in each other's presence."

"Lady, you seem to got the notion that you'd be better off out here on your own."

"Well, I certainly--"

"It gets mighty lonely out here, darlin. Trust me, I'm the man to know. There ain't a friend out there for miles. Not in any of those towns or any of these hills. The desert's a mean mistress and loneliness makes her surly."

"Slim, really. I have been travelling on my own for three years. Do you think I just appeared in the desert?"

"I don't reckon I know where you come from. You ain't said much about your past. That don't mean nothing. I ain't done much tellin myself. But this mission you got, going after MacHurdyGurdy, it ain't no carriage ride. You need as many friends as you can get."

Lady sniffed. "You speak as though you do not have the same intentions. You wish to track down MacHurdyGurdy as badly as I do. He left you to die. Have you forgotten that? Do you wish me to believe you are simply here for my benefit?"

Slim laughed, his grin uncomfortably compelling. "Darlin, I'd be a fool to stick around just for your company. You got more prickly spines than a cactus' got needles."

"Then why are you still around?"

"I figure I thought it was better than being alone."

Lady stiffened. She was not here to cater to a lonely man. "Do you honestly believe that?"

"I don't reckon so, no. You've gone and changed my mind."

"I've changed your mind?"

He crossed his arms over his chest and closed his eyes, essentially shutting her out. Lady opened her mouth to speak again, but he said, "It don't matter none anyway. I'll be headed out my own way in the morning. You got Sybil with you. I figure the two of you'll watch out for each other."

"You will?" Was he honestly going to leave? It was what she wanted, but that did not explain the sudden heaviness in her belly. It had to be nothing. A simple reaction to the departing of a companion. Nothing more. She and Sybil would fare quite well. Certainly better than they had with him. "Slim."

"Go to sleep Lady. The morning will come early."

She let it go. The man was right and she did accomplish what she'd set out to do. Curse him for making her doubt herself. She knew loneliness and she must assuredly did not fear it.

When she returned to the fire, she found Sybil curled within her linen and silks. Lady leaned over the delicate woman, removing a section of linen from her body. With silk the only fabric Sybil could tolerate touching her afflicted skin, they lined the linen with scraps of silk. It provided protection from the elements and soothed the woman's pain. Sybil suffered enough as it was, Lady hated to see her wake with a new irritation.

Pulling her bedroll from the other side of the fire, she laid it beside Sybil. Perhaps she was a fool, thinking two women could survive alone in the desert. They would be tempting prey to unwanted visitors. Lady closed her eyes. She had survived for nearly three years on her own. She did not need to doubt her capabilities. She had weapons, intelligence and a companion whose wisdom she'd grown to trust. Of course they would fare well.

4

Slim was gone before they woke the next morning. Sybil didn't ask and Lady was determined not to speak of it. The man had taken one of the horses and she supposed it was fair. A horse could mean life or death to a person in the desert. Unfortunately, that left just the one to share.

It was time to focus on the task at hand, and that was tracking down the MacHurdyGurdys. A fortuitous stop at a soothsayers crib in Silver City pointed them north, far into native territory. That was weeks ago, and unfortunately, the landscape between Silver City and the Pueblo of Zuni required a less tham direct route.

With the season turning toward winter, they needed additional supplies. Lady only hoped what she procured in the small town of Socorro would hold them until they reached their destination. Sybil would not do well in her light linen and silk when they moved into the high country. Lady hoped to acquire more, but Slim's unfortunate antics had them fleeing the town far sooner than anticipated. Damn the man and his incessant obsession with cards.

Lady worked the muscles of her back, stretching her arms and dreaming of the comforts she'd left behind. This was the penance she must pay for her juvenile naiveté.

Someday she may go back to a life of ease and privilege--if her father could forgive her. As of yet, he had not restricted her ability to receive funds from the banks throughout the west, but she feared it was more in line with keeping track of her whereabouts than any mercy for his daughter. She brought shame on the family. Perhaps her quest would soothe the patriarch's ire. It was the best she could hope for.

"Shall we continue?" Sybil asked, startling Lady with her silent approach.

"Yes. I suppose we shall. Have you had enough to eat?"

Sybil simply smiled and threw the saddle bags over the horse's back. The woman was a generous and pleasant companion, but only spoke when necessary and could go hours without speaking. The silence would be an odd contrast from the weeks of Slim's nonstop banter.

They struck out within minutes and ducked through the trees where they made their camp. In the distance, mountains rose across the horizon. Low clouds hung about the peaks, their dark underbellies portending a difficult ride ahead. Lady tightened her fingers on the reins. Only a little while longer and they would catch up with Mordecai MacHurdyGurdy. She had yet to decide what to do when they did, but for the moment, just getting there was enough.

"Lady, look behind uzz," Sybil said.

Turning at the waist, Lady attempted to see behind them, but the corset restricted her movement. Perhaps she should consider removing the blasted thing. Lady pursed her lips stubbornly. It was one of the last vestiges of her prior life and she had no desire to leave it behind.

"Lady! Quickly!"

She swung the horse around, to meet the threat face on and stared with awe into the sky. "Pinkertons."

A giant ship, held in the air by two massive dirigible balloons, coasted silently toward them like an upended pontoon boat. A pillar rose up between the balloons, a bulbous metal eye at the pinnacle, peering with eerie foreboding at the distance. The infamous Pinkertons claimed the skies over the west for decades, tracking down their prey from the heights with ominous silence. The giant engines running the grand machine released an occasional rush of steam which could shake a man from his horse, but it otherwise floated in deceptively soundless pursuit.

The last time they'd encountered the Pinkertons, they were led on a frantic race toward the Chiricahua Mountains in southern Arizona. Saved by an unexpected intervention by local Apaches, they escaped into the rocky hills. The Pinkertons were just another group intent on apprehending Slim.

"Do you believe they have found him?" Sybil asked.

"I honestly hope they have not. I do not wish him ill, despite my frustrations. I wish we could have warned him."

"He knew they were here."

Lady craned her neck around to see Sybil. The horse, unhappy with the squirming riders, sidestepped from the trail. Lady adjusted her seat and turned the horse's head back toward the distant mountains. "What makes you believe he knew?"

"He left to draw their attentionzz from uzz. He did not wish to endanger uzz again."

"He told you this?"

"No."

Lady frowned. Her skepticism was better held silent. Either way, she did wish him well and hoped the man had found a hole to hide himself in until the Pinkertons moved on. "Then it is fortuitous that he left early. They have most certainly caught sight of us. We may not be their intended target, but they make me nervous. Let us find ourselves away from here."

The horse picked its way over the rocky terrain as Sybil kept an eye on the Pinkertons. Lady couldn't help but tighten her grip on the reins, the impressions of past experience still at the forefront of her mind. There had been a number of narrow escapes over the last several months. The most harrowing the moment Mordecai MacHurdyGurdy left her for the elements, paralyzed by one of his nefarious concoctions, waiting for the hot summer sun and desert predators to quicken her death. Slim rescued her then, providing a convenient antidote to the poison obtained from Sybil. Now, with the Pinkerton's airship hovering so close, her nerves were very nearly frayed.

"Where are they? Have the gone?" Lady asked.

A moment of silence answered her, but then Sybil spoke, her voice low, "I believe we may have to run. They are following uzz and their intentionzz do not appear civil."

A boom sounded from the rear and the rush of steam heralded the airship's increasing speed. The horse jumped to the side as something hit the ground beside them in a puff of dust.

"We must run, Lady!"

"Are they firing at us?" Lady did not wait for the answer as she kicked the horse into a gallop. Sybil grabbed at her side, finding purchase in the fabric of the divided skirt. They ran, dodging boulders and threading through the brush as the horse heaved forward.

Darkness overtook them as the shadow of the airship blocked the sunlight. Lady looked to the distance, the mountains the only chance they had to escape, the peaks and ridges too hazardous for their pursuers to capture them. But the mountains were miles away.

Beware!" Sybil screamed as more projectiles landed about them. Lady caught the slightest glimpse of the brown bulges. Sandbags? Were they shooting sandbags at them? Another flurry rained down and she felt the impact of Sybil being thrown from the horse. Lady shouted as she pulled back on the reins, circling the mount toward her companion.

"No, Lady! Run!" Sybil said.

It was too late. Lady reached Sybil's side and slid from the saddle, reaching down to aid her friend. Sybil's eyes widened with fear. Spinning around, Lady watched as the steamship hung over them, the rail lined with men, their dark features indiscernible at such a height. Ropes uncurled from the rail and several men swung over the side, hurtling down the lines in a controlled fall that made Lady's stomach lurch.

"The bastard hazz found me."

Lady looked to Sybil then followed her gaze to two men standing apart at the rail. How could the woman recognize them? They looked like indistinct man-shaped shadows to her. "Who has?"

"Zhao Jin."

Lady yanked on Sybil's arm to bring her to her feet. "Then we must run."

The women fled toward the horse. If they could remount, they might have a chance.

"Lady!" Sybil screamed as her arm was torn from her grasp. Lady spun as two men bore down on them. One had Sybil by the waist, her legs kicking in the air as he hefted her onto his shoulder.

"Put her down!" Lady lurched toward the horse, intent on grabbing her bag. Her augmented steam pistols were within, loaded and nearly primed. If she only had a little more time. Her body was wrenched back as a crushing hand grabbed her shoulder.

"Hello, sweet heart. There's no reason to be fighting," a deep voice drawled.

Lady swung her arm up and aimed it for the ugly man's chin. He ducked to the side, chuckled then kicked her feet out from under her. He pulled a large burlap bag from his belt. She yanked at the grip he had on her arm only to fall backward as he abruptly let her go. Everything went black as the bag was pulled over her head.

***

Would she never escape this man's clutches? Sybil watched Zhao Jin from beneath lowered lashes, his sense of conquest evident in his strut. With hair black as a vat of oil and a narrow nose, his appearance brought back horrid memories. With the assistance of Lady and Slim, she had fled from this Chinaman's covetous domination months past --but again, he had her.

Lady sat across the room, her limp body propped against the finely papered wall. Sybil worried for her friend, dumped so negligently onto the floor. When the ruffians captured them, Lady struggled like a fierce wildcat, necessitating her incapacitation as the men hauled them up the ropes toward the airship. Sybil's own shrieks had been silenced by a dazzling slap to the temple which still had her disoriented.

"Sir, I commend you on your crew's capabilities," Zhao

Jin said to the man seated behind a heavy oak desk. Large and slightly balding, he had callous eyes and tense lips.

Drumming his fingertips on a leather blotter, the man flared his nose as he stared at Sybil. "She looks sick."

"An unfortunate malady. Nothing to worry over, Banahan," Zhao Jin said.

"And what do I tell my men when their skin starts looking like a rattler?"

"She is not contagious. In fact, in all of my years of exploration, I have found none other like her." Zhao Jin cast an eye to Sybil and unease slid across her skin. "She is indeed, a unique specimen."

"Then you have what you wanted. But I don't." Banahan poked his thumb toward Lady. "Seems your dragon lady left her cohort. You promised me Slim Robinson."

"He was with her, I assure you," Zhao Jin said, his stance defensive.

A smile graced Sybil's lips. It seemed the man made a deal he could not deliver. Fortune favored the wily gambler and she took great pleasure in knowing Zhao Jin would be taken to task for his failure. What would the Pinkertons do now that their quarry once again evaded them? Would they keep her from Zhao Jin's possession?

"What do you need with this...girl anyway? You're a rich man. Don't seem to me like you need to be chasing all over just to find a...*thing* like that." Banahan curled his lip only to look away as Sybil raised her lashes to scour him with a glare.

Zhao Jin swung around to Banahan and said, "She is a woman, sir. Powerful with immense potential, despite her affliction." He turned and smiled at Sybil with affection. "In fact, she is so because of her affliction."

Sybil shivered under his gaze as he continued, "Do you know what strength it takes to maintain composure when all you have known is condescension and disgust? As the body is disdained, the mind grows into a sharpened blade." He turned back to Banahan. "To be held accountable as a monster for a consequence of birth or situation? I do sir. Any man from the Far East who has traveled to these shores and been successful has battled those conditions. And it has made me stronger. It has only made her more formidable as well. We are not so different, she and I."

Banahan grunted. "Whatever makes a man happy, I suppose. Now, you promised me Slim and I don't have him. Seems to me, we need to renegotiate our deal."

"I will pay you whatever you feel is fair," Zhao Jin answered and Sybil felt all hope disappear. He could afford whatever the man requested.

A knock came at the door before Banahan could reply. He shouted and a young man with a narrow chest and thin, golden hair entered. "Sir?"

"Can it wait?" Banahan asked.

"Sir, I believe it is important for you to know."

Banahan waved the man further into the room and Zhao Jin moved to stand beside Sybil. She could smell him, the oils he rubbed into his long, black braid floating about him like a fog of despair.

The young man held a paper to Banahan and Sybil caught a glimpse of a woman, drawn in bold pencil. He said, "I thought I recognized her when they took the bag off her head."

Banahan took the paper and stared at the drawing, then looked at Lady. He stood and crossed the room, squatting down beside the unconscious woman and tipped her head up from where it had fallen to the side. Looking down at the paper, he murmured beneath his breath then let her head fall back to rest against her shoulder.

He stood, a smile lifting his thin lips. "Miss Fidelia Dewhurst of the Boston Dewhursts. Seems her father has been looking for her for some time. He's willing to pay quite a bit for her safe return too. Thank you, Thomas. This has made my mood considerably better."

"And Slim, sir?"

"Send out the scouts. If he was traveling with these two, he may still be in the vicinity." He spun to address Sybil, "Unless you would be so kind as to tell us where he is?"

Sybil glared at him and he disregarded her with a smirk and continued to speak to his man, "He was with them in Socorro. Knowing the kind of man his is, I bet he abandoned them the minute he saw we were coming. Get out there and find him. I want Robinson on this ship by evening."

The man left and closed the door. Zhao Jin reached down to take Sybil's arm, but Banahan interrupted. "About what you owe us."

Zhao Jin straightened and Banahan continued, "The deal was for Slim and you did not lead me to him. So I will be wanting payment for her." He nodded to Sybil.

Zhao Jin bowed his head and said, "Whatever you believe is fair."

5

The woman stank of death and yet she breathed. Mordecai placed a lace kerchief to his nose and leaned over her prone body. The stench would never cease to invade his abode, but there was nothing else to do. Containing their stores and equipment, the other cart lacked the room to convalesce the infirm. If the blasted woman would do them the favor of dying it would significantly improve the situation.

Her lips parted and a wretched sob tore through her body. Stepping away he, grabbed one of his prized green bottles and poured another dose. Isabel had enough elixir to fell a man twice her size, and yet the terrors still sent tremors through to the bone. A knock came at the door and Charlotte ducked her head into the musty hot room. "Can I see her?"

Mordecai grunted, but moved so the woman could approach her friend. Tears built at the corners of her eyes as she knelt beside the bed. "I looked in the water too, but I didn't see what she did. What did she see, Mordecai?"

Years of wasted life at the bottom of a bottle he imagined. But he'd not be the one to tell her that. Charlotte ran a hand across Isabel's sweat drenched hair. Both women lived a life driven by excess and risk. Isabel could have been taken by syphilis for all they knew. It was a possibility that had him avoiding women of their ilk for his entire adult life. He catered to the sins of the wretched, and his strength lay in a moderate life. He'd not been celibate, but careful and that more than anything primed him for greatness.

He set the glass bottle on the side table and watched as Charlotte's eyes slanted toward the euphoric promise held within. He'd leave the bottle and when he returned it would contain less. Her concern for her companion not nearly strong enough to withstand her vice. His lip curled in distaste. The women had outrun their utility. He would need to see about their departure.

Slamming the door behind him, he left them to wallow in the recognition of their mortality. His hat shifted as a gust of wind slapped at the brim, the quick movement of his hand the only thing that saved it from blowing from his head. In the day since they'd discovered the catatonic Isabel, the weather had changed from eerie stillness to a tempest. Dust swirled and the scream of wind rattled through the carts, sending the mules into a panic which the already frazzled Beatrice could barely handle.

Without even a cursory glance at his struggling sister-in-law, Mordecai pushed against the wailing wind and approached the tallest of the three pueblos. Ducking within the solid mud walls he brushed his pants and scanned the interior. Abandoned in haste, the floor was littered with broken pottery and stone, blackened by the fire which had engulfed it nearly a century ago. The wood beams of the ceiling had long since fallen due to neglect. Three stories above was a roof, half open to the sky. Despite the inherent danger, he needed to be on that roof.

He ducked his head out the door and caught sight of his brother. "Bernard, bring the ladder!"

Beatrice shouted and he responded with an obscene gesture then barked, "Just bring it man." His brother scurried around the cart, ever the obedient servant. When Bernard arrived, he helped to prop the pine ladder against the mud wall. Enough of each floor survived to allow him to make an attempt at scaling the walls, but he would need his brother's assistance.

"I have to go back to Bea," Bernard said.

"Leave it, I need you here," Mordecai said with exasperation.

"But--,"

"We are not here for a holiday. Now, help me get to the roof." Mordecai stepped on a rung and the two men hastened up the crumbling walls. Eager to see the landscape, Mordecai stumbled onto the roof, losing his footing and falling to his knees. Angry wind threatened to send him back down into the pueblo, but he held fast and crawled to the edge.

Grass covered the plaza in a tight weave, but victory thudded within his breast. In the center of the plaza was a circular depression nearly thirty feet across, the grass a slightly different color, the soil settling in a distinctive pattern. The circle on his map had finally shown itself. Scrambling back to the ladder, he ordered his brother to assist in their descent. There was work to do.

Sending Bernard to retrieve a shovel, Mordecai strode to the center of the plaza. The dirt beneath his feet felt loose in comparison to the surrounding hard-packed earth. The grass came up easily in his hands, and when he felt beneath the soil his fingers struck the same mud and straw adobe that had been used as walls for the pueblos.

When Bernard returned with the shovel, Mordecai grabbed it from his brother and prodded the ground. When the metal struck wood, he fell to his knees and pulled the loose grass to expose a square of hastily lashed branches.

Slipping the spade between the branches, they cracked beneath the pressure. Bernard stood beside him, eyes widening as the ground opened before them. Finally, a hole, large enough to allow a man to enter was cleared and Mordecai threw down the shovel. The two men peered into the darkness, but all they saw was an empty chasm, the stale stink of abandonment rising from within.

"Bring my lantern," Mordecai said.

"But the wind."

"There is no wind below, now is there? Bring the ladder as well. I do not see another way down."

As Bernard scurried to do his bidding, Mordecai knelt, leaning his head into the stygian darkness. A stuffy silence was all his senses could pick up, but the thrum of his heartbeats built a rising excitement within his body. This was the key to his quest. It was all falling into place.

The ladder slid into the hole and found purchase before it would have been too short. Mordecai debated sending his brother in first, but this was his discovery, he would be the first to witness the glory. Sliding down the rungs, he grabbed the lantern from his brother's outstretched hands and descended. Halfway to the bottom, he paused and lit the lantern.

The room illuminated as he turned up the gas to intensify the light. He tempered the disappointment. The mud walls and thick beams were devoid of the sparkling promise of gold. He anticipated that. Had there been gold in this location, Coronado would surely have secured it. Yet he still yearned for a taste of success, anything to prove he was on track to riches. He stepped to the floor and called for his brother to join him.

A circular room, it contained no furniture or trappings. Mordecai stepped deeper into the shadows, the light striking odd patterns against the walls. Drawn by black slashes which ran across the adobe, he approached the farthest side, lifting his arm to bring more light. Thick soot ran like a brush of paint across the wall.

"A fire?" Bernard asked.

"A strange fire." It looked more like a splash of liquid than the remnants of flame. Mordecai dipped his finger into the hardened ash. Black transferred to his fingertip and he placed it to his lips. Soot for certain. Interesting.

A thorough examination of the room provided no clue to the source. Even the slab-lined hearth was absent the signs of fire. The plastered floor was pristine, as though it had seen limited use. Considering the condition of the pueblos, the entire room appeared out of the ordinary. Mordecai approached one of two raised bench-like structures on either side of the hearth. The lantern brought to light the carved images within the plaster. Peering closer, his breath caught at the image of a snake, coiled and ready to strike covering the bench. Slivers of coral, turquoise and gold were inlaid with sparkling precision.

As he reached a hand toward the image, Bernard called, "Mordecai!"

A ruby glow coalesced several feet above the hearth, the crackle and snap of fire a ghost of sound. Bernard stood to the side, his hands trembling and face a mask of horror. Mordecai stalked to his brother, grabbed him by the arm and yanked him away. "Pull yourself together. It is smoke and mirrors."

The two men had been in the business of illusion for far

too long to let the tricks of a magician send them into a panic. He circled the spectacle, watching as it intensified and formed into distinguishable images. Colors caressed the darkness and an, iridescent green serpent undulated within the smoke.

"The snakes! Isabel screamed about the snakes!"

Mordecai didn't bother to grace his brother with a response. The smoke stank of chemicals and atmosphere. Peering into the heart of the fire pit, he searched for the source. The origin of an illusion was never at the site of the show. He turned, scanning the walls then cast his eyes to the ceiling. A well-constructed trick, the naked eye could not discern its solution. A twinge of respect niggled at his consciousness; what a master its creator must have been.

The serpentine image rippled, then grew, flowing into a bloated ball of filth, soot falling from the edges like sugar from a fancy cake. A pop sounded, and the smoke filled the air to the ceiling, the roiling serpent slithering above their heads in a menacing dance. Its jaws opened, the tapered fangs dripped fire onto the floor. Bernard fell to the floor with a fearful cry as the serpent dove toward him, fire streaming in a liquid arc and slashing a scorched trail of soot against the wall. Mordecai shook his head, the show was impressive, yet his brother should know when it was clearly man's machinations. They created far too many illusions of their own.

The serpent flashed past the two men a second time, threatening and remarkably lifelike, sending a stream of liquid soot against the wall, painting a slash of black over those they'd spied upon entering. The mystery of the sooty wall solved, Mordecai returned to the bench with the serpent drawing. Upon closer inspection, he spied a circular impression within the serpent's center coil. Intrigued, he moved to the second bench. A screaming eagle with golden wings held a similar impression in its talons. He reached into his pocket, ignoring the shouts of his brother.

The lockets dangled at eyelevel, the images mirrors of those carved in the benches. Pulling his silver lock pick from his vest pocket, he pried around the edges of the snake carving. A slight pressure released the disk from the locket's hold. Repeating the same to the eagle locket, he placed it within the circular impression. When he completed the same action with the snake disk, the room plummeted into darkness.

Bernard whimpered. Mordecai waited.

The air sizzled with a lightning-like current, standing the hairs on his arms and sending a wave of anticipation across his skin. In place of the bright red serpent flame, a blue and white glow developed, ebbing like water from a river bank. The light brightened and colors expanded, spreading across the room in a spectrum of swirling shapes.

Translucent mountains formed in the far corner of the room, great volcanic cones emerging from a vast grassy plain. A wind shifted, cool and crisp, the taste of winter on his lips, surreal in the small confines of the round pit building. Then the air crackled and the image shifted, flowing toward the great cliffs, soaring toward the sky as though they sat on the wings of a great bird.

The air thickened and the scent of wet vegetation mingled with musty loam. Bernard rocked on his knees and Mordecai put a stabilizing hand on his brother's shoulder, feeling his own knees buckle with excitement. He'd never seen the like. Pictures that moved and shifted before them, he nearly missed the details among the sense of awe. The vision increased speed, spiraling toward the tallest peak, the wind suddenly audible and deafening.

It came to a sudden stop, silence tearing through the room. Mordecai stared up at the immense beauty of a tall pine swaying gently in the breeze. Dry needles gathered at their feet. Bernard reached down and grabbed a handful, then let the needles fall from his fingers. "How is this possible?"

"Smoke and mirrors," Mordecai answered, but the truth was elusive. Never, in all his years had he seen magic so real. He zeroed in on his prize and drew his attention to movement at the top branch of the tree. An eagle landed, spreading its wings as it greeted them. The magestic bird turned its head and pointed its beak down, piercing Mordecai with its black stare.

The room plummeted into darkness.

6

The pounding in her head brought tears to her eyes, but it was no time to show weakness. Lady reached a tentative finger to the small bump which had risen at the base of her head. The man sitting across the desk shuffled papers with impatient force. Apparently finding what he had been searching for, he looked up, his eyes intent and filled with triumph.

"You are a long way from home, Miss Dewhurst."

Lady stilled her features. "I do not have a home, Mr. Banahan. And call me Lady, I am not this Miss Dewhurst. You must be mistaken."

Banahan slid the paper across the desk and Lady stopped it with a single finger. Looking up from the yellowing sheet was an eloquently penciled image of herself three years ago. It was a remarkable likeness; no one could mistake her for someone else. Every detail was exact, except for the eyes. Those stupid, ignorant eyes. Lady pushed the paper away and raised her brow. "I am in my majority. My father has no authority over my whereabouts. I have done nothing wrong. I have committed no crime. You have no reason to hold me."

Banahan snorted. "You are a Dewhurst. Of course your father has the authority. And I really don't care what kind of squabble you have with the man. All I see is that he's willing to pay a thousand dollars to get you back."

Lady jerked her head back to the paper. A thousand dollars? "He is insane. I am hardly worth one thousand dollars."

"You are to me," Banahan said as he stood. He turned toward a small table sitting to the side. "Now, let's see what you have in your bag. My men have been fighting over the contents and that has me curious."

Jumping to her feet, Lady grabbed the arm of the chair and waited as the room ceased spinning. The brute who captured her used significantly more force to subdue her than was necessary. Returning the favor was on her mind. How would she escape if she couldn't stand up straight?

"What the blazes have you been collecting, young woman? This is hardly the kind of thing for someone from aristocratic Boston."

Lady scowled and stumbled toward Banahan. "I told you. I do not belong in Boston. Leave my things, they are expensive."

He held up a long rod, testing the switch with his thumb. It flared to life as the steam system heated. Lady grabbed it from him and turned it off. "You will burn your hand off."

Grinning he reached his hand back into the bag, retrieving her augmented pistols. The nodule containing the compressed air sat just above the barrel, ready for the spark from the firing pin to ignite the powder and heat the small pocket of moisture in the tube running into the compression chamber. The process took a few extra seconds, but the effect was awe-inspiring. The power and sound that came from one shot could terrify an entire band of miscreants. At least one hoped, otherwise it was just another gun, just like any other.

"Miss, I am afraid I'm going to have to take these away from you. There isn't a man alive that would trust you with these."

"Do not be ridiculous. You cannot just take those from me."

His smirk built heat at the base of her neck as he put the pistols to the side and reached into the bag again. Frustration and fury rose and her hands shook. She couldn't fight him for her weapons. Each needed a few moments of preparation to be effectively wielded and he was far too strong.

"What on earth are these?" In his hands he held three round balls, a single fuse extending from the top of each. The smoke bombs were recent acquisitions and she'd been pleased with the results. They had been singularly effective in Soccorro.

"Light them. See what happens."

"No reason to be uncivil, Miss Dewhurst." He returned the bombs to the bag and closed the flap. "Now, let us discuss your traveling companions. You have been consorting with dangerous men. Just for that I could deliver you to a number of local sheriffs. There are marshals that would be interested in having a conversation with you as well."

"I do not know what you are speaking of."

He sighed and leaned a hip against his desk. "Slim Robinson?" She lifted her head in surprise. Robinson? The man never told her his last name. Banahan continued, "Do you know he killed a man? Did he tell you that?

She thinned her lips and did not respond. He waited a moment then said, "How that man finds such loyal companions I will never understand."

A knock sounded before the door swung open and

slammed against the adjacent wall. A woman, with a narrow-waist and honey-colored hair sticking out in disarray from beneath a tightly tied kerchief, stalked into the room. A black streak of grease ran across an attractive face, highlighting hazel eyes that flared with ire. "Tommy, we got to talk. You promised me parts. I got a flywheel that's about to go and a crank shaft about to snap."

"Miss Blackwood, this will have to wait." Banahan bristled and glared at the outrageous woman.

"Wait? Like hell it can wait! You got a death wish mister? I've been telling you about this for weeks and I'm done with tyin' things down with bailin' wire and sweat. If you don't get me to an honest to god machine shop then you're gonna be walking."

His eyes strayed to Lady, and Miss Blackwood halted, finally catching sight of the only other person in the room. She wiped her hands on snug, brown pants, and slid on a stunning smile as she approached. Lady wasn't sure if the look was friendly or not, it scanned her with far more familiarity than she was accustomed.

"Well now, it's been some time since I've seen another lady on board."

Banahan snorted at the word 'lady', but Miss Blackwood ignored him, sticking out a hand in greeting. "Malphia Blackwood. And the pleasure is mine."

Lady gaped, but took Malphia's long fingers in her own. Calluses felt foreign on such feminine hands. Off guard, she responded with practiced courtesy, "My name is Lady and it is a pleasure as well."

Malphia's smile softened. "Hmm, I am sure it is. Now tell me, what is a fine…Lady… doing with a reprobate like Thomas here."

Banahan coughed and scowled. "She is a suspect, Miss Blackwood. Now I can promise you, we will be on our way shortly. We have one more apprehension before the day is out and then we will make for Albuquerque. You will have your parts."

Hand still imprisoned within the audacious woman's hand, Lady grasped frantically for options. She could not allow Slim to be captured, but more importantly, she had to determine Sybil's condition. If Sybil had been correct, then she was now in the hands of Zhao Jin. Lady's own predicament was no comparison to what the poor woman would suffer under the hand of that insidious man.

She sent a pleading look at Malphia and the woman's eyes flashed with a flicker of response, but she dropped her hand and turned to Banahan. "Tommy, you've never been the type to take advantage of a girl. What's got you doin' that now?"

The room grew silent as Banahan's lips pressed together. Lady held a breath, convinced he'd been pushed beyond his limits, but Malphia surprised them again when her eyes strayed to the bag sitting at the table beside the desk. "Is that a steam wand? Sweet Jesus, that's exactly what I need!"

Three steps took her to the instrument and in less time than it took to blink she'd disappeared out the door. Lady gaped at the empty space beyond the door. Abandoned and hopeless, she looked back to Banahan, his head shaking as he met her eyes. "A talented mechanic, she's nearly worth the irritation."

***

The blasted machine kept moving. Slim tied his horse to

a low branch and stole through the night shadows, his hat tipped so he could keep an eye on the steamship hovering above. The damn Pinkertons made it a dang challenge to keep up without being seen. Agent patrols nearly happened on him twice during the day and if the terrain hadn't supplied convenient hidey-holes, he'd be up on the ship. Granted, it was exactly where he wanted to be, but not with his hands tied and muzzles pointed at his face.

As the Pinkertons chased down the girls, he'd been shouting and making a general nuisance of himself, but the idiots hadn't noticed. Intent on their quarry they'd let him slip out of their hands. Now, instead of drawing the Pinkertons away from Lady and Sybil, he had to stage a rescue. It would have been a hell of a lot easier if the giant eye in the sky had done its job and caught him standing out in the open.

Gravel skittered down the hill as he hopped over the rocks, focused on a slight rise which would bring him within feet of the rope ladder swinging from the steamship's rail. He'd have to jump for it, but three feet was better than the forty he'd been facing for the last several hours. This would be his one chance before they were completely out of reach. He couldn't leave the girls with those bastards, not when it was his fault they'd been captured in the first place.

A thud and a bang came from the engines just as he lunged for the rope. His fingers wrapped around the rough rope and his body swung free through the air. He scaled the ladder, listening to the groans and pops from a machine that sounded like it'd seen better days. With luck it would stay airborne long enough for him to grab the girls and get away. Leave it to the Pinkertons to push a ship to its death just to catch up with one gambler. He wasn't a murderer, he didn't give a damn what they said.

When he reached the rail, he scanned the deck for guards. Not a man walked the hardwood planks. Course, they wouldn't be expecting him to sneak on board a flying fortress. It was just plain loony. But if there was one thing Slim prided himself on, it was throwing his opponent an unexpected card. His heels landed heavily on the deck and he crouched low, listening for anything that might throw a trump at his plans.

When nothing happened, he slunk down the walkway, keeping close to the walls. It had been years since he'd been on a steamship and that one had been nothing like the monstrosity that which up the Pinkton's flagship.

The groan of the engine grew louder and he stopped, listening to feminine curses over the sudden rush of steam. White hot air billowed out of the doorway directly to his right and a body scurried out, coughing and waving their hand in front of their face.

"God damn piece of shit! You call yourself a steamship? I got windup dolls that are more steamship than you are. Piece of crap." The woman turned, one hand rubbing her eye. Slim stilled, he was caught for sure. Her eyes met his and they widened, her mouth falling open. "Who the hell--"

He struck his hand out, grabbing her by the arm and swung her around to cup his palm over her mouth. "Now listen up darlin', I ain't got no issue with you, but I'm gonna need you to be quiet for me."

She went slack, catching him off guard and he lost his grip. Sliding to the ground, she spun on her side, kicking his legs out from beneath him. He landed hard and when he could breathe again she sat on his chest and smiled down at him like the cat that caught the mouse. "Well now, howdy

Slim."

"Phee?"

"Have you gotten skinnier? I didn't think that was possible." She leaned down and tweaked his nose and he grabbed her wrist. Damned if he didn't just fall into trouble. Malphia Blackwood was most brilliant mechanical engineer in the American west, hell, probably the whole dang world. Course, she was also the most ornery, mischievous, and downright devious woman he'd ever met. Damn good under the sheets, though.

"Get off me, woman."

She stuck her lip out in an exaggerated pout, but swung her leg over and stood, still grinning like an idiot. "What are you doing on this ship? You thinkin' of turnin' yourself in?"

"Not a chance. The Pinkertons got a couple of my friends. You know how I feel about people messin' with my friends."

"Well, now isn't that interestin'. You hitchin' your spurs up to a society girl? I never thought I'd see the day."

He frowned. "I ain't never hitched a spur on a girl yet. She's a friend."

"Then you won't be mindin' if I--,"

"She ain't as free with her affections as you are, Phee." He cut her off. The woman was a heartbreaker and a barrel of trouble that he wouldn't wish on his worst enemy. A smile slid across his lips. Well, maybe his enemy and it seemed she'd already done him the favor by jumping on board with the Pinkertons. "I take it you've seen Lady, but what about Sybil? The little woman in the silks?"

Malphia turned her attention back to the engine room, striding back in now that the worst of the steam had cleared out. He followed her in, wary of the temperamental machine. Grabbing a rag, she dipped it into a bucket and wrung the excess water from it before running it over her face. Her eyes were strained when she looked back at him. "I've seen her. On the other side of the ship with the Chinaman."

He stormed to the door. Steadfast as her corset stays, Lady could handle incarceration. That didn't make it sit any better with him, but she was a tough one. He liked that about her. But damned if he was going to let Sybil spend one more minute with the man who had terrorized her since childhood. There were limits to any man's control.

"You got a plan, Slim?" Malphia drawled from across the room, "Or are you interested in hearin' mine?"

Damn. He didn't trust the woman. He stopped, swiped his hat off his head and ran a long-fingered hand through his hair. Unfortunately, she was the best card in his hand at the moment. "Alright, what you got in that head of yours?"

7

Zhao Jin lit a cigarillo, the smoke swirling about his nose in an exotic dance. Across the floor, his prize sat enveloped in the brilliantly colored silks he'd provided her, the tattered remains of her previous garments thrown over the side of the lumbering steamship with disgusted haste. His key to victory would never be found in anything less than the richest trappings, a creature such as she deserved nothing less.

Green eyes glowed in the muted light of the room, her customarily plump lips pressed in a thin line. Like an unbroken mare, she resented captivity, but as all man's creatures, she would bend to his command and flourish beneath his firm hand. She could not resist his mastery.

"Your faith in prophesy will guarantee your failurezz," Sybil hissed.

Unreleased strength vibrated from her slight body, the scaly skin which covered her face taking on a shimmer that cut the colors of the light with surreal precision. He stood from the utilitarian chair and approached her. "Your powers are increasing."

She glared at him. "I have no powerzz."

It amazed him how the young could be so blind. Reaching down, he took Sybil by the elbow and hauled her to her feet. They had spent time enough with the Pinkertons. Delusions of law-abiding men made them capricious and he would be away before they chose to stand between him and his destiny. Sybil did not resist as he led her from the room, but she stiffened at the touch of his hand against her back.

Ever a dutiful daughter, she served her mother well through drug induced illnesses and alcoholic madness. A heart of gold was a rare commodity in the backstreets of Dodge City, and he'd been swept away by her sweet innocence. Taking the mother had been a simple thing. Encouraging the destructive behavior which ultimately led to her death a small challenge, but one he'd taken to with enthusiasm. The promise in the budding child was a great prize and now he knew why.

The blossom shall meet the serpent. The Silver City witch's words rang like sweet whispers in his memory. A promise and a trail to follow. To this point the prophesy led him true. He put a hand to the satchel at his side to touch the slight bulge of three rolled scrolls. They were the map, the serpent the key. And there had never been a serpent so enchanting.

Sybil's fine features and petite body held the markers for unrivaled beauty. The unfortunate affliction which turned her soft skin to scales enveloped her petite body just before he'd met her. The pain of the experience was difficult to watch, but beyond the trials of the flesh he saw the transformation of a child into a creature of astonishing potential.

And when he stumbled upon the prophesy that guaranteed his triumph over his greatest rival he knew this little woman was tied to him without compromise. She was his.

Now she would know this unequivocally.

The soft soles of her feet pattered silently besides the clicking of his finely-made boots. The deck was empty, but for the shadow of his men waiting against the far rail. Acrid smoke sailed from another part of the ship, and the loud thumps of an uncooperative engine echoed in the night. The Pinkertons would be lucky to make it another one-hundred miles. He and his prize would be far away by the time this ship fell from the sky.

Martin joined him as he approached the open landing pad. The night shrouded his prized contraption in darkness, and only the barest line of contrast with the black sky hinted that all was well. The SteamWing came at a gargantuan price, but was well worth the expense. Joseph worked with Martin to remove the tarp and unfold the giant black canvas wings. With the wings removed from their place of rest, the mini-dirigible balloon rose as it filled with air, exposing the small passenger compartment. Designed to comfortably seat five grown men, it would easily handle the small group intent on leaving the much larger ship.

Sybil sucked in a breath beside him and he smiled down at her. Running a hand down her silk coverings, he asked, "Do you like it? I assure you, it is a far more enjoyable ride than this barge."

"It izz so small."

Zhao Jin nodded. "Yes, it is the most highly advanced model of its kind. Not even the leaders of this country have conveyances of such quality. Do not fear for your life, my child. The SteamWing is perfectly safe."

She wrenched away from him and hissed, "I am *not* your child."

He responded with a mildly tolerant smile. It would take time for her to grow comfortable as his property.

The SteamWing let out a low moan as the engine engaged and tanks warmed. Martin and Jake hustled around the cabin, releasing the ropes that held it in place. Zhao Jin took Sybil by the hand and led her into the compartment.

Settling her on a plush settee, he moved to the control console and flipped the switch to the interior lights. The soft glow bathed the space with illumination. Automated gas lighting had been a challenge, but the engineers succeeded and Zhao Jin relished his pearl of technological genius. The white men who held power so reservedly within his new homeland could not compete with his wealth and ingenuity.

Sybil shifted and the sliding silk sounded as the song of angels to his ears. This glorious woman would provide him the final lynch pin to not only destroy Mordecai Kovacs, but would award him the treasure the blasted man coveted.

His heart rate accelerated at the thought of Kovacs. His old rival traveled free across the lands of the wild American West, performing for the simple-minded masses and profiting from deceitful promises. Success ever a fleeting mistress for Kovacs, he left Dodge City, changing his name to that ridiculous MacHurdyGurdy, and set out to discover the secret of wealth beyond all comprehension--the fabled cities of Cibola.

Zhao Jin sneered. Since their days in Dodge City, he had done everything to prevent Kovacs' success. And now he would destroy the man and have his treasure. With the beautiful serpent mistress as his guide, the great gold of Cibola would be his.

Martin followed Joseph into the cabin and sealed the door. Taking their seats, they prepared for departure. Zhao Jin gave them the order to leave the giant steamship behind, and then he took a seat beside Sybil. Placing a hand on her knee, he leaned in and brushed a tendril of dark brown hair away from her eyes. "Now, my sweet serpent. Where were you taking your friends? Where shall we find Mordecai Kovacs?"

She widened her eyes and her lips parted. Then a stubborn glint enveloped her eyes and she refused to speak. No matter. She would tell him before the night was done. She was his to command.

***

Slim squinted as he watched the movement across the deck. Something unreal was floating over the rail. Like a giant bird, it had wings that spanned over twenty feet. He couldn't possibly be seeing what he thought he saw.

"Dang it. That was our ride."

"What?" Slim looked to Malphia. The blasted woman insisted on changing into a completely new outfit, this one wrapping her curves in black leather and not leaving anything to the imagination. Course he appreciated the view as any hot-blooded man would. But, damn it, they'd lost precious time. Apparently the cost had been their escape. "What do we do now then?"

"Don't you get huffy. I got alternatives. But I'm thinking that we just lost one of your friends on that ship."

That was a ship? He'd never seen anything like it and if one of the girls had been on board, he'd have a hell of a time catching up to them. "Who?"

"Sybil. That's the Chinaman's contraption. I ain't never seen anything like it. Brilliant piece of work. Course, I could have done better, it could use some adjustments, but he wouldn't have looked twice at me anyway. That man's got one thing on his mind and I ain't got the faintest idea what it is."

Slim knew. The shrewd Zhao Jin hunted Sybil for years and according to the poor girl, he had aspirations for greatness which amounted to believing in the words of cracked soothsayers and witches. Zhao Jin believed Sybil was some kind of key to his destiny and the man would do anything to have her.

Slim clenched his fist and a streak of pain shot from his grinding teeth. Now he'd have to track down another flying stagecoach. Why didn't people ride in a normal way anymore? What was wrong with a horse?

Malphia stuck her head around a corner then put up a hand to wave him forward. They slipped down the back side of the ship, headed toward a brightly lit corridor that ran through the center of the ship.

They came to a staircase and Malphia listened before she headed down. After two flights, she stopped, pointed down the corridor and whispered, "That's the crew quarters and at the end is Banahan's suite. I think they got your Lady locked in one of his rooms."

An angry flush spread across the back of his neck. He'd have preferred they'd locked her up in the prisoner cells. What kind of scoundrel kept a classy lady in his rooms?

"I'm going in to distract Tommy. Give me a few minutes to get him into the bedroom, then you come in and look for your lady," Malphia said as they came upon the door.

"She ain't my lady," he said more out of an ornery sense of argumentativeness than anything else. Things needed to be moving in his direction soon. He was getting tired of waiting.

"I'm gonna leave that alone for now. Just give me a few minutes. Tommy can be a wily old coot." She put her hand on the door handle. "I'll meet you on deck soon as I figure you've had enough time to get away."

Slim made to respond, but the leather-clad woman was through the door and closing it before he could put two words together. Feeling exposed, he turned down the gas-light lantern directly to the right of the door. A click down the corridor had his hand going for his peacemaker. A skinny man with his shirt partially untucked and hat askew stumbled into the hall. Slim pushed into the shadows and waited as the man decided which way to go.

He tightened his fingers around the handle of his pistol as the man started to weave toward him. Damn, he didn't want to have to shoot someone. The hammer cocked, he pulled the pistol from the hard leather holster, but breathed a sigh of relief when the man spun around and headed the opposite direction. Blessed by a drunkard's inability to pay attention to detail, he put away the peacemaker and turned the doorknob. Malphia should have had plenty of time to ply her wiles on Banahan. And if not, well, Slim was going in anyway.

The room was quiet, and dark. Muffled murmurs came from the left where a shut door was framed by a thin line of light about the cracks. Vision was limited to dense shadows where each piece of furniture stood. His boots tread silently across a rich carpet and the scent of a recently smoked cigar wafted from the corner of the room. Striding to the right, he hoped to find Lady with little trouble. Based on the tenor of the conversation, Malphia was having little luck charming Banahan to her desires. It sounded more like they were arguing over machinery. Slim smirked--whatever worked for the man.

Slim found it more enjoyable to acquiesce to the fairer

sex. Arguing might get the blood boiling, but nothing made a woman more amenable to pleasure than believing she was right. Course, it didn't explain why he'd taken such enjoyment out of bickering with Lady. But that was something to contemplate another day. Right now, he needed to get this particular lady-friend out of trouble.

Three doors lined the far wall. The first knob turned easily in his hand. Within he found an extravagant water closet, complete with porcelain tub and honest-to-god running water. Seemed the Pinkerton life was good for Mr. Banahan. Sending this ship crashing to the desert floor was sounding more and more enjoyable.

He tried the second door and found it locked. Fairly certain it was where he'd find Lady, he still tried the third for good measure. Inside he spied a storage room, containing shelves of weapons, boxes, and what appeared to be confiscated contraband. An entire shelf of bottled whisky had him whistling under his breath. Too bad he didn't have a way to make off with all that liquor. He'd be set for a year. The familiar shape of Lady's rucksack caught his eye and he grabbed it. She'd be mighty appreciative of him returning this to her. Maybe she'd even give him a smile.

Raised voices had him closing the door before he could explore further. At the locked door, he knocked with a knuckle and placed an ear against the wood. A rustle could be heard in the room beyond and he whispered, "Lady? You in there."

More rustling sounded and then he heard a scratching at the door and her voice came through the lock. "Who's there."

"It's Slim. I'm gonna get you out of there."

"Slim? You idiot! What are you doing here? They want

you, you fool. Get out of here, I can take care of myself."

Yep, Lady was doing just fine. He rustled in his pocket for the skeleton key Maphia handed to him before they'd left her room. The metal scraped in the lock, but he had it open and Lady in his arms before she could scold him any further. Elated, he ran a hand down her arms then over her face, checking for injuries. Relieved that she appeared unharmed, he put her from him and caught a momentary flash of disconcerted confusion on her face. Damn, the woman didn't know how to let a man take care of her.

"Come on, we got to get."

"You're insane."

He grabbed her hand and strode from the room, ducking his head into the hall to check for Pinkertons. When he found none, they ran down the corridor and up the stairs. He led them to the back of the ship they ducked behind a barrel which smelled suspiciously like gunpowder. He handed Lady the bag and moved to watch for Malphia.

"Slim!" Lady hissed. "What now?

He waved her off, and grabbed for his guns when a shadow crossed in front of him. Malphia came around the corner, her lips set with resolve. "Well, Slim we got a problem."

Banahan followed her from behind, holding two pistols and a sly grin on his face. "Mr. Robinson, it's a real pleasure to finally meet you."

"Got to tell you Slim, Mr. Banahan's offer was a bit more lucrative." Malphia gave him a lazy wink and stepped aside as Banahan sent three men in to take Slim by the arms, his peacemaker wrenched from his hand.

"And please come out and join us Miss Dewhurst. The game is lost," Banahan drawled.

Slim swung his shoulder around and caught a glimpse of Lady, hoping she wouldn't do anything foolish. She rose, pointing two augmented pistols at their advisories. He should have known better, the woman had more gumption than the entire west coast. He admired it, but now was not the time for her to be showing her courage.

"Lady," he warned.

"Let him go," Lady said.

"Now Miss Dewhurst, don't be doing anything rash," Banahan said.

"Rash, Mr. Banahan? I have had just about enough of this. You will let him go now or I will blow a hole through you and your men. You have seen one of these in action, I assume?" When he didn't respond she raised her arm and pointed it at a barrel beside Banahan and continued, "Well, perhaps I should just show you what it can do."

"Lady no!" Slim shouted, but it was too late. Sparks flew, and an explosion sounded from the small barrel. The bullet crashed through the wooden barrel beside Banahan, sending shrapnel and powder through the air. The sparks caught and a second, much louder explosion erupted around them. Fire and screams filled the air and Slim was sent flying across the deck. The last he saw was the flapping of Lady's divided skirt as her body disappeared over the rail.

8

The earth tilted and the colors converged in a kaleidoscope of surreal geometry. Sybil blinked, fluttering her lids to banish the vision. The landscape returned to the sharp clarity of day and the wind that blew through the tiny, single-paned window brushed away the sense of anxiety. Clutching at the edges of her silk, she turned, pulling the fine fabric tight against her body. There was security threaded through the voluminous folds; something to protect her from the changes in her body and mind.

Her captors sat across the room. Zhao Jin's two lackeys manned the elaborate console, gliding the black steamship across the sky. Their master stood behind them, staring into the blue expanse. For the first time since he'd returned his dark presence to her life, he looked relaxed. Complacency in victory was dangerous and she hoped it foreshadowed a new carelessness.

A slight shift of her silks made his head turn toward her, his obsidian eyes boring into her. Despair threatened to bring tears to her eyes. Perhaps she misread the complacency; the man clearly had his faculties in prime working order.

"Would you like tea, my dear?" Zhao Jin said as he turned to the back of the narrow compartment. A tea service sat beside a highly polished copper tank, where a pipe rose from the tank through the ceiling and out to the tail of the ship. He twisted a knob on a spout extending from the tank and drew water into a cast iron tea pot. "One of the many amenities that I had built into this machine. It seemed simple enough to have a steamship provide hot water as well as transport. Do you take it with cream? Such a barbarous thing the white men do to good tea, but if it is your preference, I will accommodate you."

His smile twisted as he looked at her and she turned back to the window. She did not want tea. She wanted nothing from the man.

The rising sun punctured the billowing clouds that hovered over the horizon. Headed north, they made excellent progress across the New Mexico landscape. Stubbornly, she refused to give the destination to the evil men who held her, necessitating an educated decision by the Chinaman. Sybil let relief wash over her as the ship turned to the east.

Light spilled over the clouds and the sky erupted into the bright yellow and gold that guaranteed a clear day. Warmth teased fleetingly with the wind, impelling her forward. She turned her cheeks to the light, the heat sending pleasure across her skin. The autumn drive to winter wreaked havoc on her nights. Sleepless and unbearably cold, her mind slowed and senses dulled. It had made the trip through the desert nearly unbearable. She'd kept her growing lethargy from Slim and Lady, not willing to worry them. The only cure to her malaise seemed to be the bright promise of daylight.

Combined with the frequent hallucinations, she felt as though her body abandoned her just as she so desperately needed to feel human.

A tea cup slid in front of her, the small table protected

by a smooth coat of glossy finish. She stared into the tan depths, restraining a scowl. She hated cream in her tea. Turning her head away, she closed her eyes to the sunlight. Zhao Jin's cosseting reminded her of the rich, old women that attended grand dance halls, lapdogs held within their pudgy arms. To be feared and cursed for her ugliness was far kinder than the dehumanizing clucking of a pet-owner.

Zhao Jin settled into a garishly upholstered settee across from her and unfolded a newspaper. The scene was nauseatingly domestic. Turning her thoughts to the friends she lost, she sought for anything to distract her from the current travesty that had become her life.

Dark thoughts and fatalism had never been her mood of choice. Despite tragedy and frustration, she'd maintained a relatively upbeat flair to her perspectives. Unfortunately, optimism was proving far more difficult to summon with the recent turn of events. Having lost her surrogate family in the MacHurdyGurdys, her recent colleagues quickly replaced them within her heart. Truth be told, Slim and Lady had far surpassed the traveling entertainers in kindness and loyalty.

Except for Miss Chevious. How dearly she missed that naïve and beautiful doll.

Her nose twitched, as memories swelled about her, bringing images of her life on the trail to mind. The Marvelous MacHurdyGurdy Traveling Show had been a conglomerate of misfits and ne'er-do-wells and despite a significant ethical conflict, Sybil fit in. The timid Bernard was nothing but kind. The bristly Beatrice, tolerant with the occasional bout of motherly support. The comical Twins with their whirring clockwork parts and the graceful marionettes brought joy and laughter to her life. So much good existed during the years she traveled the west with the troupe.

Dark memories swirled amid the bright, bringing a rash of tears to the corners of her eyes. Syrus, a kind-hearted and misunderstood reprobate had been a shining champion of her, keeping watch and always ready with a gentle hand. What kind of madness had the troupe succumbed to that led to such nefarious misdeeds?

The ghostly stench of death filled the room, and the colors shifted as she witnessed the evil moment of discovery again. Overwhelmed, she relived the morning when she discovered the charred remains of Syrus, burned within one of the troupe's cart, his hands gripping her pillows. A tiny fragment of fabric clutched within his palm was the only remains of her previous life.

And beside him sat the melted copper pigtails and destroyed components that once made up her old friend, Miss Chevious. A mechanical doll, with a devilish curiosity and kind heart, she'd brought real joy to Sybil's life. The metal and hose which made up the girl had been created by the genius of Bernard MacHurdyGurdy, but her soul had been a gift from the heavens.

Her soul was torn from earth by the devious desires of a man who could wield kindness as lethally as he could ill-intent. Having committed murder and vice in the pursuit of wealth and prosperity, Mordecai MacHurdyGurdy deserved a traitor's death for all he had done.

The memories faded and she focused once again on her captor. Temptation made her consider the option of telling Zhao Jin exactly where to find Mordecai MacHurdyGurdy, as his was the only hate for the man which could surpass her own. But she promised that vengeance to another.

Slim and Lady would have their reckoning with the sly,

snake-oil salesman. And when they were done with him, Zhao Jin could have the carcass.

***

A horse snorted. Bolting up at the feel of hot animal breath against her cheek, Lady came face-to-face with the long nose of a majestic equine. She opened her lips to scream just as the horse nudged her shoulder, sending a jolt of searing pain through her torso. Stars formed behind her eyes and she gritted her teeth.

"Chief, leave her be." A deep voice rumbled from behind her and the horse looked up, its mane shaking as it turned to leave. Wide-eyed, Lady shifted, bringing another shot of pain through her shoulder. Booted feet came into view, and as the pain receded, she scanned up the legs, past firm muscular thighs, across a flat belly and chest into the eyes of… "Eustace?"

He squatted beside her and grabbed her hand, a grin painted across a face sprinkled with stubble. The dark blue cavalry hat pushed back as he leaned forward, the yellow tassels swaying as he moved. "Do not move. You suffered quite a fall."

Lady lifted a hand to her head and felt the bruises that covered her cheek bones. Scrapes and cuts could be seen across her arms and she looked with horror at the condition of her bodice. A giant gash had torn diagonally from one corner to the other. There would be no saving the garment now.

Eustace let go of her hand and reached for the canteen secured to his waist. He offered her the water and she eagerly accepted. The cool liquid cleared her confusion and brought her back to reality.

The explosion! She'd blown herself right off of that ship and apparently suffered a number of injuries which thankfully appeared to be less than life-threatening. Her shoulder throbbed and she reached her second hand to prod at the wounded joint.

"You dislocated your shoulder. We righted it before you woke, but it will be quite sore for several days." He leaned forward again, searching her eyes, his own swarming with concern. "What were you doing on a Pinkerton ship, Miss Dewhurst? And why in heaven's name did you fall off?"

Falling off was a mild description of what she had actually done. And explaining to an old family friend why she'd nearly killed herself was not going to happen. His fingers rubbed with a familiar tenderness into her palms and she looked down at his uncharacteristically rugged hands.

Those same hands once led her through stately dances and escorted her to dinner at the grandest of society balls. The son of a senator, he frequented the same entertainments, even being on the list of guests who attended her parent's dinner parties. Ever the discerning host, her mother only invited the most influential guests. Slim would certainly never be included at their dinner table.

Slim. Good heavens! The blasted man was in the hands of the Pinkertons and she'd left him there!

Grabbing the pieces of her bodice, she held them together as she struggled to find her feet. Eustace pushed her back. "Miss Dewhurst, I must protest. You are in no condition to rise. You must rest for a bit longer, and then we will depart."

"Depart? Eustace, what are you babbling about? I must get back to that ship."

Silence fell and his expression darkened. Lady took in a breath. Finally, reality swung into focus and she turned to look around. Ten men stood at various distances, their movements clearly meant to suggest busy industry, but the angle of their heads made it quite obvious they watched Lady and Eustace with interest. Horses were tied to branches, and the scent of a fire answered her questions. She was in a cavalry camp.

How on earth had she landed in a cavalry camp? "Eustace, where am I?"

"It is Captain Wright." His words were gruff, but when her eyes swung back to his, he softened his response. "We were a mile away when we saw you fly off that ship. It was quite the sight to see, fire roaring into the sky. There was shouting and then we saw your body fall to the ground. Nearly lost our bellies when we realized it was a woman that fell."

Lady blinked at him. But where were they now? She couldn't leave Slim to those ingrates. They'd just as likely kill him as turn him over to the law. She didn't want to see him end up with either fate. He may be an all-around nuisance, but she had invested time in his welfare and she had no intention of seeing it wasted. "Eustace--I mean, Captain Wright, it is imperative that I return to that ship. I left something quite valuable there."

Eustace pulled her bag toward him and opened the flap. Pulling out the smoke bombs, he raised a brow. "What exactly are you doing out here, Miss Dewhurst?"

Her nose flared. He had no right to question her. Grateful he had come to her rescue, she placed a hand on his wrist. "I truly appreciate the kindness you have shown, sir. Had you not seen to my injuries, I may have been the victim of the elements."

The convenience of being found by a cavalry unit was unmistakable. And one that was led by an old friend, it was nearly unbelievable. What were the chances she would run into a man such as he in this great desert? But that was a question for another day, she had a purpose. "If you could simply point me in the direction the Pinkertons flew, I will not take up any more of your time."

Eustace frowned, and placed her smoke bombs back into her bag, then threw it up to a compatriot who sidled up beside him. "It pains me that I bring you this news, but I have been sent to bring you home."

"I beg your pardon?"

"I know that you must value your freedom. It is the only explanation for why you have been gone for so long. But your father has had enough, his tolerance has ended and it is time for you to return home."

Lady gaped at him and could think of nothing to say. Return home? She wasn't going home. Without the locket there would be no future there for her. There was much to be done. MacHurdyGurdy still walked the desert on a quest for treasure. Sybil was in the clutches of the infuriating Zhao Jin. She did not have time for this foolishness.

Especially now that the Pinkertons had Slim.

9

Slim spat blood onto the floor then cracked his neck to realign the bones. Banahan's man hadn't pulled any punches and Slim figured the idiot wouldn't stop until he'd pummeled his face to something like corned beef hash. The giant stood across the room, his hands flexing with impatience, the stupid look on his face focused intently on his quarry. Slim gave him a slow wink.

"Don't antagonize the man, Mr. Robinson. I only have so much influence on his behavior." Banahan drew long on his cigar then watched as the smoke filled the stale air between him and Slim. Over the years the arrogant Pinkerton had shown his face to Slim every now and again, never quite smart or fast enough to catch him. It was a darn shame that Lady had blown that barrel up as she had. They'd be long on their way to Pueblo if she'd kept her wits about her.

It was mighty fine she'd come to his defense like that, but the girl's city-bred instincts hadn't served them well. One of these days she'd find her western legs, but in the meantime, Slim had a heck of a job keeping an eye on the reckless female. Course if he wanted to continue to do so, he needed to find himself a way out of his current predicament.

"You takin' me to Montana, Banahan? I heard they got me figured for dead."

Banahan bit the end of his cigar and spread his lips in a sneer. "They are willing to pay the most for you. After your stunt in Socorro, everybody knows you're still livin', even the governor."

No doubt the old bastard was laughing at the prospect of having Slim caught in his net. Considering it was the death of his son which had the man so intent on his capture, Slim wasn't unsympathetic to his feelings. He just preferred to keep a rope from tightening around his neck. "How much they got me going for now?"

"Three hundred dollars, last notice I saw."

Slim whistled. Damn that was a nice price. He never figured he'd be worth more than a horse.

"Of course, your pretty lady friend was looking to bring me one thousand."

Red swam before his eyes, and Slim lunged up, bringing the old wood chair with him as his tied hands strained at their bounds. "You figurin' to sell my lady friend, you bastard?"

A fist grabbed Slim by the shoulder and threw him to the ground, the chair crashed beneath him and splintered into pieces. With the wind knocked out of him, he didn't have the chance to take advantage of his relative freedom. A heavy foot pressed down on his chest, the toe of the boot poking painfully into the soft skin beneath his chin. Stupid eyes stared at him with unrestrained malice.

Banahan joined his thug and looked down at Slim. "I wasn't going to sell her. Her daddy has a price on her head just as sure as the governor has on you. Seems she's worth quite a bit more than you, but I can see how that might be the case."

More blood pooled in his cheeks and Slim spat again,

covering the boot that held him down with the thick liquid. He hoped it would stain the pretty tan leather. A man who made a livin' beatin' the tar out of folks shouldn't have nice things. It just wasn't right.

"I hear you, Banahan. You gettin' tired of knocking me around or do you got a point to this whole conversation?"Slim said.

"No, I'm just trying to decide what to do with you." Banahan squatted beside him, the stale stench of his body overwhelming Slim's nose. Perhaps he'd be knocked out the next time the fists flew. It'd be preferable to smelling the old Pinkerton. Banahan blew out another fog of smoke then continued, "Montana is an awful long way to be flying this ship for just 300 dollars. It'd cost that much just to get there and back. So I figure there had better be a good reason for me to want to collect on that."

Slim snarled. He didn't have time to be messin' with these men. Either Banahan locked him up tight and he found a way to escape, or he left him to his bruiser and Slim figured a way to outsmart the giant with sadistically beefy hands. Either way, he needed to be off this ship by the morning.

Banahan stood and continued to chew on his cigar, letting the time pass and frustration build. Slim wasn't one keen on patience. Not unless cards were in play. Maybe he could interest the man in a game. Banahan seemed to be the gamblin' type. "You up for a hand? I'll give you a chance to win that money right now."

The Pinkerton's hearty guffaw rattled around the room. "Do you think I don't know why you got yourself in such a mess? I ain't heard of a man that beat you yet at the tables. Either you got a deal with the devil or you cheat like nobody else."

It was something like that. Slim scowled. "Well, what choice do you got? You either hand me to the governor or you let me go. I don't figure you're in a mood to let me go."

"No. I'm not." Banahan pulled the cigar from his lips and smiled the first honest grin Slim had seen all day. Toothy and yellow, it turned a man's stomach. Heaven help her, if the man had a wife. Banahan continued, "I think I got a use for you and it will be quite a bit more useful than having you swing on a rope. If I wanted to see that, I'd just throw you over the side of the ship and let you kick the clouds. But, no, we'll keep you around a bit."

Banahan strolled toward the door then turned to address his man. "You can mess him up a bit more, but he needs to be in working condition. I'm going to need him to heal before we can do the tests. I want to know without a doubt that it's the elixir that kills him, not your hands."

Slim withheld the sigh of relief. Finally, they'd get down to business and he'd find himself a way off this damn sky bucket.

***

Lady hurried after Eustace, the old soldier's coat flapping against her knees as its voluminous fabric protected her from the biting wind and unconscious stares. So far all the men in the unit had been nothing but courteous, she certainly couldn't blame their wandering eyes when her bodice left nothing to the imagination. The offer of a cavalry coat was well received. She stumbled over a rocky outcrop and glared at Eustace when he sent a patronizing look backward.

If he hadn't hidden her satchel, she'd have taken off in

the middle of the night. The arrogant man made it quite clear he considered her the very same twit she'd been when they knew each other three years ago in Boston. Of course, he had a particular fondness for that twit, and with his upbringing, she couldn't find fault with his predilections.

Or his aspirations.

Her father's powerful fingers threaded through everything from the merchant trade, high society, and apparently the highest offices of politics. That this single company of men would be sent off to find one, belligerent girl of circumstance said more about her father's money than about her worth. "Eustace, slow down. I haven't the legs you do."

He spun around. "Miss Dewhurst, I told you to stay at camp. If you must insist on accompanying me, then you will need to keep up."

She felt a sudden urge to roll her eyes. Heavens, she hadn't felt that urge in years. Even Slim didn't elicit this particular response. Lady frowned. Apparently, she couldn't help comparing Eustace to Slim. They were such vastly different men, in both stature and personality.

Both men had light-colored hair, brown, but nearly blond. That was where any similarity ended. Where Slim was jovial, Eustace was morose. Laidback and steadfast, Lady might find fault with Slim's approach to life, but she never doubted his motives. He was exactly the man he said he was. And it was comforting.

Eustace, on the other hand held his secrets close to his chest and his motives were always suspect. They always had been, and no more so than when he'd asked her to marry him.

She stumbled again and stopped her fall against a palo verde that stood sentinel on the steep slope. That night had been forgotten, unfortunately dredged up by the recent circumstances. Combined with the loss of the Spanish Hope, his proposal aided in her final decision to leave her life amid the social elite and pursue her destiny in the dirty American west. It was a decision she'd never regretted. In fact, she should be grateful to Eustace for precipitating such a fantastic adventure.

Of course, she didn't feel particularly thankful at the moment. Not while he had every intention of taking her from her hard-won freedom. He would find himself on the wrong end of one of her augmented pistols if he persisted with this nonsense.

They finally reached the top of the hill and Lady sat atop a boulder as Eustace removed a long spyglass from a bag at his side. The valley rolled out beyond them, the sun rising slowly from the horizon. They marched for most of the day, making a hasty push toward Albuquerque. The day before was short and little was covered, so the desire to make decent progress had been quite clear. Lady's trail hardened stamina impressed most of the men and she kept the pains from the fall to herself. But Eustace refused to notice her hardiness and the strength of character she'd developed in the years since they'd last seen one another. It was quite infuriating.

"Miss Dewhurst, you will do well to drink from your canteen."

She withheld a derisive snort. The container was half-full due to her diligent attention to hydration. His observational skills left much to be desired. How he managed to receive this command was blatantly obvious; her father wanted a lackey to lead the charge. True to form and uncreative. He would soon discover his mistake when the Captain returned without his charge.

"You can call me Lady, Eustace. There isn't much use for formality out here."

He gave a snide look and said, "I had heard you were going by that ridiculous name. I hope it does not offend you, but I would prefer to maintain the formalities. It is even more necessary in the wilds among the savages to keep a semblance of civility. Otherwise, we risk losing ourselves to barbarism."

Good God, was he serious? She sucked in a breath and felt the pinch of her corset stays against her hips. Frowning, she thought of her last conversation with Slim. The one before their misadventure with the Pinkertons. The one where she said more than she intended and meant very little of it. Slim encouraged her to throw off the last bastion of the civilized, mocking her corset and the stiff emotional protection it provided her. At the time she'd been outraged, furious and feeling murderous.

Now she missed him terribly.

Perhaps it was time to let go of the corset and with it any intention of returning to her old life in Boston. If she had ever had a choice that would mark her direction through life, then this was it. Today she could decide to give up her quest. She could return to her father's protective, though obnoxiously controlling arms and let the last few years pass as if nothing happened. She'd return to the ballrooms and lecture halls. She'd marry and become a great hostess for her husband. And if she were reading the signs right, that husband would be Eustace.

Her father was laying her life before her and demanding she follow his command. Stubborn and dictatorial, his desires would be met, whether she wished to marry the irritatingly snobbish Captain Wright or not. It was as it had always been—her father's world.

But one thing her dear father did not count on was the Spanish Hope. In her quest for the family heirloom, she'd discovered a new purpose and a personal fortitude which surprised her. Years ago, she would never have dreamt of going against her father's wishes. His word was law and she automatically complied. But now she knew each moment was a choice. And the choice was hers alone.

Her father entrusted her with the locket in an attempt to teach her responsibility. He'd intended for her to learn the skills of a grand hostess and homemaker. If she could maintain a hold on a priceless bauble, then she could be trusted to present a suitable image to the highest society.

The old man would be terribly disappointed to discover she'd learned an entirely different lesson. Lifting her hand above her eyes, she shaded the sun from her face and stared into the distance. A shadow against the horizon suggested they were near a settlement. With luck, it would mean they were nearing Albuquerque.

Eustace believed he could keep a hold of her all the way to Denver where her father waited for her arrival. She imagined he'd purchased an ostentatious house with a full staff and all the accoutrements a man of his status deserved. She hoped it was comfortable. The man would be waiting there for quite some time.

She had business in Albuquerque, and when things were done, she'd be certain to send Eustace her gratitude for the escort to town.

10

The Spanish flavor of Albuquerque far outshone the American influence. Heads turned as the company of cavalry trudged through town, although most eyes settled inquisitively on Lady as she sat with a rigid back on Eustace's horse. The stallion was a beauty, and she longed to save him from his negligent master, but she was not keen on adding horse thievery to her crimes. It was bad enough she'd made a habit of fostering a fugitive.

The company stopped in front of a proper boarding house and Eustace entered to secure them lodging. The men stood around her, wary of the strangers that hovered about them with curiosity. A stoop-shouldered man with gnarled hands stopped beside one of the soldiers. "You boys here about the Apaches?"

The soldier, no older than eighteen, shifted uncomfortably. Lady imagined he'd far rather be here for the Apaches than escorting a woman through the unforgiving territory. The boy stuttered as he answered, "No, sir."

The old man frowned and looked toward the saloon. "That's too bad. Three of them came into town last night, been drinking in MacDougal's place. Figure they've got a mind to cause some trouble." He cast a sly look at Lady. "Don't think the women-folk are safe with them savages hangin' about. But the sheriff ain't made no move to do anything about it."

The boy's drawn face and stiffened shoulders made Lady want to roll her eyes. There was nothing like the fear of savages to turn otherwise honorable men into monsters. The one experience Lady had with Apaches was frightening, but each side comported themselves with dignity. Slim, with his usual confidence and laid-back nature got them through that confrontation with relative ease.

Lady slanted her eyes to the saloon. But, one thing about the experience still had her curious. The Apaches saved them from capture by the Pinkertons that time, distracting the monstrous steamship with their arrows and rifles. But later, when the band of men caught up with Slim, Sybil and her, they were adversarial and frightened of Sybil. At the time, Lady had brushed it off as reaction to a disease-ridden woman. It was, after all, a common instinct for the white and red men together.

She had her doubts now.

Something about Sybil particularly spooked the men. And the longer Lady spent in Sybil's company, the more she questioned the disease which cursed the young woman. Something was happening to her friend, something the Chinaman understood and something the Apaches seemed to have knowledge of as well. When she found Sybil, it was time to see about solving the mystery.

First Lady had to evade her diligent escort.

Eustace returned to the dust-covered street, righting his hat after placing it back on his head. He looked uncomfortable in a uniform and she smiled. Not everyone could adapt to the rigors of the west. He raised his arms to assist her from the saddle, his hands lingering a second too long on her waist before he set her aside. Lady brushed the feel of his touch off her waist and swished past him toward the door.

Grabbing her hand, he tucked it into the crook of his arm and slowed her movement toward the boarding house. "I have rented you a room facing the back so you do not witness the unseemly nature of the nearest establishments."

Lady withheld a laugh, certain he would not appreciate her reaction. She was tempted to describe her adventures in the Chinese brothel when she and Slim first rescued Sybil from Zhao Jin's clutches. Eustace was unlikely to see the humor in how she'd scaled the walls, snuck into Sybil's room and set fire to the garishly carpeted halls.

She replied, "Thank you. I truly appreciate your consideration."

His back straightened and chest puffed out like a feathered grouse. Lady had to bite her lip to keep from laughing. Slim never puffed out his chest, his confidence and kindness was far more genuine. Lady frowned. She must stop comparing the two men as though they were both suitors. Eustace believed he was, and never would be. Slim didn't even pretend.

Lady sighed. Her decision to stay in the west and embrace her new life of adventure would mean giving up the possibility of a stable marriage. The likelihood of securing a husband in the territories was not out of bounds, but settling down into a simple, homespun life wasn't on the horizon for her. She was far too handy with a weapon and had too much desire to explore the treasures of the land. There wasn't a man out there who would embrace a woman like that.

Eustace led her up the grand staircase, and stopped in front of one of the rooms. He removed a key from his pocket and slid it into the lock. "We will stay here for a few days and stock up for the trip to Denver. I hope you will not mind the inconvenience?"

Lady gave him a placating smile. She could work with a few days, but she would have to be careful not to arouse his suspicions. Placing her hand on his wrist, she said, "You have been the reminder of my old life that I needed. I cannot thank you enough. Your gentlemanly behavior has truly inspired me. Can you forgive me for being such a silly girl?"

His nose flared as he looked down at her fingers and Lady gasped at the sudden heat in his eyes. "Of course, Miss Dewhurst. I would follow you to the Pacific if I needed to."

Lady's heart thudded with trepidation. His grip turned possessive as his hand moved to her elbow, encouraging her into the room. When she passed the threshold he released her, sending her scurrying across the room to find solace beside the curtained window. A slight stab of fear had her gripping together the lapels of the soldier's coat.

The door clicked shut and the key turned in the lock. Eustace dropped the key into his pocket then turned to face her. Lady gaped at the predatory gleam in his eye. It seemed she failed to see the warning signs which led to this moment.

"Fidelia," he whispered.

Her heckles rose. "My name is Lady."

"Fidelia," he reiterated as he slowly stalked her. Lady glanced around the room, desperately seeking anything she could use to stall his progress. He'd taken control of her satchel and it was the first thing she intended to rectify. But now she was without the comforting protection of her contraptions. A quick hit to the head with one of her augmented pistols would certainly have put him in his place.

She moved from the window and circled the room away

from him. His smile turned devilish. "Do not pretend you are not aware of my feelings for you. Fidelia, we are to be wed. You will grow used to my presence in your bedroom."

Heart pattering, she placed her hand on the dresser, the mirror wobbling at the force of her grip. He closed the gap between them.

"We are not married yet," she said. And they never would be, though telling him that at the moment seemed unwise.

"Your father has already given his consent to our union. In fact, he has ordered that I bring you home by whatever means necessary. I do not believe that our child's early birth will worry him."

Lady's mouth fell open. He had to be out of his mind. She struggled for an answer. "I have not changed so much that I would consider this action outside of marriage. Why we would be no different than the savages if we gave into our baser desires."

"It is a savage country we live in, my love."

She cringed at the endearment and her stomach turned as he drew closer, his eyes intent on her hand grasping the coat. She said, "You said yourself that we must maintain a sense of civility if we are to survive, otherwise we fall to barbarism."

He stalled and she continued, intent on distracting his ardor. "I would not be able to live with myself if that which I have guarded so defiantly for all this time were taken before we are wed. Please, Eustace, wait until our vows have been committed."

His hands fisted and his jaw clenched. "Is it what you truly want? To wed and be as husband and wife?"

Feeling that this was her one chance, she loosened her

hold on the dresser and cast her eyes down in submission. "I have not changed so very much in these years. But I have discovered much, and most of all--" She tipped her head up and gave him a tremulous smile. "Most of all I have learned that my life belongs in your hands. That we shall be man and wife and I will return to where I belong."

His chest heaved under his forcibly restrained passion and she waited, desperate to know if her ploy worked. A moment passed and she tightened her fingers, finding solace in the heavy wool garment. Finally, the heat in his eyes diminished and he spoke, "Then I will respect your wish, my love. And I apologize for my boorishness. It has been so long that I have sought you. Finding you well has quite obviously overwhelmed my senses."

"How long, Eustace? How long have you been looking for me?"

"A year and a half."

Good heavens. Eustace did not belong in the west, and certainly not for so long. He should be in Boston, securing a willing bride and riding the road to political success. She felt pity he had been caught up in the commanding net of her father's controlling nature. Now, with only failure to face, he would suffer her father's wrath. Unfortunately, it was the bargain Eustace made. She would give her freedom up for no man.

"Let me have one thing to remember. A token of good faith?" he said.

Lady eyed him warily. "What do you wish?"

"A kiss."

She blanched. Would he believe her chaste refusal? But she knew, such a denial of his desires would simply incur his distrust and threaten her game. By dusk the next day, she would be gone. She could leave him with a kiss at the very least.

When she gave a nod in acceptance, he covered the distance between them in two steps, placing his hands on her shoulders. A sudden instinct to withdraw overwhelmed her but she stood strong, willing the deed be quick.

His lips descended and covered her own, teasing at her mouth with persistence. She remained quiet, not wanting to appear as anything but compliant. When his tongue darted out and slid along the junction of her lips, she jerked back and stared at him with wide, innocent eyes. His masculine chuckle fell down upon her. "It seems, my love, that you were not lying when you said you had guarded your virtue. I shall have to teach you the art of kissing."

That was never going to happen. She gave him a cautious smile. "I will look forward to it--on the night of our nuptials."

With that, he stepped away, his shoulders brought to attention. Then he gave her a nod and withdrew, opening the door but keeping the key with him. Turning just before he shut the door, he said, "I must apologize again, my love. I must lock you in. There are far too many men of ill intention walking free in this town. I will return to you with supper. It will be a pleasure to speak of what else you have discovered since you've been away."

The door shut and the key scraped in the lock. Lady strode to the bed and slumped onto the flowery quilt. That had not gone well at all.

***

Beatrice slammed the cart door shut and stalked away

from the two brothers. Mordecai spat on the ground and reconsidered the wisdom of allowing his sister-in-law to continue with them. The woman had always been irritable, constantly questioning his orders and generally being a thorn in his side since the days she trod the boards in Dodge City. That tendency only increased as they moved west, reaching a peak in the recent weeks.

It intensified to nearly unbearable proportions when he'd informed her and her husband they would be leaving Charlotte to tend Isabel in the ancient Indian ruin. He had not been completely unfeeling, leaving the girls plenty of supplies to hold them until they determined their new direction. The fact that Isabel was unlikely to recover and Charlotte would more than likely die from incompetence was not on his conscience. The women had grown soft under his care. It was time they grew hardy enough to be self-sufficient. He was not a charitable man.

Beatrice knew this. They all knew this. It should have been no surprise he made the hard decisions that would ensure his family's success. And despite her wedding ring, Beatrice was not family. Only Bernard mattered. Only the Kovacs would benefit from Cibola's treasure.

"Don't judge her harshly, Mordecai," Bernard said.

Mordecai looked at his meek brother, standing quietly in the shadow of the cart. They left the other cart behind, leaving many of their stores in the process. He would regret that particular action. The girls might waste away and die, and he would most certainly need the extra food. But he had done it out of kindness for his brother.

A gentle soul, Bernard had always been a timid and weak man. Illnesses during his youth made his mind susceptible to melancholy. His sympathies for the downtrodden built through honest empathy. But it was a weakness that could destroy a man. Mordecai would not watch his brother wallow in sadness only to die in misery just as they watched their own mother do in Hungary.

"Your wife is trying my patience," Mordecai said.

"She mourns the loss of her dolls, brother. You must give her time to heal."

Mordecai scoffed at his brother's plea. Beatrice's attachment to the life-sized marionettes she performed with in the traveling show, had been unhealthy--it bordered on sickness. "No, brother, she mourns for a dead child. It has been too many years. If she has not healed her soul by now, it will never happen."

"We all mourned that child, Mordecai. We still do…even you."

He swung his eyes on his brother and pierced him with a glare. "It is in the past. A family tragedy. We must learn to forget it."

"But you never have. I wonder why you mourn so deeply for that child? My child?"

Mordecai spat into the dirt and stalked from his brother. *His child.* If Bernard only knew what that child had been, how quickly the bonds between brothers would be severed.

11

His face itched. Slim growled at nothing in particular, the room empty of anything but him, the uncomfortable bed, and a bucket. He wasn't sure what the bucket was for, but figured if they ever unlocked the chains which him secured to the bed he'd use it to hit someone over the head. 'Course, they weren't liable to let him do that.

Yanking his foot up, he tested the hold of the chains at his feet and got the same response he had the last fifty times he'd tried it. He wasn't going anywhere. It was damn frustrating staring up into the dark ceiling. Since Banahan's goon last left, he'd not seen anyone for a long time. He couldn't count the hours, but he'd swear he'd been there for at least two days, the thug's sporadic visits the only company he'd had and that wasn't much to say.

Thankfully, he'd been kept hydrated. It was mighty embarrassing having the man hold a container for him to piss in, but he did his darndest to splash the asshole. He needed to find out the man's name, he was running out of things to call the bastard. Maybe he'd call him Charlie. He'd known a Charlie before and he'd been just as dumb and violent. Met a bad end too, falling down into a ravine while chasing Slim after finding him with his wife. Slim felt a little bad about it, but Charlie had knocked his wife around for years, so the man really had it coming.

Slim had just about had enough of it all and was thinking he might have to get desperate if something didn't change. His face was healing, that was obvious from the damn itchiness. And beyond being sore from lying around all day, his body felt like it was doing fine. He just had to find a way out of the damn chains.

The door creaked open and a splash of light hit the room. Finally!

Three men entered with hard expressions which suggested they had a solemn purpose. Slim grinned up at them. "Hey Charlie, you bring your friends to watch me piss?"

"How do you keep yourself from punchin' him again, Leslie?" one of the men asked.

Slim burst out laughing. "Your name's Leslie?"

The three men glared at him, but Slim just kept on laughing. It seemed the Pinkertons recruited only the finest. Leslie reached down and unlocked the chains around Slim's legs then the other two men grabbed his shoulders as his arms were released. They yanked him to his feet and hustled him into a long corridor.

Night had fallen and a cool breeze sailed in from an open door at the far end of the hall. Slim barely touched the ground as the men moved him along, turning up the narrow, internal stairwell. Banging from a distant room reminded him of the traitor on the ship. Malphia Blackwood. When he got done with the Pinkertons he was going after her. He'd never trusted the woman, but he figured she would have had more loyalty to old friends than she'd shown.

They turned onto a corridor he recognized and then stopped in front of Banahan's quarters. Whatever the head

Pinkerton had in store for him, it was unlikely to be messy. The last time Slim had been in the room he'd noticed the fine trappings and Banahan wouldn't want to get them dirtied.

Intrigued, Slim kept his mouth shut as they entered at the boss's command. The room glowed with orange light from four gas lamps fixed to the corners of the room. There wasn't much safe about gas and with the way this bucket of metal was flying lately, he figured they were all set to go up in flames. Slim wouldn't be too broken up about the Pinkertons crashing in a torched ball of copper and steel down some unmapped canyon, but if they were close to civilization when this thing finally decided to give it up for good, a whole heck of a lot of people were going to get hurt.

"Thank you gentlemen. You may put him in the seat there." Banahan walked around his desk and pointed to a cushioned chair. Slim settled against the pillowed back and stretched his legs out when the men finally released him.

Leslie stood to the side facing Slim, his eyes boring into his chest like he wished for just the right moment to send him to hell. A muscle twitched at Slim's lips, the smile he'd been holding back nearly ready to escape. Antagonizing the giant was a great sport, but he had better things to do right now.

Mainly, antagonizing Banahan.

"Now Tommy, I heard the Pinkertons paid well, but I got to figure they don't pay this well." Slim nodded to the room. "How much do you think your boss up in Chicago would pay to know you've been skimming him on his profits?"

"Don't think I care to worry about that, Mr. Robinson, considering that you won't be making it outside of New Mexico."

Slim followed with his broad, confident grin. He might not know how he planned to escape, but there were a whole lot of worse situations he'd managed to run from-- this one wouldn't be any different.

Banahan walked to a side table and picked up a blue medicine bottle, his expression haughty. "Tell me if you recognize this, Mr. Robinson. I received it from a friend of yours."

"Everybody's got medicine bottles, Tommy. Don't see much about that one that's interesting."

"Ah, but it is. You see, we've been hearing reports about this particular elixir for years. Seems the recipe originated from an old witch in Silver City. The knowledge had been thought to have been lost when the old woman died. But then things started happening in towns. Towns that had seen a certain travelling show."

The Marvelous MacHurdyGurdy Traveling Show. No doubt, Mordecai had killed the old woman for the recipe. Slim schooled his features and turned a disinterested eye to the bottle. "There's a snake-oil salesman every hundred miles, Tommy. You know that. They're just pretty bottles with sugar water."

"Not this one. It seems the medicinal qualities of this particular brew actually deliver on the promise. Quite a bit more than anyone expects. But--" Banahan paused and held the bottle up to the light, showing off the iridescent colors that floated within a green liquid. "We aren't quite sure what it can do."

"You scared to try it?"

"Oh, we've had people try it. In fact, it is a rather pleasant experience. But too much of a good thing is often quite the opposite. I'm interested in seeing what it can do when administered in high quantities."

Slim felt a throb at the corner of his jaw and he knew he'd give away his trepidation. He was well aware of what this particular elixir could do. Sybil had been more than forthcoming. It delivered a potent euphoric experience which encouraged the taster to trust unquestionably and guaranteed complacency. Mordecai used it to bring money into the troupe's hands, ensuring they left each town with a profit. It would only be much later that the townspeople would realize the truth. The elixir was genuine, but he only gave that version to a few to encourage sales, the rest were handed bottles missing the essential ingredient.

In addition, when the elixir ran out, the withdrawal was severe. Those who used it heavily were lucky to survive.

"How much do you think a man should take?" Banahan sneered from across the room. "I've heard that a single dose could last an entire week, but at the very least several days. It makes a man happy. How happy would you like to be, Mr. Robinson?"

Slim didn't bother to respond. Banahan pulled the stopper from the bottle and nodded to his henchmen. Leslie dove toward Slim and grabbed him by the face, as four heavy hands grabbed his shoulders. Figuring that fighting would only give them the pleasure of beating him to a pulp, he held still and let Leslie open his mouth with ease. Banahan dumped half the bottle down his throat, and Slim sputtered, spraying a good portion across Leslie's unshaven face.

"I thought you'd give more of a fight, Mr. Robinson."

"Don't reckon I need to break a rib over it. I'll see you in hell, Tommy." Slim's belly twisted and he figured he only had a few moments left with his mind. Grabbing onto the one thing that kept him going this far, he pictured Lady. If he was going to survive this, keeping he's mind focused on something he had to do would give him a handhold on sanity. Lady may have fallen from the ship, but he'd be damned if he believed she was dead. The girl needed him, and he was going to do what he had to and stay alive.

Tommy laughed as Slim's eyes lost focus and his body relaxed against the chair. A lazy grin flipped easily onto his lips and he slurred up at Banahan, "You know, I ain't never lost a game of cards. Lost a lot of hands though. I figure, the next one you'll be all in. We'll see who walks away from the table then."

Banahan snarled and slapped him across the face. Slim thought is should have hurt more than it did. So he started to laugh. If nothing else, he'd die happy.

***

Lady looked out the window of the second story room, catching a glimpse of a young Hispanic woman carrying a basket of linen from a line strung out across the small yard. Eustace and his adherence to the proprieties left her in the best of conditions, facing away from the busy street and spying eyes. She lifted the sash and ducked her head into the cool desert dusk, scanning the area for anyone else who might be in the vicinity. It was relatively quiet, but for the sounds filtering from the front of the building. The door below her slammed and she held her breath. A few moments more to make sure the girl would not return, and then Lady would be off.

Eustace had only left a half an hour earlier, taking their supper dishes with him. He'd been nothing but the most proper of gentlemen during their supper, being even so conscientious as to leave the door open so no one could question her virtue. Lady had done her best to play the part of a naive and willing bride-to-be. How it rankled her sensibilities to allow the twit she'd been so many years ago a chance to emerge again. When this escapade was at an end, she would do her best to banish that woman to nothingness.

Tugging at the frills around her neck, she glanced longingly at her bodice and divided skirt hung across the room. Eustace had brought her a new dress, completely frivolous and unworthy of the trail. It smelled of cloying perfume and felt as delicate as paper. It would not suit her in any way.

How easy Slim would find it to mock her now.

Unfortunately, there was little she could do until she had her bag. The bodice was a complete loss and until she could secure funds, she had no means to replace it. Figuring her father used her withdrawals as a means to track her from one bank to another, she did not imagine he'd cut off her supply of ready income quite yet. He would very soon--as soon as Eustace alerted him to her capture no doubt. So this was her last chance. Eustace made mention of stopping by the wire to send the good news to her father the next morning.

By that time, she'd have the money. Lady ducked her head out the window again and listened. When she felt it was safe to emerge, she grabbed the sides and hefted her body out and onto a small decorative wood slat lining the building. Escaping to the first floor would not be one of the easiest she'd attempted, the dress only making it more difficult. But she'd plotted her descent and even had a plan for returning.

A small porch covered the back door, and she shifted her feet, her fingernails gripping the wood siding. Paint chips flaked off as she slid along the wall and rough spots sliced splinters into her skin. Her knees quivered beneath the pressure of holding her weight against the house and she prayed for the strength to make it the next foot to the porch roof.

Just as she was ready to slide gratefully onto the gabled roof, an exposed nail caught her dress, tearing a gash from her knee to ankle. She cringed and cursed Eustace's delicate tastes. Had the man truly expected her to wear this on the trail? Distracted by the dress, she nearly missed the sound of the door opening beneath her. As it snapped shut, her heart plummeted to throb within her belly and she flattened her body against the roof.

A man walked out from beneath the porch, a cigarette lit between his lips and hat tipped forward. His head moved from side to side as he scanned the yard. With the common clothes, it was clearly not one of Eustace's boys, but she had no desire to meet this man in her particular predicament. The way he stalked the yard heightened her wariness.

His head never lifted and she watched as he ducked behind a creosote bush several feet from the door. A quiet moment passed before Lady heard the door open beneath her again, then it snapped shut and quick, youthful steps clicked against the porch floor. The young woman, tending the laundry earlier, appeared with another basket, this one weighed heavily by the wet linen.

Lady frowned and looked to the creosote. As the girl turned to pin the fabric to the line, the foliage moved and the man stepped out. Fury flared as Lady realized his intentions. This would certainly not do at all.

As the man reached out to grab the unsuspecting woman, Lady dropped from the porch roof and landed in a crouch. Springing forward, she ran to the man, tapping him on the shoulder just as he spun the terrified woman around into a forced embrace.

His accosting interrupted, he turned with a scowl, but Lady did not give him the time to notice her features. With a quick jab to his nose and a second to his jaw he fell to the ground unconscious.

The unfortunate creature that had been his target shook beside her, and Lady turned to place a commiserating hand to her arm then paused. The woman was far younger than she'd expected, unlikely older than twelve. "Dear heavens child, you're hardly out of the schoolroom."

The girl burst into tears and looked to the door leading back into the house. Lady cooed gently and ran a hand down her arm. "It is alright, it is done. He won't wake for quite some time. And when he does he will think twice about touching you."

The tears increased and Lady leaned forward to gather her into her arms. "No, please, it is all right, child. Nothing happened. It is all right. We must have you go to the sheriff. "

The girl stiffened and pressed away from Lady. "No. Dios, no. They would never believe me. They would never believe you! They never do. The last woman that…" the girl stared down at the man with terror.

"Do not be ridiculous. You are a child, he is a grown man. Of course they will believe you."

The girl looked at her as though she'd completely lost her mind. Lady sighed. Perhaps she had. "Do you have family here?"

She shook her head vigorously and wiped at the tears that which streamed down her face. Lady raised her eyes to the heavens and bit back a curse. It was certainly good fortune she had been there to witness the incident, but now she would have to add another thing to the list. Resigned, she said, "Do you wish to leave town?"

The girl nodded and Lady put her hand to the girl's waist and moved her toward the house. "Then you will hide in my room tonight. They will not suspect that you are there as they assume I have been locked away this whole time. I will devise a suitable story, and then tomorrow, we shall depart together."

The girl nodded, gripping Lady's hand with claw-like fingers. They would need to hurry to complete the ruse, but first, Lady had to rummage through Eustace's room. With luck he would have left her key there as well, it was unlikely she would get the young girl up to her room the same way she left it.

12

Delayed by a loose mechanism in one of the black wings, it had taken far longer to reach their destination than expected. Finally, Zhao Jin gave instruction to land the SteamWing just outside of Albuquerque. He would leave Martin with the ship, bringing Joseph as an extra hand as they entered town. Sybil would sleep well tonight in a fine bed. The pride he felt at holding the beauty at his side only increased. When he'd kept her locked away in his bordello in Prescott, he'd thought he'd done the best for her, keeping her hidden from view, protected from the evil eyes of the town. The people never understood the beauty which radiated from her, drawn to her grace, repelled by her disease.

But he knew and he understood. It was no pestilence that ravaged her body. Rather, it was a blessing from the heavens, a promise of good fortune and prosperity. And she was growing close to completing her transformation, he could feel it.

Joseph opened the door to the SteamWing and stepped out into the desert as the sun sunk closer to the horizon. As he and Martin secured the ship, Zhao Jin reached to take Sybil's delicate hands. Elegantly exquisite, her fine bones would have been envied by women the world throughout. If the heathens could learn to see beyond the oddity of her skin, they would see everything about Sybil was designed for perfection.

She pulled a stray corner of silk across her face, leaving only her bright, moss-colored eyes exposed to the light. As usual, they betrayed nothing of her thoughts. He'd ceased attempting to read the mysterious woman years ago. The only true emotion she'd ever shown had been the searing hatred directed at him over her mother's dead body.

Zhao Jin let the memory fade, unwilling to examine the mixed emotions of regret and satisfaction that threatened. Martin busied himself with tying down the SteamWing for the night and Joseph pulled together the few supplies they would take with them into town. When the men were ready, Zhao Jin left Martin with orders to be ready to fly by mid-morning and led Sybil toward town. With an hour of day-light left, he intended to have Sybil tucked away for the night and well rested for the morrow.

Her refusal to point them in a direction hadn't been un-expected. Zhao Jin intended to rectify her uncooperative-ness, but it would take far more time than he could to spend at this junction. Her nervousness receded when they'd turned east. After sending Joseph out to the tables tonight to seek information on possible sightings of the Ma-cHurdyGurdys they would wake in the morning and return the way they had come, continuing on into the west until Sybil gave her next clue.

Zhao Jin had all confidence they would encounter his old enemy within the month. Mordecai was brilliant in many things, not nearly as brilliant as Zhao Jin, but brilliant none the less. However, the man had the theater in his blood and could not stay behind the scenes for long. Zhao Jin, on the other hand, was quite accustomed to pulling the puppet strings and waiting for the right moment in the shadows. Mordecai would make his dramatic entrance and Zhao Jin would be there to sweep the rug from beneath his feet.

They approached the town of Albuquerque, the bustling movement of hooves and boots on the road kicked up a layer of dirt that floated above the ground. Sybil sneezed as they passed a group of curious cattlemen, their gazes predatory as they followed her swirling silks. Zhao Jin tightened his hold on her elbow and continued toward a boarding house.

When they walked into the entry hall, Zhao Jin removed his fine. beaver top hat and handed it to Joseph. Luscious carpets covered the hardwood floors and elaborate floral paper clung to the walls. Zhao Jin took in a long breath of respectability. The European designs were an aesthetic he had grown to appreciate. It lacked the opulence and pure richness of his homeland, but it screamed affluence in this dirty country. This was how he was meant to live.

A woman stood behind an elegantly carved desk, hands clutching at a pen, her eyes shifting nervously toward the back door. Zhao Jin ignored her discomfort, leading Sybil to the desk. "I have need of two rooms, beside each other if possible."

The woman opened her mouth to protest, but he threw several coins on the desk before she could utter a sound. "I believe that will be enough to cover two rooms for one night?"

It was far more than enough. But he'd learned long ago he would pay a higher price to live in a white man's world. He was willing to pay for the privilege of comfort and thought little that other men paid less. That their inferior minds could not comprehend a method to procure enough wealth to pay for everything desired was of no consequence to him. He always had plenty.

The woman stared at the coins, clearly torn by her choice. Zhao Jin threw another coin on the table and slid on an appeasing smile. "Please, madam. We are weary from our travels."

Her quick fingers snatched the coins and she stiffened her shoulders. "This way."

They were installed in two rooms, one across from the other. Zhao Jin would have preferred to share a wall with Sybil, where he could hear the woman's movements, but the situation would do. As he left Sybil to her nightly ablutions, he closed the door and turned to his room. A flash of white caught his eye down the hall and he paused. Another guest, no doubt, but he waited, curious to see who else shared this house with them.

When no one appeared, he assumed they had entered their own room and continued into his. But a niggling suspicion kept his eyes open most of the night. All the money in the world could not replace the treasure that slept in the room across the hall. Was he a fool thinking a locked door would be enough to keep her secure?

***

Lady paced the room, unsure and torn. Of all the blasted timing. It was certainly convenient to have Zhao Jin show up with Sybil. But how would she manage another rescue, protect her new charge and retrieve enough money to last them the coming months? Lady released a frustrated snort. The girl winced, her knees pulled up against her chest as she huddled in a worn upholstered chair, worry a constant crease across her brow.

Stopping mid-turn, Lady looked at her new companion. The girl had soft brown hair and wide, overly expressive brown eyes. Dark shadows covered her eyes, and her long lashes and pouting lips enhanced the look of fragility. Lady frowned. At twelve, Lady lived under the autocratic rule of her father, hidden behind the veil of respectability found in the houses of the affluent. But she had not known hardship. Not like the creature huddled in front of her.

Lady tightened her lips. Despite whatever travesties had befallen the girl, she would have to show her mettle and be the determinate factor in her future. Lady would help, but the girl would have to pull her own weight—there was just no other way.

"Carmen, do you know this town well?"

The girl nodded and Lady continued to pry, "How long have you been here?"

"Two years, miss."

"Then where is your family?"

Tears filled at the corners of the girl's eyes and her nose reddened with sadness. Lady closed her eyes, drifting between sympathy and irritation. She did not have time to deal with a weepy child. "Carmen, I have the best intentions to assist you, but you must help me as well. We cannot let our feminine tendencies be the weakness that prevents our success."

Carmen hiccupped, and covered her mouth with her hands, tears streaming down her face. Lady released a massive sigh, and closed the distance between the two of them. Falling to her knees, she pulled Carmen into her arms. "I know that you have been through too much. I will let nothing happen to you, I promise that. But the time for fear and sorrow is at an end. If you want to survive this, you must discover the strength that I know is within you."

The girl silenced her sobs but her body still shook with the emotion. Lady pulled away and did her best to keep her eyes calm and kind. What terrible luck she had this day. Discovering Sybil was only a few feet away was fortuitous and she could not scold the heavens for delivering her friend so conveniently. But she had one night to accomplish her tasks and an uncertain future. If she was unable to secure funds…

Lady cringed. She had no idea how to survive without her father's money. She'd learned so much in her years traveling the west, but that had always been her salvation. Her father's accounts were accessible across the country, a unique benefit of being a tycoon's progeny. Now, believing her firmly in Eustace's grasp, her father would no doubt discontinue her ability to retrieve money.

Lady blew a strand of hair from her face and patted Carmen's back. Zhao Jin was unlikely to stay in Albuquerque for long. Just how long might ultimately determine her success. Lady needed to speak to Sybil.

A knock sounded at the door. Carmen's head shot up, nearly clocking Lady on the chin. With a finger to her lips, Lady pointed to the bed, motioning for the girl to shimmy under the metal frame. As Carmen moved to comply, Lady called out to her unwanted guest, "Who's there?"

A key turned in the lock and she gritted her teeth. Kicking a few stray inches of Carmen's skirt under the bed, Lady grabbed her own skirt and whisked into a position that hid the long tear from the blasted nail. Eustace entered, his eyes entreating. "I stopped by to check on your welfare, Fidelia."

"That is quite kind of you, Eustace."

"You have not dressed for bed?"

Lady raised a brow. He knew quite well that she owned nothing suitable for sleeping. The cad had no doubt hoped to find her in some form of undress. "I rested for most of the evening after supper and find I am not quite ready for bed."

"I could keep you company."

That would be absolutely out of the question. Lady covered a grimace and countered, "I found a book in the dresser, I imagine a guest left it and I am quite eager to read. It has been some time since I have sat down with a book."

He began to turn his head toward the dresser and she realized her satchel lay in plain view. He would know for certain she escaped her room earlier that evening the moment he caught sight of it. Closing the distance between them at a run, she drew to a halt inches from him, turning his gaze solidly to her heaving chest. Letting her hand flutter above her breast, she allowed a blush to spread across her cheeks. A blush risen from fear rather than pleasure. She doubted Eustace could tell the difference.

"It pleases me that you are so considerate of my welfare and comfort."

He groaned and leaned toward her, his eyes sliding to half-closed. "Fidelia."

She stopped him with a hand against his chest. "I do not know how to thank you. But I promise I will give it my full attention as we travel to Denver. I am certain to come up with something by the time we are wed."

He blinked at her, drawing his breath deeply between weathered lips. With an innocent smile, she placed her free hand on the inside of the door and firmly pushed him toward the hall, closing the door slowly behind him. "I do believe I have suddenly become sleepy. I must have been waiting for you to return for the night, but now it seems I am able to put aside my worry. I will be retiring now."

A solid hand halted the door's progress and he frowned at her. "How did you know I had left?"

Fear settled against her spine and she sought an answer. She knew because she had listened intently to the hall, picking out the voices and discovering the perfect moment to make her escape. Securing her bag and the key to her room had been relatively easy. Replacing the key and returning through the window was more challenging. But what answer would he believe?

"I overheard your men discussing their plans in the hall. They mentioned you had gone out."

He stared at her, his suspicion evident in the heavy brows. But he could find no fault with her answer and he replaced his frown with a pleasant smile. "I will see you in the morning. Would you care to share breakfast with me?"

"Will it be very early?"

"Just after dawn I imagine. I have much to do tomorrow to prepare us for our journey to Denver. If we move quickly, we can expect to be ready by the next morning."

Lady let her bottom lip jut out and she threw him a practiced, doe-eyed glance. "I do not know that I will be ready to leave my bed so early for breakfast. It has been so exhausting on the trail and I find my body is just ready to give out."

A gullible sympathy filled his face and she felt a spasm of distaste rise from her belly. Did the man seriously believe her to be such a vapid ninny? He reached down and pulled her hand to his lips, lingering at her knuckles longer than customary. Fluttering her eyelids, she retrieved her hand from his without snatching it away as her instincts demanded. If luck held, this would be last time she would have to evade his advances.

"Good night, Fidelia."

"Good night, Eustace. I shall see you on the morrow."

He turned to leave and she held the door as he continued down the hall. His step was springy and she sucked in her breath as he stopped at his door. He paused before entering, turning his head back toward her room. She smiled and gave him a wave, hoping he wouldn't notice that he hadn't locked her in.

She closed the door then waited as she listened for his to close. The soft snap of the door sent waves of relief through her body. Finally, luck was on her side.

Sending a whispered command for Carmen to stay put, Lady sat on the edge of the bed, resolved to wait to see whether her luck would hold out. After twenty minutes, Eustace had not returned to lock her door and she finally believed fortune was there to stay.

Carmen coughed as Lady assisted her from the floor. Brushing the dust from the girl's clothing, Lady said, "I must secure our escape. You will wait here. From the commotion we heard earlier, we can only assume your employers believe you have run from town. But we cannot be sure they would not check the rooms should they not find you soon."

Carmen nodded and glanced worriedly at the door. Determined to reassure the girl, Lady added, "I will only be gone a short time and then we will make our escape. You do not need to hide beneath the bed." Lady put a hand out to Carmen's hair. "In fact, you should sleep in the bed."

The girl gave a bracing smile and threw her arms around Lady. Stiff and unsure, Lady patted her on the back then set her aside. Lady returned to the door and opened it with caution. The night had grown late and not a sound could be heard. She spent several moments listening on the chance Eustace would stir.

With no more excuses to hold her back, Lady stepped into the hall and turned toward the room where she had seen Zhao Jin escort Sybil.

13

Slim had never seen a more beautiful sight. The black smudges about her eyes made her look like an exotic temptress, destined to be his downfall. But damn would he die happy.

"Damn it, Slim." She slapped him across the face. A tingle rushed from his cheekbones to his nose and he licked his lips. A coppery taste exploded against his tongue and he closed his eyes, reveling in the sensation. The filly could torture him to death and he'd only die of pleasure. A guttural growl vibrated beside his ears and he opened his eyes to the most exquisite breasts he'd ever had the honor of caressing. He blinked, remembering how those phenomenal mounds felt beneath his hands.

Hot breath brushed against his neck before a splash of water crashed over his face. He grinned. Now she would drown him with love. A sharp voice scolded him, "Are you out of your mind you blasted man? How much of that devil piss did they give you?"

Something niggled at the back of his mind, something insistent, but fleeting. He pushed it aside. Everything was just fine in the world. He had a bed to sleep in, a beautiful woman holding him in her arms, what more could a man ask for? Reaching a hand up, he drew his finger down her face, tracing her lips and becoming entranced in her perfection.

She jerked back and wrapped hands around his wrist. "That is more than enough of that. What the hell did they do to you?"

He tried to speak, to say that whatever it had been, he'd gladly beg for more. Just to feel this absolute euphoria, this complete happiness, the outright promise of no pain and no sorrow. It was intoxicating. And now he had her. An angel disguised as a mortal woman encased in men's clothing. But of course an angel would not know they were men's clothing. He would not be the one to tell her, she was perfection and a single kiss would promise him life everlasting.

She prodded him with questions again, but he could not answer. His smile kept the words back, his happiness mute in the wake of such beauty.

With a frustrated huff, she dumped him on the bed and stood, her hands propped on her glorious hips, her chest heaving with intense emotion. His hand rose as he beckoned to her, pleading for her to join him again, to share her touch. Just for a little more and then he would die the happiest man on earth in the arms of a woman whose name he could not remember.

"I'll be damned if I'm gonna be able to get you off this ship myself. I hope your lady friends have a better idea of saving you than you did of saving them. If Tommy hadn't heard you rustlin' about last time, we'd all be long gone from here."

The woman, with hair curling out from underneath a tightly tied kerchief, rubbed a hand over her forehead, leaving a smudge of dirt against sun-blessed skin. Her lips were tightly pressed, and eyes narrowed with calculating intensity. A warning tried desperately to pry into his euphoria drenched spirit, but the lid to his sanity closed firmly over common sense.

Pushing up from the lumpy mattress, he leaned on an elbow and flashed his best grin. The ladies could never say no to that smile. He'd perfected it over the years, testing it on young, old, beautiful, wretched, sensible and silly. It couldn't be denied and he'd never failed. Never, except…

A memory tickled his mind and another face flitted at the edges of his consciousness. A memory of brown eyes blinked at him in condescension, a hard edge framing a soft body. Competence and vulnerability warred within the same perfectly formed figure and she looked to Slim in a silent plea. Something about her appearance had him questioning everything he knew about himself.

Shaking his head, he banished the memory. Whoever the brown-eyed woman had been, she'd demanded things of him he had no intention of giving. Not today when he held the key to absolute bliss in his hand. A haze gathered at the edges of his sight and he blinked lazily.

The woman who shared his room frowned down at him, her eyes a dark green. So very different from the woman in his fleeting memory. She sighed and said, "I'm not gonna lie to you, Slim. You've looked better. And I don't think Tommy plans to stop giving you the elixir. I had bigger things planned and you sure made a mess of them for me."

She sat on the bed again and stroked his hair. The nerves of his scalp tingled and he nestled in closer to her, inhaling the scent of grease and femininity. She continued, "Well, looks like I'm just gonna have to do my best to make sure you don't die so you can pay me back for saving your ass."

A laugh escaped his lips and he smiled at her, hoping she'd stroke him a little longer. He couldn't' get enough of her touch. She frowned. "You're gonna smile your way to the grave, ain't you, you damn fool man."

***

Remnants of terror tickled her spine, the settling of the building and hush of a town saying farewell to the day adding to her unease. Huddled beneath the covers, Sybil prayed the nightmares would not come, then prayed even more that the visions would be absent. She couldn't decide which were worse, the horrid memories or the new fears.

Years ago, when the affliction first took her, she'd worried for her health, her life, and her safety. As the years passed and she never took ill, she learned to live with the outward appearance of infirmity, content to know she was not dying. The sickness of human nature had been her only symptom, cruelty the fever which surrounded her in each town where they stopped.

Now she feared death again.

That morning brought the most intense of her new symptoms. As Zhao Jin escorted her to town, a trance took her, transforming her sight from the base colors to signatures of warmth and movement. The landscape had blended into a smooth sea of nothingness, spiced with moving colors in shades she'd never encountered before. The sun's rays pierced through her veils, encouraging her to throw them aside and bask in the glory of its golden promise.

Somehow, she'd held a grasp on her sanity and tightened her grip on the fabric, touching the reality of her surroundings despite her inability to see it. She'd stumbled along, led by the hand of her adversary, helpless and terrified until they'd reached the boarding house. And then it all just disappeared, as though the episode had never been, her mind mocking her fear, her heart convinced she'd lose her life--or her humanity.

Which would she miss the most?

A soft scraping came at the door and Sybil jerked her head up, baring her teeth. A click sounded as the tumblers in the lock fell and the door knob turned, agonizingly slow. A shadow appeared at the crack between the door and the jamb and Sybil felt her body quake. Zhao Jin would not have made such a cautious entry.

"Sybil?"

She did not move, the voice too hushed to recognize. There was nothing for her here with which to defend herself, nowhere to flee. Waiting to see what her future held, she felt regret cross her heart. To leave this world as a tortured soul might truly be a blessing, but she had made promises that she would never keep.

"Good heavens, Sybil! What has he done to you?"

The shadow moved with haste, softly closing the door in its wake. The bed sagged beneath the added weight of a lithe body at the foot of the mattress. A hand reached out, but snapped back when Sybil hissed.

"Oh Sybil, it's me, Lady. Can't you see?"

Sybil blinked and leaned forward. Squinting in the soft light, she made out the features of her dear friend and let her heart fall into a less chaotic rhythm. "I did not see, no."

Lady leaned forward, pulling Sybil into her arms, brushing the blankets away from her hair. "You look like the devil was coming for you. Has he hurt you? What has he done?"

Sybil shook her head and clasped her hand over Lady's to stop her from brushing against the scales along her cheeks. The pain of touch had intensified over the weeks, and she still refused to let her friend see just how much it hurt. "He hazz done nothing beyond keep me captive. Why are you here? How could you possibly have followed uzz? Did the Pinkertonzz not have you azz their captive?"

Lady pulled her hand away and said, "That is a long story, but we have little time for it. All I can say is fortune has paid us a kind favor and we must accept it with due haste. I fear we have a bit of a quandary, but we shall find our way out."

"Lady, we cannot escape him. Not by foot and not even by horse. It will take a trick even more clever than what we performed in Socorro."

With her head turned to the door, Lady sat quietly, her breath barely discernible above the quiet sounds of night. Footsteps creaked beside the door, steady with purpose and as they receded into the distance both women released relieved sighs.

"Sybil, we shall have to come up with a clever plan for certain. But leave that to me. Do you know when Zhao Jin intends to leave?"

"Late morning, tomorrow. Hizz ship izz waiting outside of town."

"A ship?"

Sybil nodded and explained to Lady the SteamWing and everything that transpired since they last met. Lady then described her own situation from her encounter with the insistent Captain Wright and rescue of the timid Carmen.

After several minutes, Lady stood and brushed her hands down her skirt. "I believe I may have an idea to bring about our rescue. And perhaps someday we will be able to thank the black-hearted Zhao Jin for providing us the opportunity. From a distance of course."

Lady shuffled silently to the door and pulled it open a crack. When she looked back the soft glow of the hall light illuminated her mischievous smile. "It is always an adventure with you, Sybil. Wait here. I will return before dawn."

As the door closed behind her and the tumblers clicked into place, Sybil let herself relax for the first time in weeks. Lady may not have her entire plan devised, but there would be no doubt it would work. Lady had the mind of a maverick and the heart of a crusader.

Sybil lay amid the covers, determined to find some rest before the excitement to come. It could very well be the only sleep she found for a long time.

14

The wind whipped across the grasslands, striking its nails along the cart's weathered wood walls. Mordecai flipped up his collar, one gloved hand clutching the reins, his top hat pushed down over his ears as snow flurries fluttered around his face, driving beneath his clothing. Beatrice and Bernard huddled together beside him, their noses turned down into their clothing, as tortured by the wind's wrath as the poor beasts who trudged along in front of them. A dark, foreboding cloud filled the horizon promising a kind of unholy retribution only the sky could produce.

They needed to find shelter. The three would not survive a blizzard within the thin walls of the cart. A shadow to the right drew his attention. In the distance he spied movement and the straight lines of civilization. Nature did not create straight lines. Humanity did. Mordecai estimated the distance to be at least a mile away. With the speed the distant clouds were gathering, they would cut it close. He snapped the reins and goaded the mules forward.

Darkness enveloped them and the snow slapped what was left of the visibility away just as they approached a modest ranch. With doors and windows sealed against the oncoming onslaught, the place felt abandoned. Mordecai knew they could not be so lucky. Pulling the cart to the front porch, he hopped from the bench and directed his brother to secure the cart and mules for the storm. Then he turned to the door. Beatrice jerked when he took her by the elbow. His lips had descended to snarl into her ear. "Time to utilize your dramatic training, my dear sister. You must act as though you are likable."

A silky smile slid across her lips as she fluttered her lashes. "Why my dear brother? Do you believe I would waste my energy on others when my hate only knows one direction?"

He pushed away her arm and strode up the stairs. The hatred was shared and spanned decades. If only his brother and his damnable honor…no, it did not require his effort. Someday, Beatrice would provide her departure. The vitriolic woman would be but a passing shadow in memory.

Three knocks and no answer. The howl of the wind would likely require a more emphatic signal to their presence. Mordecai raised his walking stick, swung the tip toward the window to the left of the door and snapped the copper tip against the glass. He repeated the performance several times, before a sound could be heard beyond the door. Stepping back, he returned the stick to its proper place, bracing his hands on the elegant knob and he dressed his face with an enigmatic stage smile. He sent a quick glance at Beatrice to find her demeanor meek and feminine. If nothing else, the woman could act.

Cautious eyes peered from the crack of the partially opened door. Mordecai changed his expression to a hopeful naivety, encouraging trust in the homeowner. The door opened more fully, just enough for the two men to take stock of each other. Mordecai adjusted his stance to minimize any sense of threat. Tired age and weariness of strangers fairly oozed from the gentleman. Mussed white hair, receding toward the back of his head complimented sun-ravaged skin. The conservative cut of the clothing and stiff back suggested a religious man.

"My good sir, I do apologize for the intrusion. But we have found ourselves driven to your home by the most unfortunate storm," Mordecai said.

His brother came up the stairs at that moment, his shoulders hunched and face red from the ferocity of the wind. The kindness in Bernard's eyes immediately reassured the man at the door and he stepped back, allowing the three into the warmth of his home. Grateful for his brother's innocent view of the world, Mordecai stepped across the threshold.

The front room was square and heated by a healthy fire in a hearth across the hardwood floor. Three chairs sat around a small table, and the scent of beans boiled to mush mingled with a sharp hint of pork fat. Two women stood warily beside the hearth, a child in each of their arms and three dirty-faced urchins clinging at their skirts. The number of dresses told Mordecai that the man who let them in was woefully outnumbered by the weaker sex.

"Thank you sir, for your hospitality. May I introduce my brother, Bernard and his wife Beatrice." Mordecai swept off his hat and held it softly in his fingers, smile mild for the women across the room. "And I am Mordecai. We are traveling to Flagstaff to meet with my dear wife and our children. Your generosity shall allow our homecoming to go on without tragedy I am quite certain."

Beatrice did not blink at Mordecai's artful lies, but his brother cast his eyes about the room, eager to avoid the family's gaze. The gentleman held out a hand and said, "I am

Levi and my family, Esther and Joy." He did not introduce the children and Mordecai did not press. Levi continued, "Please sit. We were just about to share our meal."

Bernard eyed the three chairs and looked up to his brother. "We could not intrude on you. Please. We can settle ourselves out of the way and wait out the storm."

Mordecai narrowed his eyes at his brother, but Levi insisted, prodding Bernard toward the table. "Do not be concerned, Our Heavenly Father would not abide by such actions. Please sit and my wives, Ester and Joy shall share our bounty."

Wives? Mordecai's interest was drawn in a way which had been dormant for some time. He smiled at the woman who slid a meager bowl of beans onto the table before him. She quickly looked away, a wash of red across her cheekbones. Private and protected, these women were the embodiment of purity. They wore their faith as a shield from the evil of the world. What would it be like to hold something untouched by the sins of the gross humanity which overflowed into the west? He felt the subtle flicker of desire, but tempered it beneath a hearty spoonful of beans.

When he attained his goal, he would surround himself with purity even more rare than these two. None of the evils of the world would intrude on his sanctuary and the sins of his past would melt away with salvation. Mordecai slanted his eyes to Levi, wondering at the kind of salvation a man thought to find with two wives.

A small hand tugged at his elbow and Mordecai looked down into the unwashed yet rosy cheeks of a child barely old enough to walk. His toothy grin frightened the child, and she turned hastily toward her mother, eyes welling with imminent tears. The very young were always the least foolish. They knew a dangerous man when he smiled.

Mordecai turned toward Levi. Above the sound of rattling windows, he brokered conversation. "I was not aware of any communities in the area. We were quite lucky to happen upon you just as the storm approached."

Levi's lips thinned. "Yes, we are in an isolated land. The building of the railroads have brought many new settlers, but we still have our peace." He exaggerated his final word, a silent message or plea, Mordecai did not care. These people would serve as little more than a boarding house until the weather allowed them to continue the journey. There was little value in the common chattel.

Mordecai stood and nudged his brother to stand, their meal complete. "I thank you. Please, do not let us prevent you from breaking your own bread. My family and I shall settle beside your fire."

Levi shook his head. "No, we shall share our home. The loft provides you a bed to rest your weariness"

"We would not wish to displace any of your family." Mordecai offered out of politeness. Whom he displaced was the furthest from his mind.

"We insist. The children will join us this night."

Inclining his head, Mordecai graciously accepted and the three of them were led to a ladder that disappeared into the darkness above the room. A chill crawled beneath his collar as soon as he rose above the fire's direct influence, but the bed was large and blankets plentiful. Evidence of childhood stood all around him.

A roughly constructed rocking horse creaked as their steps on the wood planks disturbed its rest. Rag dolls were scattered across the bed and Beatrice stilled as she reached down to pull one into her arms. Mordecai turned away as his brother pulled his wife close, the comforting gesture an uncomfortable reminder of the past. Mordecai had grown tired of the two and their mourning. It had been too many years.

The covers rustled as Bernard prepared for sleep. The bed would just hold the three of them. But Mordecai would not sleep this night. The screams of the wind would release the demons in his mind; there was no use in fighting them. The shadows proved effective blankets and he sat beside the rail that separated the narrow loft from the open air beyond.

The murmur of prayer filtered over the howling wind and Mordecai spied the family gathered about the table, the children perched on the laps of the women, the meager meal a testament to poverty. The portions seemed significantly less than had been offered their guests.

The firelight mellowed and no additional wood was added to feed the heat. As their dinner closed, the family moved quietly from their seats, the children hustled through a door Mordecai spotted as they'd ascended to the loft. The two women bustled about the room, cleaning with reserved and efficient movements, one still holding a child on her hip. A sudden cry from the child was hastily silenced with a finger.

Mordecai's memories sent him flying from the room, the golden firelight turning blood red. His mind's eye blinked at a gory scene from his past. A child motionless in Beatrice's bloodied arms, her exhausted body lax, hair plastered across her forehead where sweat and exertion ravaged. That child never had the chance to be silenced by a mother's comforting touch. He blinked and the horrid remembrance cut to the maid, pressed into service as midwife, her fear an expression she would wear after death. Mordecai strangled her with the force of his fury, unable to lash out at the woman who'd ignited his wrath. It had been the one and only time he'd used his hands to destroy another.

No one in Dodge City would know what happened in that room. No one but Beatrice and she had yet to tell him the truth, hiding behind claims of innocence and mourning.

That day the Marvelous MacHurdyGurdy Traveling Show was born. The day that child died.

Mordecai turned his head, and the small loft came back into view. His vision now turned to the bed where Bernard and his wife lay. The blankets shifted as a body moved beneath their folds and he narrowed his eyes. There had been a time when the hope of a new country, so different from their home in Hungary had been enough.

He and Bernard worked the great stages of the American east where the elite men mingled with the wretched masses to catch the eye of an enchanting doxy treading the boards. Bernard's mechanical sets and genius contraptions brought in the more discerning audiences. And Mordecai had been master of them all, directing the emotions and desires of the public, giving them more but never all.

A single blond curl appeared from beneath the covers, a glint of what had been a tease in the dampening firelight. Mordecai's lip curled. Two brothers, both intoxicated by a fantasy of their own making. Beatrice had once been enchanting.

Never again. Mordecai controlled illusions. He would never be seduced by them again. Had Bernard not let his honor demand her hand, Beatrice would have been left behind, a broken dream that rotted beneath her duplicity.

But soon Mordecai would break the spell. His destiny lay in the deserted lands of a people who squandered their gifts. The ancient gold would be his and this new west would be his empire.

Another violent gust rattled the walls and he turned his attention back to the central room. The women had disappeared, safe in their obscurity. A new day would rise and they would be forgotten as Mordecai led his brother to their destination. Then nothing that had happened would matter.

15

Sunrise painted a strange effect across territorial buildings. In Boston, Lady rarely saw the daylight in its infancy, more often sleeping away the morning hours after a night of frivolity and inane conversation. But on those rare occasions when she'd fallen victim to wakefulness at dawn, there was a soft lightening of the sky, the darkness seeking refuge between the brick buildings and narrow lanes. This yellow bathing of skylight painting the land gold had an eerie effect. A promise of warmth and new beginnings.

If only the bank would open before the streets filled with people bustling about their business. Her white, frilly dress stood out like a lone cloud in an otherwise blue sky. First order of business would be procuring funds. Second would be replacing the ridiculous dress.

Lady leaned against a plank wall, hoping the lingering shadows would facilitate a few more minutes of obscurity. The men who followed the command of her well-meaning captor were early risers and their preparations for the march to Colorado would no doubt begin in earnest. The opportunity to procure financing for her escape into the desert would be short-lived as the risk of discovery grew.

The bank sat lonely and uninhabited, the few pedestrians about during the early hours not giving it a second glance. Lady had no idea when the doors would open and wondered at the wisdom of attempting one final withdrawal. Eustace had no doubt sent word to her father by telegraph. What if he blocked her ability to procure funds?

If she were apprehended in the bank, there would be no saving Sybil or Carmen. Lady stilled her quivering fingers. Never had the risk been so great and the outcome so unpredictable. A frustrated urge to give in and follow Eustace back to her father's iron hand billowed within her belly. The sudden clench and familiar fury followed. She would not meet her father; not until she could hand him the Spanish Hope. And certainly not until she held her life solidly in her own command.

A flurry of movement at the bank fixed her eyes on the doors. A rotund and hurried man ruffled through his clothing and pulled a key into his hand. The dirt road between stood empty and Lady considered rushing in to follow the man into the building. Would he suspect her desperation? In this case the fluffy white travesty she had been forced to wear might be a suitable disguise. Fugitives did not wear innocent lace.

The silence which permeated the road broke just as she stepped out of the shadows. Her heart stopped when a line of soldiers came into view, their heads turned toward the opposite side of the road. "Blast." Lady slunk back against the wall, her hand pressed against her breast. Eustace's golden hair and thin-chested figure stepped into view, prompting her to slink further down the narrow alley. There would be no way to enter the bank now.

A soft keening floated from the street and stopped her retreat. She tiptoed back to the front of the building. With horror, she watched as Carmen was pushed roughly in front of two soldiers, tears streaking down her cheeks, fear and despair a cloud about the miserable child. Lady clenched her fist and reached the other hand toward the satchel that hung by her hip. She froze when the sheriff arrived, Carmen's assailant from the day before at his side. With no recourse available, Lady felt the inevitability of confrontation. She could not leave Carmen to the town's mercy. The augmented pistol slid easily into her grip, the cool metal no assurance that they could escape this most recent setback. But she must do something. She slid it from the satchel.

The sheriff grabbed Carmen's arm, but froze when Eustace placed a hand on the girl's shoulder. Lady could not hear the exchange, but she let her arm relax. Perhaps the captain's intervention would give her a little more time. Ideas swirled like a flurry, each discarded as they proved impossible. Devising rescue schemes were so much easier with Sybil as her companion.

Sybil. She must retrieve her friend. Together they could determine a course of action. The pistol uncocked as she removed her thumb and slid her hand from the bag. A few more steps backward and she would be completely swallowed by the shadows in the alley. When Eustace completed his obligation with Carmen, he would no doubt set out to find his missing charge. Lady had no desire to find herself back in his autocratic grasp. Sneaking back into the boarding house would prove a most vexing challenge.

Two granite hands fell onto her shoulders and the shock of contact sent a gasp from her lips. A voice floated toward her ear. "You are a might too pretty to be on the run from the law."

Lady swung around and pulled out of her silent attacker's arms, searching the shadows for his identity. "What do you want? I am no easy prey, I warn you. There is a very good reason that I run from the law. Do you wish to discover it?"

He stepped into the light and answered her with an amused smile. Dark-eyed and solidly built across the shoulders, he dressed as a white-man, yet his coloring marked him as foreign. A soft-brimmed hat was tipped low, shading his expression, but Lady could see the mischievous steel lurking beneath his relaxed stance. He advanced another step, but she did not dare retreat. If she stepped away from him, those milling in the street would see her. Lady slipped her hand back into her satchel. "I am assuming you have no desire to bring attention to yourself either. Perhaps, it would be best to go our separate ways."

"But I don't have any issues with these lawmen." He took another step closer, their bodies touched and heat mingled.

Lady's heart pattered, but she kept her head. "That would change should they find you with me." She slid on her own mischievous smile.

He lifted a finger to her hair and twirled a stray tendril with his index finger. "A pretty girl like you would be trouble for any man."

Her eyes rolled and she coughed to hide the sound of her augmented pistol engaging. Just a few moments and it would be ready to fire. Not that she had any desire to bring attention to the alley. But it was always better to be prepared. "I have little patience for smooth-talking devils. Step away, sir."

"Are you not afraid, pretty lady?"

Exasperated, she dropped a massive sigh and pulled her pistol from her satchel. The hiss of steam from the tiny valve gave a fair warning that what she held was no ordinary weapon. "As I mentioned previously, there is a good reason the law is interested in my whereabouts. Are you afraid, sir?"

He chuckled beneath his breath. "I am beginning to understand." Then his eyes cut suddenly to the wall to her left. When her own eyes followed his, she felt a sudden piercing pain in her wrist and her elbow twisted to the side. When her attention was returned to the smiling man, her pistol was pointed at her chest.

"Blast," she said. With one eye on her pistol, she scanned the alley for options. A six-foot fence sealed the far end. Tall walls lined the sides, with only a single window on the second floor to the right as an alternative entrance. Lady had scaled walls before, but the man before her would unlikely allow her the opportunity. She shuffled to the side. "Are you the law, sir? I know few men with the skill to unarm me."

"Flattery won't help you."

Lady shrugged. "It never does."

"What is your name?"

She took another miniscule step to the left. "Why?"

"I'm intrigued."

"Lady," she slid on a silkily sweet smile and he frowned. "And yours?"

"Sir."

Lady stopped her move toward the fence and laughed. The banter did much to release the tension and she shook her head. "If you wish to turn me in, may we get on with it? I find I am beginning to enjoy this far too readily, and there is too much to be done."

"I don't want to--,"

The thunder of horse hooves racing through the street drew their attention. A cavalry man hustled past the alley. They were searching for her. In moments she would be discovered and all hope for escape would be gone. There would be no helping anyone.

A hand clamped on her wrist and tugged her toward the back of the alley. Lady said, "What do you think you are doing?"

Rather than answer, he wrapped a strong arm around her waist and hefted her to the top of the fence and pushed. An uncharacteristic squeal fell from her lips as she hurtled toward the ground. Dust engulfed her when she landed. As soon as her head grasped what had happened, his hand clamped about her wrist again and he yanked her up and into a run. A door barely opened, before he slammed them through it and slammed it shut.

Three sets of black eyes stared at her from a corner table. Cards in hand, the men turned their heads to Sir. One spoke rapidly in a language she could not place. Sir answered with a surly bark and dragged her across the room. The interior door stood open a crack and he peered into the hall. Lady looked back at the men. The bandanas tied around their heads and long braids reminded her of the Apaches they had met in the Chiricahua Mountains. They continued to stare at her with narrowed eyes.

"They don't look happy to see you," Lady said to Sir.

"It isn't me."

"Of course not." She wiped her hand down her skirt, the white fabric turning decidedly brown. "Are you going to turn me into the authorities?"

"No."

His terse reply should have provided more relief. "May

I have my weapon?"

"No."

Lady yanked at her hand, but his grip did not loosen. "If you will not be turning me into the authorities, then we have no business together. Let my hand go. You are wasting my time."

A thunderous expression met hers but he did not respond to her. The door clicked shut and he turned back to his associates around the table. Their conversation proved as unintelligible as it had previously, prompting her to bite her lip to prevent a frustrated growl. One of the men stood, his movements showing his own irritation at the scene. Trudging to the door, he glared at Sir before he left.

Sir still held her hand in a bruising grip. Determined to be free, she tried tact. "Please. I have people that depend on my success here today. It is imperative that you release me."

His features softened and he reached a hand toward her hair but stopped before making contact. "Trust me. I'll get you out of here."

She frowned, then jumped as another of the men stood and strode toward the door. Without a look back he exited as well. Lady said, "I do appreciate the offer, but I am confident that I can--"

A shout echoed from the room beyond and a crash shook the wall. Lady's eyes widened as the third Apache ran to the door, a slight smile on his lips. Sir led her back to the door, waiting a moment after his comrade left to follow. Lady sputtered, "What are we doing, what are you, what is going on?"

As they moved through the hall, Lady stopped in astonishment. A mob of bodies flew around the room, fists swinging and furniture crashing around the combatants. A tug on her arm drew her focus back to Sir. "Come on. This will bring your friends in from outside soon. We only have a few moments."

He finally released her wrist and gently prodded her toward the stairs. A body flipped over a long bar, just as she passed, a bottle of whisky poured across her skirt. She blinked down in consternation. Now she'd smell like the saloon. She may enjoy the freedom of the west, but she had no intention of smelling like some half-bit doxy. Another push to her back and she hustled up the stairs, Sir following close behind. When they reached the second floor, she ran along the hall until a gentle hand touched her elbow and directed her into an empty room.

He shut the door and pressed his ear against the wall.

Finally free of his grip, Lady put several feet between them. A handsome man, Sir took command naturally. Unlike Slim, this man held a steel edge within that appeared barely contained. She had little trust for this man but her choices were scarce.

Lady moved to a window which looked out toward the street. Two of Eustace's men ran toward the violence roaring beneath them. Across the way she caught a glimpse of the man who had accosted Carmen arguing with the sheriff. Beside them Eustace stood, his hands propped on his hips, a dark expression directed toward the saloon. Lady ducked from the window and turned back to Sir. "Well, now what do you suggest we do?"

"Get naked."

All the color left her face then returned in full force to her cheeks. "I beg your pardon?"

His eyes sparkled as he reached for the buttons of his linen shirt. "In about ten minutes, those men on your trail will start checking all the rooms in this town for you. The captain is particularly attached to the notion of marrying you, Lady. So I doubt he'll give up. And now that their attention is on this building, I figure they will start here."

"How do you know about the captain?" Fear sent bumps across her skin. Had she run from a demon into the arms of the devil?

Sir chuckled, and turned away from her. "I know an awful lot about you, Lady. But I ain't here to hurt you. We share a common goal. So get undressed. This is just for show."

Lady did not move as her eyes skirted the room for a weapon. "What common goal?"

"Sybil."

Lady nearly fell to her knees at the name. Then she spun around as he dropped his pants. Lord have mercy. What had she gotten herself into?

16

The sound of angry men and quiet weeping woke Sybil from her slumber. Boots thudding against the hall floor brought her to her feet. Once the noise receded, Sybil began to worry and now she wondered if all was lost. Had the men left with Lady? It would have been quite out of character for her friend to cry so wretchedly. Lady fought like a hell cat and would never have let her enemies see her weakness. No. It could not have been Lady.

But who then? And why was the cavalry on the move? Sybil recognized the sound of men in uniform. And the rushed orders from their commanding officer had been urgent. Whatever had happened, it did not bode well for Lady or for Sybil.

With the sun rapidly lightening the sky, Sybil wrapped her body in the silks. Her situation within Zhao Jin's grasp may be the least desired, but she did have new silks. The intensified pain felt soothed beneath the smooth fabric. Sybil slid toward the window and arched her neck as the warmth of the sun played against her skin. A smile touched her face.

The noise outside her room ceased and the quiet sank around her, taking the pleasure from the sunlight and wringing it into a nauseating worry. If Lady were discovered missing, the men would find her. Where could a woman hide?

Sybil shook herself. Never had she doubted her friend's ingenuity. This morose negativity no doubt came from too many days in Zhao Jin's company. Sybil paced the room, eager to be on the move. Lady had said she would return before dawn. That time had passed and now they waited for a new opportunity. Born with a mind designed for the ballroom, Lady learned her devious tricks from social intrigue and bitter battles of intellect. Accustomed to hiding her mind behind an illusion of flighty superficiality, she had taken wing the moment her intelligence was an asset without the ruse of idiocy. Sybil knew the woman well, despite the short time together.

A hidden soul recognized another with little prodding.

But now Sybil wondered if their dependence on intellect may have finally failed beneath the circumstances of evil persistence. Slim was lost to them. Now Lady may also be beyond her reach. Vengeance may never be theirs, but would they also lose their freedom?

Booted feet stomped across the hall again, this time ordered and with firm intent. Doors slammed open, the wood protesting under heavy hands. Sybil tightened the wrap of her silk and waited. They would come and find nothing but a woman wracked with sickness. But perhaps there was some way she could assist Lady? Some way to redirect their search?

Her door flew open. A young soldier, chest heaving at the exertion, stood at the door. His eyes darted across the room, stopping when they reached Sybil.

Sybil lowered her eyes and smiled. "Would you like to come in? I assure you, there izz nothing here that I hide. Perhapzz you would like to rest between roomzz?"

He froze, his eyes wide with horror as she removed the silk from her face. Sybil had grown used to the shock her appearance inspired. Such reactions said much of a man...or woman. The initial shock was honest and true. But the second moment, when the reason within the mind returned, proved the mettle of a soul. This man had grit. He composed himself in seconds, straightening his back and thinning his lips. "Ma'am, I apologize for the intrusion. I must search your room for our charge."

"Your charge? You have lost a child?" Sybil sang the words, swishing the silk as she moved toward the bed. "Do you believe I have your charge?"

The soldier coughed, uncomfortable as he stepped into the room. "No ma'am. But I must check all the rooms."

"That izz quite an assignment. You must be truly trusted by you commander for such an important duty."

The young man blushed then began to search the room thoroughly. Sybil sat as he crouched down to inspect under the bed. She hummed to herself as he returned to his feet. Then she said, "Izz thizz child very important?"

"Yes. Her father is extremely influential."

"Oh my," Sybil cooed. "I imagine it izz very important that you find her. Hazz she gone missing before?"

The young man shifted uncomfortably, so Sybil pressed on. "Children can be so vexing. They hide in the most unexpected locationzz."

"She's not exactly a child." He scratched his head as his eyes darted out of the room. With nothing left in the room to search, he no doubt felt eager to move on. But as long as Sybil continued her questioning, she could keep him from his goal. Perhaps a few more moments could provide Lady a window of escape. But there were so many soldiers at the captain's disposal. What would deterring one soldier do for any of them?

Sybil ignored her doubts and continued, "Not a child? How strange. You did call her your charge. Are you saying you have an adult woman azz your charge?"

He switched the weight from one foot to another and refused to make eye contact. "Her father is very important."

"Yezz, you have mentioned that. Do I make you uncomfortable?"

The man's eyes shot to hers. "No ma'am."

"It izz quite alright if I do. Most people find my appearanzze unsettling."

"No ma'am, it ain't that. It's just…my orders ma'am."

"So you are not uncomfortable in my presenzz?"

He shifted uncomfortably again and Sybil nearly felt pity for the poor boy. But his actions threatened her friend and that she could not abide. "Perhapzz you would like to sit with me?" Sybil purred, lengthening her legs in a smooth, sensual movement. Dance had always been her most enticing tool of communication. Perhaps this young man would like to see her dance.

A clenched hand suggested that he warred within himself and that made Sybil wonder why. Given a choice he should wish to leave. Politeness kept him standing beside the door. Nothing more for certain. Ceasing her movements, she asked, "What izz your name?"

"Samuel." His hands unclenched but his eyes never left hers. A warmth spread across her chest at the open expression. Fear had vanished from his face and for once she wondered…

"Samuel, you seem to be a good and honest man. I will not keep you from your businezz."

Confusion crossed his eyes then he stepped forward. "Ma'am, I know you would not believe--"

"What is this? What are you doing in this room?"

Sybil stood at the sound of Zhao Jin's voice. His obsidian eyes bore suspicious bolts into Samuel's chest. The boy straightened his shoulders and took a step toward Sybil. "I am under orders, sir, from Captain Wright of the 6th regiment, to search all the rooms of this establishment for a fugitive."

"Do you see a fugitive in here?" Zhao Jin gestured to the whole of the room. "No? Then you must leave."

"He izz simply doing hizz duty," Sybil said. "Do you deny him that?"

Zhao Jin narrowed his eyes at her. "He has completed his duty. He may now leave."

Samuel took another minute step toward Sybil. "Is this your husband, ma'am?"

Sybil smiled at the young man's brash bravery. "No."

At that, Samuel straightened his back even further. "Then if you are not her husband, sir, please tell me by what authority allows you to order me from her room?"

"Sam, what is going on?" Another soldier stood at the door, his uniform marked him as an officer. Sybil lowered her eyes, but examined him with intense interest. Sandy blond hair, neatly trimmed, complimented sun-ripened skin. He was not unattractive, but thin lips and weak eyes marked him as a man who did not command his own life. However, the stern set to his shoulder and unwavering sense of purpose suggested he followed his orders to the end no matter the cost. This was the man they must outfox and with more resources at his disposal, he might prove as challenging as the brilliantly deceitful Zhao Jin.

"Captain, I am merely asking your man to leave, now that he has completed his duty," Zhao Jin said, his words silky and smile venomous.

Samuel's jaw tensed and the captain's brow rose, but he moved to the side to allow room for his man to leave. The captain said, "I assume you are done, Samuel."

Sybil smiled and inclined her head at the young man when he made a move to resist. The two alpha men confronting him would not treat Samuel well. Not when his sympathies were for a broken woman. The captain would assume she was of no consequence, and Zhao Jin knew no mercy. She slid toward Zhao Jin and stood at his side. He could not hide the look of approval that reflected back at her action. Someday that approval would prove his undoing. She would simply need to bide her time with patience.

As Samuel exited, Zhao Jin stopped the captain from following with his question. "This fugitive, is he dangerous? We are to leave town and if we were to encounter such a man, we would wish to be forewarned."

The captain's nose flared and he looked distastefully at the Chinaman. "Dangerous? Hardly. She is simply a spoiled heiress that refuses to acknowledge her station. However, it would be unfortunate if someone were to think they could use that knowledge to their benefit. The United States Cavalry are not forgiving over such matters."

"Certainly, Captain. I wish you the best in your search. I do not envy you the charge of an uncooperative female."

The captain grunted then shut the door with a thud, leaving her with a seething Zhao Jin. Sybil took a settling breath, composed her expression, and stepped away. Zhao Jin swung on her. "Do you think I do not know who their fugitive is? The Pinkertons have proved incompetent it seems, but I am far from it. Grab your things. We are leaving."

Sybil lifted her head and smiled at him. "You may not be incompetent. But your talentzz pale in comparison to my associatezz."

He lifted a hand to strike, but she did not flinch. When the slap failed to come she inclined her head toward the door. Sybil said, "Shall we continue our game?"

***

The water hit his face and Slim laughed, choking as some of the liquid splashed down his throat. Who needed a bath? He needed a bath. Slim lifted his arms, but they slammed back down on the bed. He twisted his head to see the restraints which held his wrists. Laughter welled up and his chest ached. The pain made him laugh harder. "Oh Leslie my boy, did anyone tell ya, you remind me of Clementine?"

Banahan's brutish assistant snarled and threw another bucket of water on Slim. The laughter kept coming. Slim sang, "Oh my Clema, Oh my Clema, Oh my darlin Clementine. Now you're gone and lost forever. I 'm dreadful sorry Clementine!"

"If you don't stop that, I'll hit ya with more than water," Leslie said.

"Oh my Clema, Oh my Clema, Oh my darlin Clementine!" Slim crowed. The walls had stopped spinning, but now the water droplets on the wall slid together into globules of menace. Crawling along the cool metal, the sinister intent of the water creature became evident. Slim snorted another laugh. He would die by water monster. How fitting an end.

Perhaps Banahan would give another round to ease the pitch into death's bottomless pit. It seemed only fair. "How 'bout another bottle, Leslie?"

The hulking man growled and threw another bucket of water on Slim. The monster on the wall grew, long columns turning into eerie tentacles. Didn't Leslie see it? But the big man just glared, ignoring Slim's pleas for more elixir. If that's how the man wanted to play this hand, then Slim would throw down another card. He sang, "Her lips were like two luscious beefsteaks. Dipp'd in tomato sauce 'n brine. And like the casha'mere goat'es coverin was the fine wool of Clementine!"

Leslie threw another bucket of water on Slim.

"What is going on here, Leslie? We can hear him all the way on deck." Banahan strode into the room and Slim gaped at him. Certain he had something to say to the man. But he just couldn't remember. Maybe he'd want to play cards?

"He's gone and addled his brains. Wants more of that devil's piss." Leslie spit on the floor as he replied to his employer.

Slim looked down at the floor and watched the spittle dance like a sprite on forest moss. "Come 'ere sprite. Ya can save me from the monster on my wall."

"I see what you mean. Give him another."

"Are you sure?" Leslie asked.

Banahan took a moment before answering. Then Slim heard the words which made him crow with victory. "Yes. We want to see how much it will take, don't we? But come get me if he takes a turn for the worse. I don't want to miss the final moments."

"Don't see how it could get much worse," Leslie murmured as his boss left, but Slim ignored him. He had another bottle comin'. Lordy things were lookin' up.

17

Lady decided she'd had far too many encounters with arrogant, stubborn, self-important men to last her for many years. Would she be tortured this way for the rest of her days? Destined to struggle against men who exemplified all the characteristics of her father that she abhorred?

Sir ordered her to disrobe again.

Lady crossed her arms over her chest. She'd already removed the dress and corset. That was well enough. "I am not going to remove my chemise. It isn't proper"

"Lady, running around the west burning down buildings, blowing up steamships and rescuing outlaws ain't proper. You still did that." He opened the door a crack and peered into the hall.

How could he know what she had done? Could he have been sent by her father? But Eustace was sent by her father. Sir had to be someone…"You are a marshal!"

"I ain't a marshal."

"You know too much. There is no way you could know all that you do and not be a marshal!"

He turned toward her and she spun around, blushing at his nakedness. Heaven help her, she'd had little experience with men in undress. To be true, she'd never seen one. Her mother would be mortified. Her father furious. The thought was strangely fortifying and she turned back to confront the dreadful man.

His hands reached for her chest and she gasped. Fingers tucked into the neckline of her chemise and he ripped the thin fabric to the knees. Her mouth hung open in shock and her body stood frozen as the remnants of her chemise fell to the floor.

"Sweetheart, you're just gonna have to forgive me." He grabbed her around the waist and threw her on the bed. The sheets flew over them as he crawled over her body.

The heat of skin against skin felt foreign and frightening. Lady said, "Get off me!"

"Pretend you like my company."

"I hate your company." Her hands met a solid and smooth chest but no amount of shoving removed him from her body. The fear receded as her fury rose. "You are a despicable, unredeemable toad."

"That's why I said pretend." He kissed her. Heaven help her, he kissed her. Lady froze again, her body tense. His lips felt like silk and molasses and if she were honest, it tasted sweeter than her favorite tart. This was unacceptable. No one kissed her without permission! Not even if it were a pleasant kiss. Lady struggled, pushing with all her strength against his chest and growling into his mouth.

His lips lifted and he glared down at her. "Shush. Don't you hear them?"

"Hear who? I can't hear a dang thing with you attacking me."

"I ain't attacking you. I told you. This is just for show." He stopped her ready reply with a hand over her mouth, then he nestled his head into her neck just as she heard the door slam open. He whispered, "Giggle for me, Lady."

"What?" she hissed through his fingers.

His hand moved down to her waist and he poked a finger into her side, eliciting a surprised squeak from her.

A strong, masculine voice came from the hall. "Stand up, mister. We got orders to search this room."

Suddenly, Sir disappeared from the bed and the sheets flew up to cover her face and slid up to show her quite obviously bare leg. Lady bit her lip. How had things gone so wrong? Not only was she to be discovered, but her clothing was gone. Eustace would throw a fit.

Freedom had been lost, all because of a chance lunatic encounter.

"What the hell are you doing in here?" Sir roared. "I done paid my tab and this lady and I are gonna settle up when we're done."

An embarrassed cough answered him. She listened to thuds and the rustling of clothes as Sir continued his tirade. "I ain't never been…you better have a damn good reason… where are my boots. Rosa, where are my boots??"

It took a moment before Lady realized he'd addressed her. What was the blasted man up to?

"Damn it, Rosa. Don't you know there's a soldier here? Where are my damn boots, woman?" Another thud sounded, but she dared not look out to see what he'd done. He'd started this ruse, she would play her part. With an exaggerated giggle she poked her hand out of the sheets and pointed to the corner of the room. She had no idea where the man's boots were, but it was as reasonable a guess as any.

"Dang, there's only one there." She felt the bed move slightly and heard the sound of his body crawling beside the bed. "Here it is, under the bed. Damn, Rosa. You sure are a wild cat."

Despite the obvious fabrication, she blushed at his insinuation. There was a playfulness in his voice reminded her of another rascal. Her mood darkened. Too much was at stake to let the humor of the situation sway her. Too many people depended on her freedom. Sybil, Carmen, Slim.

"Rosa, I don't think you're gonna be able to wear this again." This time Lady could not withstand the urge to look and she pulled the blanket away just enough to peek at Sir holding up her torn chemise. The shocked expression on the soldier standing by the door prompted another short laugh from her lips.

The young soldier covered another uncomfortable cough then said, "I believe we are done here, mister. It is obvious you are not harboring fugitives."

"Fugitives? Why in the devil would I be harboring fugitives?" Sir dropped the chemise to the floor and stepped over the fabric, blocking Lady's view. She covered her face again, satisfied that for the moment she was safe.

"We apologize for the intrusion." The door clicked shut and Sir threw a few more expletives at the retreating man before pulling the sheet away from Lady's face. A smug grin accompanied sparkling eyes.

"Sir, you are a devil." Lady fought the urge to pout. This had to be the first time she felt this put out. The man had been right, using their undress as a convincing disguise. But he didn't need to resort to such a demanding tone. Had he been reasonable, surely she would have listened. She gave a crooked smile. Even she did not believe that she would have listened. She said, "I think you may have enjoyed that."

Sir chuckled. "Perhaps a little. Would you like me to kiss you again?"

Lady's eyes widened and she shot up, clutching the sheet over her chest. "Certainly not. Now please, hand me my corset. It will be dreadfully uncomfortable without the chemise, but I suppose I can forgive you that."

"You can go without the corset."

Lady huffed then pulled the sheet around her like a dress. Sir was going to be no help. And now a second man had made derisive comments about her corset. Honestly, a woman just did not go without a corset. She stepped over the rags that had become of her chemise and pulled open the dresser drawer where she'd tucked away her clothing.

As she adjusted the strings that would pull together the corset, she heard a rattling from the street. Sir already stood at the window and she joined him. A sudden shift in his stance forced her to look into his stark face. Brows drew tight over his eyes and his jaw tensed. The man looked purely furious. Her gaze followed his line of sight and fell on a small Chinaman in elegant clothing escorting a diminutive figure wrapped in silks.

An irritated breath caught in her throat. She whispered, "Sybil."

Lady threw down the corset and ran to the drawer for her dress. There would be time to properly dress at another time. The white confection she draped over her body would be an unfortunate beacon to all the men currently searching for her, but there was nothing to do. She would have to risk it.

A whoosh sounded before a ball of fabric hit her chest. Lady looked up in shock at Sir. He stood bent over the bed, his hands rummaging through a well-worn bag. The fabric unrolled into a slightly wrinkled linen shirt. Lady raised a brow to Sir, only to duck as a pair of trousers flew toward her head. "What are you doing?"

"You can't go out in that dress. They'll spot you the moment you leave this room."

"Won't it be strange for two men to walk out that door? Honestly, have you thought any of this through?"

Sir stood, grabbed his hat and stomped toward her. He shoved the hat on her head then tipped her face up with a finger to her chin. "Do you give all men that try to help you this kind of trouble?"

"It has been mentioned in the past, yes." By a certain gambler with a devilish grin and personality that rivaled this particular man's penchant for mischief.

"Get dressed. We don't know where they are going, so we need to move fast."

Lady removed the hat and replaced the hated dress with his shirt. As she stepped into the trousers she replied, "You said we had a shared interest. That you know Sybil. If you are truly not a marshal then what is your interest in my friend?"

"Your friend?"

His quizzical expression irritated her. "You are surprised that she is my friend?"

"Yes. From what I have seen, she has had few true friends in her life. And someone with your pedigree does not seem the type to count her as one."

Lady snorted in as unladylike a fashion as possible and glared at the dark-eyed stranger across the room. Exotic cheekbones with an austere jaw-line made her wonder what exactly this man wanted. "My pedigree does not shape my decisions anymore. But what of yours? What kind of man tracks a traveling show dancer? You are not the only man that has coveted my friend. And none so far have been good men. Why should I allow you to come any nearer to your goal?"

His lips turned up and his eyes shone with cleverness. Lady took a step back and decided this man was not one to trust so readily. He said, "I have no ill-intentions against Sybil. Her safety and happiness is of the utmost importance to me."

"I find that hard to believe."

"Then you will have to do your best to stop me from reaching her before you do." The door swung open and he left the room before she had a second to blink. Lady gaped at the empty floor where he'd only just stood. Damn if the man hadn't thrown her off guard again. Now she'd have to chase after him.

Or perhaps not. She knew exactly where Zhao Jin was taking Sybil. If she could move quickly, she could beat them all to the Chinaman's steam contraption. Lady snatched her satchel and ran to the door. Before she left, she cast another look to the room and caught sight of the corset. With a quick dash, she grabbed the garment and stuffed it into the bag. The question to leave it would come again. Just not now. She wasn't quite ready.

The sun rose well above the dawn horizon and she had to duck from one hiding spot to the next each time a soldier drew near. When she'd accompanied the cavalry into town, they hadn't seemed quite so numerous. Now, she couldn't go two steps without running into one of Eustace's men. The clothing Sir provided helped to mask her appearance, but no close inspection would mistake her for a man.

Once she reached the outskirts of town, she broke into a run, hoping to pass Zhao Jin and Sir among the desert brush. The over-large shirt snagged in the prickly branches and the trousers dragged along the dirt, picking up burrs which worked their way into her shoes and tore irritating scratches into her ankles. Lady stopped to hitch the trousers up again, the fourth time in the span of her run from the saloon. Rolling the waistband only assisted in pulling the burrs farther up her legs. Luck had not been a friendly companion in quite some time and now she sent an oath into the sky. Something good had to come of all this.

Movement to her right sent Lady sprawling on the ground. Muffled conversation carried over the mesquite and palo verde trees. A soft lilting accompanied a brusque male voice and Lady sighed in relief. Sybil and Zhao Jin had yet to reach their destination. Perhaps luck was a slight kinder mistress than she'd assumed.

A flicker of movement to her left startled Lady's heart, the thuds reaching a new height. Who?

"Mister, you need to let the girl go."

Lady slapped a hand to her mouth to keep from reacting to Sir's proclamation. What was the idiot thinking? Zhao Jin wouldn't simply let Sybil go. He was far too clever.

True to his character, Zhao Jin replied with calm derision. "I assure you, there is no cause for halting our progress. Whatever slight you have imagined, I can guarantee it is unfounded."

Lady threaded through the brush to a more suitable location to overhear the confrontation. Determination to remain unnoticed schooled her motions to silence.

"It is far from unfounded, Mister Jin. That woman has never been a willing accomplice in your plans."

Pausing in her movement, Lady listened intently to Sir. How did he know the identity of Sybil's nemesis? The man proved more intriguing than she originally thought and his brash intervention may prove more fortuitous than anyone would have predicted. Lady caught a glance of black wings in the distance. They only had another one-hundred feet to the SteamWing. If Lady could sneak around while the indomitable Zhao Jin was distracted, she might abscond with both his contraption and his captive. She slipped through the brush toward her new objective.

Zhao Jin answered coolly, "You have me at a disadvantage. I do not know you. What business do we have?"

"I have no business with you. My business is with the lady."

"I am afraid her business is my business."

"Not anymore."

The silence prompted Lady to peer toward the party of foes and nearly stumbled. In Sir's hand, pointed at the rather unruffled Zhao Jin, was one of Lady's augmented pistols. She whipped open the flap to her satchel and found both of her weapons missing. The bastard ran off with her guns! Damn him and his unrequested assistance.

18

Sybil did not know the man. Broad-shouldered and imposing, she would never have forgotten a man so feral and menacing. His dark, exotic-colored skin and deep brown eyes highlighted an otherwise anglo face. Something familiar in his features made her search her memories for a clue to his identity, but she found no answer. Depth of courage warred with blistering hostility in the eyes he pierced on Zhao Jin. Only when his gaze flickered to her did his expression soften. Taken aback by the subtle affection, she looked away, into the desert brush, unsure of her place in this particular game.

No man fought for her without reason. What unknown piece to the puzzle confronted her now? For once, she missed the lonely obscurity she had endured as a social outcast.

Pain lanced up her arm. Zhao Jin held her elbow, his fingers pressing with punishing pressure into the tendons. There would be no escaping his grip. Had she known an offer for assistance were in the waiting, she might have prepared more fully for the opportunity. But now, her position held no advantage.

The guns the unknown hero wielded were held steady in expert hands, but Sybil could not help but recognize the make. Only one in her knowledge possessed such unique pistols. What connection did this man have to Lady?

Sybil cast down her lashes as the man and Zhao Jin verbally sparred, neither paying much attention to her. Despite her person being the topic of contention, she felt unneeded and inconsequential. Had Zhao Jin not maintained his clasp on her person, she could have simply walked into the brush and disappeared among the sage and palo verde.

"I am in no mood to continue our conversation. Remove your hand from her and be on your way," the stranger said.

Zhao Jin gave no reply and made no move. Oddly enough, he had few options. With the nefarious weapons pointed at his chest, the Chinaman dared not move. Sybil reveled in his uncertainty. Unfortunately, the moment did not last long.

Beyond the far stand of mesquite, a flash of movement exposed the presence of Martin and Joseph. Sybil gave a sharp sound of warning as the two men stepped into view, weapons drawn and pointed at her prospective rescuer. Zhao Jin's manner changed, his confidence returned and sly smile slid on easily. "Those are interesting weapons. I would very much like to examine them. Please lay them on the ground."

Martin came forward, his weapon still trained on the adversary. Sybil tested Zhao Jin's grip on her arm with a slight tug. He sliced a quick glance her way and shook his head. Disappointed, she felt hope sink from her grasp. When the man stepped away from his weapons, Zhao Jin urged her toward the SteamWing waiting in the distance, the sound of releasing steam testament to their imminent departure.

"Unfortunately, you are not the only foe we must avoid

at this time, so I will not have the time to determine your purpose. However, violence is not my purview, so please accept my apologies that we will not be present for your demise." Zhao Jin turned his head from the stranger and pushed Sybil forward. "Martin, please wait to dispatch our friend until we have entered the cabin."

Sybil's hand shook. Another death would weigh heavily on her soul. Between MacHurdyGurdy and Zhao Jin, the west would be a bloody mess from their arrogance and ambition. What could she possibly do at this junction to prevent another unfortunate tragedy? As she wracked her mind for options, Zhao Jin opened the door to the SteamWing then turned back to the men waiting in the distance. With her captive momentarily distracted, she was able to remove her arm from his possession. But what could she do with her freedom? There was nowhere to run.

A hand snatched her wrist, yanked her into the cabin, and the door slammed shut.

"Quickly Sybil, we must be off!" Lady shouted as she slid the lock into place then ran to the steering console.

Sybil blinked at her friend then grabbed the arm rest of one of Zhao Jin's overstuffed chairs as the SteamWing jerked into motion. The release of steam nearly deafening, Sybil looked with worry at her friend. If there were a chance that they could escape, she would trust Lady and her ingenuity to discover it.

The ship jerked again, and rose into the air. Sybil ran to the windows and watched as Zhao Jin and his accomplices struggled to maintain grips on the ropes hanging from the SteamWing. A dark figure dashed across her peripheral vision just as the ship made a final jerk and rose to a height to catch the wind. The ship settled as Lady adjusted the angle and the ship sailed with ease through the sky. Zhao Jin's furious dark silhouette shrank into the distance. Sybil said, "How did you know to do that?"

Lady turned to her, face ashen and uncommonly frightened. "Honestly, I had no idea what I was doing. I am grateful it seems to have worked."

Sybil released a pent up sigh and returned her gaze to the window, watching Zhao Jin disappear into the distance. "That wazz unusually effective."

"Indeed. And now we must endeavor to do the same again. We must return to Albuquerque for Carmen."

Carmen? Sybil did not know this woman. "I am not familiar—"

A face pressed against the glass of the door, startling Sybil into falling backward. Lady rose and shouted, but Sybil heard none of the words as the world spun. The sky turned a dusky yellow, the warmth of the sunlight that filtered through windows pouring like molten energy into her body. The scales across her skin tightened and her teeth bared.

She curled into a ball and looked frantically about her, scanning the room for anything familiar. Her world had disappeared into rapidly moving waves of color and heat. What had once been solid turned liquid. Silence felt like thunder in her ears and her scream came out empty. What was happening to her? Had the madness finally come?

A sudden sensation crept across her shoulder and the sense of danger swirled into every one of her pores.

Sybil struck at the threat.

***

He had need of a guide. Mordecai scanned the room where roughened miners mixed with railroad men, each focused intently on his drink and personal trials. Bernard and his wife, waited beyond the door, watering the mules. He took advantage of the brief respite before he would bundle them back onto the cart and push on toward their destiny.

With the air so cold with autumn's icy winds, there was little to keep the spirits up. Even his brother had resorted to grumbling. Beatrice always did enough of that for the both of them, but now their voices grated into his persistence. Mordecai considered leaving them in Flagstaff while he continued on to where the mysterious magic in the Zuni village had directed him.

But any moment that Bernard spent with his wife and not with Mordecai increased her influence over the changeable man. The urgency to maintain his hold on his brother kept his options limited and slowed their progress. Each of the previous hindrances to his plan were easily discarded--except Beatrice. As always, she continued to stymie his operation.

But not for much longer. There would be an opportunity. Of that he had no doubt.

A young man, made ancient by the harsh reality of western labor, slumped against the long, rough wood bar. Mordecai approached gingerly, laying on an act of eastern naiveté, keeping his hands lax, his nose turned up, and his mouth pinched in moderate distaste. "I do say, sir, do you know this hamlet well?"

The man looked at Mordecai, his eyes glassy from exhaustion and too much drink, and grunted. Mordecai scanned the room as though counting the worth of a cattle herd. His voice rose as he continued, "I find myself in need of a man familiar with the local area. There's money in it, if you are."

The man cleared his throat and sat up with more obvious interest. "You lookin' for something particular?"

Mordecai sniffed and looked down his nose. "Of course. Gold. Is there anything else to look for?"

Greedy eyes flickered across the room, and Mordecai knew he would find just the man to lead him to the next step in this mystery with little trouble. And when it was done, none would be wiser to his intentions. Confident men on the make were sloppy and would remain unaware of their quarry's duplicity. Men with gold on the mind were doubly susceptible.

With a flick of his wrist, he pulled a gold coin from a small pouch attached to his hip, and laid it on the bar beside the young man. "If you know of someone that can take me to the top of that mountain we can see from the street, then this coin is yours."

Several eyes shuttered and an uncomfortable cough highlighted the sudden silence in the room. A raised eyebrow from Mordecai made men shift in their seats, their excitement about the prospective easy take from an eastern gentleman oddly stifled.

"Sweet gold, sweet gold, can't go there, can't go there. Bring the baby, bathe the baby, grab the eagle born and butcher."

Mordecai swept the room for the mad rambling and he was drawn to a man, rocking in the corner, his hair greasy and long. The others in the room refused to make eye-contact and Mordecai knew he'd found his man. The coin scraped against the bar as he plucked it from where it lay and he tossed it back into his pouch.

As the man rocked, the men that surrounded him inched away, their faces ashen. Mordecai approached the table and pulled out a chair. With a stony glare, he sent the rest of the audience scurrying into the shadows, leaving himself and the madman alone in a room full of strangers. Mordecai said, "What do you know of eagles?"

Frosty eye's flared with fire. The man said, "Butcher baby, grab the eagle, tear the skin, it tears the skin."

Adjusting his seat, Mordecai reached into his vest pocket and pulled out the eagle locket. The gold and coral flashed in the dim light and caught the madman's attention. Mordecai moved the locket and watched as the glassy eyes followed with an unnatural fascination. He flipped open the lid as though looking at a watch and the spell broke.

Vividly lucid eyes looked at him from across the table. "Hello, Butcher."

Mordecai smiled, baring his teeth and the man pushed back in his chair, eyes wide and frightened. Mordecai said, "How much gold to show me the eagle?" The man shook his head and Mordecai leaned forward to say, "You've been to the top; that much is clear. Take me there and you'll walk away with gold in your pocket. It will be more than you find in the dirt here."

The man shook his head. "The spirits don't like men. Men make them angry. No men. No men. No men."

"I have business with those spirits." Mordecai snapped the locket shut and held it up, pressing the red coral image toward the madman. He pushed gold coins forward with the other hand. "You know this eagle. You will take me there."

The man's eyes glazed with madness again, but his hand closed over the gold. "The butcher grabs the eagle.

Butcher baby tears the skin."

19

Blood streamed down her arm and the skin burned from the ragged scratches that tore through cotton and into flesh. Lady bit down, her teeth grinding as she struggled with Sybil, the woman's body a writhing mass of fluid desperation. Lord save them, no one was steering the mad machine.

The window above the door shattered, the shards of glass raining down on the two wrestling women. Lady glanced up as a body flew through the door only to scream in agony as Sybil's nails sliced down her cheek.

Sir's familiar form rolled and came up beside Lady, his hands frantically reaching for Sybil. Lady shouted, "Do not be daft! I have her. You must save us from falling!"

He froze before clarity sent him scurrying toward the steering panel. Lady's belly rolled as he regained control of the spiraling ship, the sense of nausea momentarily replacing the pain of Sybil's attack. Wrapped arms did nothing to still her companion's terror-filled struggles. Lady cooed into her ear, humming and pleading—anything to ease the fear.

A sudden dive by the ship sent Lady rolling into Sybil and both women careened toward the open door. Legs tangled with skirts and silk. The air rushed from her lungs as she slammed into the door jamb. Sybil's weight pressed Lady into the wood. Lady's legs flew out the door and hung into nothingness, the wide legs of her borrowed trousers flapping like leaves in a tempest against her ankles. The pressure of Sybil's weight against her body provided the only hold she had on the ship. If there was even a slight change in their position, Lady would fall into the sky.

Very human and tender fingers wrapped around her wrist. Lady looked up into Sybil's kind and concerned eyes. "I have you, my friend. Calm your fearzz."

Sybil rolled back into the ship and pulled Lady with her. Heart beats crashed against her ribs, and Lady rested on her back for several moments, hoping time could still the shaking of her limbs. When did the possibility of death at any moment become a constant occurrence? Perhaps returning to Boston would be the more prudent choice. At least she would be guaranteed making it through the year alive.

"Lady, I do not know how to keep us in the air," Sir said.

This was a shared dilemma. She knew nothing of how this contraption worked either. The fact that they were in the air was a mixture of luck and providence. Lady sat up, cradling her arm where the impact had bruised the skin. The shredded white fabric of her sleeve had stained an ugly red. Sybil stared, her face stricken with remorse and something far more eerie.

Lady asked, "Are you alright?"

"I do not believe so. But there izz little we can do, izz there?"

Lady had no ready reply and turned her attention to Sir, grappling with the ship's controls. Lady said, "I can promise you, manhandling this machine will do nothing but send us to our deaths. Loosen your grip."

"Perhaps you should take them from me?" He pleaded and despite the pain, Lady complied. Sybil moved to one of the velvet chairs and wrapped her body with the silks, hiding her face behind the soft blue fabric. Sir gave up the controls and stepped away with haste.

Lady eased the lever into a neutral position and the SteamWing settled into a soft glide, catching the wind and leveling its flight. An unconsciously held breath hissed through her teeth as she stared into the distance, the past moments painfully incomprehensible. Sybil's behavior straddled a fence between defensive action and evil intent. The blood still oozed from Lady's wounds, but she was not ready to acknowledge them. How do you accept the pain when a sinister curse lurked beneath the surface of a good and compassionate soul? What demon had taken control of her dear friend?

A gentle hand took hold of her arm. Sir said, "Let me help." The fabric of the sleeve tore beneath his fingers at the shoulder and he applied a cloth to the wound in her upper arm. Then she felt the cool relief of a wet cloth against the scratches on her face. Their fingers touched as she raised her hand to hold the cloth in place and when their eyes met, he quickly looked away.

Confused, Lady fought to control the sudden urge to rant against them both. Sir looked to Sybil, his eyes soft with compassion. Lady lost the hold she had on her anger. "You will tell me who you are. Now. I am tired of the puzzle and secrecy. If I am correct that you care something for Sybil, then your actions should shame you. We could have all died."

Sybil said, "My reaction to hizz appearanzz wazz not hizz fault. I wazz startled. I do not know who you are, but I am grateful for your assisstanzz on the ground. Had you not distracted my captor, we may not have made our escape."

Lady stared into the distance, grumbling at Sybil's easy acceptance of the stranger. Sir was simply another man intent on taking advantage of whatever he thought to gain from Sybil. With so many charlatans and bounders roaming the deserts of America, it was a wonder that the region didn't just fall into a pit of lawless anarchy. With the SteamWing suitably stable, Lady swung on Sir. "Your name. It is not Sir, is it?"

While she'd been navigating the ship, he'd composed himself and stood confident and aloof again. Lady narrowed her eyes and contemplated brandishing her steam wand on the rascal. And there was a certain issue to be dealt with concerning the theft of her augmented pistols. The man owed her quite a bit more than a name and an explanation.

"And you are not named Lady. Does it matter?" he asked crossing his arms as he leaned against the ship wall. The door no longer hung open, but the rush of air still flowed through the broken window, making it difficult to hear his rumbling response.

Lady frowned and crossed her arms as well. "My name may have been different at another time of my life. But it is Lady now. You however, I do not believe would ever be known as Sir."

"Is that a slight on my character, Miss Dewhurst?"

As her real name slipped past his lips, Lady's nose flared and she clenched her fists. The man knew far too much. "You are not the law. You are not with any of our known enemies. You know far more than anyone ought about both of us. Who are you?"

"Would you accept that I am simply here to assist you?"

"No," Lady growled.

Sybil let the silk fall from her face as she cocked her head to the side. Curiosity swam across her features with something nearly like recognition. "You will forgive my friend. She hazz little reason to trust anyone. But you do yourself no favorzz hiding behind an aliazz or subtle insinuationzz. What are your motivezz, Sir?"

Softened eyes looked at the slight woman in the chair and Lady's sense of protectiveness flared. What manner of mysticism did Sybil possess that encouraged the covetous nature of men? She said, "I do not like how you are looking at her, Sir."

"You have made your distrust quite clear, Lady." Sir turned toward her, his expression unyielding. "I admire your loyalty, but you are unprepared and unqualified to assist in the menace that follows you. Your instincts are good, but your penchant for attracting attention will do nothing but harm Sybil's chances of surviving what is coming. And while Zhao Jin has played a minor role, his has been but a simple irritant compared to the coming storm."

"That is the most ridiculous and inane explanation of nothing I have ever heard," Lady said.

"Lady, pleazz. Hold your hostility. We will discover more from our friend here if you would mute your suspicionzz."

The rebuke silenced Lady's next comment, a slight feeling of betrayal welling up beneath her breast. Did her friend not see that as much danger stood within this very cabin as there was on the desert floor? To be truthful, Sir saved them from Zhao Jin, to a certain degree, and he had assisted her in avoiding capture in Albuquerque. But his behavior had been nothing less than highly questionable. If he did not provide a suitable answer, she would have to find some way to take the matter over. She stared at the door. Perhaps she could simply push him back out…

"I am your brother."

Lady nearly choked, and swung her attention back to Sir. "I beg your pardon? I do not have a brother."

He laughed. "Not your brother. Sybil's"

Sybil pressed back into her chair, the open curiosity suddenly closed. "I have no family."

Fury rose and Lady reached for her satchel. Things had gone quite far enough.

"Lady, the mountain!" Sir shouted and ran for the console.

She turned in time to see the ominous rocks only feet from their path. Reaching for the controls, Lady grabbed the control stick and yanked it to the left. The room dipped and spun as the ship careened out of the way of the oncoming bluffs. The quick move proved to be overcompensation and the ship rattled as it spun, the wings flapping in distress. Lady wrapped both hands around the lever and held tight, praying her strength would be enough to straighten their path.

Sir's strong and calloused hands covered hers. The urge to push him away lost to their need to survive. The combined effort urged the machine into a weaving path that avoided the jutting rocks and rugged cliff faces which had seemed deceptively distant only a few minutes before. She should never have lost focus on their escape. Lady berated herself for putting them in danger, yet again.

A delicate hand reached in beside them and touched several of the controls. The blue silk slid across the console as a sudden flurry of activity engaged a previously unknown function and the SteamWing rose in a large arch, the wings flapping with great beats and a gush of steam pumped from the giant pipes to exhaust into the sky with a noisy hiss.

The mountain disappeared below them and the great expanse of blue sky fell out in front of the windows, the danger of imminent destruction sliding away in a hush. Lady stared at the distance in disbelief, her voice ragged when she said, "You have known how to fly this thing all along?"

Sybil slipped away from the console with a soft rustle of silks. "I wazz able to observe much under Zhao Jin'z hand."

"But why did you not assist sooner?"

"You were doing quite well without my aid."

Lady could argue that she had been doing no such thing. She slumped into the narrow chair that had been bolted in front of the console. It swiveled on its base, but Lady kept it oriented toward the window. To this point, she had felt relatively competent. But as each day and event passed, the doubt grew. Each decision had been made to keep them all alive. She…Sybil…Slim. But had she really done anything but put them further in harm's way?

At what point would she realize she had no clue to what she was doing? Was the Spanish Hope worth the risk? Was the quest to prove herself a competent woman capable of functioning outside the purview of her father's control nothing more than an exercise in futility?

"Lady, what must we do next?"

"I beg your pardon?" She looked back at Sybil. The lithe woman had curled into a ball, the silks once again wrapped about her body as she nearly disappeared into the upholstered chair. Sir took a seat in another chair only a few feet from Sybil, his expression contrite and cautious. Lady did not know what to do about him. Nor did she want to approach the issue of his lineage. Not now. Not while her nerves vibrated with fear, doubt and anxiety.

Too much counted on her.

Suddenly an idea formed and she turned a mischievous eye to Sir. "I do not trust you. But I shall give you an honest hearing, if you do something for me."

A quizzical brow rose but he nodded. Lady looked to the sky again and said, "I made a promise that you will help me keep. Sybil, tell me, can you control this mad machine enough for another of our reckless adventures?"

The soft chime of Sybil's giggle rang across the cabin. "For certain I can."

Lady let a soft smile touch her lips for the first time in days. When this endeavor was over, she could think again of her choices and the plan for the future. In the meantime, there was a campaign to plan.

20

The captain's boots squeaked as he stalked across the room. Zhao Jin considered pacing the mark of an ill-prepared man. Unfortunately, he was once again forced to partner with unlikely allies in his quest to maintain a hold on the slippery Sybil. Again, he was thwarted by the pernicious Fidelia Dewhurst. The advantage to Captain Wright's assistance lay in his unquenchable desire to lay hands on the spoiled lady.

"Do you believe she will make an attempt to rescue this man? This Robinson?" the captain said.

"It is likely. They have established a relationship. The exact nature I am not privy too. However, if all patterns continue as they have, she will undoubtedly stage a clever rescue," Zhao Jin said.

Wright cursed. "She made no indication that she had tender feelings for this scoundrel. What hold must he have over her? Fidelia is not the type to allow a man below her station touch her. Any man for that manner. She is…"

Zhao Jin nodded in commiseration. The man could believe what he wished. The girl was no mindless doll destined to cling to the arms of great men. She had the cognition of a clever player, having stymied both Kovacs and he in their battle of wits. An unexpected complication, Zhao Jin did not take her skills lightly. And if the captain underestimated her capabilities, it was not his concern--once she was well and completely out of the way.

In the meantime, the captain had the manpower Zhao Jin lacked. The captain could continue to believe he held the command. As long as he bowed to the greater mind, they would work well together.

"The Pinkerton's have no doubt captured the outlaw. While he had slipped through their fingers readily enough, I do not believe he was able to duck from their eye for long. The 'lady' will more than likely assume the same. If we find the Pinkerton's we will find your ward. And with her, my daughter."

"I still do not understand how your daughter and she came to be companions." The captain was no fool, despite being of a slow and limited mind. Zhao Jin knew the story held many inconsistencies. But the fewer the details the more believable the ruse.

"My daughter took ill in a town where Miss Dewhurst had taken rest. They were in adjacent rooms, and Miss Dewhurst came to our aid when my daughter took a turn for the worse, calling the doctor when things had seemed most unlikely to end in anything but tragedy. Had she not intervened on our behalf, the care for my daughter would have lacked even the base consideration."

The captain frowned and Zhao Jin ducked his head in feigned contrition. Men and their expectations rarely melded with reality. Captain Wright could understand a compassionate and bumbling flirt far more readily than the capable and intelligent woman he was actually pursuing. It was a wonder he had ever caught up to the enigmatic Fidelia Dewhurst.

And with Zhao Jin's aid, he would come upon her again. It was unfortunate her freedom would be yanked from beneath her, simply because she crossed the wrong Chinaman. But that was the fickle nature of fortune. He stood and crossed to the door. "I shall leave you to your preparations. I am certain that you will find the information on the Pinkerton's whereabouts readily from the locals. Please advise us when you wish to embark. We are ever at your service in locating the dear girls before they do themselves some sort of irreparable harm."

He snapped the door shut and strutted to his room. The emptiness of the room across the hall mocked his purpose. The girl would discover his patience was limited. Her charm would not protect her from his fury this time. She may be his key to thwarting Mordecai, but Sybil would learn her place and expectations. He obviously kept her under too gentle a hand.

***

The engine whirred, creating a muffled dissonance to the evening's sudden silence. Lady waited by the back of the machine, hiking her trousers up around her waist every few minutes, more out of a desire for distraction than for a real need. A quick tuck and cinch by Sybil's delicate yet competent hands prevented the troublesome articles from drooping further. With luck, they would stay in place when the time came for quick action.

A rustle in the bush precipitated Sir's arrival. She let out a long breath then stalked toward him. "You have been gone far too long. Time is one thing we do not have in spades."

"Do you want this done right? Or do you plan to simply

storm the town like you have every other time?"

Lady clenched her fists. "Did you find her?"

Sir nodded and stepped toward the SteamWing's door. Sybil rested inside, her energy waning as the day progressed. Lady couldn't help the worry as she watched her friend's eyes grow tired and wasted. Something dire happened and if not for a promise to a young and vulnerable girl, Lady would have spirited her friend away to the nearest doctor.

She followed him into the cabin, the room turning a brass orange under the gas lights. Sir approached Sybil and said, "Are you certain you can do this? We can find another way."

"I can manage well enough. We have been through many adventurezz, Lady and I. We will make do. But what manner of man are you, Sir? You keep your secretzz fast against your chest. Do you think we trust so easily one that hidezz liezz behind subtle truthzz?"

"I promise, when this is done, I will tell you the truth." He turned his head a fraction, enough to lay a wary eye on Lady. "I will tell you both the truth."

Lady moved to the table where she laid out the munitions for their campaign. "I trust you will do your best to make your truth as palatable as possible." She turned up the corner of her lip. Never, in all the frustrated dealings and irritating debacles had she ever felt such hostility toward Slim. Both men practiced charm, only one of them succeeded at wearing it honestly. "But as I said, do this and I will listen. Sybil can make her own decision whether to give you the time. Now, where do they have Carmen?"

Sir lowered his head an inch in acknowledgement. "The sheriff has her in a cell on Main. The captain gave the girl a good work over, trying to get information about you. Poor thing's been crying most of the day if you can believe her face. I got a look at her through a window on the side of the building. Wasn't easy sneaking around there. The whole town's excited about this latest nonsense since they haven't had a good shoot up in months. Western folks are getting right melancholy over all this law and order."

Lady smiled. Well, they would certainly show the town a bit of excitement. "You are able to get her out?"

"With the right amount of distraction, I can get her out of solid glass."

Sybil giggled from beneath her silks. "That particular rescue may be necessary if you spend more time with uzz, Sir. Our excapadezz have only become more complicated over time."

He looked down, his eyes sparkling with a familiar mischievousness. "Seems to be that way."

The satchel Lady swung thudded against his chest. "You may need these. Stores left by Zhao Jin and his men. There is extra ammunition for the pistols in the bag. But do please try to avoid using them. I may have need for them later."

A strong hand closed over her hand and he yanked her toward him. He lowered his voice and said, "Anyone ever tell you, you're pricklier than a cholla? I know snakes with less venom."

Lady pushed him away. "It has been mentioned. Now, get on. There is a girl in need of rescue. You can tell me of your tender sensitivities when this is done."

The room fell quiet when he left. Lady shuffled her feet as she fussed with her supplies. Two smoke bombs would create only the slightest of screens. The colors, a vibrant red and deep blue held less impact in the night, and so their utility would be quite a bit less valuable. Her augmented pistols conveniently returned by the rascal after much cajoling, always had the potential for impressive showcases, but there were only two shots. If things were not timed to their best advantage, they would be little more than ducks flying through the street.

Perhaps she could simply lean out and squawk.

Lady closed her eyes and steeled herself to the inevitable. They would be flying underprepared this time.

"Do not question your instinctzz, my friend. That which takezz much contemplation izz often the least trustworthy." Sybil uncurled from the seat, her silks falling around her as she stepped gingerly toward the console. "I have every confidenzz in our succezz."

"Sybil, are you..." Lady paused, unsure how to ask...what to ask.

The slight woman caressed the smooth copper that lined the console, its shine reflecting like glass in the lantern light. "I am not certain. I am only sorry that I cannot control that which hazz come over me. When thizz izz done, we shall discover itzz purpozz. Perhapzz our new friend shall provide a clue to thizz affliction."

Lady's stomach clenched. "When this is done, all of it shall be done. We cannot continue to put you in danger. Not with so much that ails you."

"And would you leave Slim to his fate? And your birthright? Izz that not all worth the sacrificezz?"

"Not at your expense. No."

A fingernail clicked on the panel as Sybil narrowed her eyes at Lady. "It izz my expenzz, my friend. Not yourzz. We have much to discuzz, but giving up thizz quest izz not open for debate. I am azz committed azz you."

"Sybil."

The hum of the engines rocketed to a roar as Sybil pulled a lever. Steam hissed from the exhaust pipe and the sound of the machine preparing for flight cut off any thought Lady had for argument. She bit her tongue and let it go. They could revisit the issue once Carmen was safely in hand and many miles lay between them and their pursuers.

The flapping of the SteamWing rocked the nearest trees. The branches creaked and leaves fell in a torrent toward the ground as the machine beat its way into the sky. The sheer power that rattled from the engine terrified and astounded her. Each move the SteamWing made appeared counter to the laws of nature, its move into the sky a testament to the stubbornness of man. Only a bird of the utmost resolve could compete with the sheer audacity of this contraption's design.

Lady could hardly contemplate how the thing could fly.

As they gained altitude, the SteamWing quieted and the wings shifted to a gliding position. Quiet settled around them as they soared through the sky, the town of Albuquerque a hint against the horizon. "We must bide our time. Sir will need time to reach his position."

Sybil nodded her head and shifted a lever, sending the SteamWing into a graceful arc. "Then we shall have them look in another direction."

Circling the town, Sybil kept them at a distance from town that allowed for a stealthy approach. They would enter from the opposite end.

When they reached the first building that lined Main Street, Sybil shifted another lever and a gush of steam erupted from the exhaust. Lady grabbed hold of one of the tables bolted to the floor. "Goodness. What was that?"

"I am simply knocking at the door. Let them wonder what monsterzz are out tonight. We shall show them soon enough."

"Your enjoyment of this is a tad unhealthy."

Sybil laughed heartily. "Ah, but I live for the stage. I do mizz the show."

Lady could not help but join in the laughter. It was far too absurd otherwise. "Are you certain you can pilot this through the streets?"

"We shall see." Sybil's eyes flashed a bright yellow and Lady blinked. When she looked again, a mossy green looked back.

Lady switched her gaze to the dark streets which lay ahead of them, their approach far faster than she'd anticipated. A few figures milled about as they approached, each moving slowly, heads turned toward the oncoming noise. Few would recognize the contraption that hurtled toward them, trains and the giant Pinkerton steamships their only experience with steam vehicles.

Where the steamships sailed like great sea liners, the SteamWing soared with the ominous grace of a bird of prey. How fortunate Zhao Jin delivered such a beautiful tool for their distraction. Lady whooped as the SteamWing swooped into town, the long wings spread across the street, each tip slipping past the second story windows of saloons and mercantiles.

Several bystanders fled as they flew overhead and Lady felt a grin spread across her face. She strode toward the door and swung it open. Below she caught sight of the sheriff, his hands held aloft, waving in an ineffective attempt to bring order to his town. Lady blew a kiss toward him. "Hello sheriff. Do tell me if you've seen Captain Wright. I have something to say to him."

A flash of shadow slithered behind the sheriff and snuck into the jail. Lady felt a rush of pride, knowing the plan worked to this point. But it was not done. Not by any means.

Sybil flew the SteamWing over the buildings and turned it in a tight arc, readying them for a second pass. Her voice hissed over the sound of steam, "What on earth do you have to say to the captain?"

Lady smiled and leaned out of the cabin, her hand gripping the brass bar bolted beside the door. "Oh there you are, Eustace. Wait right there!" Lady ducked back into the cabin. "Do you think you can bring us around one more time?"

Sybil shook her head in disbelief but pulled a lever and sent the SteamWing higher into the sky. "I believe we shall have time for one more pass."

With a hoot of laughter, Lady reached for her bag, ecstatic they hadn't had to use her stash of weaponry. Shock at the SteamWing's appearance had, to this point, proven to be enough. But Lady had one more thing to do. A flash of white at the corner of her eye sent a sense of freedom coursing through her, and she knew it was time.

The SteamWing fell toward the sheriff and the Captain. Lady hung her head out of the cabin as they approached and shouted, "I am terribly sorry Eustace, but I simply cannot marry you. We are far too different."

With a shout, Lady swung her arm out of the cabin and let go of the fabric in her hands. Laces fluttered in the wind as her corset flew toward Eustace. His awestruck expression froze as he realized what sailed from the ship and into his arms. Lady laughed at the stricken and horrified sheriff.

Heavens, that felt amazing.

She waved, ducked back into the cabin, and secured the door. "I think that is far and enough of that. Let us make our way from this town, shall we?"

Sybil grinned and shifted the lever again. "That izz a fabulouzz idea."

21

Twenty years in America and Mordecai still had not acclimatized to the terrain. Tall pines surrounded him, but still the desert encroached on his peace. How he missed the rolling hills and green expanse of his homeland. The simple people of Hungary haunted his soul, scolding his betrayal. But opportunity lived across the seas for men intent on capturing the flame of success. There was no home for him in a village of farmers.

Now they scaled yet another western mountain, this one riddled with black rocks and dry brush ripe for burning. The cold wind tore at their clothing, breaking their skin with its fierce fingers. The snow from the storm that raged only a day earlier clung to branches and boulders, unimpressed by the sun's pitiful attempt at warming the desert land. But even the snow here felt dry, like white powdered bones, it sucked the moisture from the body and promised a death for thirst. He could never grow used to the desolate lands which promised gold.

Mordecai blew into his hands. The cracked skin of once elegant fingers stung with the dry cold. He did not bother to look at their distressed condition. It would only serve to remind him of the sacrifices he must continue to make.

He took heart in the truth that the others in his party

faired as badly. Ahead on the trail, Bernard stumbled, his hands slipping from the reins he clung to more out of his own need than in an effort to lead the weather-exhausted mules. Beatrice trudged past her struggling husband, arms wrapped about her midsection and head tucked to her chest. Her once fair, blonde tresses frizzled out in a state of disarray which reminded him more of straw than soft flowers.

The only fool who appeared unaffected by time and hardship stood at the ridge they approached, his nose to the air and wild hair flying in the wind. For not the first time, Mordecai questioned the wisdom of following a madman up a mountain.

But madmen knew more than most about the ethereal mysteries of the world.

"Butcher has a box for babies. Where's the eagle flown her coup?"

"That does appear to be the question." Mordecai encouraged the madman's ramblings. Each verse drove them further up the mountain; each step the man took seemed surer, more directed. There had been enough madness in his life that Mordecai could see the difference between a man lost to all things and one held captive by forces unknown.

This man had the hand of the otherworldly leading him into insanity. And as had been seen with Isabel, that madness lay along the way to Cibola. He had no doubt.

The troupe stopped at the edge of a ridge as the man sniffed the air, weaving his fingers through the wind, a guttural moan singing with the creaking branches. Beatrice grumbled beside him about lost causes and idiots following the like.

Mordecai found her easy to ignore. "What do you see, old man?"

The madman scurried to the edge of a ridge, cocking his head to the side and closing his eyes to the wind. Mordecai turned away, looking for signs of promise himself, despite knowing the clues which showed themselves to the mad were invisible to the sane.

Bernard stared into the distance, his eyes void of the spark of ingenuity that once drove him to build great and miraculous things. Mordecai worried more for his brother's sanity than for the man who danced like a child toward a previously disguised trail. "Do you wish to rest, brother?" Mordecai asked.

"It is cold, Mordecai. Has it always been so cold?"

A sudden heaviness sunk against his chest. Mordecai said, "It is only this American weather. We are nearly there and soon we will not worry of the cold or whatever ails us."

Bernard turned his empty eyes to Mordecai. "I see mama. She is sad, Mordecai."

Frustration soared. "She was always sad. Pull yourself from this melancholy, my brother. It does not suit you. There will be creatures to build and crowds to entertain once again. I cannot do this without you."

"I think we have dropped the puppet strings."

Mordecai had nothing left to say. He must persevere. When this escapade concluded, he could heal his brother from the hereditary melancholia that struck so many of his people. The sight of gold and rich comfort would do much to brighten a mind drawn to darkness.

One must rule the darkness or it would drag you beneath its murky waves. And Mordecai would rule it all.

"Tell the Butcher the Eagle flies from her babies," the madman crowed.

Mordecai hurried after the madman, ducking beneath

the branches of an ancient fir tree. The foliage stood beside a flat face of granite, the branches and brush hiding a small entrance to a cave. "Brilliant. Come along Beatrice, bring your husband. We shall at the very least find respite from this blasted wind."

Darkness enveloped the four as they slid between rock and rubble. The madman's ramblings echoed against the rock face, the sound disappearing down a dark, empty chasm. Mordecai put out a hand to stay his brother. The man ahead of them may be led by a hand that could see through darkness, but they could not. "Do you have the lantern?"

"I left it in the cart. I did not anticipate darkness, it is still midday," his brother replied in a surprisingly lucid tone.

Heartened that mystery may yet bring Bernard back to him, Mordecai chuckled. "Do not fret, my brother, I did anticipate just such a situation." Mordecai reached into his vest pocket and retrieved his flint and steel. With quickness in mind, he hurried to the entrance of the cavern and found a sturdy branch and affixed a fuel soaked cloth to the tip. The cloth had been prepared days earlier in the event they would need something to fight away the monsters of the night and had been hidden in his satchel. Mordecai, once again convinced of his divine purpose, lit the makeshift torch. Flame illuminated the rock room.

"We must hurry. Our guide has already left us and I suspect he will be difficult to track after some time."

"Only fools follow the mad," Beatrice said.

"You are welcome to remain behind," Mordecai answered.

"I suspect you would relish the opportunity to leave me behind, dear brother."

Mordecai turned a corner where the cavern narrowed into a tunnel, natural fissures showing the violence of the earth's forces on her petrified body. They reached a branching trail and Mordecai paused, listening over the sounds of their own shuffling feet for their guide. Pebbles skipping against rock directed them to the right. As they hurried, the muffled murmurs of the man's insane monologue lightened the concern they had lost their chance.

Eventually, a shadow of movement appeared several feet in front of them, the crazed hair and jerky movements familiar. The man cackled and sang, "Do you see the Butcher man? He brings the serpent to the eagle. Brings the serpent, brings the serpent."

"This is ridiculous," Beatrice muttered.

The woman may believe so, but Mordecai knew they were on the right trail. He followed the serpent and eagle as devoutly as this man. The difference lay in his ability to maintain his faculties. The quest for lost gold had taken many a man's mind, but those who kept their focus and control could succeed where weaker men faltered. The lockets burned in his pocket, desperate to show him their secret, he knew this.

Lead the way, madman.

A sliver of light hit the far wall and the scent of cool autumn entered the musty cave interior. The man danced toward the light, his hands flailing about him, flapping like a bird just from the nest, unsure of the movements but convinced it can fly. "Eagle, eagle, bring your babies. Butcher's here to take you home."

They continued toward the light and found a narrow break in the rock. Crumbling pumice fell away as their guide slid between the walls and into the daylight. Mordecai followed, slightly irritated at the rough stone catching the fabric of his vest. Months on the trail and he'd managed to keep it relatively pristine. It would be some time before he could find a suitable mercantile which provided the quality of cloth he preferred.

His distracted mind returned to the event at hand the moment he emerged into the light. The grunts of his sister-in-law's efforts fell into the background as he stood wide-eyed in a small clearing. Pines of remarkable height surrounded the area in an unnatural perfect circle. The grass waved in the wind, golden and lush. At the very center, their guide skipped around a monument, a smooth and perfectly formed cone. The top was flattened just enough to provide a perch for a stone eagle. Mordecai approached slowly, his eyes never leaving the rock statue.

Carved with a precision rarely accomplished, the type of rock was unfamiliar to him. It shined with a glossy depth of color that rivaled the most exotic marbles of the old world. Mordecai circled the monument, suddenly curious about the peoples who left such a testament to their culture for him to discover so many centuries later. Had de Vaca felt the very same awe at the mystery of an ancient people unable to tell their story with words? If they could, what would they possibly have told their discoverers?

He reached out a finger, the cold rock sending shivers of anticipation through his spine. When he removed his finger, they felt wet and slick. A shimmer appeared on his skin and he brought his fingertip closer to see. A gold tint flashed in the light and he widened his eyes in disbelief. What matter of material could show gold where there is none?

"What now, brother?" Beatrice's voice broke the spell and Mordecai wiped his finger on his lapel. A wet streak very like water soaked into the fabric, but no gold transferred. When he returned his eye to his finger, it was devoid of the promising color. He frowned. Perhaps the madness of their guide was catching. He coughed and responded to his sister. "Find a seat, I must examine our surroundings."

She huffed, but took her husband by the hand and led him to a small outcrop of man-sized boulders. There they sat, as patiently as to be expected, Bernard with his head buried in his hands, Beatrice with her hawk-eyed stare pierced on their guide's every movement. Dancing and skipping through the grass, their happy madman made a suitable distraction and Mordecai took advantage.

He shifted his weight then pulled the eagle locket from his vest pocket, dangling the chain through his fingers and playing with the cool metal as though lost in thought. But he was far from lost. The great eagle carved in stone drew the eye much as the great charred walls of the subterranean snake pit in the Zuni village. Light cast its spell here just as darkness had in the other. Mordecai searched for signs of the mystery monument's engineers.

The breeze picked up to a more or less constant irritant as the day waned. Still he paced the meadow, eyes casting along the ground for impressions in the soil, divots in the stone--anything that would lend a clue to what to do next.

Nothing. Everything was a natural perfection, frustratingly devoid of mechanisms to engage with his locket.

"We will freeze if we stay here much longer. Do you even know what you are looking for? Damn fool man dragging us up this mountain with no plan and nothing to keep us from dying in the night."

Mordecai looked to the smooth stone eagle, pleading for deliverance from his harpy sister-in-law. It stared down at him, eyes hardly sympathetic in its ferocity. "What do you see, you glorious beast?" he muttered.

"Baby, Butcher. Bring the baby, hold the baby in your hand. Sweet, sweet, Butcher baby. Mamma's calling me home." The madman stopped beside Mordecai, and stared up at the eagle, cocking his head like a chicken. He turned his head back to Mordecai and said, "Mamma's calling me. Have to go. Have to go."

Mordecai reached out a hand to stay the man as he was about to walk away. Suddenly violent, the man screamed, throwing his arms in the air, frantic and frightened. They tussled, and limbs flew in various directions, and Mordecai was only just able to keep hold of the locket. Scratches appeared on the man's face where he'd pulled his nails across the skin. Mordecai dropped his hands in horror as blood dripped as rivulets into the sand, the man's eyes flashing with something familiar. Something that left his heart stony with unbidden regret.

"God Almighty, not again." Beatrice came up between the two men, her appearance breaking the spell and sending their guide skittering into the shadows, down into the cavern where they'd emerged hours before. "He looked just like poor Isabel. What did you do? What have you done, Mordecai?"

He stilled his heavy heart and watched as the sun's rays left the clearing in a graying dusk. "Nothing, dear sister. It is the nature of the mystery that some souls do not have the fortitude to persevere."

"What are you looking for?" Beatrice asked.

Before he could respond, Bernard came up and grabbed his shoulder. "The baby. The Eagle's baby."

"I do not understand," Mordecai said as he followed his

brother's eyes to the stone bird of prey.

"He was insane and perhaps you have to be just a little to understand." Bernard pointed to the talons, carved as though perched on a petrified nest. "You brought the baby to the eagle. The stone, Mordecai. The stone goes in the nest, just as it went in the snake's den."

"Brilliant." Mordecai drew the locket forward, prying the stone from its metal housing. "Do you see a way to the top?"

Twenty feet stood between him and the nest. The smooth rock would prove an unconquerable obstacle if they could not scale its heights. They circled the stone, but no answer was forthcoming. As the sun dipped further into the recesses of the mountain cliffs, Mordecai felt the first inklings of failure strike him cold. They could not be unsuccessful. Not now that the puzzle had been solved.

"There's nothing for it. We shall have to return with supplies when it is light," Mordecai said as he looked to Beatrice, her eyes shining with anticipation. The woman could smell promise of fortune and there certainly was bright promise in that stone. He tightened his fingers around the coral eagle. Tomorrow they would return. But he would not let his key leave his person, not for a second would he lose his focus on what was his by right of purpose.

22

The escape proved a success. Once again defied, Zhao Jin could languish in his loneliness without his prize. How Sybil wished she could celebrate the moment. But her heart felt the tug of disbelief. This could not last, not when so many wished to drag them down to the fiery pits of the earth where evil men sought their ill-chosen dreams.

They should turn away now, while at the crossroads. It was their only chance for survival.

"Carmen, dear, why do you still shake? We are safe, and they cannot harm you." Lady ran a gentle hand down the young girl's back, a strange expression of protective empathy in her eyes.

Sybil glanced at Carmen, then slid deeper into her silks, torched by the hotly intense antagonism directed her way. Even the tragedy of her life had not created such visceral hate in her eyes at an age so young.

"Dear, it will be quite alright. You have nothing to fear," Lady persisted.

But Carmen hissed, her voice lowered, but the words clear. "Ella esta serpiente. Maldito."

"I beg your pardon?" Lady raised a thin brow.

"Cursed. You have killed me more certainly than any man."

Lady sat back on her heels. "Well, that is rather melodramatic for one of such tender age. I suppose I was the same. Either way, we shall have none of that. Sybil is a gentle soul. Did your parents not teach you to look beyond the skin to the heart beneath?"

"There is no soul within the heart of a serpent." Carmen paused to glare up at Lady. "Her people have killed mine. My mother, father, brothers."

"I don't understand," Lady said. "Her people? There are no people like Sybil. It is simply an unfortunate malady." Lady continued to prod the girl for more details, but Carmen staunchly refused. There would be no details from that avenue, and Sybil felt the fear melt deeper into the recesses of what was left of her humanity. Carmen's stony glare returned to Sybil, causing unease to raise the scales along her arms. It itched and she wished desperately she could scratch beneath the surface. Whose truth could she believe? Was she a cursed creature, destined for an evil existence? Or a poor soul wracked by an unfortunate disease?

Lady stood and wiped her hands down her baggy slacks. Not having made any further progress with the frightened girl, she wandered toward a window, periodically adjusting her stance and unconsciously hiking the waistband higher. Still, the pant cuffs never rose above the ankle.

Sybil turned to the man who stood at the pilot's console. She hadn't observed much of him through the night as they hid in the dark skies, deciding a course and catching what rest they could after their adventure escaping Albuquerque. An enigma, Sybil wondered at Sir's sudden intrusion into their party. Tall and strongly built, his back flexed beneath a shirt strikingly similar to the one Lady wore. The trousers held a remarkable likeness to Lady's as well. Sybil banished a smile, knowing whatever story lay between Lady and their new companions would be undoubtedly entertaining and to Lady's eyes, mortifying.

He showed an interest in her own wellbeing, claiming an affiliation she never hoped would be true. She may not believe he was her kin, but he still proved to have a concern for her welfare she'd never experienced before. And that was stranger than anything else. No man thought twice about her, even in a platonic way. No man beyond Slim, and he was an oddity for certain. Zhao Jin was a completely different story, one who didn't bare thinking of.

She approached the console, her silks swishing against the floor in silence. Despite her quiet movements, he turned just before she arrived beside him.

His smile flashed with sadness. Sybil frowned. "And now it izz time for you to explain yourself. I do not have a brother."

His voice was warm, calm, and sincere. "You do. Though only half. We share a mother. Maria Vargas."

Sybil lifted a brow. That was a name she hadn't heard for a very long time. When they'd lived in the great cities of the east, long before she'd developed her affliction, her mother changed her name, claiming an exotic personage to entice the audience. Cassandra was born. But in her drunken slurrings, Sybil had discovered small pieces of a past that Maria Vargas sought to drown. A home in the west with a man who loved her.

But that love hadn't been enough and Sybil never learned why.

"Your name, it izz not Sir azz you have told Lady."

He chuckled as he cast a quick look toward the pacing Lady. "No. But she gets so prickly when things do not go her way, I just could not stop myself." He looked back to Sybil and grinned. "I am Juan Caesar Vargas. Son of Carlos and Maria Vargas. Half-brother to the infamous Sybil."

"I am hardly imfamouzz." Despite her statement, she could not prevent the blush that spread across her cheekbones. The scales flexed with the sudden warmth and she lifted a finger to rub the sensation away. "You have been following uzz. Why?"

"You do not believe I wish to be reunited with my sister?"

"Not a sister like me. There izz alwayzz more to a man's motivation. What do you gain through knowing me, Juan Caesar?"

He did not respond, his attention focused on the windows in front of the console. Thoughts flickered across his face, and she let him have his moment. She had quite a few thoughts of her own to corral.

The clouds beyond his head billowed and spread across the blue sky blocking the view ahead and causing her concern. What obstacles lay ahead of them? Were they as treacherous as those that existed within the cabin? Sybil wondered when time would let the secrets be known. "If you know anything from following uzz, then you do know neither Lady nor I suffer from sensitivitiezz or illusionzz. Do not think to gild your responzz with circumspection."

"You are well spoken. Mother seems to have imparted some of her schooling on you. Do you know her history? She was quite remarkable. Elegant. The most beautiful woman in the west."

"I knew her azz a different woman. She wazz a broken soul."

"She was the strongest of women. Had she stayed in

Spain, she could have married a prince. Her beauty and talent was so revered"

Sybil did not respond, fascinated by his conviction. Could he be mistaken? His version of her mother did not match hers. Not in any way beyond the name. And he could not be much older than she. What memories could he have?

"Our mother left her life of privilege to love my father."

"My mother wazz a dancer."

"Our mother loved to dance."

Sybil frowned. "My mother wazz a broken and tortured woman. There wazz no happinezz in her eyezz that wazz not found in drink or Zhao Jin'zz dragon smoke. You must be mistaken. No such thing could turn what you say your mother wazz into the creature that gave birth to me."

"There is one thing." Juan raised his hand and pulled away the silk, exposing her scales to the sunlight. His reaction was strange, unique, unexpected. There was no surprise or disgust. There was not even curiosity. He looked at her as though he'd seen her before, and thought nothing of her disease. He said, "What happens when the best of humanity meets the most hideous of monsters?"

"I do not understand."

"You are the offspring of that mating. And you are the key to a mystery that is older than this land itself."

Sybil reached up and grabbed his hand. "Speak plainly. I have had enough of masked wordzz and prophesy from Zhao Jin."

"Sybil, is everything well?" Lady called from across the room, concern blanketing her words.

"Quite," she said, her answer clipped. She lowered her voice as she addressed Juan. "You will need to provide better answerzz or I am afraid neither I nor my companion will suffer your presenzz."

"It is a difficult thing to explain and begins with legends that have proven far truer than any person could dream. I ask that you listen to the story before casting judgment."

"I cannot promizz you anything but to listen."

"Then I will take that." His shoulders relaxed and fingers released their tight grip on the console. "What do you know of your affliction?"

"Nothing but what I have observed." Sybil leaned in closer. What could this man who claimed to be her half-brother know that no one else did? Was there truth in Carmen's accusations? She had seen doctors and scientists, men of religion and great seers. None could tell her much of her condition. Few could do much more than recoil at the sight of her skin.

Juan opened his lips to continue, but was interrupted by Carmen's sharp query. "What is that?"

"Good heavens," Lady said.

Visible beyond the side window a great flame erupted across the sky. Sybil ran to press her nose against the glass window. Black smoke billowed among the white clouds. The SteamWing changed course and they drew toward the scene. Lady ordered Juan to bring them even closer, determined to solve the riddle of the fire in the sky.

"It looks like a ship," Carmen whispered, forgetting her fear of Sybil to stare in awe at the scene before them.

"Oh my child. That izz most certainly a ship." Sybil watched in horror as the great eye of the Pinkerton's ship came into view. Flames licked at the giant pillar that held the eye, blackness covering the outer shell of the two great balloons that held it aloft. The fire would soon burn through the protective covering and there would be no hope for the men scurrying about the deck.

"Slim!" Lady cried. "If he is still on the ship--" She covered her lips.

The SteamWing swerved away just as a violent explosion rocked the Pinkerton's ship. Debris and smoke filled the air, engulfing their significantly smaller ship. Carmen screamed as the SteamWing rocked in the wind and Sybil ran to the console to assist Juan with steering. Sybil shouted, "We must land away from the wreckage! Quickly!"

Glass shattered as another blast came from outside, hurtling shrapnel into their cabin. The SteamWing dipped heavily and spun. Through the smoke, the rocky ground spun toward them. Sybil grabbed the nearest lever and pulled with all the strength she had and prayed.

***

"Dang it you ornery bastard. We got five minutes to get off this bucket and you're acting like this is some country dance."

Her voice sang sweetly like bells on a Sunday morning. If she'd stop fussing with his clothes, he'd give her a kiss. A hand snaked out and yanked his hair. A pleasurable pain lanced across his scalp, focusing his mind for a moment on the door. A yellow glow flickered in the hall. Something tickled his mind. A warning. Something he should be concerned about.

Then her soft body pressed against his again and he was lost. "Come 'ere darlin'. Why are ya puttin' my clothes on? We should be takin' yours off."

"You are a damn rascal, Slim Robinson. And I like that. But not now. I have no intention of dying in your dirty arms.

I got plans. Big ones. So get your skinny arse off that bed and git movin'."

"Oh darling, don't be so harsh. There's nuthin' to worry about."

The brown-haired beauty dropped him and stood, perching her hands on her hips. A charming frown pointed at him as she sucked in a breath, raising her breasts toward the ceiling. Lovely, yet small, he yearned to reach out to them. Suddenly her expression changed, replaced by a secretive smile. A tingle at the back of his head encouraged him to be wary. But the smile was seductive, endearing. He would follow that smile anywhere.

"Slim, darlin. I know what you want to do. I do too, but if my husband comes in."

He narrowed his eyes. "Husband?"

"Yes darlin', don't you remember? Mr. Pinkerton, my husband with his big brothers. I don't want nothin' to interrupt us. Let's get you dressed and find somewhere safer to..." She let the words trail off, but he was already pulling on his trousers. He didn't remember a husband, but damned if he was gonna let this little filly out of his hands. If she wanted to find a better spot, he was all for it.

"Good, darling. Now, don't forget your shirt. You're gonna need it."

Need his shirt? Why in tarnation would he need his shirt? Despite his confusion, he slipped on the shirt and secured the first few buttons. She ran a hand through his arm and led him toward the door. "Now, be quiet. I know my husband in near. I heard him only a moment ago."

The blood in his veins pumped like wildfire, clearing his mind for a moment. "Damn it Phee, you don't have a husband."

She froze. "Slim? Damn, I thought they'd plum turned you into a lunatic."

"What's goin' on?"

"We got to get out of here. The ship's goin' down."

He blinked as her face shifted and oozed. Damn it, he was losing it again. He reached out and grabbed her arm, tightening his fingers around her wrist. Knees buckling, he stared up into her wide eyes and flashed her a silly grin. She sure was a pretty thing. "Hello darling, what's your name?"

A snarl left her lips and she closed her eyes. "Damn it Slim, I really was hopin' I wasn't gonna have to carry your ass."

"I'd let you carry me anywhere," he said, the words slurring as his lips suddenly felt thick and swollen.

"Tell me that when the damn devil's piss wears off."

His eyes fell shut and he tried desperately to raise the lids. But darkness felt too sublime. Perhaps she'd forgive him a small nap.

23

Smoke burned her lungs and pain pierced Lady's shoulders as she struggled to crawl from beneath the remains of the wood table. The crunch of glass beneath her elbows drew her up short and she peered through the haze to survey the damage. The shirt Sir had leant her was torn in several places and blood mixed with the linen. She squinted at her arms. The injury to herself appeared minor. Blood trickled from several shallow cuts, but the worst of it lay in the bruises she felt forming beneath the skin.

A layer of glass spread ahead of her, the sun glinting off the shards from the open door, piercing the smoky haze with knifelike streams of light. The console stood in place, slightly tilted, but as she scanned the room, she realized they landed at an odd angle. The gas-lights had burst but if the room had filled with the illuminating gas, they would have been lost in a far more furious ball of fire than they experienced. She thanked the ruthless Chinaman and his desire to pay for only the best. In this case, his best included essential safeguards which prevented the worst calamities.

A frightened, youthful face filled the doorway. Carmen said, "Lady! Are you hurt?"

Before Lady could stall her, the girl ran across the floor, her shoes crunching on the littered floor. Her hand flew out to steady herself against a partially upended desk. Lady said, "Stay back. I am quite alright. Where are the others?"

"Sybil is outside. She and I were thrown through the window. But I cannot find the man. He's disappeared."

"His name izz Juan and he izz my brother."

Carmen stiffened at Sybil's words but Lady breathed in a sigh of relief. "We must search for him. Now that I know his name, I do not relish finding his corpse."

Sybil considered the room with reserved eyes, her stance solid and unmoved. Strength radiated from Sybil and Lady watched as Carmen stepped away from the silk-clad woman. Sybil gave her a sympathetic smile, then murmured instructions Lady could not hear. Carmen hastened away and the lithe woman tip-toed across the glass-littered floor, her silks rustling in the breeze that slid through the damaged cabin.

The acrid stench of scorched wallpaper glue and wood burned Lady's eyes, streaming tears down her cheeks. Something new had caught fire and black smoke billowed through the room. When Sybil's long fingers closed around the table leg to lift it from Lady's body she could hardly see. The weight of the table fell away with ease and she heaved a sigh in thanks that heavier woods were not used in constructing the swift machine.

The firm grip of Sybil's fingers above her elbow drew Lady to stand and they maneuvered out of the smoldering ship. Lady said, "We should douse the reminder of the fires. If they continue to burn, there will be no saving this ship."

"It would serve Zhao Jin well to never find hizz prize again. I should like to see it burn to dust."

Lady fell to the ground outside the ship, grateful as Carmen handed her water and a rag to wipe away the soot from her eyes. The grit would take days to fully disappear, but at least she could see.

Despite her reluctance, Sybil moved to smother the last flames within the cabin with canvas pulled from a cracked chest. The thump of the fabric against wood and metal rang across the surrounding landscape. Lady surveyed the area, gathering bearings and hoping things were not nearly as bleak as anticipated. Where had the Pinkertons landed and had anyone survived?

Carmen kneeled beside Lady. "What shall we do Miss? We have not gone far from Albuquerque. Those men are sure to follow."

Lady coughed, the remnants of smoke and dust scraping against her throat. With the SteamWing a mangled wreckage of steel and copper, they would be left to their own devices as they moved through the New Mexico landscape. With luck they may be able to procure mounts... except Lady abandoned her attempt at securing funds in Albuquerque when the rescue had taken precedence. That choice meant they had no means to purchase supplies. With the cavalry on their trail there was little likelihood for friendly assistance.

Hope tenuously held on the precipice of their future and she fortified herself with a ragged breath. "First we must discover Juan's condition. Then we shall worry over the next step. I fear the daylight will quickly disappear if we continue to lick our wounds and stall our action. Quickly, show me where you have already searched. He could not possibly have fallen far."

Carmen stood, her hand firm as Lady held it to struggle to her feet. The girl should not have the work-scarred hands and strength developed through persistent labor. She belonged in a schoolroom. Lady frowned. When she was Carmen's age, she'd thought more of ribbons and sweets than of survival amid the wild lands of this country.

There would be time to determine a brighter fate for the girl. Lady must first ensure her survival. With a few tentative steps she tested her strength and found herself fit and able. Sybil stepped from the SteamWing's cabin. "It izz done azz much azz can be. I fear we may not find much of use still inside."

Lady gave a reassuring smile. "That is all we can expect. Take rest beneath the mesquite, Carmen and I shall search for Juan."

Soot covered much of Sybil's silks and she coughed quietly as she moved toward the largest of the mesquite in the area. Its long branches stretched a canopy against the harsh sunlight. The warmth of the sun was welcome on cool days such as this, but the solace of the protective shade provided a more insulating peace. Lady turned away once she saw Sybil settle beside a shallow basin Carmen discovered among the wreckage. The water she found would more than likely be the last they would find after such a disaster, but Lady could begrudge none of them the ability to remove the evidence of the crash from their bodies.

Lady would fret over each challenge only as it presented itself.

First they would find their mystery accomplice, a man she had yet to trust and did not anticipate changing her opinion of any time soon. However, a lack of trust did not justify leaving a man to die amid the thorny brush and water-starved land. Lady pointed toward a large gash in the vegetation where the SteamWing had bounced prior to settling in its current, mangled condition. "Explore that area there. Be cautious, we do not know if any of Zhao Jin's evil machinations still lie in wait."

Carmen paled but took several steps in the direction of the scarred foliage. She stopped and looked back at Lady, her hands wringing, and lips pressed in thin, trembling line. "Do you truly believe something..."

"No. Of course not. I would not send you into danger. Just practice caution and call if you see something you are unsure of. Time is not something we have in excess. A man's life could depend on us finding him."

Carmen steeled herself against the fear and turned toward her assignment. Juan could very well be in that tangled bit of brush, but Lady doubted the young girl would find much more than broken branches. Cutting a wider circle about the crash site, Lady scanned for signs of life. Nothing stirred. Birds had quit the area when they had careened into the brush, fire and screams as effective a banishment as anything. They would return as the threat diminished, but in the meantime, Lady took advantage of the silence to listen for movement.

A soft hiss came from the SteamWing's damaged boiler, the heat of the smothered fire still warming the immediate vicinity. A breeze picked up the leaves and played with the tendrils of the long, chestnut-colored hair that had knotted about the crown of her head. The timid sound of Carmen picking her way through the branches covered the deceptively quiet undercurrent of sound that Lady searched. If she could not hear him, then she would have to take a more systematic strategy to the search. How far could the man have flown from the ship?

The last she'd seen of Juan, his hands rigidly gripped the console, struggling to maintain control over a spiraling doom. Strength and determination were the words which came to mind, but blind stubbornness would creep in as she feared they might find the worst. As she completed the first circle around the crash site, she walked further out, ready to search a broader circumference. As she stepped gingerly over the dented remains of an elaborately decorated tea pot she nearly missed the tell-tale groan of a man in pain.

She stopped to listen. The sound weak, she was only just able to determine the direction. At twenty more feet from the crash she discovered his body. Blood poured from his temple, a cut fattened his lip. Lady fell to her knees, reaching out to test for further injury. A groan echoed from his chest as she prodded his arms and legs. "Do say you are conscious, Sir. It would be quite a bit more convenient if you could tell me what hurt."

"Always concerned about your convenience, eh Lady?" His tone was light and she sighed in relief. But that sudden positive feeling evaporated as his chest shuddered under a wretched cough. She grabbed his hand as he convulsed beside her, shifting his position and spitting up blood beside her. After the episode quieted, he turned a bashful eye to her. "I apologize. I think I may have bruised a rib."

Lady felt around his midsection, eliciting a sucked in hiss as she prodded the tender spots. His skin turned ashen and eyes held the glassy look of intense pain. His light hearted comments aside, he was most definitely in bad shape. She said, "We must get you to a physician."

A sudden chuckle instigated a second bout of coughing and Lady bit her lip as she held his shoulders. When he was able to speak again, he said, "Do stop making me laugh, I don't know that I can survive it."

"I am hardly making a joke of the situation. I can't see

what you find humorous at a time like this."

A slip of a smile peeked from behind his fat lip. "I don't suppose the SteamWing survived?" At her head's curt shake he continued, "Then you will not find it all that easy taking me to a physician. How are the others? Oh God Almighty, Sybil!"

Lady pressed a hand against his chest as he struggled to sit. "She is quite fine. I have her resting only a little way off." Once he settled in relief she said, "Now we must consider what is to be done about you. And us for that matter. The night will come swiftly and I do not suppose we will be able to move from this spot. At least not until after tonight. You would not happen to have any of your grand schemes in that tossed up head of yours?"

His frown was only slightly disheartening. Lady figured they had a few hours still before night would shroud them from pursuers. That might be enough time to create a suitable shelter against the cool autumn night. With Carmen in reasonably hearty condition and Sybil still strong, the three of them might whittle something positive out of the SteamWing's demise. At the very least, the ornate wood furnishings would burn well enough to keep them warm.

Lady simply hoped their escape from Albuquerque by air provided enough distance between them and the Captain. She had no doubts he was on their trail and based on his past behavior, Zhao Jin would be close behind as well.

Their bruised party did not have much time to gamble. If only disaster had not struck.

"Let me see if I can find something to bind your ribs. Perhaps then you will at least be able to join us further in. I do not see much advantage to the location you have chosen." In truth, Juan's landing had been a fortuitous one. To the right an outcrop of jagged boulders glinted dangerously in the sunlight. To the left a copse of prickly bushes would have ripped him apart had he landed with any speed. The clear, sandy wash where he'd come to a stop had indeed been the only one not to promise death. Lady wondered at his luck. She'd only known one other man that could court disaster so well and survive.

A shout sent her scurrying to her feet. Juan followed suit, but doubled over under the pain. Lady spared him the scold she had ready when Carmen's frantic call sounded closer and more urgent. "Sit down. I will return shortly."

Lady went to follow Carmen's call, but had to turn back to glare at the struggling Juan. Sweat slid along his browline, his fists were clenched in determination. He said, "It could be dangerous."

"I believe you passing out would be far more of a disadvantage. She is merely shouting for me to come to her, not screaming in terror. I will discover our plot and return to you. I assure you this is no emergency needing the aid of a man about to die."

"I am not about to die," he growled, but stumbled to his knees, heaving in deep, painful breaths.

Lady turned from him. Even if the stubborn ingrate decided to follow, she would discover the trouble and be back before he made it five feet. Sybil ran into Lady as she passed a particularly full mesquite. "Good heaven's Sybil. You walk softer than a cat."

Sybil frowned. "I am concerned she hazz discovered…"

"It isn't Juan. I found him in the brush behind those boulders. He's injured, but has more fight in him than intelligence."

Sybil sighed and continued toward Carmen's voice. "I

wonder what hazz the child so anxiouzz."

They stopped when they turned past another set of boulders. Carmen stood several away, her feet shifting with barely controlled nerves. Her wide eyes looked from the smoking field to the two women frozen in shock. Carmen said, "I don't know what to do. I think they may all be dead."

It was certainly a possibility. Smoke filled the air and the noxious scent of burning flesh sent Lady's stomach into a rolling turmoil. Bodies lay blackened amid the fire reddened steel of the Pinkerton's ship. Across the field, mocking them with its surreal existence, the Pinkerton eye lay unblinking on its side, smoke seeping through the black pupil. Nothing moved but the smoke. She could count twenty, perhaps thirty men in disparate degrees of disintegration. Twisted and burned, the sight of the bodies made Lady turn away as her stomach threatened to empty.

"Dear God, Slim," Sybil whispered.

"Do you believe he is there? Do you see him?" Lady asked.

"No. God in heaven I hope hizz izz not among thezze men."

Lady's heart plummeted. Oh how she hoped her friend was right.

24

Beatrice tapped her foot impatiently. With the dawn slipping behind late morning, Mordecai felt the frustration of unanticipated detours just as strongly. Regardless, he eyed his sister-in-law with suspicion. The morning was uncharacteristically void of her complaints. Now, as they approached the cave entrance discovered the evening before, he wondered at the wisdom of sharing the next hour with her. What catastrophe would her interference bring?

A clatter sounded behind them and Mordecai swung around to see his brother tangled within the ladder he'd diligently hauled up the mountain. Mordecai held out a hand to assist his brother to his feet. "We shall rest before proceeding."

"I am fine," Bernard said.

"It is for us all. We do not know what to expect once we reach the eagle's nest," Mordecai said.

Beatrice sighed, swinging the newly lit lantern toward the cave's darkness. Her eyes shined with a strange youthfulness reminiscent of so many years ago when they had all been far more innocent. As she stared into the depths with unrestrained curiosity, Mordecai moved with disguised nonchalance, scanning the area for signs of mankind. The trees rustled beneath a breeze significantly gentler than the prior evening. The ground surrounding the cave entrance was blanketed with leaves, undisturbed by any feet beyond their own. The oddly spaced steps of the madman stood out amid their more consistently even prints from the night before. Despite his vigilance, Mordecai worried that others would grow interested in their trek up the mountain. But so far their luck held--for now.

The madman had disappeared. He did not show in town the night before nor had they discovered his direction as they retreated the night prior. Even now, there was no evidence of the man's escape from the cave. Perhaps he never left. Mordecai focused on the distant peaks partially visible beyond the pine's prickly foliage, letting the implications of the mystery surround him. They had no need for the guide with the eagle monument's secrets already discovered. But he was uncomfortable with unsecured strands of circumstance. What had been left undone could haunt their success, leaving chance as their only ally.

Mordecai never left anything to chance.

"Can we go now? Can't we rest on the other side?" Beatrice said.

Bernard stood at her insistence, tucking the ladder under one arm and throwing the satchel of supplies over the other shoulder, he disappeared into the cavern. Beatrice followed, her hand held high as the lantern swung above her head. With the possibility of riches, the woman drove those around her with unswerving domination. Perhaps the mercurial behavior had been the draw that caught his eye so many years ago. But like repelled like and he'd be damned if he'd lose this game to a woman such as she.

Mordecai took position behind the pair, covering his sullen glare with the shadows of the cave. As they turned the corners toward their destination he struggled to focus on the task at hand, his ire strangling his most avid fantasies of riches and rest. What did it matter that the woman continued to plague them with her presence? She was nothing more than a failed actress, washed ragged with age and stepping vicariously through life on the coat-tails of greater men. She was nothing. A pawn. A dark memory.

An obligation of which he would soon be free.

"Mordecai, come quickly," Bernard said, his breath thin and exhausted. "I believe I discovered what kept our guide."

Mordecai pushed aside his sister-in-law and joined his brother. The tunnel split in two directions, the furthest to the right their intended trail. But to the left, a moist breeze ruffled the thin frills that graced his neckline. The light from Beatrice's lantern flickered against the dimpled rock, casting shadows that glistened with a damp sheen. Mordecai sucked in a silent breath when he spotted a foot turned unnaturally under a thigh. A hint of white shone from the area of the knee where bone had broken through skin. Above the limbs lay a mass of stone, terrifyingly neutral in its resting place.

"I never heard it fall. Did we miss this when we left last night?" Beatrice asked.

Mordecai shook his head. The mystery of their guide's disappearance was solved with only a slight hint of unease. It was remarkably convenient. "Come along. We have much to do and I do not wish to wrestle with the night like we did yesterday."

Snatching the lantern from Beatrice's hand, Mordecai continued toward the hidden meadow, a sinister smile tipping his lips as his companions scurried to follow. Within a few minutes he entered the cool and sunny air beyond the cave's exit. The eagle stared down at him, eyes intent on a prey it could never capture in its stone talons.

"Bring the ladder," Mordecai said as he sidled up to the monolithic cone, his attention focused on the heights crowned by the nest and stone bird. "Careful now, we do not know how old this is. It could be more fragile than it appears."

"That thing could withstand Noah's flood," Beatrice said, her hand shading her eyes as she too stared into the majestic bird's gaze.

Bernard bustled around the monolith, securing the ladder against the stone, and setting the feet firmly in the soft ground. The locket slipped easily into Mordecai's hand as he reached for the nearest rung, his heart pattering with an unfamiliar nervous thrum. Anticipation took control of his hands, and the ladder shivered beneath his shaking fingers. With flared nostrils he placed his foot on the first step, determined to school his body into a reasoned control—not even his own excitement could distract him.

"Stand back, I am not certain what to expect," Mordecai said as he reached the top, the smooth stone talons cold beneath his fingers as he anchored himself against the monolith. Beyond the protruding claws, an intricately carved nest sat beneath petrified feathers, each stone twig exquisite in its execution. Even the artists of the day would struggle to create such fine detail. Mordecai let his mind marvel at the work as his hands prodded, searching for the divot.

A heavy breath escaped his lips when his fingers found the prize and he slipped the stone from the locket into place. The birds in the surrounding trees silenced their natural serenade and the trees stilled their gentle sway. Silence stormed Mordecai's ears, the pressure mounting as they waited.

He descended, his eyes never leaving the eagle, watching eagerly for the next clue to his quest. What secrets did de Vaca's trinkets have for him this time?

"Well?" Beatrice said with irritable venom. "Did you do it correctly?"

"Do quiet down woman," Mordecai said.

"Quiet down for what? Your show is lacking—-as usual."

"Bea please," Bernard said, his eyes plastered to the predator in stone. Beatrice shook her head and stalked away, mumbling beneath her breath. As her skirts rustled against a boulder a second, equally hushed sound tickled the air. Mordecai smiled and stepped away from the stone.

A golden glow started from the eagle's talons and spread over the legs and up through the feathers. Bright white pierced through previously unseen cracks, shattering the illusion that the animal had ever been alive. Beatrice gasped from behind the two men, a satisfied warmth filled Mordecai's belly

Rock rending in two halves sent all three stepping back as the smooth cone splintered. Shards ricocheted across the meadow. Bernard grabbed his wife's hand and tugged her toward the safety of the cave, but Mordecai spun in wonder as the world around him fractured and fell. The whole meadow shivered with the force of a thousand hammers, the ground crumbling into fissures and sink holes. His feet gripped the trembling floor, his shoulders thrown back in blatant challenge.

Suddenly the ground quieted, the silence once again seeping eerily about him. The bird stood triumphant, untouched by the violence, perched on a thin column of stone, all that was left of the once immutably solid cone. The land shivered with one final gasp, then settled. With a flash, the eagle lost all color, drab stone once again standing immovable. Mordecai frowned, certain he had missed something. That could not be all. What was his next step? It was impossible!

Then the eyes came alive. Piercing white light sliced through the air from the eagle to the floor at Mordecai's feet. He skipped to the side, surprised by the suddenness. Several feet away, he waited, watching. Nothing moved.

Intrigued, he stepped to the side, staring at where the light hit the ground. Illuminated by the light was a great spiral, previously hidden by the meadow's loose soil. He took a step toward the carving. Crude figures danced around the spiral, each pointing to a cardinal direction. Mordecai sank to his knees. His fingers traced the spiral to the end, landing beside a serpent pointed to the east.

He traced with his finger to the east and met another drawing, this one far less crude. Elaborate outlines of dwellings, mountains, rivers cast an elusive tint on the mystery. In the center of it all, above a great semicircle was perched an eagle. Mordecai grinned. This was his destination. He had no doubt.

"What is it?" Beatrice asked, her fear overcome by her curiosity.

"It seems, dear sister, we will be back tracking a bit. Retrieve the ladder, we must be on our way," Mordecai said.

She stepped up beside him and looked over the etchings in the hard stone ground. "I do not understand. How can you know what any of that means?"

He stood, dusting off his breaches as he dismissed her with a wave. "Years of study, my dear. While you played with your dolls, I prepared for this moment."

She puffed out her chest and strode away, but could not

prevent the spiteful response, "All you have done, dear brother, is discover new ways to destroy lives."

***

They were lost. The blasted cavalry, complete with men trained in cartography, tracking, and warfare, were a worthless lot. Zhao Jin barked for Martin to fetch his spyglass. Over the last two days they squandered the advantage of knowing their quarry's direction with poor choices and youthful exuberance. Zhao Jin flexed his fingers, irritated he could not take command when it was quite obvious the captain lacked even the most elementary skills necessary for their task.

"I do not understand. How could we have gotten so turned around?" the captain asked one of his men, fury evident in his flushed neck and clenched fists. The unfortunate soldier flinched as Wright snatched the map and pulled it closer to study in the dying daylight. "This is ridiculous. We know the Pinkertons were within a day of Albuquerque. How could a ship that size disappear?"

It helped if the tracking party was inept. But Zhao Jin kept his thought behind hooded eyes. Martin returned with his glass and Zhao Jin took it in hand, scanning the distant horizon for clues. Enough time had been wasted, it was time to make a move.

The captain sent his man away with a frustrated order. They would hunker down for the night and prepare to set out at dawn. Zhao Jin knew Wright still had no idea where they would go, but hid that truth behind bald arrogance. Had his company not shared his incompetence, they would surely have mutinied at some point in their travels.

Zhao Jin had seen many of the elite placed in seats of power, despite even the most miniscule competence. The elite loved to believe their wealth ensured a level of intellect unattainable by those less fortunate. It made them particularly susceptible to his maneuvers. The captain may have the best of intentions, but he belonged in the ball rooms of the eastern shores, not matching wits with outlaws and maps.

The horizon glowed red as the sun sought her evening rest. To the east, dusk clamored over rolling hills. Zhao Jin swung his glass to the north, then the west. Clouds, darkened with rain, billowed over a rocky mountain range, distorting the land, but something caught his eye. Something unnatural.

"Captain, tell me what you see beyond that ridge," Zhao Jin said.

Flustered, the blond man pulled the lapels of his coat down and took his time to draw his own spyglass to the distant horizon. While they were in the company of the captain's men, Zhao Jin kept his superiority in check, but felt no such compunction when the two men were alone together.

"I see nothing," Wright said. "It is simply a storm approaching. Do you fear a little rain?"

"Not in the slightest. But if you look closer, you will see that something rises from the ground. That is a strange behavior for clouds, do you not think?"

Wright scrunched up his face and took a second look. Zhao Jin continued, "That is smoke, Captain. And it comes from a rather large source. I believe we have discovered what became of our Pinkertons."

The captain blanched and dropped his hands. "How do you know that is them?"

Zhao Jin stilled a triumphant smile. "It was only a matter of time before that behemoth fell from the sky. What remains in question is whether the ladies reached their prey in time to be caught in the catastrophe."

"We must search for survivors. I will prepare the men for a night march."

"Captain Wright. That is at the least a day and a half march."

"It cannot be more than five miles," the captain dismissed him and struck out toward his men.

Zhao Jin shook his head and looked through the glass toward the rising smoke. The western desert did astounding things to reality. What the captain believed to be five miles was closer to twenty. He would exhaust his men before the night turned to dawn and they would take even longer to reach their destination.

Zhao Jin sighed and looked to the sky. If he could discover where Kovacs was headed, he would have no need to track these women all over New Mexico. But Sybil, with her affliction gaining intensity, would direct them true. And until the indomitable Miss Dewhurst was dealt with, he would have to maintain the tenuous hold on Captain Wright.

His patience had frayed, but he had not achieved so much by letting misfortune rule. Within the week, Sybil would be at his side again and this time, he would chain her inescapably to him.

25

The heat from the wreckage cut beneath the scales on Sybil's arms, stinging the tender layer of skin. The Pinkerton's ship split in several segments, landing across a mile of rolling hills and arroyos. Dry patches of brush caught fire but lost roaring momentum as it came in contact with the long steel beams and dense hardwoods. The glass in the giant Pinkerton eye fractured, the crack as it split echoing across the area. Sybil took solace beneath a large palo verde, unsure of what to do next.

Lady stepped across the arroyo, scanning the area with an intensity that bordered on frantic. The emotion and worry rippled off her shoulders, crying for providence to deliver her good news. In the few months they knew him, Slim, had grown solidly in their regard. And despite the recent separation, the connection held strong. Affection was hard won from Lady, and no matter the circumstance, Sybil understood the grief of a relationship severed long before its time. That it had taken an adventure in the west to bring Lady a family of the heart said much of her past and more of her character.

Sybil sent up a prayer they would find Slim alive and well.

She emerged from beneath the tree to join Lady in the

search. Carmen had been sent to assist Juan to spare the young girl further exposure to the horrific sights found among the twisted beams as well as from the woman she appeared to fear more than death. Sybil drew her silks tight against her body. The frightened eyes weighed heavily on her. Was the child simply remarking on legends passed down to explain others afflicted as she? Or was there truth beneath Carmen's vehemence?

Sybil turned her head and covered her nose as she passed another corpse, the body bent in an unnatural position, the eyes wide and glassy. Most of the men they found were unfamiliar, faces without context. But a few struck true to her memory. One man, accomplice to her capture, lay bent over a fragment of the boiler, half of his body charred beyond recognition, the second half terrifyingly familiar.

Sybil turned away, the scent of death growing unbearable. Lady called from ahead, "Have you seen him? Do you believe he escaped before they fell?"

A hardwood beam crackled to her left, a small fire smoldering, slowly breaking down the wood's resistance. The silks flared as the heat rose from the ground, threatening to add her to the fuel. Sybil moved with haste toward Lady, an elemental fear traveling up her spine. As she came to stand beside Lady, Sybil said, "I have not seen him. And truthfully, we do not know that they kept him onboard much beyond our own escape. We may find that he hazz made hizz way to another town, far from our enemiezz clutchezz."

"True." Lady let a tenuous smile touch her lips. "Or we may find him behind another poker table. Would be just like that blasted man."

Sybil reached over and touched her friend's arm. "It

would be, indeed."

"Damn it Slim! Get yer dirty hands off my breasts!"

Lady jumped and Sybil swung around in surprise at the raised voice. The two women stared at each other in wide-eyed confusion then ran toward the sound of rustling in the arroyo to their left. As they ducked beneath the thick mesquite and cottonwoods which escaped the torrent of fire and metal, they stumbled across a deep, sandy wash. In the bottom, two bodies struggled in a mess of tangled limbs.

Sybil raised her hand to her lips and stifled a laugh. Slim had a lazy smile and rugged look of mischief plastered unapologetically across his face as he wrestled with the Pinkerton's mechanic. The two painted a ridiculous picture that nearly superseded the relief she felt at seeing Slim alive and well.

"Get away from him you traitorous harpy!" Lady pulled her augmented pistol from her satchel, aiming it with unusually shaky hands. Sybil gasped as her friend slid down the embankment, sending sand and rounded stones cascading toward the writhing pair. "Slim, get away, I have her. She will not escape us this time."

"Lady. No!" Sybil shouted then recoiled in shock as Lady landed, took aim and pulled the trigger. The shot went far right, but the boom brought everyone to a standstill. Ears ringing, Sybil was caught off-balance, and as she lost her footing the ground beneath her crumbled. The sand provided little cushion as she fell.

Suddenly, the world took on the eerie tint and shade of unreality which tormented her so often of late. Bodies moved in the distance, faceless forms shimmering in a range of colors unfamiliar and frightening. She withdrew, curling within herself and tucking the silk around her body, insulating her skin from the torrent of sensation. Vibrations rose from the sand, each step from the others sounding like a thousand trains charging across the country. Tears threatened to fall, fear tightened the skin about her eyes, and once again she knew the last glimpses of sanity lay in the eyes of those around her.

A hand settled on her shoulder, warm and coaxing. A breath seeped through the silk wrapped about her face, a rumbling voice unintelligible but calming brought her focus to a pinpoint. The thud of her heart slowed, the vibrations stilled and slowly the colors sharpened and lines of detail fell into order. A hand slipped along her silk and removed it from her eyes.

Juan smiled back, his expression unlike any she had ever seen. Understanding.

"It is all right, sister. This does not mean the end for you. You will learn to control it."

"You know what it izz? What hazz been happening to me?" she said, her words breathy.

He nodded, sadness punctuating his knowledgeable eyes. Sybil wanted desperately for him to explain. It had been too long. She'd known nothing of her life, her heritage, or her affliction and finally she had the chance to know. But Lady popped into view behind his shoulder, worry furrowing her brow and guilt weighing heavily in her stance. Sybil gave a tremulous smile. "Pleaezz tell me you did not kill the mechanic. She may be of use to uzz."

Lady released an exhausted laugh. "She is alive. But I cannot promise she will remain so. It depends on the story Slim has to give."

"Well, sweetheart, he won't be givin you his story any time soon." The mechanic sidled up to stand beside Lady, her audacity as apparent as when Sybil first met her on board the Pinkerton's ship. Her hands were propped on shapely hips, sand clinging to the side of her face where it stuck to grease left from her profession. "Tommy gave that boy some nasty potion that got him all addled in the brain. You can think about me what you want, but that man's gonna need some help and I don't know if there's a doctor in this country that could help him. I ain't never seen nothin' like it."

"Phee darlin', come dance with me. Show me some of that sweet molasses smile."

All heads turned toward Slim who still lay sprawled in the sand. The mechanic shook her head, auburn tendrils peeking from beneath a kerchief flipping with the movement. "I told ya. The man's been stoned as a town drunk for over a week. At least he knows my name. Half the time he don't know where he is." She turned a sparkling eye to Lady. "But he's been happy. Ain't never seen a man happier, and I've seen plenty of men in their best moments."

Lady pursed her lips then stalked away from the group toward Slim. He was less than cooperative as she attempted to bring him to his feet. Sybil frowned and asked, "This potion, wazz it in little blue bottles? And did it smell sweet and earthy? Like sugar and grazz?"

Phee narrowed her eyes and said, "Yes, that sounds about right."

Sybil's heart fluttered and she moved to stand. Juan put out his hand, assisting her as she struggled with her tangled silks. He said, "You know this poison?"

"Oh very well. And I imagine the Pinkertons have given him far more than any man should have. It will take some work to excise it from his body." Sybil squeezed his hand in thanks then dropped it to adjust her silks and brush away the sand. "I believe we all have important stories to tell. But first we must attend to our friend."

Juan left to help Lady manage Slim and Sybil looked beyond Phee up the arroyo where the smoke from the wreckage began to clear. So much had happened and so much was still unanswered. With luck, some answers were forthcoming, but they were still far from their destination. Had they lost the trail of the MacHurdyGurdys? With the excitement, tracking the elusive Mordecai seemed ancillary, but with his elixir practically dooming her friend to a premature death, her resolve tightened. What Mordecai had done could not be undone. But she could save Slim and she could guarantee Mordecai never reached his fortune.

No one should suffer from the man's evil, even if she must unleash her own unholy curse to its full potential. If Zhao Jin were to be trusted, she contained a potential yet unrealized. With Juan's help, she may yet learn what it was and use it to protect those souls from all the devilish men who tortured her in this life.

***

Pain sliced along the back of his neck, piercing like a jagged knife into the back of his eyes. One moment euphoria sent a cloud of numb joy through every limb, the next he felt excruciating agony to such degree he hoped for a sharp blow to the head to knock him senseless.

Feminine voices and soft curves surrounded him, an experience which in more favorable circumstances would have been pleasurable. As it were, he steeled himself against the roiling stomach threatening to unpack his last meal.

When had he last eaten? He couldn't remember. Truthfully, he couldn't remember a damn thing. Unlike the throbbing mornings after a drunken night, this lack of memory stank of sweetness and something unnatural.

The euphoria seeped into his head and a silly smile replaced his grimace. One of the woman groaned beneath his weight as his legs fell out from under him. "Stop teasin' me with those lovely noises, sweetheart, I'm in no condition to do anythin' about it." He chuckled and tried to focus on the woman to his right, his arm slung over her shoulder and weighing her down. The features were familiar. Fair skin and chestnut brown hair, she was elegant and composed with only a slight hint of irritation in the lowered brows and pinched lips. Something niggled at his mind, a memory teased at the edges of his consciousness. An important detail about this woman wanted to be remembered.

She turned her fine-featured face his way and he forgot himself. "Damn darlin', I ain't never seen a lady so pretty."

"Your wits are quite obviously addled," she said with a sneer.

"Shoot Slim, I thought you found me the prettiest thing this side of the west."

He turned to his left where another lovely lady held him upright, her sparkling eyes flashed beneath a kerchief tied over hair that fought to escape the restraining cloth. Her features were darker than her companion, stronger and rigid. She had the beauty of an Amazon, regal and unyielding. Something warned him not to turn his back on this one.

Neither were known to him, yet a familiarity seemed natural between them all. Why did he not remember these women? How could he possible forget such beautiful examples of womanly charms?

Shoot, what did it matter? He had both of them in his arms now. "How 'bout you lovely ladies take me to my room and I'll show you how beautiful I find you both."

His fair companion huffed and shifted, sending a shock of pain through his shoulder and toward his head. The euphoria evaporated as the intensity of pain hit a new high, his eyes watering beneath the lightning heat. He stumbled to his knees, dropping his arms from the women and reaching up to press his palms into his eyes. What was this? Why did it hurt so much?

His control over his belly was lost and he leaned forward to let loose the contents of his stomach.

"Damn it Slim, did you have to do that on my shoe?"

"It is quite obvious that he is ill, perhaps your sensitivities could wait? It was your actions that did this to him."

"I didn't have nothin' to do with this! That was the Pinkertons. And I don't care if you believe me, but if we don't him help soon, he'll probably die. They gave him a whole lot of that poison."

A gentle hand brushed against his forehead, the fingertips soothing his brow. When he looked up, a frightening face surrounded empathetic, moss-colored eyes. Her lips moved slowly, and he just heard her words beneath the pounding in his head. "Juan, pleazz assist me. We must move him to a place where he can rest azz the elixer workzz through hizz body. I must find suppliezz. I am not familiar with thizz landscape, but I suspect we will find what we need here. Thizz potion izz a product of thizz land, the cure is azz well."

Rough hands gripped Slim's elbows in a crushing grip, prickles shot through his arm. Slim said, "Hey now, that's enough of that."

"Please, Juan, be cautious." His fair angel came to his defense and Slim smiled beneath the pain. Unfortunately, her plea didn't help much. In fact, the man seemed to be in more of a hurry to throw him into a ditch. It wouldn't be the first time, but he usually had enough sense to be able to run. Seems his luck may have run out.

Damn. His luck should be turning around anytime now. He never had a slump this long. And he had a lot of winning still to do.

In the distance, he heard his lovely ladies bickering. The man hauling his uncooperative body up the steep embankment grunted and swore. Slim didn't like his attitude. What were three beautiful creatures doing with a reprobate like him? He murmured his displeasure, but was ignored. 'Course, he sounded more like a drooling child at the moment.

Another piercing pain struck his head and he shouted, reaching up to press his hands into his temples. The man lost his grip and the two of them tumbled back, falling in a heap at the bottom of the wash. Head pounding and eyes burning, Slim looked up into the blue sky, hazy with dispersed smoke. Had there been a fire? Was that why he hurt so bad?

His fair-skinned angel looked down at him, her nose flaring with amusement. "Oh Slim, you certainly are a mess, aren't you. I do hope that Sybil's concoction can save you. I far prefer your ornery self."

"Sweetheart, you find a way to make me feel better and I'll be as ornery as you want me."

She lifted her head and laughed, then reached down to assist him back to his feet. Slim much preferred her aid to their disgruntled companion. The man sat beside him, staring sulkily into the sand. A sense of satisfaction flowed in and dulled the pain. He'd sure enjoy making the man irritable if it meant he got more time with this pretty lady. Slim smiled; she sure did look like a lady.

26

The strains of the hurdy-gurdy melody trickled across the camp, the firelight flickering off the elaborately painted, wood body of his cherished instrument. Mordecai loved the night, when the breeze blew softly and the birds quieted. It was a time when he could almost believe he was home. He turned the handle and let the old song of Hungary play into the darkness. If he had a soul, it lived in this ancient instrument, trapped forever in the keybox, released only when he played.

In the distance, the skeletal remains of the homestead could be seen casting shadows in the moonlight. Mordecai had hoped to take rest with the family a second time, their hospitality so graciously offered only a few days prior. His companions refused to accompany him to see the grisly remains of the once happily active house. Perhaps it was been just as well. His brother maintained a far too melancholy disposition of late. The sight would have only worsened it.

A rustle alerted him to his brother's arrival, as the man joined him by the fire. Bernard smiled.

Taken aback, Mordecai ceased playing and covered his surprise with a cough. "You seem well, brother."

Bernard's answer took time, but his tone was light. "I'm remembering the old country. You're music always takes me back there. Do you miss it?"

Mordecai cleared his throat and returned to the song, letting the sound distract from the honest question. "We always remember that which was good in a way that seems brighter than it ever truly could have been. Tragedy melts away with time. Does it not?"

"Tragedy is only a brief companion of a good life. There wasn't so much bad when we lived with mother." Bernard stared into the fire, his thoughts turned inward as surely as Mordecai's. It was true. Life with mother had been pleasant. Simple, but pleasant. So little to recommend it, but even less to despise. However, that time had passed along with their mother many decades ago. He and his brother were orphaned and lost. No mother and certainly no father of any consequence.

"Life will be better soon, I promise you. We are nearly there and nothing stands between us and a life of little care."

Bernard turned to his brother and smiled again. It was an eerie sight, so foreign and unexpected. Could the thought of riches be enough to pull him from his melancholy? The whites of his brother's teeth disturbed him and he looked away, the shadowy remains of the homestead a more comfortable sight.

"Bea believes it is your doing, their home burning down."

Mordecai snorted. "How could I have had anything to do with that?"

"I wouldn't know. She has as many theories as you have schemes. Bea's an unhappy woman. I wish I could have made her happy." Bernard released an exhausted sigh. "But I suppose that was an opportunity that left her many years before she met us. I don't know that she ever could have been happy."

"Quite insightful. It is a wonder she remains with us at all." Mordecai felt his brother's gaze on him again and he shifted uncomfortably. He coughed and continued, "Ten years is a long time to feel beholden to someone when the debt was long ago paid."

"I knew the child wasn't mine, brother."

Mordecai's fingers slipped from the keys and his other hand tightened on the handle. What on earth had come over his brother? The man was a mechanical genius, but never one for insight or keen observation. He traveled through life focused on his projects, quietly existing among men who moved the world in circles. Mordecai turned unblinking eyes to his brother. "I don't know what you mean."

This time, Bernard was the one to look away. "I did not know if the child was yours or another man's. It could never have been mine. But if there was any chance that the blood of the Kovacs ran in its veins, then it had to remain with us."

"What are you saying? That you believe I would not have stood up for a child of my own blood? You married that shrew of a woman because you did not trust your own brother to be a man?"

Bernard chuckled. "You could never have claimed the child."

"Why on earth not?" Anger stormed across his brow and for once he questioned all he knew of his brother. Had he fallen into madness even then? Quietly maneuvering inside his fantasies, pursuing his own crazed agenda while Mordecai planned for their future?

"Because you are the master of all and beholden to none. You drive this family forward, always seeking the next town and our fortune. I am simply a tinkerer but I had hoped that I could have also been a father." A note of sadness entered Bernard's words and it silenced Mordecai's furor. He could not fault his brother for a desire he never entertained himself. Was it truly worse that his brother had entered into his marriage knowing the risk and the truth?

"Either way, it was for naught. You are trapped in a torturous marriage and we have no heir."

"It hasn't been altogether torturous. She is a good woman, within her heart, but her past is no less dark than our own. It is never easy to come from nothing. We at least had a warm hearth for much of our youth."

Whether the harpy had a difficult childhood or not meant little to him. What did matter was the inevitable moment when he must decide whether to share their fortune with the meddlesome woman. If she remained Bernard's wife, then what choice did he have? But if Bernard knew she never truly valued their marriage--was it possible? "I can see how you could sympathize with her plight, and I do as well. But surely she cannot be happy following two vagabonds on fruitless journeys? Would she not be better off where she shines, in the eastern cities?"

"That has always been for her to decide. And yet she stays. Why do you think that is?" Bernard asked, an undercurrent of something far darker than Mordecai cared to examine lying beneath the words. He did not have an answer and let the quiet settle between them.

With the sun down, the warmth of the desert evaporated into the clear, star-filled sky. A cold seeped into the bones, promising a silent and freezing night. Mordecai missed the comfort of his bed, but he had to give it up as the trip required consolidation of their supplies into the one cart. As the master of a traveling show, he'd grown accustomed to the small luxuries they'd afforded. The Marvelous MacHurdyGurdy Traveling Show had been relatively solvent, between the performances and the sales of his mystical elixir. It was unfortunate they had to give up the small amenities they'd won. But it was a sad necessity that one must give up any degree of comfort for the opportunity of greatness. It was a lesson he'd learned many years ago.

The sacrifices would be rewarded.

"How long before we reach our destination?" Bernard asked.

"A week, perhaps two. I am unfamiliar with the terrain, and this weather concerns me. I do not relish finding ourselves stranded in the snow. I am certain I know the ancient ruins the eagle unveiled, but the map I have of the area is old and I am not sure how trustworthy."

"I am certain you will find it in due course. You have always had a remarkable sense of the landscape. I just wonder if you will find all you have been seeking when we finally reach the end."

Mordecai placed his hand on his brother's shoulder. "There will be more gold then any man knows what to do with. We shall want for nothing and live a blessed and righteous life."

Bernard shook his head and stood. "Do you truly believe we can clear our dark souls with gold?"

"Undoubtedly." Gold could give them everything.

***

Zhao Jin had little time for delays. Three horses and two mules danced in front of him, reins swinging free in the air beneath their head, frantic wide eyes flashing in panic.

Among the mounts heaving bodies, several cavalrymen grabbed for control of the slashing leather, their hats flying off in various directions only to be trampled beneath the hooves. Martin spit on the ground to his right, Joseph stood with arms crossed on his left. Neither man were impressed with their companions any more than he.

"Should we take care of this?" Martin asked.

"No," Zhao Jin said as he stepped away from the fray. "Let us make camp. We are unlikely to make much distance after this fiasco."

Captain Wright brushed past Zhao Jin and his men as they retreated, his hand raised to direct the struggling soldiers. His interference would more than likely worsen the situation. The captain did little to improve Zhao Jin's initial assessment of his character. Now, that another day stood between them and their quarry Zhao Jin reconsidered striking out on his own.

With the sun falling toward the horizon, the last remnants of the distant smoke dissipated. The only chance they had of catching Sybil now would require her broken body amid the carnage. The death of the woman provided no value to him. If she were to lead him to Cibola, she would need to be very much alive.

And if she had not died in the smoking rubble of a ship, then she may still be surrounded by capable allies. Zhao Jin underestimated the competence of the elegant Miss Dewhurst, but after the debacle in Albuquerque he refused to do so again. Her resilience and fortitude would have made her an excellent companion in his endeavors. Unfortunately, the heiress had taken up with the uncouth Slim Robinson. From what Zhao Jin knew of the man, he could charm the cards off a poker table with a smile. He'd undoubtedly found it a simple thing to do the same to a girl more familiar with Boston balls than western boom towns.

But Slim was out of the way. Now, he must only mitigate the damage Miss Dewhurst could wage. With the well-intentioned but incompetent Captain Wright he had a better chance of neutralizing her threat. But it would only be possible if Zhao Jin took control of the campaign.

"Martin, see to the settlement of camp. Show these men how it is done properly."

Finally able to spread his wings, Martin puffed out his chest and prepared to take command. A capable sergeant at arms, Martin bellowed commands like a man used to compliance. The young cavalrymen, green and unused to assertive orders hopped to obey without thought to whose authority they answered. Zhao Jin pulled out his snuff box and dipped his finger into the powder. That Captain Wright was saddled with such young and inexperienced men suggested the level of confidence his superiors had in his talents.

By all accounts, the captain had one mission and to this point he had failed miserably. He snapped the lid shut and replaced the box in his vest, smoothing the fabric and feeling for his cigarillos. By tomorrow these men would be marching in line and they'd easily make their destination. If luck held, he'd have Mordecai Kovacs in his sight before the month's end.

"What is going on here?" A ruffled Captain Wright stomped into view, his insecurities worn on his sleeves as clearly as his emblems.

Zhao Jin flicked ash from his cigarillo and nodded to the quick work Martin had made of camp preparation. "With your attention drawn to the emergency with the mounts, we thought to assist with preparation. All is in order, Captain.

Would you like to join me for a drink?"

Ready to object, Wright had opened his mouth only to close it quickly, a dark cloud of confusion crossing his face before he said, "A drink?"

"Indeed. It has been a long day. There is no harm in two gentlemen enjoying a whisky while we wait for supper."

Wright shifted and watched his men working diligently to set camp. Fires came to life and tents were easily erected. Zhan Jin imagined the captain had never seen such an efficient ten minutes in his entire life. "Come Captain, I have a few questions about our quarry that I would ask. But I feel that for the sake of the lady's reputation, we should speak privately."

"Of course. It appears my tent has already been set. Would you join me?"

"It would be an honor, sir."

Two young cavalrymen, fresh-faced and likely just out of the schoolroom completed tying down the captain's tent as they approached. A third and fourth entered with a cot and writing desk, hurriedly completing the set up. Wright held the heavy canvas flap open for Zhao Jin to enter. Joseph entered a few moments later carrying two glasses and an elegantly incised bottle, the gold liquid swishing as he moved.

Once they were alone, Zhao Jin poured two glasses and found a seat on a rugged stool. Captain Wright took the desk chair, the creak of its joints only slightly less strained than Zhao Jin's. Wright said, "Your men are quite efficient."

"They are adept at their positions. I imagine you and I have similar expectations of our servants."

Wright looked toward the flap and sighed. "I look forward to this campaign's end. It has been a struggle."

"What do you plan to do with the lovely Miss Dewhurst when you have her in hand?" Zhao Jin asked.

"I had hoped…but it seems my affections were misplaced. I have been tasked with returning her to her father and I will do so." A steely glint hit the captain's eye and it gave Zhao Jin a spark of hope that the man could accomplish his side of the deal.

"It is unfortunate when a young woman is placed in a position that requires she make decisions well beyond her capacity. You cannot blame her for missteps when her only influence has been the lowest sort of humanity. Truly, her behavior could simply be attributed to that reprobate Robinson."

"Robinson?"

Zhao Jin hid his a smirk behind a solemn bow of his head. "An unsavory sort and a gambler. He took advantage of both Sybil and Miss Dewhurst's naive and trusting natures. Once they have been removed from the savagery of the west, I have no doubt they will see the truth of their youthful misadventures."

"It is possible. I do hope she has not done anything irreparable." The dark shadow across the man's brow darkened and Zhao Jin intended to encourage the fury. An uncompromising arrogance would do much for them with what was to come.

"I am certain that anything can be repaired by a man of your intelligence. Her father wields such wide influence that I do not doubt the two of you will have her settled in her rightful place before the month is out." Then he and the Dewhurst chit would be effectively out of his way. It would be none too soon.

Wright stood with an air of dismissal, his drink complete. "We shall leave before dawn. Prepare your men for a quick march. I intend to arrive at dusk when they will not suspect us."

Zhao Jin stood, clasped his hands and bowed before the captain, making him shift uncomfortably. It was all going to plan and soon, he would be on his way to fortune once more.

27

Slim stank like fifty saloons, but they had no water to spare. Lady lifted his head to adjust the rolled up canvas which provided the least bit of comfort. With everything burned in the wreckage, there was little to repurpose for treating his condition. She replaced his head on the canvas and pressed a hand to his pock-marked cheek. He looked like absolute hell.

Tucking a loose tendril of hair behind her ear, she leaned back and sighed. Sybil had concocted an evil-smelling poultice for his chest and a potion he'd spat up more than drank. She made no promises, but then, Lady would never have believed them. Now they waited with Lady sitting sentinel at his side.

Sybil retreated into the desert, hunting for ingredients for her potions. Her confidence in Slim's ability to fight the effects of MacHurdyGurdy's elixir was low. Lady could tell. This was the second time the bastard Mordecai MacHurdyGurdy would nearly kill Slim. Even though his hand had not delivered the poison, his evil products landed Slim in a pain-filled stupor which threatened to turn him mad. Perhaps death would be more kind. Lady took the gambler's hand and held tight. If only she hadn't fired her weapon into the barrel of gunpowder. There may have been a chance she could have prevented the abuse caused by the corrupt Pinkertons. She could have done something. She should have.

"He doesn't look good," Juan said, his voice gruff.

"Better than he did before." Truthfully, he looked no better than he had when they'd discovered him, but at the least he looked no worse. Lady smoothed the hair plastered across his forehead. His skin burned beneath her fingers. "We need water to cool him."

"We hardly have enough for ourselves"

"I know that." She bit back the frustration. "Have you searched the area? The wash? Surely there is water to be found somewhere."

The shade shifted and a bright slash of sunlight crept toward Slim. The tall cottonwood provided a subtle shelter from the warmth, but it would not last long as the sun moved further across the sky. Lady did not wish to move him from the only soft grass to be found. The rest of the area had either been blackened by the fires or was covered with inhospitable, prickly plants. If the SteamWing survived in better condition, she would have easily commanded they carry him the distance.

A loud bang came from the direction of the ship. Lady narrowed her eyes, but Juan quickly explained, "Seems your friend from the ship has a mechanical background. She says she'll have it ready to fly by evening."

Lady dropped Slim's hand and stood, ready to stalk toward the SteamWing. "She has no business stealing our ship. That woman should be tied to a cactus."

Juan put out a hand and stopped her. "What other choice do we have? If she can fly, we can get out of here." He nodded toward Slim. "How long do you think he will survive out here?"

"I do not trust her. You do not know what she has done." That Malphia Blackwood still lived was more a testament to Lady's desire to stay by Slim's side than by any sense of mercy. Lady scanned the area for her satchel. They were gone. "Juan, where are my weapons?"

"I thought it better if you were not tempted."

"What do you mean? You took my things?" Lady turned on him and he took a quick step back. His height and broad shoulders shrank beneath her building fury. "You have no right to take my things. This is not the first time. I was willing to forgive you that instance for you had not yet developed an understanding of my expectations. But too many have laid hands on what is mine."

Had he continued to back down or even hinted at apology she might have eased her ire, but he stiffened and stood fast. Lady came to a stop in front of his iron chest and stubbornly set mouth. She lost her mind and set forth a volley of scathing curses which had never once left her lips prior. Had she listened, she might have wondered where she'd heard half of them. But it did not matter. Too much had happened, too many men stood between her and her goal. What right did any of them have in treating her like a child? Did her sex truly deserve this constant interference?

"And furthermore, if I deem it necessary to shoot a woman as a traitor, I can damn well do so. It is my neck to hang, not yours!" Lady stepped around him. "You will watch Slim. Should he turn worse, I shall hold you to blame. I am quite done with duplicity and secrets. Hold yourself fortunate that my ire is directed toward Miss Blackwood at the moment, for your own deceptions are only a step beneath her in promising my wrath."

He called out as she stormed away, "Please, believe me,

nothing is as it seems."

"It never is, is it?" she murmured as she continued toward the SteamWing. At some point she lost the handle of control and now she must pull order from the chaos. The safety of her companions depended on her maintaining her faculties. Sybil's sporadic behavior had Lady frightened, and now with Slim so very ill, she could let no evil come to them. Mordecai MacHurdyGurdy was slipping away and their pursuers were no doubt making good time on their trail. Even a cavalry on foot could overtake them while they waited beside the remnants of the Pinkerton's ship.

Snakes in their own nest only complicated the matter.

The bang of a heavy strike against metal echoed around the trees that hid the SteamWing. Lady ducked between two branches and came upon the awkwardly positioned ship. The door clung to place with a single hinge. Glass crunched beneath her feet where it landed when it spilled from the windows. That Miss Blackwood believed she could fix the crippled conveyance was ridiculous. A noxious scent came from the direction of the tilted steam chimney. Lady wrinkled her nose, but continued toward the sounds coming from the leeside of the ship.

When she came around the giant wing folded in an unfortunate tangle amid the branches of a spiny palo verde, she spied the athletic shape of Miss Blackwood clinging to the outside components of the ship's boiler, her legs wrapped around a copper pipe, and her head hanging over the edge. In one hand she held a wrench, in the other a steamwand that looked suspiciously like Lady's.

"Miss Blackwood," Lady said.

Malphia's head swung up and she grinned before letting her legs loose and flipping to the ground. "Good, I need a second hand." She disappeared around the boiler and crawled through one of the broken windows.

"Miss Blackwood, really, we must talk," Lady said with a huff. A hand reached out the window and gestured rapidly for her to follow. "Oh for heaven's sake."

She dropped to her knees and crawled into the Steam-Wing. Light filtered in from the shattered windows, casting odd shadows at angles that should not have been possible. Furniture lay in huddled piles at the low point of the room. Carpets and light fixtures nailed in place looked awkward with the entire room tilted to the left.

Malphia swung to the top of the room and called for Lady to join her by the interior components of the boiler. Lady protested. She did not have time to fiddle with the ship. Malphia cut her off and said, "Please, Miss Dewhurst, it will only be a moment. Hold this."

Lady grumbled, but complied. Malphia removed a wrench where it had held a valve. A hiss came from the seal and Lady reached for the valve. Heat warmed her knuckles and she gritted her teeth. Malphia tossed the wrench to the side and leaned against the nearest wall, hands braced on the tilted window sill.

"Now we can talk," Malphia said.

"I beg your pardon?" Lady moved to remove her hand but Malphia jumped forward with a panicked shout and froze Lady in position. "What?"

"If you let that go, the valve will burst and we'll both be shot higher in the sky than man was ever meant to go. Right now, you're the only thing keeping this ship in one piece." When Lady tightened her hand, Malphia smiled in victory and leaned back against the wall. "As I was sayin', now we can talk."

"You're quite mad," Lady said.

"Well sweetheart, you don't do much listenin' and so I figure I had to put you somewhere that made you have to listen. I got some words for you and I figure you got some words for me too, so we're gonna do that here and now." Malphia removed the checkered cloth from her hair and wiped it across her sooty cheeks. Brown hair lay half matted and half spiky, giving her a rather urchin-like appearance. A younger version of her would have easily fit on the streets of Boston, selling newspapers or holding gentlemen's horses.

"Miss Blackwood, if this is your attempt to kill us all, I can assure you I will find a way to thwart you."

"I don't got no reason to want to die. At least not for real, believe me. But you seem to think I want you all dead too, which I don't, thank you kindly. Now, I've known Slim longer than you by a long shot, and he ain't done nothin' to me to warrant I kill him. Lord know he's tried though." Malphia, crossed her arms when Lady snorted in disbelief. "What makes you so high and mighty Miss Dewhurst? You figure money makes you better than me?"

"No, the fact that I am not a traitor to those I claim as friends makes me better than you. Do you forget that you betrayed Slim to the Pinkertons?"

"Ah, that. Now ain't that a funny thing. See, there I was, coming up with a plan to get you both off that damn death trap when you go and nearly blow us all to kingdom come. I don't see how blowing a hole in a barrel of gunpowder makes you any more effective as a rescuer."

"At least I tried to save him. You would have had us in the laps of our enemies. You certainly delivered Slim. Now look at him. What did you get in return, Miss Blackwood? Or was it a gift for your employer?"

Malphia rolled her eyes. "You make about as much sense as your pretty little corset."

"I will have you know, I have left my corset behind." Lady pouted. The sweat on her palms had built up between the nerves and the tiny stream of steam working its way around the valve. If the woman would just get to the point, she could figure some way out of this predicament. Letting the woman go up with the ship was not an unpleasant thought, but Lady had no desire to join this turncoat in death. "Would you kindly tell me your point?"

"Think you can shut up enough to listen?"

"Why you nasty little--"

"Honestly Miss Dewhurst, quiet." The first honest expression of exasperated impatience showed on Malphia's face and Lady flapped her mouth shut on another burst of protests. It was true she had not willingly given Miss Blackwood the freedom to explain. But what other explanation could provide an alternative conclusion? Lady's fingers twitched on the valve. Apparently she had time to spare and was going nowhere in the meantime. It couldn't hurt to listen. For the moment.

"Once Banahan discovered the ruse, I knew there was no way to get you two off that bucket. I did some quick thinking and figured if I could convince old Tommy to trust me, then I could sneak y'all off later when he weren't lookin'. I know I don't got no proof, except that Slim and me ain't dead and all the rest of them are."

Lady blinked at Malphia and waited. But the woman just stared back at her. Finally Lady said, "That is it?"

"That's it."

"You want me to believe you with nothing more than the coincidence that you did not die? What kind of idiotic nonsense--"

"That ship went down for a reason. And if there was anyone knowin' it was gonna happen, that was me. Now, if you were still on that mess when we went down, you would have gone off with us. You just got lucky and ended up in this--" She gestured at the room, "sweet machine."

"If you knew it was going down, why did you do nothing to stop it? To warn them?" Lady asked

"How else was I gonna get Slim off that boat?"

Lady stared in confusion. Then her expression quickly switched to horror. "You let it happen? You let all those poor boys die?"

"Those poor boys signed their life away when they saluted that jack-ass Banahan. If a man is crazy enough to sign with the devil, then he's in charge of his own damn survival."

"But you were a mechanic. Surely you could have done something. What kind of sick soul lets so many die just to save one man?"

Malphia gave her a dark glare then pushed away from the wall. "Look, I really don't care if you believe me or not. But we've got trouble comin' and you got to decide if you're gonna to take me up on my offer to get you and yours out of here before that trouble catches up to us. I'm takin' this ship and I'm getting Slim and me the hell out of here."

Lady watched the woman scale the sloping floor, her boots slipping across the hardwood as she headed for the far corner. She made for a large steel bar sticking out of one of the upended cushioned chairs Sybil had perched on only the day before. Malphia wrapped her fingers around the bar and pulled, releasing a flurry of padding as the bar broke free. "You got a choice, Miss Dewhurst. Either you decide to hold your grudge with me, or you figure a way to let it go. Slim's got enemies and I don't exactly keep many friends. We're on our way out, with you or without. I'd rather have you along, cause I figure there's a good reason you ain't dead yet. And I figure that's cause you ain't exactly a fool."

Lady narrowed her eyes, unsure if she'd been insulted or complimented then realized it had probably been both. Malphia Blackwood knew her way around machinery and no matter Lady's opinion of the woman's questionable moral compass, Malphia could move them all along their journey with significant speed.

It was a risk. But what choice did she have? They were running low on water. Slim was a bad case and they were surrounded by death. Someone would come looking for this ship or notice the remnants of the crash from the distance. At the very least, Eustace or Zhao Jin would make the miles from Albuquerque and close in on their prey. There was little which argued for Lady's continued argument against Malphia.

But she did not have to like it. "I concede your point. We shall join you and take you up on your offer."

Malphia grinned. "Well that's just fine. I'll be gettin' back to my work then." With that, she threw her leg through a window sill and disappeared.

Lady stared, confounded. What was she supposed to do now? After a few moments, she considered shouting for Malphia, but she closed her lips stubbornly. Yet, if she stood their much longer, her fingers would cramp and they'd all die anyway. Perhaps she should rethink her pride.

Malphia's kerchief-covered head popped back in through a window just to Lady's left. "Oh, you can let go of that now. I may be mad but I ain't daft. There ain't no way

I'd ever let this baby blow. She's far too pretty. Now get on out of here and make sure Slim's doin' alright. I don't trust that man y'all got with you."

Lady stared open-mouthed as Malphia disappeared from the window again. That deceitful little... honestly, when had she lost absolute control? If they made it out of this alive, Lady decided she'd find a nice, quiet cabin in the most far distant mountains and wash her hands of all this madness.

As soon as she retrieved the Spanish Hope.

28

Madness followed wherever she ran. Sybil could not remember a time when her life did not spiral with endless machinations of evil and manipulation. She strove for goodness and peace, but always lost to the forces which spread their infamous desires like disgruntled painters with brushes filled with life's insidious offal. In the wake of Mordecai's destruction, Sybil had grown used to offering a small respite to the effects of his magic. What a fool she'd been to think distance would lessen the need.

A flash of reddish orange drew her eye and she changed direction, heading for a small cactus clinging to an outcrop beside the arroyo. The rare succulent tasted acidic and in many cases would induce vomiting, but combined with the leaves she'd collected, they'd flush the system of the evil potion. The tonic she prepared would bind with the more treacherous poisons and sweep it safely from Slim's body. The poultice would ease the ache in the chest that would result from the heaves and shakes which would soon come.

It wouldn't be pretty. But considering the amount ingested, he would be lucky to survive. In truth, she worried she was already too late.

Ingredients in hand, Sybil trekked back to where Slim lay beneath a leafy cottonwood. The sun had crept in as the angle shifted, but with luck, it would keep its most aggressive rays beyond the mask of foliage. There simply was nowhere else to take refuge in the ravaged landscape.

When she returned to Slim's side, Lady was missing and Juan paced in the shade a few trees away. "Where hazz she gone?"

Juan blew out a disgruntled sigh. "Had something to say to the mechanic."

Sybil frowned. A confrontation between Miss Blackwood and Lady would not be pleasant. But she heard nothing to spur her worry. At the moment, the pale-faced Slim was a far more worrisome priority. She kneeled beside him. "Hazz he said anything since I left?"

"Nothin' that made a lick of sense. Sybil, why are you bothering with this man? He's got the look of trouble."

He certainly did, but she supposed the gambler was born that way. "Outcastezz of many colorzz have a way of finding each other. Would you pour me water?" She held up a small tin bowl, confiscated from the remains of the Pinkerton's galley. "He will not appreciate the medicine azz it goezz down, so I will require your assistanzz."

Juan provided the water and then knelt across Slim's body with a begrudging huff. "I had different expectations when I found you. I had hoped--"

Sybil gripped the back of Slim's head by his hair and lifted him up, opening his mouth. She poured the liquid down his throat, causing him to jerk violently in her arms. Juan moved to hold him down, grabbing his flailing arms, effectively changing the direction of his thoughts. Sybil had many questions for her brother, but none that deserved answering above a man in dire need of a miracle. The paleness of Slim's face drew his cheeks deeper, enhancing the pockmarks easily overlooked when he flashed his irascible smile. She felt more sisterly affection to this gambler than she imagined she'd ever feel for the stranger across from her.

Dark and sullen, Juan may have an easy smile, if his thoughts steered away from the burden he attributed to her. What truths did he expect to share? Did she wish to hear them?

"Sybil, beware!" Juan shouted as Slim twisted out of his grip, hands slicing through the air and toward Sybil's throat. She cried out just as his long fingers raked across her skin, tearing a streak of blood with his nails.

Her mind withdrew and she shivered as something foreign struck out from within. She felt her teeth bare and heard an inhuman hiss vibrate from the top of her nasal passages. Her body lunged forward to strike back, but she was hauled backwards and she gave thanks for prayers answered. Something had her mind, the same thing that turned the world around her a faded existence of brilliant color without detail. She could see nothing, but felt everything.

And now, someone on the outside struggled with the beast within. Had she finally lost all control of herself? Had the demon finally staked its claim?

"Sybil, darling. Please. You can control this. You can own this. Do not run. Ride the beast."

She shivered, the voice a deep rumble beside her writhing body. Her hiss echoed through her ears from the inside, her eyes casting about widely, hoping to see something she recognized. A rock, a tree, she did not see them. But they were there, as clear as any bright day.

Something covered her arms, held her tight and vibrated against her ear. A voice, a vibration. Sound and movement. She could hear him, and yet she could not. What madness had overtaken her? Would she ever find a way to sanity again?

"Sybil, do not hide from this. I know you are still there. Come back and I can tell you so much. Come back and I can show you how to command this."

The ground stilled, her body frozen at words she wished to hear. Did the hope in her mind create a fantasy from nonsense? Or perhaps the demon within simply wished to draw her closer to a final confrontation.

"Your friends need you. Do you wish to abandon them so soon?"

Her head snapped to the side, anger and frustration building a rampart from which to see her position. The colors fluctuated with images, the sensations shifting in focus and fighting to gain strength. A face came into view then shifted again into a range of reds and orange. Her angry hiss changed, deepening and moving from her nose to her throat. A victorious and human growl rumbled and she scrambled for the surface of her consciousness. No demon would take her mind from her. No madness could command her.

"That's it, Sybil. Oh you darling girl."

She blinked into the darkly relieved eyes of her brother, his arms still wrapped solidly around her body, her own arms pinned against her side. Her voice emerged as a croak. "Juan, what is happening to me?"

"I wish I could have told you sooner. Perhaps it would have helped."

His arms tightened just before he released her, then he scooted from her side. Slim lay lax beside them, his breathing shallow but unlabored. Guilt fell across her shoulders and she leaned over him to feel his cheeks, hoping that in her madness, he'd at least received a portion of her potion. "Do you know if he drank?"

Juan chucked. "A good half of it came back up, but he kept the rest down."

She sighed in relief. "That should do--for now. I must find more of the flowers. It is so late in the season, I was lucky to find what I did. I suppose I could go further out."

His hand reached out to stop her from rising. "Don't you think it is time that you heard my piece?"

It was time. But she did not relish the idea. Truth could bring clarity and yet knowing might only add mortar to her prison. "What do you know?"

"Did our mother tell you nothing of your condition? Where you come from?"

"Where I come from? I am the daughter of a midnight assignation. My mother wazz a dancer, there wazz nothing unusual in my parentage and azz for my condition, it izz an illnezz that even the most curiouzz physicianss could not identify."

"I imagine shame can make us do terrible things." Juan reached out, but stopped his hand before making contact with her arm. "Our mother was a dancer, yes. But she trained in Spain decades ago where she met my father. Their marriage sent them to the New World, my father a Don, our mother a common but enchanting woman. The Vargas family has a long history in New Mexico and we had beautiful life. We lived in a hacienda in Santa Fe. You would have loved it there."

"Then why would my mother leave? You paint a lovely picture, but you do not look like a man softened by a life of privilege. And my mother would not have chosen such hardshipzz willingly."

His face darkened and she sucked in a breath. He said, "What do you know of the serpent-men that live beneath the mountains?"

"Nothing," she said. But her memories flashed unbidden to Zhao Jin and his insane ramblings. Serpents and gold. There could be no credence given to his belief in the gypsy tales. It simply could not be true.

Juan continued, "There are so many things in this world I would never believe. Had I not seen … Sybil, you must believe me. Our mother was taken by the serpent-men. You are what came of that night. When she was returned to us pregnant, she could not face living with the shame. The next morning she disappeared and I have been searching for her since."

"I do not understand."

"If you continue to seek the land of Cibola, you will understand all too well."

Irritation flared. What nonsense. "You speak in riddlezz and give me no reason to believe you. I know that I am ill, but that izz no cauzz to play easy with my trust." Struggling to her feet, she flung dirt from her knees with a flick of the silk that clung to her body. Too many assumed her simple because of her size, sex, and illness. She did not suffer cruelty such as this well. "Unless you have something with which to prove your allegationzz, I have no further need of your conversation."

"Sybil please, your transformation is only going to get worse. The closer you get to Cibola, the sooner they will gain hold of you and what you are."

She flung her arm in the air and shouted, "You have no clue to what I am! No one can! Not you! Not Zhao Jin, and not MacHurdyGurdy. You are the snakezz in the grass. I am no serpent-child!" The world flushed and shimmered, but for once she did not fear the shift. They wished to warn her of what she was to become? Perhaps it was time she discovered for herself. Fury flexed the skin beneath her scales, the muscles loosened and she stepped toward her quarry, fluid like a dance. No one would prevent her vengeance. No one would stop her from discovering the power of the madness. No one would…

A warmth touched her foot, soft but firm. Kindness pierced her heart and cleared her mind. When she looked down, the vivid colors receded to be replaced by the dust and dirt of reality. And Slim stared up at her, pain in his eyes cloaked in worry. "Hello darlin'. Seem's things have gotten a might out of hand for us all."

Sybil fell to the ground and hunched over her friend, tears streaming down her face. "Oh Slim. What are we to do?"

***

Damn his head hurt like a five day spree at the dirtiest, rowdiest and downright unholiest saloon he'd ever had the chance to frequent. It didn't help that the man making eyes at his girls insisted on droning on and on as Slim clawed his way into consciousness. Course, he didn't have to worry none about the girls takin' care of themselves. Shoot, if he hadn't put out a hand to cool Sybil off, she'd have likely torn the poor sot's arms clean off. Maybe he'd pay to see that. Maybe not.

"What's got you seeping tears, Sybil? You never cry, sweetheart," Slim said.

Sybil wrapped her silks tighter about her body, but he

could still see the drops of tears soaked into the fabric. Her eyes showed bright against puffy red skin. Relieved that her eyes showed green instead of the eerie yellow, he shifted to glance at the unwelcome stranger.

Honest truth, he'd never seen the woman even come close to crying. What had the bastard done to get under his friend's defenses? "This dude givin you trouble, darling?"

"I ain't no dude, friend," the man growled.

"He izz my brother, Juan Vargazz. Half-brother," she said, the last word muffled beneath her breath.

"Well it looks like the half of him that ain't your brother is causin' you trouble," Slim said.

"I rather think it izz the other way around," Sybil said, but her voice lost the frantic fear he'd hated to hear in someone so precious. Hell, he was more brother to this woman than the varmint standing around like a drunk on Sunday morning. "Really, all izz well. The anger izz no doubt a reaction to such difficult experiencezz. It haz not been easy for any of uzz."

"You just give me a word, darling, and I'll take care of him," Slim said. More words sprang to mind as Juan snorted in disbelief, but Sybil's hand on his kept him quiet.

"I would prefer you spend your energy getting well. We have worried so about you. I do believe the Pinkertonzz meant to kill you," Sybil said.

"Sure as hell they did. Don't know how I got out of that mess. Shit, I don't even know how long I've been up in that damn bucket of metal," Slim said.

"Over a week and you smell like it too," a familiar voice said from a short distance away.

Slim craned his neck and swore when he caught sight of the flashy kerchief and wicked grin. "Damnit Phee, what the hell are you doin' here? You nearly got us killed."

"I got you off that damn bucket, and don't you forget it. Ain't nothin' left of it, so don't give me lip about my methods. I already had it out with one of your sweethearts, I ain't in no mood to tackle with you. What I did worked didn't it? You're back with your ladies, right?" The arrogant hussy sniffed at him. Hell, there'd been a time when he'd had that woman smiling like a cat that stole the cream. There wasn't no reason for her to sniff at him.

Slim lifted his head and shifted his hips. When his stomach didn't empty he tried for another inch. Sybil reached under his back and helped him sit up. At least someone still seemed to have a positive opinion of him. With the reception he'd received so far, he'd hate to see how Lady would react. Speaking of Lady… "Where's?"

"What are you all doing sitting around? Good heaven's Slim. You should not be sitting up. Sybil are you certain?" Lady ran toward Slim and he couldn't help the smug grin that spread across his face. When she stopped suddenly, the world tipped and he couldn't stop the roiling sensation in his belly. Damn, she looked just fine. Softer though. Something was definitely different, and it wasn't the man's clothing. Where had she gotten a man's shirt and trousers? He sent another glare toward Juan. Damned if he would let that rotter cause more trouble with his girls.

Lady knelt beside Sybil and helped him sit a little straighter. The attention felt nice, but he wasn't an invalid. Slim said, "I got it. I got it. Come on now, I ain't dyin'."

"You could have fooled me you blasted man," Lady answered, her nose flaring in a frustration. That more than anything made him feel that everything was just right.

"Had you a bit worried, did I darlin'?"

"I just didn't have a shovel handy for your grave. I'm not comfortable leaving a body to the elements."

Slim busted a laugh and grabbed his ribs. Hell that hurt. But damn, she was as prickly as ever. "Missed you too."

"Lady!" A young voice screamed from a distant hill. Slim twisted around to find the source, but Lady had already jumped up and stood between him and the call. The voice continued, growing closer with each word, "The Chinaman and the cavalry. I saw them. I saw them coming across the valley! They've come for me. I know they have."

Lady huffed. "That is hardly likely. They've come for all of us."

Phee reached down and grabbed Slim by the arm. As she pulled she looked at Lady to say, "Seems it's your luck I know a thing about that broken ship of yours. Let's move. I can get us in the air, but I ain't gonna be able to do it on my own."

"Ship?" Slim asked, "What ship?"

Malphia's smile was as mischievous as ever. "Sweetheart, you've missed a whole heck of a lot."

29

Zhao Jin lowered the eyeglass. "Captain, if you want to catch your prize you will ride with due haste."

Martin rode up to Zhao Jin, leading the extra mount they'd procured from the cavalry's ranks. The men to their rear scurried to prepare for a rapid assault. They were tired, pushed beyond their limited training and endurance. Despite the long months on the trail, these men were not yet toughened to the needs of the campaign. Zhao Jin shouted for those ready to embark to follow his lead.

The flash of movement he'd spied the mile across the valley proved that surprise was no longer their ally. The women knew the company was on them and with access to the SteamWing, they would no doubt be in the air long before the horses made the distance, a mocking escape into a cloudless sky.

Unless fortune proved a more generous mistress.

He threw his satchel over his shoulder and mounted the side-stepping steed. With a kick to its flanks, he was off, dust kicking up in their wake, leaving the cavalry behind to find their feet amid the tangled disorder. The sound of Captain Wright's voice carried a short distance as he attempted to bring the men to speed. Only a few joined Zhao Jin and his men.

Martin and he took a swift lead with Joseph close behind. The thundering hooves on approach would mark their location, but there was no time for caution. The serpent would not escape him again.

The horses veered to the left to avoid a dense stand of cacti. Two well-intentioned cavalry men drew up short as they tangled with the unsympathetic plants. Martin shouted a derogatory comment, but sped on, following close to his master. As they drew closer to the crash site, Zhao Jin scanned the area for clues to the women's whereabouts. The green streak of trees to the north would have served as a suitable staging area, one he would have chosen for himself. He pushed that direction, urging his mount on, gritting his teeth as the weight of his braid slapped his back.

The sense of urgency spurred them forward, a quick look to the rear confirming the captain's men were far behind. Perhaps enough of the Pinkerton's men would have survived their ship's demise to assist in the capture. Zhao Jin would not depend on it. He turned his head to Martin as the line of trees came within reach and he nodded. The man reached within his drover coat and pulled out a long-barreled pistol.

"Beware of Sybil, we do not know her condition. I want her unharmed. The others are of no consequence," Zhao Jin shouted above the pounding hooves. Wright would not appreciate injury to Miss Dewhurst, but they could not risk losing the key to Cibola again. By all accounts, Mordecai Kovacs would have discovered its location by now and Zhao Jin could feel the opportunity to thwart his rival slipping away with each delay.

Martin broke to the right to enter the trees as Zhao Jin dove in head on. The heavy rustle to his left indicated that

Joseph also followed the unspoken strategy. They would outflank the women if nothing else.

They emerged from the first line of leafy cottonwoods and entered a narrow clearing, a great scar left by the doomed Pinkerton ship. Zhao Jin pulled back the reins at the sight of the bodies broken in the wreckage. Burnt foliage and twisted metal scattered across the ground, requiring the horse to step tentatively through the wreckage. Martin and Joseph entered the clearing and halted as well, their experienced eyes taking in the situation with swift, unmoved precision.

Zhao Jin valued men of staunch manner.

Shouts further north spurred them forward, beyond the gore of bloody bodies and unsalvageable ship components. A familiar face drew his focus for a split second, the sightless eyes of Banahan peering up from beneath a heavy beam. Zhao Jin sniffed and carried on, the bastard deserving little more than an acknowledgement of his passing, carrion of the least quality.

The trees thinned and they rode down into a shallow wash, the horses losing their footing in the soft sand, slowing the progress. Martin was the first to ride up the embankment, his head down and determined, lust for success heavy on his shoulders. Joseph followed, his seat on the horse more relaxed though no less intense. As Zhao Jin's own horse struggled up the embankment, he heard the cry of a woman caught in fright, the harsh shouts of his men as reply.

When he crested the wash's edge it took a moment to take in the activity. Several figures ran between the horses, a young girl, an unfamiliar man, and an unexpected acquaintance. Zhao Jin calmed his horse and raised a brow at Slim

Robinson, his arm slung over Miss Dewhurst's shoulder as the unknown gentleman attempted to protect them from Martin's charging horse.

The Pinkertons did a shoddy job disposing of the irritating gambler. A girl sprinted from behind a palo verde, startling his mount into throwing its front legs into the air, and forced him to remove his eye from the madness in the clearing. When he had his horse settled, Miss Dewhurst disappeared into another stand of trees, the dark-haired stranger swinging a large metal sheet at Martin in defense of their retreat.

But where was Sybil?

Zhao Jin kicked his horse into action, sweeping around the standing man and following the slow-going Miss Dewhurst. If anyone knew where the serpent slept, it would be that lady. As he came upon the struggling pair, he reached down to grab her by the collar. Miss Dewhurst shrieked, her hands losing hold of her struggling companion. Slim crumpled to the ground beneath the horse hooves, the animal dancing gingerly out of the way. Zhao Jin said, "Tell me, Miss Dewhurst, where is my Sybil?"

"Nowhere you will find her," she spat. A thunderous flap proceeded black wings rising beyond the line of trees where they fought. Miss Dewhurst grinned, "That would be her chariot. Do you recognize it?"

A black snarl lifted his lips and he yanked her hard against the horse's flanks, her feet flying into the air and buckling her knees. He hauled her over the saddle as the horse spun, attempting to avoid the rolling man cursing at its feet. Zhao Jin shouted, "Joseph, stop that ship. Put a hole in it if you have to!"

His men disappeared beyond the branches, followed by

shots and the ping of ricocheting bullets. Miss Dewhurst wriggled, but an assertive slap kept her in place as he led his horse to a vantage point which would keep him clear of battle, but close enough to see the action.

The heavy thump of the giant black wings resounded against the air, trees shivering beneath the force as the cabin came into view. Glass gone, the ship had the vacant look of an abandoned home, evidence of violence sliced into the once extravagant wood exterior. What did they do to his beautiful ship?

A figure stepped into the exposed doorway, silks flapping in the wind, chin lifted in defiance. When Sybil's gaze hit his position, she stiffened and he smirked, his hand stroking his captive's hair. Miss Dewhurst growled, but another sharp slap to the rump quieted her challenge.

"Release her, Zhao Jin!" Sybil shouted from the door. The sound odd for a creature so soft-spoken.

"I shall be happy to make a trade, my child. Come down and we shall negotiate," Zhao Jin said.

"Like hell!" A man swung into view, grabbing the reins and turning the horses head. Zhao Jin grabbed for leverage, but the horse, unhappy with its treatment, bucked and twisted. A sudden shift by Miss Dewhurst made her fall beyond his reach. The pockmarked face of Slim Robinson grinned up at Zhao Jin. He said, "Bout time you started fighting men instead of taking advantage of the little ladies."

"All I see is a broken outlaw," Zhao Jin said, raising his hand to strike at the fair-haired man dodging the horse's hooves. His hand glanced off Slim's shoulder, but the man fell, his condition vastly weakened by the Pinkerton's hands. "What kind of a man must continually be rescued by women? You flirt with a winning hand, Mr. Robinson. But when it is all done, you always end up the loser."

"That's where you are wrong." Slim grinned up at him and flicked his eyes to the right. A sudden flurry of action drew Zhao Jin's focus to the new threat. The great black wing of the SteamWing swung to the side, a massive metal strut headed right for his head. He ducked before the beam struck, but lost control of his seat and fell heavily to the ground. Slim had already risen and said, "I flirt with disaster, but I always win."

"Quit messin' with that bastard, Slim, and git your damn pretty arse on board my ship." The Pinkerton's mechanic piloted the SteamWing, her grim lines bespeaking a competent captain. His nose flared with fury at the theft of his property. That Sybil dared steal his ship, he could forgive, she was a creature of limited humanity and unique characteristics. This new foe would pay for her thievery.

The door of the SteamWing drew closer, the bottom step just above Slim's tall shoulders. Sybil's elegant fingers reached down to take hold of the gambler's hands. Zhao Jin jerked to his feet, determined to reach her before they escaped--again.

"Quickly, Slim." Their fingers met, and the gambler swung into the air, his free arm grabbing hold of the door's metal frame.

Ready to curse in frustration, Zhao Jin stumbled toward Slim's swinging feet, but a third body flew into the scene. Heavy shoulders barreled past Zhao Jin and grabbed hold of Sybil's wrist and yanked. Zhao Jin crowed with the certainty of victory as Martin took control. His man would come through--not all was lost.

But no, he stood stunned as another man jumped from the interior of the ship, dark hair twisting in the wind as his legs kicked at Martin. The stranger fell forward, tumbling from the SteamWing taking Martin with him and leaving Sybil safe within the ship's confines.

"No!" Zhao Jin shouted. But it was too late. Sybil was pulled into the ship by Slim, as it climbed higher into the sky. Her voice cracked in despair, calling out a name--Juan.

Zhao Jin looked down at the man crumpled on the ground at his feet, the impact more severe than expected. Martin scrambled beneath the man's heavy body, but shook his head when asked if the man were dead.

The ship drew away quickly, disappearing into the fading sunlight. There would be no catching them now. What chance was there to predict their direction? Zhao Jin had nothing. The scrolls only told of following the serpent. But if he could not follow her.... how would he--

The man groaned and Zhao Jin threw him a dark scowl. But then his thoughts lightened. Perhaps all was not lost. "Take this man, see that he is cured of his headache. I have need of his clear mind."

Martin nodded as he brushed the dust from his pants. Joseph grabbed the man by the arm and hauled him to his feet. "Boss only said he needs yer mind, stranger. Don't figure you'll be needin' your body for much longer."

Zhao Jin strutted away, determined to reassert his dignity before the cavalry arrived. Had the blasted captain been capable, they may have actually assisted in the doomed maneuver. Damn fortune and her fickle nature. He swatted away a branch and stepped toward more of the Pinkerton's wreckage. There was little left of any use. The ship flew far beyond its expectations, and by the look of the pieces it crumbled into, it had no life left.

"What happened here?" An astounded Captain Wright

stood awestruck across the field. "All these men… did Fidelia have something to do with this?"

"Miss Dewhurst? No I doubt that. It is more likely the work of Slim Robinson," Zhao Jin said.

"The man you mentioned earlier? The one that has her enchanted?"

Enchantment was not a talent one would normally ascribe to the irritating gambler. "The same."

"We must hurry! I did not realize he was capable of such villainy. If she remains under his thrall for much longer, I fear she will end…" Captain Wright paused and the weakness of his spirit showed beneath a false façade of bravado. "We should contact the US Marshalls. They will undoubtedly be interested in this travesty. The Pinkertons have served our country well for many years. To see so many of them cut down so young."

Zhao Jin doubted there were many men financed by the Pinkertons who cared if they benefited the country. But it was neither here nor there. "It is indeed a sad set of affairs. Perhaps you should seek their aid. My men and I will continue on the trail and report the whereabouts of the outlaws as we can."

"That would seem the wisest choice of action."

"Indeed."

"I shall prepare my men. Some will remain here to deal with the dead. I do not suppose we will be able to send the bodies home."

"That would not seem feasible."

"No, I suppose not." The captain looked into the distance, his posture unsure. Zhao Jin imagined the young man warred with the cowardice which would have him give up the fight. There was honor in reporting the wreckage. At least, it would be seen as such. Wright said, "You will be sure to send word of their location."

"Of course," Zhao Jin said. Pleased, when the captain finally took his leave, Zhao Jin turned toward where he'd left his men. They needed to move quickly if they were to keep the SteamWing within reach. When he emerged through the trees into the next clearing, he found Joseph roughing up the captive. Zhao Jin pursed his lips. "That is enough. We have no use for a beaten man."

The stranger spat blood onto the ground at his side. He leaned his head against the cottonwood at his back and narrowed his eyes at Zhao Jin as he approached. Dark hair and brown skin bespoke a native connection, but the aristocratic jaw and arrogant eyes suggested a more European descent. The man said, "So you are the demon that has tormented Sybil for so long."

"Demons are apparitions from faiths I do not ascribe to. Now, tell me, where is she headed?"

"Tell me honestly, Mr. Jin, Are you more interested in where she is or where she is going?"

"That is an interesting question. Why do you ask it?" Zhao Jin considered the man carefully.

"It matters, and will determine how helpful I am." The man's hand rose to sweep away the drop of blood that fell from his nose. Swelling had begun around the eyes and Zhao Jin wondered how recently he'd acquired the injury. He sent a sidelong glance at Joseph.

Zhao Jin said, "Sybil has always been a means to an ends. But she is the only means to that end, so the question is moot."

"If I could prove otherwise?"

"Then that would certainly change things."

The man smiled. "I can take you to Cibola."

30

The trail grew wearisome. Mordecai desperately craved the comforts and conveniences of the city life. Once, long ago, he'd nearly grown compliant within the ease of a civilized life. At the time he'd thought it a bad thing. Now, he was not so certain. His hat over his eyes, Mordecai let the rocking motion of the cart soothe his anxious spirit. As they drew closer to their destination, the fear of failure mixed with the anticipation of success. Much like an opening night, the promise of treasure held a mystical sense of unease which only came with things where you risked it all. There is nothing comfortable about victory. One must give it all up to win it all.

A hushed murmur came from his sister-in-law as she leaned toward her husband. Tucked together on the cart bench, one would think she would worry that her drowsy brother-in-law would hear her. Not that he'd ever attributed more than the most modest of intelligence to the woman, but she displayed tact at higher levels in the past. Now, she grumbled over the slightest infringement, determined to wreak havoc on his tirelessly prepared plans.

"He will be the end of us, you know that Bernard."

"Hush, Bea. That is nonsense." His brother's voice sounded tired. With the lessening of Bernard's melancholy,

Mordecai had been heartened by the hope they could soon enjoy the benefits of their labors. But if this trip exhausted them beyond recovery, what point would there be in it all?

"Don't be a fool. He is leading us to what? A city of gold? If Cortez could not find this place, what makes him more likely?" Beatrice huffed at Bernard's noncommittal reply. "Even if we do make it to the city, do you truly believe he will include us? He has always taken the largest share of all we have done. Do you forget the distribution of our earnings with the traveling show?"

"The bulk of sales came from the elixir. You know that. Besides, he always reinvested the money into the show. We wouldn't be here without him, Bea." Bernard's nearly limitless patience finally appeared at its end and for once, Mordecai rejoiced over Beatrice's waspish nature. He would never doubt his brother's loyalty, not even a wife could come between brothers. Nothing tied two people together quite like blood.

The snap of reins against the beast's neck echoed in the following silence. Mordecai smiled beneath the hat's rim. They would arrive at the entrance to Cibola within the week. And soon, everything would fall into place exactly as it should be.

The brother's Kovacs would be kings on earth.

***

Death clung to her, its stink a halo over her head like a promise. None of the tragedy would have occurred if she simply let them free of their obligation for vengeance. Had she simply offered Slim a respite from death and left it at that, neither Slim nor Lady would face the imminent threat of their destruction. Had she never left the covetous hands of Zhao Jin, Juan might still be well.

Now, with her choices bound to this adventure and the fates of those she loved, Sybil knew she would never find peace in the madness.

Not while the madness curried favor with evil.

Sybil huddled in a corner of the SteamWing's cabin among torn cushions and shredded carpet. Across the floor, Slim lay with his back against the wall, a window without glass just above his head. The howling of the wind made hearing the conversation difficult, but by Lady's harried expression, she and Slim were arguing once more. The two would not be happy if they did not have each other with which to bicker. If nothing else good had come of the escapade, at least Slim and Lady were back together.

The walls rattled and floor vibrated as Malphia wrestled with the controls, admirably maintaining altitude in a ship that fought her every moment. The audacious mechanic had more fight in her than half the American army and Sybil figured her twinkling eye caused more mischief by half.

And they were each on their way to ruin. All because of a malicious man with a cart full of seditious intentions. What point was there to vengeance if no one survived? What use was a promise of revenge for slights done to their person if they were destroyed in the process? Slim may think he deserved recompense for Mordecai's attempt on his life, but the continued suffering and persistence made no sense. Perhaps if she gave up this game, he would too.

But what of Lady? She too suffered a near death at the hands of Mordecai Kovacs. Would Lady easily forget? What of the locket she desperately sought? Could Sybil plead that she let the past lie?

Sybil watched the two across the way. The set shoulders and conviction in their eyes rarely faltered. The inevitability of disaster swirled like a fractious storm of sand and glass shards, impending failure closing in on her intentions, promising an end to an otherwise unremarkable life. The font of positivity which had spurred her forward beyond the constant barrage of adversity wavered on a precipice she had no desire to fight.

What was left for her but misery?

"Dios," a short cry sounded as a stumbling form tripped beside Sybil. Carmen reached for her shoulder to halt her fall, causing a wrenching pain so deep within, Sybil lost sight of the world and fell deep into the image-devoid world of color and sensation. She felt a scream vibrate and for one brief moment before losing herself to the cursed monster within realized the scream belonged to her.

Bright light fluctuated with dark, menacing shadows, amassing the fear in an amorphous puddle at her feet. A strange power flowed through her skin, prickling nerves that sent fires of sensation across her scales. Once soft and tender, they tightened, growing like a shirt of chainmail surrounding her with a certainty of purpose. Beyond the limited scope of her vision she felt something pull, its call demanding and yet comforting.

Words unspoken came as a hiss across her subconscious, beckoning her forward, calling her name, speaking in a language unfamiliar yet comprehensible. Serpent's daughter. Child of the ancients. Savior from the sun.

Suddenly, a vision stuck her mind with such vivid detail it rivaled any of the moments in her most lucid state. A great city soared into view, abandoned and yet remarkably pristine. Great walls rose toward the bluest of skies, cloudless and shining in the glory of the sunlight. Sybil soared above, staring into hundreds of round depressions, their purpose unknown. Stone walls built with exacting precision bespoke a dedication nearly inhuman.

Beyond the walls a rocky stream cut through a long canyon, severe cliffs climbing high and shading the city. Long roads led through the land, empty but lined for procession, promising a great migration, supplicants on their way to something greater than the meagerness of life on earth. A great shiver took Sybil as the enormity of the place gathered as a storm. The canyon screamed for her presence.

Figures rose, slithering through shadows at the base of the cliffs. Flashes of yellow eyes blinked in the sunlight then disappeared beneath giant boulders. Not human, not animal. Sybil cried out.

A scream replied, wrenching her from the vision. Danger slashed a warning, bright lights returned in red and orange. Sybil coiled, turning her head to the vibrations that threatened. Flaring heat sources came at her from all sides, threatening, urging her to strike.

Her hands rose, nails bared like talons, slashing forward and connecting with self-preserving force. Something clamped onto her arms and she wriggled in desperation, seeking freedom, terrified of the mysterious forces that held her captive. Sybil bared her teeth then bit down, tasting metallic liquid as it met her tongue.

A heavy force knocked her head back and darkness erupted behind her eyes. The back of her head slammed against the floor and the world paused, all motion slowed, and sound shifted back to the crazed cacophony of a normal day.

But nothing was normal. It never had been.

Furious eyes glared down at her, Malphia's hand clenched and her lips turned up in a snarl. Sybil struggled to make sense of it all. "Pleaz."

"Please nothing you crazy bitch. You nearly killed that poor girl."

Sybil turned her head and found Carmen held tightly in Lady's arms, her head hidden from view. Horror covered Lady's expression; Slim's a mirror of the same. Her brother's revelations prior to their harried escape from Zhao Jin fell into focus, thoughts of his fantasy turned tangible. Could she truly be the spawn of something unworldly? Could that explain her now?

Uncomfortable beneath the accusatory stares, she moved to sit, but Malphia stopped her with a foot to the gut. "Don't get any ideas. You got a mean streak and I ain't about to let you loose on anyone else."

"You must understand, I do not mean any harm. I do not know what izz happening to me any more than you do," Sybil said.

"Even more reason for you to stay right where you are."

"Get your foot off of her, Phee. She ain't gonna hurt anyone," Slim said, the shock of the experience wearing off. Ever the resilient man, he bent down and assisted Sybil to her feet. "Come on darlin', let's get you settled and we'll all figure out what's goin' on with you."

"She's gone mad, that's what's wrong with her," Malphia answered with a jerk of the head.

"Man the controls. We can take it from here," Lady said. Malphia grumbled with discontent but turned her back nonetheless. After a few hushed words to Carmen, Lady sent the frightened girl to a cushioned corner of the cabin, far from further threat. Haunted eyes accused her from beneath darkened brows. Perhaps there had been truth behind Carmen's fears. At the moment, Sybil felt more monster than human.

Slim ran a comforting hand down her back, then guided her to one of the hastily repaired chairs. The wood creaked with her slight weight, but she held still and it made no more complaints. Lady joined them, crouching to put a hand to Sybil's knee.

"It is time we know what is going on. Do you have no idea of the cause of your fits?" Lady asked.

Oh there were so many ideas. Were it madness she could accept it, but this new doubt, this unbelievable suggestion, it hardly bore thinking. "I am not certain. My brother...he said many thingzz that I could not believe. But now..."

"What things, darlin'?" Slim asked.

"I find it more palatable to be mad."

Lady sniffed as she stood and crossed her arms over her bosom. "I find that unlikely. You have been at times the most sane of us all."

"Izz it sane to encourage your quest for vengeance? Izz it sane to put you repeatedly in harmzz way? No, I fear I am far more the villain than Mordecai Kovaczz could ever be."

"That phony don't got nothing on you. You're damn near a saint compared. Now, stop that nonsense and say what your brother told you," Slim said.

Sybil blinked at her friends and wondered at the easy faith they had in her. Had months on the trail truly formed a bond so strong that they would ignore the warnings and press on foolhardily? Perhaps it was her duty to end this. "He believezz I am turning into a serpent."

Silence followed her pronouncement. Those words had

not been entirely true. Juan made allusions to such a notion, but in truth, his suggestion was far less bald. But by far, her interpretation was more appropriate. She felt the serpent crawling within her. What else could explain the behavior when she was taken by the madness? Whether it be a madness that made her feel akin to the slithery reptiles or a truth in her transformation, it was the only way she could explain it. She wore the skin of a serpent, why not complete the turn.

"That is ridiculous. I do not believe it," Lady huffed

"I can feel it calling me. Thizz serpent within me. I lose sight of my humanity and strike out at thoze I love. How else can you explain it?"

"I think that Chinaman's evil words have finally won their way into your mind. You are beginning to believe his foolishness. You are no more a serpent than Slim or I. You may be ill, you may be troubled by the unimaginable events we have endured. I myself have not gone without a touch of madness from this all. In truth, the only solution I see is setting forth and completing this quest and finding our peace."

"Why do you seek Mordecai? Do you truly desire vengeanzz? Would you not find peaze together, away from the evilz that man and Zhao Jin have wrought? If you leave now, you will all survive unscathed and live a good life."

Lady and Slim stared at her and for once she was able to catch the flicker of doubt, their reserve of conviction fraying under the tension. With a prod in the right direction, she might end this now. But then Slim cocked his head to the side. He narrowed his eyes and said, "If we were to give this up, darlin', would you come with us?"

Sybil could only stare back at him. The call to the great stone city still hung heavily in her heart. There would be no stopping her journey, not until the she had met the end of this story and learned what truth was there for her.

Slim grinned and tipped his hat up. "Well then, I suppose that's my answer then. You gonna tell us where we're headed?"

31

Sybil told them to go north. Lady knew as each mile passed, they only drew closer to a confrontation she hadn't yet prepared for completely. As the sun settled into the horizon to the left, she wondered if her pride and familial obligation were truly worth it all.

But when she saw the sad desperation in Sybil's eyes, she knew there would be no stopping now. If Lady could guarantee Sybil would quit the search for Cibola and MacHurdyGurdy, she might do the same. However, something new and undeniably compelling had Sybil streaking toward an unknown future. A future which held the unfortunate tint of doom.

The SteamWing tilted forward and gently descended toward the ground. Flat and lacking plant life, it would be a suitable landing zone. But why? Lady strode toward Malphia, rigidly standing before the controls. Lady said, "What are you doing? We have not reached our destination."

"Nor will we tonight or even tomorrow." Malphia yanked at a lever and the steam hissed from the tall pipe at the back of the cabin. Heat swam across the floor and Lady sent a concerned look at the source. The machine had held for the time, but now she worried. Malphia continued, "It will be a dark night, even with the moon, and we have no forward lights. I'm in no mood for dodging mountains blind. Are you?"

"Landing would seem wise."

"Quite. It'll give me time to make a few adjustments. This ain't like the Pinkerton's monster; it's efficient, but can't carry fuel for long trips. So expect to be haulin' wood." The ship shuddered as the ground grew frighteningly close, but Malphia handled the controls with confidence. Lady tried to take comfort in that. "Hold on, this might hurt," Malphia shouted over the groans of the reluctant landing sleds as they untucked from the sides of the ship.

Lady grabbed for the nearest solid table, but miscalculated and stumbled. A steady hand grabbed her by the elbow and held her secure as the ship rocked. A sudden jarring bounce sent her feet from under her and she fell back into a solid chest. Slim grinned down, but said nothing, being strangely courteous.

Once landed, they disembarked, but Lady noticed Carmen hang back. Concern sent her to the girl's side. "Do not fear. Sybil does not mean you harm, it was an unfortunate accident."

"They come for me. The serpiente. Mama always told me beware the serpientes. I only thought…" Carmen glanced toward Sybil. "I thought they would be men."

"Please, Carmen. Sybil is a good woman. She will not hurt you."

Carmen narrowed her eyes. "How can you be certain?"

"She can't, which is why you will stick with me." Malphia stepped in from where the others had departed, her eyes stern as they took in Lady's response. But all she received was a slight nod in reply. Lady had hoped to bring Carmen to a better place, and yet all she did was put her in danger. It would have been best to find her a home, far from the insanity of their quest. Perhaps Malphia's watchful sentry was the best they could offer.

If nothing else, it might keep the mechanic occupied.

Lady followed the woman and girl from the cabin, a strange uncertainty to her steps. When she set out, three years ago, she felt the excitement of adventure and the rise of self-assurance that only comes when one is convinced of the rightness of things. Then as the adventure drew out in a succession of lost trails and missed opportunities, she'd developed a sense of righteousness that comes with adversity.

All of it felt suddenly fanciful. For the sake of a bauble, she'd left her home, a comfortable, albeit restricted lifestyle, and risked everything.

When she held the cold metal locket in her hand, would it feel right?

A soft touch to her shoulder startled her from the depth of her thoughts. Slim said, "Come eat, I doubt you've had more than hard tack in days."

Lady scanned the area, unable to find the woman in flowing silk. How could someone whose clothing flowed like flags in the wind just disappear? "Where is Sybil? She really shouldn't be alone."

"That's one woman that can do alright alone. She won't go far. Now, I'm more concerned about you. I ain't never seen you look like a washed up prairie dog before."

"A washed-up prairie dog? How dare you? Despite our obvious troubles, we have not fallen so far that common courtesy is not called for. I swear, Slim Robinson, you have to be the most brutish, uncivilized, uncouth, un...un--,"

Slim belted out a laugh and she stopped in her tracks. Damn the man, he was deliberately goading her. "Sometimes I truly worry about the soundness of your mind."

"Seems we're all worried about our minds lately. Come on, I'm gonna get a fire started then make us some real coffee and if you're lucky, something more than them stale crackers." He led her to a small patch of cleared grass. Several large boulders lined the area which would serve well as a wind-break. Lady leaned against one, the fatigue hitting her with a swift intensity.

When time slowed and the fright of the chase dissipated, the body remembered the aches and pains in great detail. A twist to her wrist indicated a strain where she'd pushed the ligaments beyond usual. She couldn't remember when she'd injured it. She'd survived in relatively decent condition, though she'd not anticipate feeling her normal self for quite some time. The fact that Slim, so soon since his incapacitation, moved with a practically youthful exuberance was suspect.

She saw a flash of her father in Slim, a slight resemblance which until now remained hidden. By any other eye, they would see a no-account drifter with no purpose and no prospects. He played the part of a gambler with no home and kept his interactions light and uncommitted.

Slim Robinson was a liar.

Realization stained her cheeks red as she realized how much admiration she'd developed for him in the time they'd been apart. Despite his mischievous antics, he'd kept the three of them on the trail with little worry and less danger than she'd seen in the short days since he'd been captured. He watched the world with a wary eye when no one looked his way. Calculating and clever, he'd covered himself with an illusion and even she'd fallen for it. Damn the man.

Lady asked, "Why do you continue this? What do you

mean to do when we find MacHurdyGurdy?"

"Man's got a right to confront his murderer." Slim stooped over the fire, encouraging the flames to burn down to coals to facilitate the boiling of the pan of water waiting to the side.

"He did not succeed. It would seem that is revenge enough." Lady closed her eyes, feigning disinterest in the conversation. But when she opened them, Slim stood facing her, his expression frank.

"You want to quit?" he asked.

"No," she huffed. "But we could. I simply wonder why, after all you have suffered, you would want to continue on. I at least desire to retrieve my property. What could a man like you want with Mordecai MacHurdyGurdy? You won't kill him. You are no killer."

"You don't know that." He turned back to the fire.

Lady chuckled. "Oh but I do. So why are you still on this quest?"

Slim's shoulders relaxed and she knew she'd lost before his words came. "Darlin', there ain't nothin' complicated about it. I just don't got nothin' better to do."

Another lie. Heaven help her from stubborn men. Lady pushed away from the boulder and stalked to the chest of supplies Slim had foraged from the SteamWing. Thankfully, Zhao Jin prepared for a long trip and stored the contents well. The exterior of the ship barely survived the adventure, but they would do with what had been found within. Lady threw open the lid and sighed. At least Slim hadn't lied about feeding her better food.

A beautiful collection of canned peaches stared back at her. Oh heaven, she hadn't had peaches in quite some time.

***

The pemmican took a while to soften in the stew, but Slim figured they could all use a little patience. Time had run so hard, none of them knew which way was up and where the devil was comin' from. At least, he had lost track and by the looks of her, so had Lady. Shoot, the girl looked like a lost lamb for a good portion of the day, and it sure as hell wasn't like her.

A pain sliced into his gut and he sucked in a breath, cautious to hide the spasm from the women sitting around the fire. Sybil's concoctions did a lot in to help him recover from the damn demon piss Banahan poured down his gullet, but he was a long way from feelin' fine. Didn't serve them any good if the girls caught on though. They had enough troubles as it was.

"Where exactly is it y'all think your snakey friend will take you?"

"Bite your tongue, she is no snake." Lady glared at Malphia and Slim hid a smile. He would love to see Lady put that sidewinder in her place. Phee hadn't met many women who could take her on and he'd bet a good hand Lady would come out on top. Lady continued, "And she is leading us to rendezvous with an old enemy."

"I've never known anyone that thought following a madwoman into the desert was a good idea."

"You do not need to come. We can do quite well without you."

"Well, I know you can't, not after seein' what you did to that beautiful ship. Poor thing would be buried in ten feet of sand by now if I hadn't come and brought it back to life."

Lady snarled. "We did well enough."

"Here." Slim handed Lady a tin cup of coffee, the interruption enough to throw her off guard. He looked to Malphia. "You done riling her up? We got plenty of troubles, we don't need your bad attitude to make it worse. Now, you got something on your mind, so just say it."

Malphia's catlike smile stood up the hairs on his neck. He'd seen that look before. She was ready to make a deal. "You always did know me and my moods, Slim, darlin'. And you're right. I do want something. The Pinkertons ended up not being as lucrative an employment opportunity as I'd hoped. But here I am, with one of the prettiest ships that's ever been built practically dropped in my lap. I could say I'd claim salvage rights, but I don't think your haughty friend would go for that."

"You are correct in that, at least. We claimed it from Zhao Jin. It is ours," Lady said.

"And without me, you'd still be fightin' off the cavalry on the ground. Not to mention, it was your fault I lost my job in the first place."

"How do you figure that, Phee?" Slim asked. He stirred the stew again. Damn he was hungry. He finally had a settled stomach and he couldn't get the food to cook fast enough. Out of the corner of his eye he watched Lady shift uncomfortably. The men's clothing had to irritate, but he was glad to see she'd removed the corset. That she'd done so in the company of another man created an altogether different feelin'. Well, she wasn't his woman. She could change clothes for just about whoever she wanted.

"Before you all came on board the Pinkerton's ship, we were headed for a town with replacement parts. Then you show up and old Tommy got so distracted, he didn't care that we were all gonna die. I told him, but damned if he didn't listen." She paused and smiled again. "Course, I might have helped things along the way, seein' as how you needed to get off that boat before they killed you."

"You saying I owe you my life?" Slim asked before Lady could jump in with her own comment.

"Nope. I'm sayin' you owe me a ship. And I want the SteamWing. I'll get you where you need to go, but after that, you give me that ship and we'll call it even."

Lady sputtered with indignation, but Slim stood, straightening his entire tall frame. Malphia raised a brow and Carmen shrunk back, tucking herself into the side of the crafty mechanic. He gave his own wolf-like smile and said, "Well, it ain't my ship. So I can't make that deal."

Lady said, "The way I see it, we saved you from the cavalry. By your own admission you helped that ship fall from the sky. What would stop them from holding you accountable? You were the mechanic were you not?"

"Who do you think you're gonna get to fly that thing? And you don't even know where you're goin'. It could be months before you find that damn city of gold. Not that I think you'll ever find it to begin with. You think you can keep that thing runnin' without me?"

"I think we could do just about anything without you." Lady sneered, leaning forward, ready to jump to action. Slim wondered if he should interject or just let the fur fly. He coughed and another piercing pain hit his side. That settled it, the girls could fight it out between them. Honestly, he wasn't sure which had the advantage, having seen both in action.

"It izz a good deal. We shall take it."

Silence fell around the fire as all four heads spun around to see Sybil standing in the shadows. The woman walked with grace and poise, a cool reminder of the exotic beauty Slim spied so many months ago in Tucson. She could take a man's breath away by simply walking into a room. Without the affliction, she could have courted the most powerful of men. Slim was just happy she'd thought he was worth knowing.

"Sybil, it is our ship," Lady said.

"Yezz, and we need a captain. Mizz Blackwood izz one we can trust, even if she hidezz it well. It will not take long, a few dayzz at most. She will have her ship and we will have Mordecai."

Lady blinked at Sybil, but did not protest. When Phee realized she'd won, she held her victory close to the chest. Slim would have to congratulate her later on her restraint. Something hot splashed against his hand and he looked down to see the stew bubbling furiously. With a hoot of success, he bent over the pot. Finally, now they could eat.

32

"You know that we are being followed?" Juan said.

Zhao Jin knew and had known from the beginning the captain would not leave them to their purpose. Half an hour earlier, Martin began to lag behind, stalling enough to gauge the extent of their pursuers. The report Martin brought back and relayed under hushed tones only confirmed expectations. One man followed, keeping no less than two hundred feet at their back, his movement untutored to covert tracking. Zhao Jin was only slightly surprised the captain assigned himself the task.

"It appears someone has abandoned their post," Zhao Jin answered, stopped and nodded to his assistants. They immediately swung their horses around and raced back the way they'd come. Juan jumped from his horse and wrapped the reins around a palo verde branch then leaned against the trunk, his arms crossed over his chest.

Little had become apparent about the man, beyond the shared desire to catch up with Sybil. The two had developed a watchful compromise, but Zhao Jin knew in the end, they would be competitors for the same prize. What motivated the man, however, remained elusive. Juan was a random player, a new detail that did not fit in the neat patterns he'd come to understand. Despite looking to be in his early twenties, the man lacked the usual impetuousness of youth, his eyes holding a familiar glint of old world knowledge.

"How do you come to know of Cibola?" Zhao Jin asked the young man.

"Who does not know about the ancient cities? Cortez's failure."

"Ah yes, but most men know them only as stories."

Juan simply smiled. But before Zhao Jin could prod further Martin and Joseph rode forward, leading a distressed Wright by his horse's reins. Zhao Jin said, "Captain, we are surprised to see you."

The only man to react to the blatant lie was Wright. He protested incomprehensibly and Zhao Jin cut him off. "I am certain there is a brilliant reason for abandoning your command, I trust you left behind a capable successor?"

"My orders are to find Miss Dewhurst, sir. Not be nursemaid to boys wanting to chase Indians."

"I imagine those that provided your commission would think differently," Zhao Jin said.

"Do you know Mr. Dewhurst? He is no man to disobey. His orders are to secure Miss. Dewhurst."

Zhao Jin did not answer. He had extensive knowledge of the shipping magnate. Anyone at all interested in business knew of the man and his power to wield the highest bureaucratic influence. It meant little to Zhao Jin the weasel-like captain would risk court martial for the Dewhurst woman. However, having the man ride with them only created another detail to track. Another's whose goal may conflict with his as they approached the end.

The captain was useless and would be disposed of, when the time became appropriate. As the Dewhurst pawn, it would be only a piece more difficult to orchestrate.

"Are you done? Or should I go on ahead while you all have tea?" Juan asked.

Martin and Joseph exchanged glances, but Zhao Jin said, "Please, lead us forward." A look from their master kept Martin and Joseph in check, but he would release their talents soon enough.

By the way Juan kept his thoughts shrouded, he was aware of the danger. The captain—not so well.

Zhao Jin kicked the horse into action, mind open to the situation, waiting for the right moment. It would come, it always did and then he could focus his attention entirely on the problem of Kovacs.

***

The valley was less than impressive. A green scar cut through the center, a small testament to what had once been a river with enough power to carve such a wide canyon. Now, brown grasses and rocky sand covered the majority of the valley floor, showing pockets of green where a few plants eked out enough moisture to grow. The cottonwoods lining the central creek were shorter than those they'd encountered throughout the southwest, dense, and withered. Mordecai doubted they'd find water on the surface.

Water was a sparse commodity in much of the west, here it was practically non-existent. He lifted his lip in distaste. This was hardly the place he imagined to find a golden city. But perhaps the very nature of its inappropriateness kept it hidden all these years.

Perhaps...

"What is that?" Bernard asked, his hands shading his eyes as he looked to the east. Against the northern canyon wall tall structures rose unnaturally high, casting angular shadows and impressions of civilized settlement. The silence implied abandonment.

The cart rumbled across an alignment of stones, half buried and overgrown with the same dry grass that covered the rest of the valley. But when the fourth wheel settled on the other side of the stones, Mordecai held out a hand to his brother and ordered him to stop. He stood and looked to either side of the cart. An impression in the ground ran for miles to the west, clear of anything taller than the knee-high grass. To the east, it continued toward the strange walls Bernard had pointed out. "It's a road."

"If this place is such a secret, why would they build a road?" Beatrice asked.

"It would not have always been a secret, now would it my dear?" Mordecai said. Roads did not lead to nothing, and if not Rome, perhaps this road led to Cibola. "Let us follow this."

Beatrice grumbled then held onto the bench seat to keep her balance while Bernard encouraged the mules forward. "It will be an easier ride, Bea, hang on," Bernard said.

They followed the overgrown road for a good mile before they approached the entrance to what looked like a large pueblo, much like those they'd encountered in Zuni. Except, at the same time they were nothing like Zuni. Tall walls with immaculately cut and sized bricks rose three to four stories up, perfectly straight and rivaling the masonry skill of anything built in the great cities of Europe. These walls lined the entire settlement, and Mordecai jumped down from the cart to take a closer look.

One crumbling section provided an entrance leading into a large inner courtyard. He stepped into the surreal town, empty and mysterious without a look to his brother. Something drew him forward, a new urgency, much like a fever. He could feel the power of the place, the promise intoxicating.

A few steps in, he spied several large round walls, covered in lattice and earth, they reminded him of the subterranean room they'd found in the Zuni pueblo. But these were significantly larger. When he stood beside one such wall, he could spy through several crumbling holes into the room below. Plastered floors, beautiful in their cleanliness sparkled in the light of the harsh sun. Great care went into the building and maintenance of these structures.

He continued his tour, ducking into a doorway, opened to the elements, but short and narrow so that he had to bend to enter. The interior of the front room provided relief from the sunlight and the temperature dropped by several degrees. A second doorway across the room beckoned, and he followed the impulse, exploring a vast array of rooms. Ladders, still standing after what had to be hundreds of years, led to the subsequent floors which he imagined led to even more rooms, but Mordecai resisted the urge to test the ancient wood's hardiness.

Beautifully hewn and clean, the rooms were awe inspiring--but empty.

Whatever the rooms were used for, habitation was not one. The buildings felt permanent, but the presence of humanity felt temporary, as though they were never quite welcome. He left quickly, certain the mystery of Cibola was not to be found within the walls of those buildings, and returned to the cart.

Bernard stood beside the mules, his eyes staring vacantly into the distance. Concern settled heavily in Mordecai's belly when he caught his brother's lapse into one of his morose moods. Mordecai said, "It is quite remarkable, brother. The craftsmanship is far beyond anything we have seen in this savage land. I do believe we are close. Closer than we ever have been."

"It shouldn't surprise you. There is something about this place. Something different. I think you may be right. We are close to the end of our journey."

"Then why the sadness? It is not as though you have particularly enjoyed this journey. Is not being at the end a cause for celebration?"

Bernard turned slowly away from the horizon, the smile at his lips not quite touching his eyes. "It is indeed. But first, I would settle my stomach. Bea is setting camp. Do you believe we will stay here into the night?"

"I would not wish to sleep within those walls," Mordecai said, indicating the settlement he had just left. "Another night beneath the stars would be wise. We have plenty of light, however, so I will continue my reconnaissance. Do you wish to join me? There could be clues to our fortune behind any of these walls."

A slight sparkle finally reached his brother's eyes. "I do believe you are nearly giddy. I have not seen you so excited since we were boys."

Mordecai lowered his brows. "Don't be foolish. If you do not wish to come, see to the mules. We may have need of their assistance in the days to come and they should be well rested."

"Of course." Bernard put his back to Mordecai and worked to release the mules from the cart. Mordecai tried to think of softer words before they parted, but he could feel frustration working its way into his mind. It would be better to do this on his own. It always had been.

After a quick stop in the cart to retrieve a canteen and provisions for a short trek beyond their camp, he pulled his hat low over his forehead to ease the wind which rose to bite his skin. A short distance away, his sister-in-law struggled to start a fire as her skirts lifted to tangle in her legs. If the wind continued to rise, it would be an uncomfortable night, enough that he might reconsider the benefits of sleeping within one of the abundant, abandoned rooms.

Determined to worry about the coming night at a later time, he struck out to explore the backside of the structures. As he walked, he marked the curve of the layout, finally coming to the conclusion that the entire settlement was built as a large half-moon shape. It was an odd shape and unlike any he'd seen previously. While the walk proved interesting, he was no closer to solving the riddle of Cibola.

It had to be here. This was the place they'd seen in the mountain clearing, he was sure of it. So why was the answer so elusive?

He tucked his fingers into his vest pocket and retrieved the lockets. They hung like pendulums, swinging from his outstretched fingers as he lost himself in thought. What clue had he missed? There was no hint of gold in the settlement. No paintings, no symbols. Nothing but a perfectly designed community with the look of never being lived in.

Why would they make such beautiful walls and never live within them?

Flashes of light shot from the lockets to the walls of the canyon, only twenty feet from the exterior of the settlement. Mordecai watched as the light played over the rock, giving nothing but a sense of useless exercise. The feeling he'd come all this way to be stymied by empty rooms and a dry valley weighed heavily. But it took years to get to this point. He could not expect the city of gold to give up its secrets the moment he set foot in its vicinity. There were miles of canyon to explore, crevices to investigate, more settlements just like this one to explore. Any number of locations within a ten mile radius could give him the answers he sought.

The biggest question was whether he could keep Beatrice out of his way long enough to find it. Her traitorous comments over the last week grew more frequent. If he wanted a justifiable reason to be rid of her, she'd provided plenty. But still, he could not see his brother forgiving him should she experience some mishap at his hand. Unfortunately the woman was far too clever to put herself in harm's way without his assistance. The removal of that particular nasty baggage would have to wait until after they'd procured their fortune.

It might even be more pleasurable that way. One could hope.

"Mordecai!" His brother's voice echoed against the canyon walls, the tenor of his voice sending shocks of warning through Mordecai's spine. Without thought, he ran toward the cart, conscious enough of his movements to tuck the lockets back into his vest pocket. Whatever made his brother shout his name would no doubt be of great concern. Bernard rarely raised his voice above a soft murmur let alone call across great distance.

When he reached his brother, Beatrice had also joined them, staring curiously into the distance. She said, "What on earth is that? It looks a bit like a black eagle, doesn't it?"

"It's far too big to be a bird. Look how far away it is. Those wings have to be twenty feet long," Bernard said.

Mordecai stared into the distance, a sense of dread in

the pit of his stomach. Only man could create such a monster of the sky. He had many enemies, though few knew his true purpose. The few included his rival Zhao Jin. It would not be beyond the Chinaman to track his foe to this spot and attempt to steal his glory from beneath his grasp.

"We may have use of our shotguns," Mordecai said. "There is little point in hiding from them. So we must prepare to protect our discovery."

"Discovery? And protect from whom? You cannot believe those are people in the sky," Beatrice said.

"Of course it is people. Now move. We haven't much time." Mordecai stepped to the leeside of the cart. The ship, beautiful in its darkness moved slowly across the sky, but he would expect it to meet them by dusk. If it were Zhao Jin, he anticipated a long evening dodging double meanings and cautious interrogations. Unless he brought his goons. In which case, he might be beaten quite severely. Mordecai was not certain which he would prefer.

For once, it was advantageous he had yet to discover the final clue to Cibola, for as it were, he had the promise of discovery as barter. It would give him time to settle his feud with Zhao Jin. Preferably a final settlement--if fortune proved sweet.

33

The world felt lighter, like all the hinges failed and a door fell open, never to close properly again. Sybil stared across the valley, the vast and empty settlements peppering the borders, silent in sound, but glaring in purpose. She was stepping from a dream into a world that felt more real, more solid, more right.

She felt strangely at home.

"Do you see that? I think that's a cart. We couldn't have found him this easily," Lady said with disbelief, bending over the console to draw closer to the only glass to survive the crash days earlier. Malphia grunted and asked for room, sending Lady several paces away. The two women developed a working truce, but neither had moods that melded well. In another place and another time, the two may have been quite good friends. Sybil imagined they'd make the most impressive team. But the situation painted a much different path for the two of them.

Lady said, "Should we go right up to them? Perhaps an assault from the sky would be effective."

"You plan on killing him, darling?" Slim asked.

Lady blanched and looked away quickly. "I honestly hadn't thought this far ahead."

"Revenge ain't a simple thing. You want to kill him or

just get your locket?" Slim leaned against the console, ignoring Malphia's grumbles about not having enough space to breathe.

"I don't really wish to kill anyone," Lady replied and Slim smiled.

Sybil eyed them both warily. She'd come quite a long ways for them to find their vengeance. But then, perhaps it was a far too selfless way to see things. There had always been an unseen force drawing her along this course, just as it had so many years ago as she ran from Zhao Jin to only find a new cage within the MacHurdyGurdy's Traveling Show. It was a relatively pleasant cage, yet something kept drawing her forward, pushing her toward something she never quite understood.

Cibola. She could feel it thrum deep within her blood. The scales along her arms flexed and the beast within held itself at bay only out of courtesy for her companions. The cliffs surrounding them had the look of earthen walls, but a purpose reminiscent of the heavy canvas curtains used on stage. All the mystery and anticipation would soon be released in a torrent of grand showmanship. A play for the ages.

Sybil shook with the energy of the place.

"Are you all right?" Lady asked. "Perhaps we should turn back. It may be that none of this is truly worth it."

"Land the ship, Malphia. Ensure that we are within range of MacHurdyGurdy," Sybil said.

"Is that wise? What if we were to simply sneak in, under the moon tonight?" Lady said.

Sybil cocked her head at Lady, her heart struggling to remember the affection she'd felt for the aristocratic young woman. Yet a numbness built within her breast. A sense of loss... no, that was far too emotional a description. It felt more like a loss of memory, what she felt was not being replaced by anything, she simply felt...nothing.

Lady held out a hand and Sybil took it with strong fingers, tightening the grip in a sudden need to explain. "What you see, you will not be able to forgive. But remember, all wazz done in memory of uzz."

"I don't understand," Lady said.

"Land the ship. MacHurdyGurdy knowzz we approach. Hiding would be of no use. And prepare yourselvezz, he will not give up hizz secretzz without encouragement."

Malphia nodded and grinned. "Well I think I got just what you need." She motioned for Carmen to take the controls, then strode to the far wall, opening a thin cabinet built into the wall. "This thing was locked up heavier than my grandma's purse, so I knew we'd find something worth havin. And I'll be damned if it wasn't."

The door swung open with a quick jab from her fist, metal and polished wood glimmering in the light. Weapons of various types were tucked within compartments, each with enough ammunition to last several years on the trail. Sybil was certain Zhao Jin collected it for more than hunting purposes.

"My goodness. That's a Bennington Scatterblast rifle." Lady's fingers reached out, but Malphia hit them with a sharp strike of her hand.

"That is mine. Figure it's part of the ship, I get to keep what's in it. But y'all might find a use for these." She held up a Peacemaker, much like the one Slim used to carry.

"Always liked 'em more classic lookin'," Slim said.

Lady pouted, but grabbed a knife and extra Colt. "I

suppose it will come in handy after I have used my pistols."

"Always good to have something that is useful for more than one shot," Malphia said.

"If you do it right, you don't need more than one shot," Lady answered back.

Malphia just grinned and shut the cabinet. Carmen called from the front as the ship came within close range of the cart. Sybil stood and wandered toward the window, her eyes wide with awe. Familiar yet alien, the land beyond the cart brought memories to the surface. Images which had no right to be in her mind swam before her, illusions of grand gatherings, people supplicating themselves before something they didn't quite understand.

Gatherings so infrequent and so brief, the brilliantly crafted buildings only heard the sounds of footsteps once in a generation. Beyond the structures, built in a large, halfmoon shape, stood a tall, natural cliff, promising entrance to something incomprehensible.

And a people unlike anything anyone could imagine. For once, in a life of adversity and doubt, anguish and too little love, Sybil felt at home.

***

The ship damn near fell out of the sky. Slim might have chided Phee on her handling of the machine, but he'd seen the glint in her eye. That was one woman who had been pushed a little too far out of where she was comfortable. He'd known her for years and one thing you don't do is tackle a wildcat when she was ready to wrestle.

Lady shouted something about wanting to rethink the plan, but they'd made the descent and there wasn't anything left to do. Slim had a score to settle with MacHurdyGurdy, though just like Lady, he didn't have the stomach for killin'. Not that he'd rule the option out if absolutely necessary; he just preferred to let the good Lord sort out the real sinners.

Sybil stood to the side, solid and unaffected by the sudden dips and turns. Something odd had come over the woman, and this was beyond the odd she'd already displayed over the last several months. He'd gotten to the point where he'd expected the change in her eyes from green to gold when something big was happening. The fact that the others had yet to notice it was something he just couldn't figure. But today, she had the look of a bride on her wedding day, or a condemned man on his way to the noose. Neither made Slim feel any safer.

The ship dipped again and hit the ground hard, bouncing back into the air for a quick moment, then jarred right back into the earth. The gears groaned as Malphia threw one of the various controls up and pulled another down. Slim figured it would have taken him ten years to learn how to fly something like this, and honestly, if luck held, he could keep his feet on the ground for some time. There was nothing wrong with his feet that made him think he needed to be up in the air like some damn bird.

"I am still not certain about this," Lady said.

Slim laughed then threw his arm around her shoulder. "Come on now, you didn't show no sign of yellow when you came to my rescue in Socorro."

"Well that was--,"

"Or Las Cruces," he continued.

"Yes, but that was--,"

"Or Deming," he finished.

"Oh alright. I get your insinuation. Just don't die today?

Alright?" She glared at him, but Slim had a pretty good idea she still liked him. Though she probably wanted him to survive just so she could yell at him more about his bein an idiot. Slim was alright with that.

The two of them ran from the relative safety of the ship toward a stand of bushes. There wasn't much to hide a person in this land. Everything was dry and brittle. The tall, yellow grass rustled as grasshoppers fled from the two new invaders. The bugs probably had the right of it, but Slim wasn't goin' to let Lady in on that particular feeling.

"Do you think they know where we are?" Lady whispered.

A bang, followed by a thud in the ground at their feet answered her question. Slim grabbed her hand and threw her into action, pointing toward the cart. From the flash of movement several yards to their right, it appeared the MacHurdyGurdys took refuge behind the shorter walls of the old Indian ruins. That left the cart open.

Another shot sent Lady to the ground in a panic. The woman was great with technology and weapons, but put her in a real fight, and she damn near disappointed him. "Come on, Lady. You ready to quit?"

"Is this really the time for you to be giving me difficulties, Slim Robinson?" she shouted back at him.

"Figure I better get it in before you die. Which is likely to happen with you crawling around like a newborn pup."

"Newborn pup?" Outrage stirred her courage and she leapt to her feet, beating him to the safety of the cart. As they stood with their backs to the thick wood wheel spokes, her chest heaved, but she still was able to say, "Don't think I do not know what you are about. You're keeping me riled will only distract me. Quite the opposite of what you intend."

He just grinned at her. She was safe behind the cart now wasn't she? He wasn't a man to argue with success. "You got any of those fancy smoke bombs in that bag of yours?"

"Two, but one got wet, so really, just the one. Though if I had a little time, I suppose I could dry this one out in the sun. If we had taken the time to plan this, we would be in a far better situation."

"Course we would, but then we wouldn't have surprise on our side."

"Surprise? What on earth has surprise done for us?"

Again, Slim grinned and held out his hand for the one smoke bomb she had. The nice thing about smoke bombs, though he knew little of them, they tended not to set things on fire. Now he was fan of a good fire any day, but in a sense, there was no good that came of burning down the walls which protected you.

But if MacHurdyGurdy didn't know that, then it would be just the kind of surprise Slim was looking for. Once lit, he took the smoke bomb, opened the door to the cart, and threw it in. It would take a few minutes for the compartment to fill enough for the smoke to start slipping through the cracks, so he pulled Lady to a position behind one of the tall wheels and shrunk down.

"What good will that do?" Lady asked.

"Not quite sure, but we'll know soon enough."

They waited and then waited more. No shots came from the wall for several minutes. Slim looked around the cart, watching for movement. Nothing. Would MacHurdyGurdy just wait them out? He did not seem the most patient of men. But then, Slim didn't know all that much of the snake-oil salesman beyond what Sybil shared along the way.

And Sybil never shared much.

"What the devil is she doing?" Lady shrieked, and stood, her hands clenched as she stupidly moved away from the protection of the cart.

"Damn it woman, get back here." But he stopped short of jumping up to pull her back just as a dark shadow fell across them.

The SteamWing struggled to gain altitude over their heads. Malphia stood at the controls, her face impassive and determined. Slim shouted for her, but she kept the ship pointed east. Carmen ducked her head out one of the windows, tears streaming down her face. She said, "We are so sorry. So sorry."

"They're leaving us?" Lady shouted, then released a string of curses unlike anything she'd ever uttered in his presence, and he figured in her life. Malphia's abandonment was not out of character. Shoot, he'd been surprised she'd stayed as long as she had. The woman was a lone-wolf, focused on her life, her needs, and her desires for as long as he'd known her. It made her easy to know, but impossible to trust.

A shot hit the ground at Lady's feet and she scrambled back to where Slim sat. "I cannot believe that woman. Now what are we do to? We're stranded."

"Darlin', I am more concerned about the man with the gun at the moment."

Her mouth flapped shut. "Yes, I do suppose that is a bit more important."

Slim coughed, then swiped at his eyes, before he realized the smoke had started to slip through the cart's cracks. It rose into the sky, white and grey with a noxious scent. Slim grabbed Lady by the hand. "Let's hope there's somethin' in there MacHurdyGurdy cares about, or we just wasted a good smoke bomb."

They didn't have to wait long. An angry shout came from the wall. Slim stood and peeked around the cart. Mordecai MacHurdyGurdy stood as well, his face red and hand gripping his shotgun with tense strength. A sudden decision made MacHurdyGurdy run toward the cart. With a quick word for Lady to stay back, Slim moved to the side of the cart and pointed the Peacemaker at the running man. "If you want to get to this cart, you're gonna need to drop your gun."

Mordecai stumbled to a stop, his mouth a grimace. "You fool, do you realize what is in there?"

"Don't figure I care."

Movement from the wall took his attention from Mordecai, but Lady soon joined him and pointed her augmented pistol at the rest of the MacHurdyGurdy party. "Please stand and place your weapons on the ground. I do not wish to fire as it makes an awful racket. I am in a poor mood now that I have no ship so I would not test my patience," Lady said.

Two figures stood, their hands rising to the sky. Slim asked, "Where are the rest of you?"

"This is all we are now," Mordecai answered. "Unless you plan to kill me, I would appreciate being allowed to save my property."

"You have something of mine. Return that first, and then we may let you pass," Lady said.

Slim looked at her incredulously, unable to play the hero, he'd step back and let her take command. As long as in the end he won this bout with MacHurdyGurdy, he didn't really mind, but some day she and he would have a conversation about her letting a man be a man on occasion.

Mordecai dropped his head and rifled in his vest pocket, but when Lady's attention moved from her targets to the dark-eyed man, a shot rang out. The woman by the wall pulled out a pistol and shot at Lady. At least, it had seemed to be aimed at Lady. It had gotten awful close to hitting Mordecai. Luckily, neither were hit and Slim was able to grab Lady as he shot back.

The air filled with gunfire and the cart thunked with a few hits. Slim had two shots left, and he was concerned they were about to end this badly when something out of the corner of his eye had him standing in disbelief.

The shots stopped on the other side as well as five heads all turned to watch the apparition in silks move through the center of where they were firing.

Sybil. And she walked as though nothing else existed. Slim stepped out to retrieve her, but Lady put a hand to his arm. "Look."

He did, and he blinked. It couldn't be real. The tall cliff face behind the settlement had opened, exposing a dark and foreboding entrance to a cavern. He looked to Sybil again, intent on stopping her, but his hand shook as he spied the yellow shine to her eyes.

"What the hell is goin' on?" Slim asked and Lady just shook her head.

34

Once he secured the cart, Mordecai breathed deeply. The bastard gambler played him a mighty bluff, and it very nearly worked. Faced with the choice between his livelihood and the locket, he'd been forced to take serious stock in his faith. Ultimately he had not had to choose, but for one moment, he'd realized his faith in Cibola had a small chink in its wall. What if Cibola did not exist? What if there was not golden city to guarantee his future?

In the end it did not matter. The glorious beauty, Sybil, opened the portal to a subterranean mystery. He watched from the door of the cart as the others followed her slow advance toward the cliffs. Trance-like, she weaved in the wind, but her footsteps were sure.

Had he known that Sybil was the key, he would never have made the trade with Zhao Jin. What misadventure had fallen upon his rival for him to lose his prize? Zhao Jin was not a man to misplace such a valuable piece.

And now, Mordecai was certain he knew Zhao Jin planned the entire thing. The trade, the acquisition of the locket, all to ensure Mordecai lost his opportunity. It would have been the key to thwarting his plan, and the Chinaman knew it.

What more did the Chinaman know that he did not?

The party drew closer to the cavern entrance. Mordecai sprang into action, grabbing the last of the papers he'd kept from his research on de Vaca. Never having seen the actual cities of gold, de Vaca nonetheless provided brief descriptions of the interior as recited by his sources. What lay ahead would very likely make even the most talented explorers lost within an hour. With labyrinthine passages designed to disorient the invader, it could keep the greatest of the world's treasures a secret until time ended.

Unless you had a map. And these notes were the closest anyone could come.

He hurried after the others, catching up as they entered the cavern and disappeared into the depths of darkness. Beatrice held her husband's shirt, shuffling behind him with an uncharacteristic timidity. Mordecai scowled when her eyes met his. The traitorous bitch shot at him, he was positive. The shot came far too close to him for there to be any doubt. And though the young lady and the gambler had been close, no one could argue with him should he accuse her.

But accusations were not how he liked to operate. There were other ways, more convenient ways to deal with his sister-in-law. And now, little could justify his brother's support of her.

"Sybil, please stop. Wait for us," the young woman pleaded. She and the gambler were only a few feet ahead of his brother, but as they followed the diaphanous flutters of Sybil's silks into the cavern, it grew more difficult to see the tall, gangly man and his companion. If they became separated from Sybil they would have to depend on the de Vaca notes--something he was prepared but not eager to do.

"Did you bring a torch?" he murmured to his brother.

"I did not think before following her. Should I return for

a lantern?"

"That would be wise. Beatrice and I shall continue on with Sybil and the others. Move quickly and you should have no trouble catching us up. Sybil's movements are slow enough," Mordecai said.

Beatrice tightened her fingers in her husband's shirt. "I should go back with Bernard."

"Certainly not, I may need your assistance in subduing our new companions. We do know how skillful you are with the pistol," Mordecai let his voice drip with the implications and his brother, as expected, heard none of it.

Beatrice blanched and her fingers shook as she let go of Bernard's shirt. As he turned and headed back toward the surface, she straightened her back and squared her shoulders, staring down her nose as haughtily as ever. Neither Beatrice nor Mordecai spoke as they continued into the cavern, the final stages set in their game, the only unknown the place of their confrontation.

Bernard faded into the distance, his silhouette growing smaller in the last of the light from the cavern entrance. When Mordecai turned back, Beatrice disappeared along with the others into the darkness. A raised brow was his only reaction. He could still hear them shuffling ahead, and he used the knowledge as a guide.

They continued on, the sound of their breathing mingling with the scrape of shoes against pebbles and sand. The cavern grew narrow, becoming a long, spiraling passage where the walls touched his shoulders if he stepped left or right of center. On occasion, the young woman sent out a plea, begging Sybil to stop, to acknowledge her, or to beware.

Eventually, the pleas ceased and everyone focused on

the uncertainty of their trail. Every few hundred feet Mordecai felt the emptiness of a new passageway entrance, at times, faced with multiple choices. The sound of the others prodded him forward, but the disorientation could cause even the most courageous of men to lose control over the fear. It was at this point he found himself, when the noise ahead grew silent and the air grew so dense his ears throbbed with the pressure.

What an ignoble end to a great quest, suffocated by darkness, led to his death by a woman in silks.

But then something changed. The air felt suddenly sweet, clear, and welcoming. The darkness shifted from the complete absence of light to the feel of a shadow. Not quite able to see, he sucked in a breath, realizing what had once been black now was grey.

Something was waiting for him ahead. His steps quickened. His heart beat a rapid staccato. When he caught up to the others, he pushed past a feminine shoulder, brushing them aside in his impatience. The passage curved to the right and the darkness receded in a blaze of firelight.

Firelight which shined brilliant against a remarkable display of gold.

Mordecai froze, the sight impossible to comprehend. A massive chamber, with ceilings that rose hundreds of feet into the air, rang with their arrival. The walls glistened with gold, streaks of it like great gashes across a stone skin.

Yet the natural gold, impressive in its own right, meant little compared to the giant citadel that stood before him. Stone walls, carved from the granite and quartz. Stalactites, dripping from above, met the great stalagmite columns that rose from the ground. The columns were ingeniously integrated into the building design, great spires and jagged teeth among terraces and exposed halls.

And everywhere were gold-plated walls, hammered in intricate designs of geometric complexity. Spirals and mazes made the mind unconsciously follow each direction, losing the self in the nearly infinite possibilities. Blinding light flickered across every inch, as giant torches roared in their sconces.

A true city of gold. A man could go mad from the beauty of it.

Beatrice gasped and grabbed his arm, her wonder making her forget their animosity. He could not blame her and took advantage, throwing an arm around her shoulder and pulling her close. "Isn't it everything as I promised it would be?"

Breathless, she said, "It is that, and so much more. We're set, brother, completely set."

It was true, but not for her. Drawing her forward, he smiled, "Let us explore our new discovery. I am sure Bernard will be eager to have you share what you find when he returns."

Looking back the way they came, she frowned. "Will he be able to find us? There were so many twists."

Mordecai would find his brother should he not find them in due time. But there was something to be done first. "He will, I am sure of it. Come, let us see what Cibola has for us."

***

There had been a number of times when Sybil had behaved unnaturally. To be honest, Lady lost confidence she even knew what was natural for the enigmatic woman. But even in her most violent fit, they'd always been able to bring her about.

Sybil walked toward the great structures, her feet moving as though bidden forward by an unseeing force, her eyes yellow and unfocused, her nostrils flaring with a scent no one else detected. Lady wanted to cry in frustration, fearful she may lose her friend to madness. Her tears and pleas for response had gone unnoticed.

All the strength and confidence Lady garnered over the years seeking out MacHurdyGurdy and her locket were flushed away in one moment as she realized something far larger was at play.

This place. This dreadfully beautiful place had put a spell on them all. Even Slim stared in wonder at the gold shining in mesmeric glory. Everyone seeming to forget their guide.

Everyone but Lady.

"Sybil is getting ahead of us. Please, let us hurry." Lady tugged on Slim's shirtsleeve.

"Hold on. Do you see this?" Slim said.

Sybil sidestepped a thick stalagmite, and silks swam about her feet as though some current had taken hold and played with the air as she passed. Lady frowned, determined to catch up. "Yes, of course I see it. Do hurry, I think we may lose her in that forest of stone."

He chuckled. "Forest of stone? That's a might dramatic. It's just rocks, she can't get lost in that."

"But it will not hurt if we continue on, will it? Perhaps even more wonders exist where she is going. I am worried that in this condition, she will fall or injure herself."

A darkened expression crossed his face and she felt confident Slim had finally broken free of the spell of the place.

Something did not sit right with Lady. The place was far too glorious to be unguarded. Yet nothing moved but their small party. Who lit the torches? What call mesmerized Sybil so?

Mordecai and his companion disappeared into one of the doors leading up to the giant structure. A part of her worried they lost their opportunity to remove him as a threat.

Silks fluttered and then Sybil disappeared through a different door. Lady ran to her friend. Sybil could very well be in danger. The locket was forgotten, all she wanted was her friend safe and well and back on the surface.

"Who do you think built this?" Slim asked as he ran beside her, his head craned up to take in the entirety of the immense building. Lady withheld the urge to stop and shake the man. Did he not realize the danger? Could he not feel the threat which oozed about them?

Something was very wrong in this place.

A long ramp of natural quartz led to the door Sybil entered. Lady cast a cautious eye to the sides and reached for Slim's hand to keep him from stepping over the side. Plumes of heated steam rose, a slight noxious scent tickling her nose. Subtle, but threatening. An effective moat, should a person fall into the depths. Her imagination designed a slithering dragon, waiting below, impatient to swallow the prey that would inevitably come to its den.

She sped her steps toward the door, fear for her own safety growing as intense as her fear for Sybil.

They entered the door and immediately stopped. Within, the walls shimmered with quartz and gold flecks. Panels of hammered gold lined the floors with stunning artistry, giving slightly beneath their weight. Lady picked up her feet to see the impression of her foot ruining a gorgeously intricate design.

"Oh my. I hope the inhabitant is not home," Lady said. Slim looked down and shook his head in wonder.

Lady reached out to touch the wall and came back with fingers coated in gold dust. Incredible. Had they carved the remarkable structure from the existing stone or brought it in? She couldn't tell. What kind of people could design such an engineering phenomenon? Lady could imagine the stir the discovery would make in the halls of the east. Even her father would be overwhelmed by a feat such as this.

A deep distaste entered her thoughts. Her father would no doubt find every way possible to profit from such a discovery. At the expense of anyone that got in the way. Be it the culture that left this behind, Sybil, or even his own daughter.

Determined to mitigate such damage, Lady refocused on her purpose, realizing too late that Sybil left no trail for them to follow. Long corridors branched in four directions. Slim pressed his hand against a wall and pulled it back, his grin wide as he played with the light on his hand, flickering the gold and crystals like a child entranced by his mother's earrings.

Lady slapped his arm. "We have lost her. Come on. Which way should we try?"

Slim blinked at her, then shook his head. "I don't know."

Lady chose a direction and stalked away. Gold madness settled in Slim's head. Blast him for the weakness. It was the most inopportune time. "I suppose this is as good a choice as any."

When she turned the corner into a large, grand hall, she wished she'd chosen better words. A mass of creatures stood in flickering light, faces peering at the two who just entered, curious and frightening. Lady held back a scream.

Men, but not. Their skin shimmered with the gold of the walls, but the texture was reminiscent of Sybil's scales. Eyes wide and eerily yellow, they watched them as a blind-man might, hearing but not seeing, yet altogether aware of every move. There had to be two dozen, all stepping gingerly, gliding on the floor as though they barely touched the ground, weightless and surreal. And each of them male but for the single form surrounded by their numbers, her silks still dancing about her ankles.

"Looks like they are home, darlin'," Slim drawled.

"You are ever the voice of the obvious," Lady said.

35

Gold everywhere. Damn, he'd never expected to see this much gold in his life. If the miners that hung about the saloons across the west could see this now, they'd just about fall into an apoplectic fit. Shoot, he felt like swoonin' himself, and he was the type who preferred to win his fortune at cards. There just wasn't enough time in the world to contemplate all this gold.

And damned if Lady didn't see a bit of it.

Slim figured the snake-men across the hall warranted that kind of attention, but heck, didn't she see all the gold? Every wall, every floor, even the air seemed to be covered in gold. Giant gold streaks cut through the natural rock that used as a foundation for the building. Hammered gold sheets, with fancy designs coated the floor and covered the walls. Columns with rosy quartz added accents to the overwhelming yellow. There was so much to see of the gold, he really couldn't keep his attention focused on anything else.

Lady tensed beside him. There was so much anxiety steaming off her, she'd be able to teach an engine a thing or two. The girl had more spunk than anyone he'd ever met and he just couldn't see what scared her now.

Snake-men. Yep. It was a new one for him too. But considering they'd been livin life on the trail with Sybil, it really shouldn't be much of a surprise. Granted, he wasn't sure if they were the friendly type, but they hadn't done anything to have him too worried. Not yet.

Slim snuck another look at the walls covered in glittery fortune. Maybe if the locals were friendly they'd let him take one of the smaller panels when he left.

Lady tugged his sleeve. "What are they doing? Can you see her? All I can see is her silks. I cannot tell if she is frightened. We have to do something. What can we do?"

Slim looked down at her. A crease marred her forehead and her lips thinned unconsciously, saying far more than her words. What had Slim missed? As far as he could tell, no one was in any danger. It looked more like a family gathering than a threat. "I think it's alright. She don't look worried to me."

"Of course she doesn't look worried. She is in a trance. You saw her. She has the yellow eyes she gets when she's in a fit. She can't control herself when she's like that. We have to do something."

"What exactly do you think we should do? There's got to be twenty of them," Slim said. The men weaved about Sybil, their eyes not exactly seeing, but they seemed pretty interested in her. One reached out and touched a corner of the silk, then immediately drew his hand back. A hushed hiss reverberated around the room, reminding him of the soft fall of water across sand. Sybil weaved as well, her silks swaying about her ankles.

It was like a dance. Something that spoke more than words, but only understood by the participants. The only dance he'd ever excelled at was between the sheets and this was a far cry from that. The language was way beyond him.

Lady took a step forward then froze. She looked back to

him for assistance, and he really had no idea what to suggest. If Sybil were in trouble, he'd be the first to run in, whether there were twenty snake-men or not. But, what if they set something off by doing so? He shook his head then nodded to the side of the room. If they circled around the group, maybe they could get a better look and determine how much help Sybil really needed.

They were hardly noticed. Despite their caution, both Slim and Lady made noise, and no one seemed to care. Occasionally, one of the snake-men would cock his head and turn in their direction, but he would quickly return his attention back to Sybil and the strange undulating dance of the crowd. Lady reached for Slim's hand as they drew to a point in the room that brought them nearer the men. The wall jutted out, pushing them to slide around a thick, stalagmite column.

As they came around the other side, Lady stifled a scream and jumped toward his chest. Slim stilled, staring in fascination and awe. An old woman sat within a brilliantly adorned alcove, the artistry of the hammered gold that surrounded her even more extravagant than they'd seen. And Slim figured it would have been damn near impossible to do.

He took a step forward and she turned, cocking her head in his direction, her eyes a bright yellow similar to Sybil's but with a milky film. Her legs were tucked beneath her, arms pinned to her sides and hands pressed to the ground. The ragged silks she wore swayed like tattered fringe as her body rocked, backwards, forwards then swung sided to side, a raspy hum rattling from her throat.

"Do pardon us, ma'am," Lady said.

The only reaction was the cocking of the woman's head,

toward Lady, dropping the silk from her face. Lady sucked in a breath, and Slim nearly gasped himself. Thickly scarred skin, very much like scales covered her cheekbones and forehead, and as her mouth moved, papery flecks of skin fell from her chin, the loose scales turning white about the edges.

Slim put his hands on Lady's shoulders and steered her around the woman, and toward a more secluded section of the wall. His attention turned back to Sybil, her skin not nearly as scaled as the woman, but similar in makeup. Was this a picture of what Sybil had to look forward to?

Lady shook beside him. "I don't like what is happening. This place frightens me."

With a quick glance at the shining gold, he said a wistful goodbye to an easy life and said, "I'm beginnin' to feel the same way. Let's grab Sybil and get out. If we're lucky we'll run into MacHurdyGurdy on the way out." The old snake oil salesman still had something of Lady's and Slim would be damned if they'd come all this way for nothing. Mordecai MacHurdyGurdy was one man who deserved to lose and Slim was gonna make sure it happened.

After he had his two ladies safe, of course.

"You got anything left in your bag? Slim asked.

"Just the water-logged smoke bomb and my steam pistols."

"Bomb won't do us much good."

"No I don't believe it will," Lady said, her eyes shifting uncomfortably toward Sybil. The group shifted, forming a tighter circle around her, still swaying, but something changed. The mood seemed darker, more intense, as though waiting for something momentous that was highly anticipated but also feared. Slim didn't like the look of that crowd.

Things were about to get mighty interesting.

He grinned and reached for the bag hanging at Lady's hip. "Well, the pistols will do something, at least. Let's show these snakey-men that they got no call crowdin' in on her like that."

"Do you think that is wise?" Lady asked.

"Course not. When did you ever see me be wise, darlin?" Slim pulled out her steam pistol, pressed the small latch that engaged the steam and slipped the barrel into his waist band. Pointed down his left leg of course, there was no use in blowin' off his sensitive parts. He could deal with a shot leg, but some parts a man just couldn't live without.

Lady pulled out her second pistol and engaged the steam as well, her lips suddenly set in a thin, determined line. Slim nodded with approval. 'Bout time the girl found her stiff lip. She didn't do well as an insecure maiden. Raising his hands, he adjusted his hat, tipped the rim in her direction, and turned toward the crowd of snake-men. They were completely oblivious. Hopefully, with a few well-placed shots into the air, the noise and panic would create enough confusion for them to grab Sybil and high-tail it down one of the various passages. Something would get them back to the surface. They'd be blinder than the old woman who still danced like a cobra several feel to their right, but if they kept running they might just have a chance.

Damn this had to be one of the dumbest plans he'd come up with in a real long time.

A hand grabbed his arm just as he was about to throw it all to the wind and run in like a madman on fire. He looked down at Lady and she blushed. A raised brow was all he was able to do before she pushed up on her tip toes and planted a swift kiss to his lips. Firm and far too short, he hardly had a chance for it to register before she'd withdrawn and turned her back to him, setting her shoulders in preparation for the fight. Damn. Now she kissed him?

He pulled the pistol from his waistband. Well, if she was gonna go and declare herself like that, he'd damn well better make sure they all made it out of this alive. "Alright, let's go. And stay with me, I don't want to have to rescue you too."

"That would be a welcome turn of events," Lady said, an unusual smirk painting her lips as she turned to seek out Sybil's whereabouts in the crowd. "Shall we simply rush in?"

"Bandits without a plan, of course. It's my usual method."

"Quite true," she said then furrowed her brow as she scanned the crowd of men. "Where has she gone? I do not see her?"

Slim lifted his head and searched for Sybil's silks and lithe movements. Dang it. She was gone. The men still swayed as though caught in a strange, invisible current, but they now faced Slim and Lady, their heads all cocked toward them, the attention eerily intense. Lady grabbed his arm and took an unconscious step back. Slim wanted to do the same, but he squared his shoulders and started to raise his pistol. A quick shot to the ceiling should distract them enough for them to make their escape.

But what had they done with Sybil?

"Pleazz lower your weapon. They mean you no harm."

Slim swung around to find Sybil standing behind them, her eyes a shade closer to green, but still primarily yellow. Her body swayed, but there was something there, something that still felt human. Slim lowered the pistol, but held

Lady back from rushing toward Sybil.

"The night izz nearly upon uzz and you will be tired. Tomorrowzz festivitiezz require that you be rested. Come, I will lead you to a place to lie."

"I really think we should go," Lady said.

A flash of fire and sudden tensing at the corner of Sybil's eyes preceded her next words. "I cannot promizz your safety should you leave now. Trust me, pleazz. You are my friendzz and I wish no harm to come to you. Perhapzz, I will someday be able to explain, but for now, pleazz believe me when I say thizz izz the wisest decision."

Slim was not prepared to argue with the elegant woman, and as it happened, neither was Lady. They followed their friend from the hall, down a winding corridor into a darkened room where several depressions had been dug into the floor. Large enough for a man, the depressions had the look of a well-maintained flower bed.

"It izz not what you are used to, but I assure you, it will suffice for thizz night. Sleep well. I shall come for you in the morning."

Sybil left them to the empty room and odd sounds of the night. Damn, this was definitely not how he'd hoped this would go.

***

The sunlight behind them turned the canyon ahead a graying yellow, where shadows merged with the highlights of dusk. A single cart stood outlined against a large, walled city--empty, unmoving and promising Zhao Jin an end to a journey that spanned decades.

So many years he'd dreamt of a rival worth his effort,

someone with intelligence and ambition. On the great stages of the east, he'd found that man, a mysterious showman from Hungary, with a head for business, a flare for the dramatic, and a stomach for the inevitable dirtiness of prosperity.

How far had Mordecai Kovacs fallen to achieve his goal? Zhao Jin would have wished for a far deeper crevice, but a lone cart amid the desolate canyon foretold at least some hardship befell the man along his journey. A sly grin slipped across Zhao Jin's lips. The anticipation of tearing away the final strings of Kovacs livelihood made a heady potion for the mind.

"Mr. Jin, do you see this?" The captain's slightly effeminate voice bounced against the canyon walls, creating an echo that ran spikes of irritation across Zhao Jin's back.

"Do keep your voice down, Captain Wright. The walls have ears," Zhao Jin said. The man had the decency to look contrite. What drew the captain's attention was a grand wall, chiseled brilliantly to the millimeter, each stone placed in exquisite precision. The effect created a building so fine it was on equal footing with any of the great accomplishments of the western world. Being from the Far East, Zhao Jin was quite used to the astonishment of white men when faced with miraculous craftsmanship which did not originate from Europe. Such fools, they truly believed civilization began with them.

Zhao Jin did not blink when he saw the glorious ruins of the ancient peoples of this land. Like he, they were simply waiting for the great men of Europe to grow lazy in their confidence. And soon, their empire would be a wasteland, to be plundered by greater men with patience and the sight of a future beyond the white man's reach.

"We have far more interesting things ahead, gentlemen. Keep your eyes sharp. Kovacs may have seen us, though he is unlikely to be looking for what comes from behind." His men nodded in solemn understanding, however, Zhao Jin knew them far too well. "Do not engage them until I order it. There is a treasure to be found, and I want Kovacs to see it before we steal it from him."

Martin flashed a wide grin. The man was nearly as demented as he. It made him an excellent second in command.

The horses stepped across the rocky terrain, diligent in the darkening light. Their guide, Juan, kept quiet since they'd arrived, his shoulders relaxed and demeanor non-committal. The man had a plan. One he would keep secret. Zhao Jin made a small motion toward Joseph to watch him closely. With the moment of his victory at hand, Zhao Jin did not wish any extra players making moves he could not foresee.

Shadows unmoving, Zhao Jin halted their progress on a low ridge just before the cart. No fire. No sign of humanity. Uncertainty hit and a foreboding menace settled into his belly before he gave the command to move forward. If they were too late, he would be greatly disappointed.

Juan rode toward the cart far quicker than Zhao Jin liked, but Joseph followed him closely, ready to stop the man should the need arise. The captain stopped beside Zhao Jin and watched as the two men circled the cart. "I don't see anyone. Can you tell if Miss Dewhurst made it here?"

"Do be quiet, Captain, and let my men work."

"Who is that Juan, anyway? He does not seem to be one of your men. Can he be trusted?"

Zhao Jin closed his eyes and asked the heavens for blissful intervention. Perhaps a sudden numbness of the captain's tongue? Would that be too much to ask?

"They are waving us over. Come on, Mr. Jin." The captain kicked his heels into his mount's flanks and sped off. Zhao Jin stifled a labored sigh and followed.

At the cart, Joseph pointed to several holes in the wood panels. "Looks like someone got to them first. No bodies though. Seems like bandits. Or maybe savages. Don't see any arrows. Could have been anybody."

It hadn't been just anybody. No doubt Miss Dewhurst and Sybil arrived before them. But where had they gone?

Juan opened the door to the cart and poked his head inside. He withdrew quickly, his nose wrinkled with distaste. "Smoke bomb. Someone smoked out this whole thing. There's whole crates of bottles in there. Not sure what they got in them. But no bodies. They had to go somewhere. Maybe they camped in one of the ruins?"

"Possibly." But unlikely. Zhao Jin lifted his head to scan the canyon. It was far too dark to find them now. They would need to wait until the first light of dawn to begin their search. "We will camp just over that ridge. Martin, you will keep watch for the first hours then switch with Joseph. Nothing can escape our observation. We will make a more thorough search in the morning."

36

Lady woke to a strong hand across her mouth and hard brown eyes glaring down at her. Juan put a finger to his lips and she nodded as he lifted his hand. Slim sat up beside her, nose flaring and his jaw uncommonly clenched. Juan whispered, "Where is Sybil?"

Her back spasmed as she sat up, reminding Lady of the uncomfortable hours curled in the dirt depression. Body yearning for the soft bed she'd left behind so many years ago, she worked a kink out of her shoulder. "She left us here and returned to the snake-men I imagine. She promised to wake us before dawn. There is something happening in the morning. We aren't sure what it is, but Sybil seems unconcerned."

Juan raised a brow then looked to Slim. "Why did you not get them away from here? Can't you tell how dangerous this place is?"

"Doesn't seem any more dangerous than it has been lately. What are you doin' here?" Slim said.

With a disgusted grunt, Juan stood. "I'm here to rescue my sister. She should have never come here. If you knew what was about to happen, you would never have let her enter this place."

Lady stood as well, her hackles rising and pain from the

night forgotten. This man had no right to command anyone. Sybil guided them on this journey and Lady trusted her far beyond this stranger. "Sybil brought us here. I believe she would know if this place were dangerous to her."

"Of course she brought you here. She cannot help herself." Juan pulled off his hat in frustration, slicking back his long black hair with a rugged hand. "If we do not remove her before dawn, every part of her humanity will be gone. The woman you know as Sybil will no longer exist."

"You are out of your mind." Lady wanted to argue, but if she were honest, he only spoke the fears she herself had within. Since they'd arrived, she'd felt the sense of impending disaster. The snake-men terrified her, the gold city an illusion which simply could not be real.

"Anyone that has lived here as long as my family knows of the serpent-men. My mother and father may have arrived only in our lifetime, but the Vargas family has been here for generations. We were raised on the stories of the men that steal our wives and sisters. Our mother was taken by the serpent-men. Sybil is the offspring of that abduction."

"I don't understand. Are you saying Sybil is one of them?"

The look Juan threw at her was insulting, but Lady was beyond concern over his opinion. If Sybil were half-human and half-serpent, what would they want with her? What could possibly happen in the morning to cause Juan such concern? "Why did you not warn us before? You had time."

"Would you have believed me? You already distrusted me. Had I spoken of monsters and called Sybil one of them, you would have thrown me off the ship."

"If I'd been around, it would have happened before you told us," Slim said.

Lady gave Slim a censoring look then moved to the door, poking her head into the darkness. A faint glow came from down one of the corridors. Even if Juan were correct in his worry, snatching Sybil from the band of snake-men would not be simple. "What happens at dawn?"

"Every generation the serpent-men must replace their queen. Two decades ago, they left this place to find human women to carry their children. They cannot have girl children without a human female, so they raid the communities in the area. Did you not wonder why there are no settlements for hundreds of miles of this place?"

Lady turned to him. "But the ruins--"

"There was a time when the ancients would bring the women here for the purpose. It prevented the violence of the raids. But with time, people forgot and only a few know to keep the women safe during the serpent moon." He's face filled with past regret and anger. "We did not know, not at the time. And they came for our mother. They traveled a long distance to do so and we were caught unaware."

"Then Sybil couldn't be the only one."

"Most of the children do not survive."

Lady blanched. But that still did not answer the question. "What happens at dawn?"

"She will be taken as the new queen and will become the mother for the next generation of serpent-men."

"Hold on. You said they needed human women to make babies," Slim said.

"To make female children. The males come from the queen." Juan's look was dark and hooded.

"Good heavens. Sybil can't want that. We must find her!" Lady said.

Again Juan threw her a disgusted look, but she waved it

off. Her satchel lay on the floor beside where she'd slept. They were woefully lacking ammunition, but at the very least a single shot from her augmented pistols would provide a diversion. Slim pulled his own weapon and moved toward the door. Lady looked to Juan. "I assume you have a plan to retrieve her?"

Juan nodded. "We will need to move quickly. There are others here that may prove challenging in our escape."

"Mordecai," Lady said. "He will be glad to see us leave this place. I imagine he wants the gold for himself."

"Zhao Jin may be less eager to let Sybil go," Juan said.

"That bastard? Who the hell led him here?" Slim said.

Juan shrugged and added, "And your friend the captain came along as well, though I do not believe Zhao Jin has much patience left for the man."

"Eustace? Oh for heaven's sake, can't anything go our way?" Lady said. Lord, if she could get through this unscathed, she'd find herself a quiet life in a small western town. Perhaps she could teach the local children. She'd find herself a good, unexciting man to marry and live a long, unexciting life.

***

The cavern passages curled into even more complex spirals and spokes. Each turn brought more wonders to view. Gold and quartz were the most plentiful, but interspersed within were various gems that crossed the spectrum of worth. A handful of the precious stones and metals could set Mordecai and his brother up comfortably. Just one room could make them lords of the land. The entire complex guaranteed them a kingdom.

Beatrice scurried ahead of him with more energy than she'd exhibited in nearly a decade. They'd explored the caverns under a tentative truce, neither completely comfortable in the company of the other. There were still questions he had for the woman and she had answers he anticipated she'd keep past death.

"Now that you have found your gold, what do you plan to do with it?" Beatrice asked.

"What would you suggest?" he asked, as he ran a finger across an elegant gold panel, inlaid with tiny red coral and amethyst tiles. The red coral reminded him of the lockets held safe within his vest pocket. They had yet to give their final clue and something kept him wary of the miraculous discovery. There had to be more.

"If I had this much gold, I would sail away to the palaces of France. Perhaps Italy? My mother told me so many stories of Italy, I think she would have liked it if I ended my days there." She looked over Mordecai's shoulder, her eyes uneasy, her expression undisguised. Bernard could return any moment, and they both knew he was all that stood between them. All that had ever created a barrier to their mutual antipathy.

Mordecai crossed his arms and leaned against the nearest gold panel. "If I could guarantee you a future in Italy and enough gold to keep you till death, would you tell me the truth?"

Her brows drew together and lips thinned. A slight flaring to her nose betrayed her anxiety over the question, yet when she responded her voice was light. "What would you wish to know, brother? I have been nothing but forthcoming."

Mordecai snorted and said, "I am sure. But tell me, how

did the child die that night?"

Her face blanched and it seemed that even her soul had escaped in a single moment. This secret, this one question had driven him to near madness through the years. Only the thought of pursuing Cibola kept him sane. Had they lost a child? Had it been his, a Kovacs? Had fate stolen his child from him?

For once, her voice shook. "It was not yours."

"How did it die, Beatrice?"

"Why does it matter?"

Because he did not believe her. The child had to have been his. There had been no one else. Even Bernard knew. "It is time you told me everything. What did you do to my child?"

"It was not yours, you damnable man!"

"How could it not be! I was the only--,"

"You were not." Her hands trembled and tears gathered around her lashes. Age and sorrow sunk her cheeks and pulled the effects of time into the foreground. Had they all grown so old? Could he have missed the impact of years on the road, to the agony of past tragedies? What a lot of despair they had become, and now, surrounded by the promise of gold, the color of their souls were exposed.

"Who else?" Mordecai drew in a ragged breath. This woman held nothing over him. Desire for her young, exquisite body slaked years before when his conquest meant something. He'd solidified his reputation as the greatest of men among those who tread the stage. He could have anything he desired, everything he commanded immediately obeyed at a simple flick of his wrist. She'd been nothing more than a symbol of his power.

Even his brother had known. "Who!" he said with a guttural growl.

Her eyes lost their focus and she grabbed for the wall. "I smothered it, brother. Against my breast, it cried out once and when I saw the eyes and knew whose child I had carried, it could not live. I smothered it, holding its tiny head tight against my own body as it struggled for life. I became a monster in that moment, brother. I became the same as you."

"Who!" he roared.

"Zhao Jin!" she screamed back.

All the breath in his body fizzled from his lips as though a long needle had been stuck in his belly, deflating him, sending him sinking into distraught anger. His voice lowered. "The Chinaman? How could you let him touch you?"

Beatrice erupted with hysterical laughter. "How? How could I not? The two of you traded chattel like the fine men traded stocks in their clubs. I was the queen of all the women on the stage. With you both entranced with me, I had it all."

His hand struck her face with a force he would normally reserve for men. Blonde curls bounced as her neck snapped backward, her cry cut short as her knees buckled and she fell to the ground. Blood from her lips painted a trail down her chin and dripped into the gleaming gold floor, her reflection a mere shadow in the orange metal. She continued to laugh, "The two kings of the stage, fighting over slips of flesh and talent that could bring you gold. You had a kingdom and you left it for nonsense and legends. You could be running Dodge City. You could own half the town. Now you have nothing, but this city of gold. What will you do with this? Live like Midas?"

"I will buy a life where I never have to see the likes of you ever again."

She laughed again, the sound desperate as she finally met eyes with him again. "You won't let me live long enough to see you do so. We both know that."

"Of course. We have always known that, have we not, sweet Bea."

Blood flew through the air as she spat at him, splattering his clothing with red. A swift kick to her head snapped her neck back again and she fell to the ground. Mordecai turned from her still body, certain she no longer lived. A sudden elation spread across his body and he repressed the urge to erupt with glee.

Finally free of the past, he could look to the future with no worries of haunting memories. The relief the child had not been his mixed with the irritation at her unfaithfulness. Zhao Jin had nipped at his heels since they first met. The man had an uncanny ability to know exactly what Mordecai desired and strived to step in to steal every victory. The stink of the man still hovered about his shoulders and Mordecai swore he could hear his condescending voice at every moment. But Mordecai came to this place knowing he could win this battle and walk away the only victor. No one stood in his way.

A shuffle of feet against the golden floor pulled his attention down the corridor. Bernard stood staring, a lantern swaying from the chain that hung from his hand. Of course his brother would arrive at just such a time. Mordecai strode forward, his confidence shrinking with each step. What had been done was done. It had always been a necessity and inevitable. "You heard her confession. Could I in good conscience let a murderess live? It is one thing to take a life of man, fully grown and capable of committing sin. It is quite another to snuff out the life of a child, barely alive, innocent and without defenses."

Bernard's expression held no condemnation, nor the fury Mordecai might have anticipated. Yet, something flickered behind Bernard's eyes, and it worried him. It was a strange, new light--something he'd never seen, something he could not decipher. His brother kept his gaze on Beatrice's broken body, unblinking and breaths even and unhurried. Bernard said, "I believe we left the right to make choices by conscience behind us many years ago. She lived her life no more righteously than you or I. It is a fitting end to her life. Here, beneath a mountain of gold far from the stage and admirers. What kind of an end do we face, brother? Who will make the choice to see to our end?"

"You are falling into melancholia again. Do you not see the glory that surrounds us? We have made it! We have discovered Cibola!"

"And what of Sybil and the others? Does your conscience say nothing of them?"

Mordecai swung his hand from one end of the ceiling to the other, a wide-toothy grin reminiscent of his greatest performances shining bright against the firelight from the nearest torch. "There is so much, it can make kings of us all!"

Bernard raised a brow, but said nothing. Of course Mordecai meant none of it. What kind of man would share such wealth and trust the others would stay true to the bargain? A fool. And he was no fool.

A rumble shook the walls, vibrating the gold and inciting a high-pitched whistle which buzzed against the ears with gnat-like insistence. Both men looked to each other in consternation, neither sure of the origin. Bernard put his hand to the metal floor then stood, shaking his head. "Something is happening. It is like a great engine has started or perhaps the applause of a thousand men."

"Do not be whimsical. There is no machinery here. All we have seen is a city of gold, with no people. It has been abandoned for hundreds of years. Perhaps thousands! It was no doubt empty long before de Vaca ever heard of its promise."

"Could Sybil be the cause then?"

"Their ship left. What more could they have brought with them? It is far more likely a natural disturbance. A quake perhaps?"

"I have not heard of quakes in this area."

"Who would have known? No one but natives live in the vicinity. Come, let us look, but I can promise you there is nothing to fear of men here."

They left Beatrice's body against a wall, blood pooling about her head. The sightless eyes made Mordecai uncomfortable enough to look away, leaving his brother to maneuver his wife into a serene position with a soft promise to bury her with the respect due an angel. The child had not been a Kovacs, making Bernard's sacrifice as husband irrelevant even had it lived. And yet the man's loyalty remained kind and unbroken.

Mordecai would never understand and for once he wished he could. "Come brother, let us discover this disturbance. If nothing else, we must make contact with Sybil and her companions. They will, undoubtedly be wishing to know our intentions."

With luck, they would play into his hands and force the confrontation to facilitate their end. Only then could he and his brother walk from this place with a future unfettered by others keen on stealing their glory. Mordecai was more than ready to begin his life anew.

37

Joseph hung back with embarrassment as Martin led them forward. Zhao Jin held his men to the highest of expectations. Keeping watch being of the most important of activities, a failure there guaranteed his ire. Had the situation not required he keep his men close and able, his punishment would have been fierce and quick.

Joseph had let Juan escape unsighted in the night. And now they were down a guide and unaware of his activities. Zhao Jin disliked losing any advantage. Joseph would be dealt with once the day was done and Mordecai's downfall complete.

"Are we certain they came through here?" Captain Wright said.

Zhao Jin looked at him with an incredulous glare. "A cavern of gold appears in the side of a mountain and you wonder if they bothered to investigate? I know that you have been insulated by your wealth, but are you truly an imbecile?"

Wright sputtered, but failed to provide a response. Zhao Jin was further saved from continued inane conversation by a turn in the corridor that opened into an awe-inspiring cavern brightly lit by torches and sparkling with quartz and gold. The previous corridors only alluded to the possibilities of a treasure trove, but this one room took all the promises of legend and prophesies, compounding them twenty fold.

They had discovered Mordecai's city of gold.

"Good heavens," Captain Wright said. He took several unconscious steps forward before a hand from Martin stopped him. A large crevice stood between them and the towering walls of a gold structure, columns framed in gold and glittering gems at the highest points. "Surely there is a bridge?"

Zhao Jin scanned the room, laying eyes on the long ramps that led to doors into the great structure. But no bridge from their corridor crossed the chasm. Other halls opened into the great cavern with easy access to the ramps. If they doubled back and tried a different route, they may find entrance into the structure. He was about to suggest the action when movement across the cavern stopped him and took his breath like a hit to the chest.

Mordecai Kovacs stole into the cavern, his tell-tale top hat tipped to the side in an irritating slight to convention. Behind him, his brother followed, head facing down in compliance as he always had. Such loyalty for a brother that deserved none, Zhao Jin spat in disgust. With a nod, Martin crept forward, his eye on their quarry. The crevice served as an unfortunate barrier, but one Zhao Jin was certain his man would circumvent.

They needed to find a way to catch the two dark-haired men across the room before time fled and everything Zhao Jin worked for slipped from his grip. The captain tried to catch Zhao Jin's attention, but Joseph pressed rough fingers into his shoulder and kept the man quiet. Within a few moments, Martin waved from the side, beckoning them forward.

The man discovered a small ledge that allowed them access across the crevice. After a few harrowing steps, they were on the opposite side. Zhao Jin murmured directions to Martin, sending him around the structure to find entrance where they might prevent Kovacs' flight. Once the two Hungarians realized the danger, they might very well flee in cowardice rather than fight for their gold.

Mordecai disappeared into the structure, his brother on his heels, neither turning to check the trail behind. Zhao Jin felt the flutter of inevitable success. With a slight flick of his hand, he and Joseph strode forward, the Captain quick to follow, but thankfully quiet. As they neared the entrance, a strange hum rose around the room, vibrating against their ears like insistent insects.

"What in God's name is that?" Captain Wright asked.

It came from within, inciting trepidation, halting their steps, and stopping their hearts. Zhao Jin pushed forward, determined to discover the source and continue toward his goal. He'd not become a wealthy man by cowing to fear of the unknown. The entrance required that he duck, a strange experience for a man so used to being shorter than all of those around him. Joseph found the action even more difficult, being of significant height and broad shoulders.

Within the structure, several narrow corridors drifted out in various directions, but one seemed to draw them forward, widening in the distance and growing brighter with each step. Zhao Jin stepped forward with confidence, but looked down as the ground gave slightly under foot. The floor was covered in the same gold plating which adorned the walls, depressing under his weight. It seemed a strange waste of energy, unless the ground was never meant for walking.

The buzz built and he let the wonder of golden floors slide away as he hurried down the hall, determined to catch Mordecai unawares and solve the mystery of the unfamiliar sound.

When they reached the end of the corridor, a great room opened in front of them, the ceiling rising high and glittering with brilliant gold and quartz, blinding with magnificence. Captain Wright gasped and pointed. "I think you may have some competition."

Across the room two dozen men, oddly shaped and wriggling unnaturally, surrounded Mordecai and his brother. The buzzing originated from the mob of men, more creature than human. None touched the two men in their midst, but the obvious tension alluded to immanent violence.

"Should we do something?" Joseph asked.

Zhao Jin shook his head, and held up a hand to stall Martin who'd appeared from another corridor across the room. They would watch and see. Moments like this required patience and extreme prejudice. The slightest movement could set off a collapse as effectively as a cannon blast.

***

The men had Mordecai surrounded. Lady held back a derogatory comment. How convenient it would be if the snake-men were to remove Mordecai from the equation. Slim slunk along the wall and Juan followed, encouraging Lady to do the same. Sybil had yet to make an appearance. This caused concern for Lady, the images from Juan's warning making her nervous and sick to her stomach. Across the room, the old woman rocked just as she had the day before.

Lady looked away, trying her best to remain calm. The ancient woman was no doubt the former queen, destined to be cast off as Sybil took her place.

The snake-men were horrid creatures, fiends who threatened to take away her greatest friend. Lady clenched her fists, and felt confidence rise as she prepared to battle against a foe of unimaginable powers. If they were indeed serpent-men, they would need to be prepared for just about anything. She had no idea what these monsters could do to them or even if they stood a chance against them in a fight. But leaving Sybil to be their slave, whether a queen or no, was completely unacceptable.

"Where is Sybil? Do you see her," Lady asked.

Juan shook his head and Slim frowned.

"Where could she be? Should we search elsewhere? Perhaps if we were to discover her beyond the reach of the snake-men we could escape more easily." Lady said.

"They are called serpent-men," Juan said, his expression distracted.

Irritated, Lady said, "What is the difference?"

"I do not know, but they have always been called serpent-men," Juan said.

Lady bit her lip, determined not to fight with the man at this time. But she could not help herself from saying, "You were far more charming when we first met. Had I known in the bedroom you were so irritating, I would have chosen to be found by Eustace."

Slim snapped his head toward Lady, "Bedroom?"

"Had I known you would question my every decision, I would never have saved you," Juan said.

"He saved you in a bedroom?" Slim asked.

"If your decisions were reasonable I would have no

cause to question them. I do not trust men that hide behind lies and deception," Lady said.

"Darlin', I don't think--," Slim tried to cut in.

"I would not need to hide behind lies if you were not distracted by your desire to track down a worthless bauble," Juan said.

"It is hardly worthless. It is a family heirloom, and if you knew a thing about the Dewhurst family, you would know a bauble to them is a fortune to another," Lady answered.

"The Vargas family has heirlooms to make a king envious. Your American wealth is nothing to men like us."

"At least we do not lose our women to monsters!" Lady's voice rose to a pitch just below a screech.

Juan swung to her, fury tightening his jaw. Slim raised a hand and said, "Now is not the time for a lover's spat. How 'bout we wait until we have Sybil and are far from here. I'll even provide the ammunition."

"Lovers? Hardly, Slim. I would never betray you with a man like him," Lady said. Both men dropped their mouths open and Lady's cheeks turned to fire when she realized what she'd said. She tried to cover her ridiculous slip by saying, "This is not the time for bickering."

"That's what I've been sayin'," Slim said.

Juan turned toward the serpent-men, his shoulders tense. "I completely agree. Do you see, across the way. I believe that may be Zhao Jin's man."

Lady stiffened and searched across the mass of swaying bodies, catching a glimpse of a weather-worn hat just as it ducked behind a massive column. "It is. I am certain of it. If he is here, then Zhao Jin has found a way in as well. If he finds Sybil before we do, it can only lead to disaster."

"What does he need Sybil for? Isn't this the end? Sweetheart, this is Cibola, they don't need any of us anymore. I figure it's every man for himself at this point. If Zhao Jin and Mordecai keep those serpent-men busy, the better it is for us. Now, let's get a move on and find Sybil," Slim said with a wicked grin.

Lady stared at him, still unconvinced Zhao Jin had no interest in Sybil. "But what if--,"

"Y'all been talkin' too much. Get your pretty little arse movin'." Slim pointed toward a corridor across the hall. "Now, them snakes keep lookin' that way and I figure that means they're waitin' for something important. If what you've been tellin' us is true, Juan, then that's where she's gonna be comin' from."

"You may be right," Juan said.

Slim grunted then said, "You circle around that way and we'll come from the other end. With luck, we'll be able to sneak through without them noticing."

"They will hardly not notice us, if they continue to stare that direction as they are," Lady said.

"Oh I'm sure Mordecai will do something stupid and draw their attention away," Slim said.

Lady shook her head. It was a lot to assume. She felt woefully unprepared and on the verge of debilitating fear. The men were a suitable distraction, keeping her mind from the monsters who swayed and hissed mere feet from them.

They slid along the wall, Slim's hand gently holding her's as he led them around the room. Out of the corner of her eye, Lady spied Juan making similar progress. Zhao Jin's man had not shown himself again, making her wonder if he'd left the room, taking the wiser road and fleeing from the cavern.

Mordecai and Bernard moved slightly, and Lady paused, tugging Slim to a stop. The serpent-men penned them in, but did nothing to threaten the two. Lady wondered at their lack of movement, and only now saw the pair of lockets swinging from Mordecai's hands. The serpent-men were swaying with the shining gold pieces, their eyes riveted, then distracted by the corridor, then drawn back to the swinging gold chains.

Lady nearly squeaked in outrage. So close, if she could simply thread through the crowd of men, she could grab the locket and run. With the mass of bodies, Mordecai would find it impossible to follow. This was her chance, and perhaps the only one she would ever see. "Slim, I must."

"Like hell you must." He tugged her toward the corridor.

Her hand dove into her satchel and fingers closed around the handle of one of her augmented pistols. "Then I shall have to kill him, and hope I can grab it during the madness."

"Are you crazy? We have to save Sybil. I thought we'd given up on our revenge."

"Have you?" Lady asked. The look on his face was more than answer enough. He had not forgotten his need to hold Mordecai accountable for his attempted murder. This was their last chance, the only opportunity, everything they suffered for over the last months. Bringing an end to MacHurdyGurdy was the only thing that would make it all seem right. Lady pulled the pistol from her bag and leveled it on Mordecai. He would never see where it came from.

She lowered the barrel. What point was there if he did not know where the bullet came from?

The buzz in the room intensified and finally the entirety

of the locket's spell broke and all of the serpent-men turned to see Sybil step in from the darkness. Silks fell from her shoulders, her skin darkened with the hardened scales. Lady gaped at her friend as she exposed her body. "Sybil, no!"

But none noticed Lady's cry for at the same moment, two men from opposite directions charged the crowd of serpent-men, one with a large knife held high above his head in preparation for striking, the other with a rifle aimed at Mordecai.

A shout from another corner revealed Zhao Jin's position, his anger visible from across the room. "Stand down Martin. Joseph do not engage." But neither man obeyed their master. One stopped and leveled the rifle, ready to shoot as the second man drew close, his knife flashing as it swung toward Mordecai's chest.

A guttural yet feminine command cut through the frantic sound of attack and hissing. Lady turned from the drama before her to find Sybil's eyes flashing with bright yellow fury, her head cocked to the side and hands held forward, fingers spread. A second sound came from her throat, not words, but distinct and clearly understood by the serpent-men swarming the hall.

In seconds, both men were separated from their weapons by swift strikes to the arms and chest. Lady anticipated that unarmed, they would be left to nurse their wounds. But she was very wrong. As the gun and knife flew across the room, the serpent-men continued to strike, tearing skin, and rending both attackers to pieces.

Lady felt her heart thud against her ribs and stomach roll as she watched the men dismembered with shocking efficiency. Blood flew through the air, landing in speckled red globules against the previously spotless gold. Sybil stood, unmoved and emotionless until the bodies lay as piles of bone and bloody muscle, unidentifiable and terrifying.

Slim pulled Lady to his side, his fingers digging like talons into her elbow. He said, "I'm thinking we may not be able to save Sybil from herself, let alone those snakes."

Lady felt the bile rise from her stomach and she feared if she could not hold it down, the two of them would be the next to face the creatures' violence. "Slim, I'm sorry I drug you here."

He turned to her and grinned in the wicked way she'd grown to know so well. "Darlin', there ain't no way you were gonna be able to keep me from following you."

Heartened by his comment, she stood straight and took a deep breath. If she were to find death today, she wasn't about to let it take her without significant effort. "Do not forget, these pistols have one shot before it works much like a regular pistol. We have six shots in all for each, so use them well." She handed him her second pistol and smiled. If they survived this, she just might kiss him.

38

Brothers, sons, fathers. Each creature part of a family she never knew until it seemed all too late. Now, blood and violence rained upon them all. The coming dawn so near, but the threat imminent. Once, she'd understood those men, the ones that walked the rays of the sun with no worry his existence might be as temporary as old skin.

What did serpent and men have but a constant rivalry? The fears of mankind for the legless reptiles grew from true terrors in the night, kingdom against kingdom. The horror of this truth only surpassed by the dawning acknowledgment that she was one of those very monsters made children scream in fear. Sybil spent her life chasing her humanity, holding it close and guarding it with jealous righteousness, only to find that she never had an ounce of it to spare.

Scales hardened about her neck, making movement difficult. Her eyes stared unblinking and incapable of finding form in the shadows. All the lovely details and colors of her life above ground seeped away into the crevices and corridors of this ancient city.

A glorious gold city she could not see.

The warmth of the radiating torches that flickered against the walls provided comfort. The cool metal floors felt as soft as the finest carpets to her tender feet and the spiraling labyrinthine corridors brought a sense of security. The creatures touched her with quivering sounds and vibrating fingers, cautious and reverent. For the first time, she felt complete and absolutely loved.

It took too many years to find her home. And now, they threatened to steal it from her. Sybil hissed another command and her people scurried from their prey, the scent of human blood a stench she'd never forget. The men, lying torn and very dead, had been vaguely familiar and a twinge of fear shot into her guts. Had they been friends? She could not tell. Had she ever had friends in the human world?

Movement at a distance showed as a haze of unfocused dark orange, menace and sickness oozing from the form. A certainty formed and she knew the man who walked there meant her great harm and would stop at nothing to attain his goal. Sybil bared her teeth and felt the scales on her back tighten and flex. Another haze emerged at another corner of the hall, this one a softer orange with smooth pockets of black and grey. This creature no doubt threatened her people, but held less antagonism toward her specifically. This however, did not lessen her desire to destroy his trespass. Another creature moved beside him, this one meek and slow to move. Sybil could read nothing of this man's intent. It was almost as though he waited for time to complete its tireless journey and lead him to the next world. Sybil cocked her head.

The man who shimmered with evil took a step toward her people, slow and confident. Sybil reacted with firm decisiveness, hissing a command to her newly acquired subjects. Each of her princes turned as one and advanced on the human men in the hall. Not one would survive the morning. A fear she might punish the innocent pulled a string within her soul, but she silenced the piteous plea. She had a new responsibility to her people.

Blood must be shed, some innocence was unfortunately forfeit.

A gurgled hiss came from her right. The sun broke through the chains of dawn's last grasp. Her predecessor keened and wailed, calling forward the new day and lifting away her claim as queen. Sybil raised her head to the ceiling, feeling the rays of light as they cast through a narrow crevice, piercing her with its warm touch and granting her rights as the next generation's commander and mother.

Sybil raised her hands to greet the sun and spun, dancing with grace and joy she'd never possessed in the past. All the memories of her childhood shattered with the promise of a new purpose. All the pain and sadness accumulated over the years seeped away, falling into the gold beneath her feet.

She was free.

The bodies undulated in a mass of violent color, reds and oranges merging with fast moving shadows and sudden flashes of yellow and white. The hiss of her compatriots rose in volume, rattling the walls with increasing intensity. Their prey moved quickly, dashing from stone columns to escape beyond the great gash that formed a nearly inescapable chasm. Sybil nodded and a group broke off and headed into the corridors to intercept their foes in the maze of tunnels.

A terrified cry brought her up short, her senses fuzzy and uncomfortably off-kilter. Something familiar rang in that sound. Her heart pounded with nervous anticipation as she scanned the room for the origin of the scream. She stopped at a pair of creatures, the colors unlike any she'd seen previously. Soft yellows and mellow reds haloed a fierce blue center. Fear and sadness enveloped the smaller of the two, containing a sorrow not unlike that Sybil had faced for so long. This creature worried over a loss, one close to the heart. The second creature stood still, protective, and vibrating with good intentions. The force of its color melding with the second, forming an invisible shield that it was likely never to acknowledge.

Sybil cocked her head at the two. Curious. She took a step forward then stopped and shook her head. They were something from her life that did not fit in this place. She did not wish harm on these two.

A swarm of her princes lunged toward the two, and frantic emotion spilled into the air accompanied by a second scream. A flash of memory hit Sybil, something so vivid she was able, for just a split second, to see images and detail.

Lady and Slim. She could not let them die!

Sybil hissed a command and the attackers paused, turning confused heads toward her. They would not understand and she could not ask them to. The two worlds should not touch. The threat humanity posed must be limited. They had exposed their existence out of necessity on the serpent moon, but what if they were discovered by others? What if the fear of the monsters of the darkness failed to keep mankind at bay?

Sybil shifted her head and peered toward Lady, willing her friend to understand, sending her a plea. But Lady stood frozen and Slim merely closed his hand around her arm. Words came to her throat, but the action scraped against her throat, her lips unwilling to form the language she'd once known so well. Air forced its way against her teeth and she tensed with the effort. Sybil struggled and fought with her changing nature for one last piece of her humanity. Her voice rumbled as she found the will to say just one word.

"Run!"

***

Sybil had been pretty dang clear and Slim wasn't about to argue with a snake queen. "If you don't pick up them feet, I'm gonna throw you over my shoulder and carry you out of here."

"Damn it, I am moving as fast as I can!" Lady replied.

Slim knew better than to remark further on her speed. Tears were streaming down her face and she could barely keep her head facing forward, but she was moving. He'd count it as a win.

They turned down another corridor, torches casting their shadows against the gold walls. It looked just as every other corridor looked for the past twenty minutes. They still weren't any closer to getting out. The serpent-men had been terrifyingly effective in dispatching Zhao Jin's men, to a point that it even turned Slim's stomach and he'd seen some pretty nasty deaths. Now, he didn't have anything nice to say about the two men who died, but there wasn't a soul out there that deserved being torn to shreds while still screaming.

Everyone that had seen it would likely sleep with a touch of terror for the rest of their days. If Slim had known, he would have done his damndest to protect Lady from that fate.

That Sybil had commanded the violence only made it more awful. He loved the woman like a sister and he refused to believe she'd changed so much she'd condone such evil. She was a good woman, a princess at heart, someone who ached for the kindness of others and only gave her best.

What kind of beast had those monsters turned her into?

They turned down another corridor and drew to a halt. Lady bent over to prop her hands on her knees and sucked in deep, ragged breaths. They'd found another damn golden passage. At the end it split off in three directions, none looking more promising than the other. Either they were going in circles or Cibola had more streets than an eastern city. They were lost, and he had no idea what to do about it.

"Are you sure this is the way?" Lady said.

"Yes." Slim had no problem with lying. Never had. Now, if his luck would finally prove useful, they might actually get out of there. He'd followed his nose so far, and he was still alive. That had to count for something. "Come on, just a little further. Once we get into the daylight, we'll be free of these damn snakes."

"Slim, if we don't make it...,"

"Ah hell, darling, we don't got time for none of that." He swatted her behind and gave her shoulders a push. Lady stiffened and kept moving. When they got out of this mess, she'd more than likely fall apart, when things were safe and she could let everything finally come out. He just hoped when it happened, he'd keep it together enough not to fall apart right next to her. A man had to keep some dignity in front of the fairer sex.

They turned left at the end of the corridor, passed another flaming torch, and headed toward another forked corridor. Something had to give. He might lose a hand, but he never lost a game. It was time for him to win this one. At the next turn he yanked her to a stop, the soft sound of buzzing a fair warning of something ahead. "Quiet, listen," Slim said.

"It is them. It has to be," Lady said. "Have we gone full circle? Have we returned to the central room?"

He sure as hell hoped not. Dragging a hand across his brow, he slipped the other onto the handle of his pistol. It wouldn't do much good against a mob of monsters, but he didn't have anything else to work with. "Come on, let's back track."

She nodded and inched slowly back, her hand reaching toward his arm for support. A rustle behind them was the only warning before a fist swung out and caught Slim against his jaw. A grunt and curse accompanied the flash of white that blinded him for a moment as he struggled to regain his footing. Lady gasped and held tight to his arm, her voice only a slight quieter than a shout. "Juan, what the hell are you thinking?"

"Damned sorry, I thought you were one of them. You were hiding in those shadows. I honestly didn't think you could be anything else." Juan sounded contrite--mostly, but Slim figured the man felt good about getting in a strong swing. Slim would have to remember to return the favor.

"Well, do you know how to get out of here? We can't go forward," Lady said.

Juan stared at them, expressionless. Slim knew what that meant better than most. The man had something he was going after, and nothing was going to stop him from heading in that direction. Lady might not understand, but Slim couldn't fault the man. "You're headed back for Sybil."

"Yes," Juan said.

"Don't be a fool. She has made her choice to stay," Lady said.

Both men turned to her incredulously. Of everyone, Slim figured Lady would be the first to send in the search party for her friend. Had Sybil's actions destroyed the bond so quickly? "We can't leave her here, darling. You saw what kind of monsters she's with."

Lady sighed and propped her hands on her hips. "They are protecting what is theirs. We have only been caught between two factions. Believe me, Sybil is quite certain of what she is doing."

"How can you say that?" Juan growled, anger the first emotion he'd shown and it nearly overwhelmed his face. "You say she is your friend, yet you would abandon her to a fate worse than slavery or death."

Lady's eyes softened and face crumpled. "No. I would never wish something like that on her. She is the only woman to ever see me as more than a bit of silliness and money. She loved me well and I loved her in return. You cannot know how difficult it is for me to let her stay here. But did you not see the expression on her face when she first entered the hall? She was so happy. I have never seen such joy, Juan. It is as though she has finally found her home. Who are we to take her away from that?"

"No. That is not how it is. No one would choose this. This is evil. They have corrupted and mesmerized her. I will not let her die here. Not as long as I live, " Juan said.

Slim felt the warning in his head before he saw Lady twitch. Things were quickly getting out of hand and he needed to get control before the serpent-men showed up to break up the quarrel. Lady lifted her hand, pistol pointing at Juan and said, "I cannot let you do that."

"You are mad! Let me pass," Juan shouted and Slim slid his eyes to the ceiling. Madness was letting the enemy know exactly where you were. They'd be overrun by man-sized snakes in half-a-minute if he didn't do something. With a swift strike, he hit Juan with the butt of his pistol at the back of the head, sending the man into a crumpled mess on the floor.

Lady gawked at him and he shrugged. "I don't think you really wanted to shoot him. But now we're gonna have to drag him out of here. I'll do the heavy lifting, but you're gonna have to shoot at anything that moves." He bent over to grab Juan. This was not going to be an easy escape.

"Interesting. For two ghosts, the two of you look quite hearty. Tell me, was it our dear Sybil that brought you back from the dead?"

Lady and he swung around to find Mordecai MacHurdyGurdy standing a several feet down the corridor, his gun pointed at Lady's heart. Behind him, a second man stood, face ashen and eyes downcast. Slim had just about enough. He raised his own pistol and said, "What the hell do you think you're gonna do to us? If you shoot, you'll bring the whole herd of them on us." Slim figured with all the shouting and arguing that already occurred, they'd be overrun in due time.

"They may, but despite Sybil's outrageous transformation, I figure she has a touch of her sensibilities left. She won't destroy that which she has grown attached to. And that, my dear, appears to be you." The slimy grin directed at Lady made Slim eager to pull the trigger. It would make life so much easier if killing a man came naturally to him.

The constant buzz of the serpent-men intensified. They had to be close. Slim sent a cautious look behind. The ground vibrated and walls began to hum. Slim furrowed his brows. That was odd. It didn't sound like men approaching--more like a giant steam engine gaining speed.

Panic flashed in Mordecai's eyes and Slim followed his gaze up. The ceiling rippled, the walls shook and the floor moved like a great wave on a stormy ocean. Gold bent and folded, exposing the rock behind and a glimpse of something more. Long pipes ran behind the gold plates and from them came a sound so perfect in pitch it became a weapon that wrenched the walls apart. Dirt and stone fell from the ceiling, tumbling around their feet and filling the air with dust. They were bringing down the walls of their city with the sound of their voices.

Slim grabbed Lady and pushed her down the corridor. He shifted Juan securely onto his shoulders and prayed he had just enough strength to get them to safety. Lady luck, be good to him now, he needed all the help she could afford.

39

Pain drew a shout from his lips, a bitter cry of emotion he'd spent years avoiding. The air filled thick with dust and ground stone. Flecks of gold sparkled against the slightest light that emanated from a torch which somehow remained lit. Mordecai coughed and while attempting to bring his hand to wipe the dust from his eyes, realized his arms were pinned beneath an unmoving pile of boulders. Shifting only settled the weight more heavily onto his body. A twist to his head sent a sharp jolt down his shoulders and into his legs.

"Bernard?" There was no reply to his call. Mordecai tried to shift again, but found no purchase to push against, his legs weakened, his arms incapable of the slightest twitch. Whatever those monsters did to bring down the walls, it had been astonishingly effective. Mordecai anticipated an ambush, something violent and savage. He would never have expected something quite so clever.

They would have a significant amount of work to repair the damage, and for what? Extermination of a few human vermin? He snarled. What a waste. But there may be a shining light on this debacle. If his brother were alive and able to remove him from his trap, they may be able to abscond with several of the gold sheets which came crashing down amid the noise.

Noise. Strange, he no longer heard the buzzing that had infiltrated every corner of each corridor. Even before they'd witnessed the monsters in person, they'd heard the sound, quiet and constant. The silence was uncomfortable and on the verge of frightening. What would make a snake silent? Death for certain, but Mordecai imagined they had not all perished under their sonic attack. It was far more likely that they had hidden to wait for the rocks to settle.

If that were the case, they had little time to meander around the place. Once the serpents were back out, they would be after the trespassers again. Weakened and injured, Mordecai would be at a disadvantage.

"Bernard? Where are you brother? Tell me you can hear my voice." Again no response and Mordecai worried his brother was lost in the rock-fall. A rustle several feet away gave him hope and he called out again. "Bernard? Is that you?"

There was no reply and Mordecai grew angry. Damn his brother and his melancholy moods. He struggled again and still made no progress. The soft sound of metal clinking against metal came from only a foot away and Mordecai held his breath. The shadow of movement was not his brother. A flash of light against his lockets drew his eye. They swung in the air at a man's eye-level. Back and forth, they spun and swung, slow and quiet, with no clue to the identity of the man who held them.

"It appears you may have lost your prize, Mr. Kovacs."

Mordecai's lip curled. "Zhao Jin. I cannot say I am surprised. Those were your men that lost their lives in such a barbaric manner, were they not?"

Zhao Jin took another step forward and stared down at Mordecai, trapped against the floor and unable to stand to meet his rival. The Chinaman's face held none of the victorious righteousness expected in such a situation, but Mordecai knew the man well. They'd spent too many years besting the other to ever think of stopping. Mordecai had moved on, to find his glory elsewhere and was slightly amused when he'd found the Chinaman followed suit. But Zhao Jin now controlled an empire of wealth and successful businesses throughout the west, profiting off the vices of white men and the desperate needs of his own people. What weakness drove him to continue to pursue his obsession with thwarting the MacHurdyGurdys?

"They were good men that made a foolish miscalculation." Zhao Jin looked away, squinting into the dusty air. "It will be difficult to replace them."

Like cattle, Zhao Jin would no doubt find the fittest stock to replace them. Mordecai said, "Have you come to steal my fortune?"

"I had considered it, but that was before I saw how elaborately the opposition has staked their claim. It is far more enjoyable to see them destroy your hopes with no help from me. It is the ultimate failure, losing to one you had once thought you controlled. She has always been such a clever girl."

Mordecai hissed in a breath, angry at the man's simple joy. But the day was not yet done and the victory would still be his. "You planned this with Sybil from the beginning. But it will not work. I have come too far to be defeated by a girl and her freaks."

"Hardly. Kovocs, you are from the old country. You know as well as I that there are creatures older than time which hold sway over events that we could never conquer. All I knew about your lovely dancer was that she was a key to a great mystery, and now we see that mystery. Your gold cities are very real. You should take heart in that. But they are not meant for mankind. They never have been."

"You are a superstitious fool."

Zhao Jin chuckled and held out the lockets. "But I am alive and able to leave this place wiser than I entered." Then he turned and walked down the corridor.

Mordecai shouted for the man to return and free him from the boulders, but Zhao Jin did not look back. The last he saw was swish of a long black braid as it disappeared into the dark haze.

He was alone. He could not remember the last time he'd truly been alone. From the birth of his young brother, they'd been together. Through childhood, across oceans and into the wild lands of the American West, Mordecai had always known someone was there to hold him up should he fall. Should he survive and his brother not... the thought wrenched a hole into his chest.

Mordecai was nothing without his brother.

A cough beside him drew a searing sense of hope across the fear in his heart and Mordecai called out, "Bernard? Is that you? Are you alive?"

Rubble scattered and the cough intensified and then went silent. Another minute passed before the reply came, "Yes, I am alive."

"Thank the Lord and all the angels of heaven. I was worried brother. Can you move? I require your assistance, the rocks have covered me completely and I cannot escape. We must move quickly before the serpents return."

Bernard did not reply immediately, the raspy sound of his breathing indication of strain. But when he did answer, his voice was even and strong. "I can move. Only a small portion landed on me, it seems you were hit with the majority. Something hit my head and I believe I was unconscious for some time."

It would explain why he had not replied sooner. Mordecai wondered how much of his conversation with Zhao Jin his brother had caught, but it truly did not matter. Whatever issues they had to overcome could be handled when they left Cibola. "Then we must make quick work of this."

A soft buzz sounded in the distance and the hair at his nape rose. They were active again. Visions of the men shredded into bloody pieces in front of them made Mordecai anxious to leave. Should they be found in the corridors their fate would be no less violent. He prodded his brother again, "Quickly now. They will be here soon."

"Yes brother. I believe they will."

When Bernard still made no move to remove the rocks from his back, Mordecai took a sterner position. "What are you dawdling for? Get to your feet and free me." Mordecai struggled again, but still was unable to make a dent in his predicament, irritated that he could do nothing.

Bernard laughed heartily and Mordecai froze. The sound was carefree, light, and happy. It was not the laugh of a man eager to escape an oncoming threat. "Mordecai, my dear beloved brother, I have loved you well. Perhaps too well. I wonder, would you have done so much and fallen so far if I had left you the many years ago when I had first thought of it?"

"What do you mean first thought of it?"

"Did you know that mama made me promise to watch over you? I, the youngest brother, with the mind for gears and gadgets, was to watch over a madman."

"What? I am no madman. Bernard, do not be a fool. You

are letting the strike to your head addle your mind. We must leave now if we are to escape."

"Then I married Beatrice. You know, I truly thought we might have found happiness together. But I was too much a coward to take her far from you and your aspirations. She could have been happy. I really believe that. But not with you. Never with you."

"Damn it, Bernard. We will die if you do not move!"

"I believe she was right, Mordecai. You destroy everything you come in contact with. Even if you do not intend for it to happen."

The buzzing grew louder and Mordecai could hear the soft hiss of a few individuals in nearby corridors. So close. They would no doubt discover them in only a few moments. It did not have to be this way. It should not have been this way. This was his destiny. He was going to bring glory to the Kovacs. They would live as kings and want for nothing. "Please brother, you know I have loved you well."

"And I have loved you as well brother. But it is over. The MacHurdyGurdys will perform no more." Bernard sounded sad, but resolved and Mordecai wept at his response.

The light of the torch went out. Mordecai turned his head toward the corridor, listening, waiting. They were coming. He could hear their breathing, a subtle hiss, the soft rustle of skin against the ground. A stale stench hit his nostrils and the heaviness in the air told him they were surrounded by several bodies. Mordecai whimpered.

"I'm sorry," Bernard said.

A high pitched hiss rose around them, deafening and evil. Mordecai screamed until he could do so no longer.

***

He felt strangely despondent. Zhao Jin had never held relationships for longer than a few years, months for most. The rivalry with Mordecai Kovacs had spanned decades. It felt akin to losing a brother, or perhaps a close cousin. Or a beloved pet. Yes, a pet was a far more appropriate description.

Behind him, the air grew thick with dust as another chunk of wall gave way and fell to the ground, filling in the corridor where he'd only just left. Mordecai was now completely trapped within his city of gold. It was as lovely a tomb as the man could ever expect and deserve. It was sad, really. The Hungarian master of performance could have been so much more. Why even his elixir had been genius. Had he used it to conquer rather than as a side note to his hunt for ancient treasure he would have been close to acquiring the kind of wealth and success Zhao Jin had found. Tragic.

A heavy buzz filled his head and he quickened his step. Not out of danger yet, he did not have time to contemplate what could have been. The serpent-men were a serious threat and had proven their intention to hold onto their treasure. With Sybil at the helm, he expected they would have little sympathy for him. She was glorious, standing before the crowd of serpents, commanding their obedience, promising vengeance on those who threatened her people. She could have been a most valuable pawn, but Zhao Jin did not win his success by continuing foolishly along a path which held no promise of victory.

Zhao Jin knew when to throw in his cards.

The sound of the serpent-men intensified and Zhao Jin

turned back to catch a glimpse of the empty corridor. Nothing. They were not pursuing him. At least, not yet. Zhao Jin tightened his grip on Mordecai's lockets, but tossed aside the scrolls he'd kept for years. They gave him some clue to the structure of the labyrinthine tunnels but with the walls coming down and monsters on his heels, they'd become useless. The only thing that would guarantee his escape was luck and his own legs. He started to run.

A few moments later he snuck another look back and caught sight of movement. Fear invaded his calm, sending sweat across his brow and dryness to his mouth. The fate of his men might soon be his. His braid swung from side to side as he pounded over the gold floor, skipping over rockfalls and crevices that opened from the force of the serpent's song. His breath came heavy and thundered in his ears, blocking out the malevolent hissing coming from behind.

He turned a corner and blessed light spilled into view. The gaping entrance was only a short distance, nearly covered in boulders, a small section still stood open. He drove forward, intent on making it, desperate to be rid of his pursuers and greet the sun again. No wealth or clever plan would save him. All that stood between him and life was the speed of his stride.

It was nearly enough.

As he approached the entrance, a great roar sounded and the room shook, throwing him off his feet to the ground. Before him, the rocks crumbled to the ground, the light slowing snuffed out as they covered the man-sized hole. Zhao Jin shouted in horror, crying for fate to deal him another chance.

Would it really end like this?

A hand grabbed his elbow and Zhao Jin jerked in terror,

certain he'd met the serpent that would tear his skin from his bones, leaving him alive to watch as they wrenched apart his body. But blue eyes looked down at him, uncharacteristically strong and competent. The captain said something that Zhao Jin could not hear, but the man yanked him to his feet and pulled him the last few feet, into the light in time to avoid the final deluge of stone.

They sat, a foot from the entrance, chests heaving, hearts running like galloping horses, and minds not quite ready to understand what just happened. For several minutes, Zhao Jin just stared at the rock, thinking nothing, feeling little.

"That could have ended very badly," Captain Wright said.

Zhao Jin turned to look at the captain, his body covered in dust, eyes wide with the realization of how very close they'd come to death. Moments like this make a man. Weak men become strong and the strong realize their weaknesses.

"Have you ever considered a career in politics, Captain Wright? " Zhao Jin said.

"My father had hopes that I would. But after this fiasco, I doubt I will be able to do so. When Mr. Dewhurst is done with me, I will have no prospects, I might as well find a claim and try my luck at mining." The man looked forlorn, and disjointed. He cast an angry glare at Miss Dewhurst, standing several feet away, her own eyes glazed with shock. "I doubt I will be able to pry her away from the gambler, and I have lost all desire to do so. Her father is a damn fool if he thinks she is worth all this trouble. He's better off leaving her to this barbaric country."

Zhao Jin grinned. He may not be able to deliver the girl to Mr. Dewhurst, but he had plenty of other options. "Captain Wright, I believe I may have a proposition for you."

40

Had she done the right thing? Lady held back a torrent of tears, determined not to lose her mind beside Slim. The whole trek across the nation had been completely useless, ending in tragedy and bringing her nothing but pain and doubts. Now, beyond the mountain of rubble, her good friend was destined to live out her life as a queen and slave to creatures she never knew existed. The vengeance they sought led to nothing. The locket gone in an earthquake of sound.

"Slim, I don't know if…"

"Darlin', it's gonna be alright." Slim tightened his hold around her shoulders and grinned down at her like the devil he was. Lady tried to respond with a smile, but it didn't make its way to her eyes. So much had happened and she wasn't quite sure she'd ever be able to think of this day and sleep again.

A groan interrupted her thoughts and Lady looked down at Juan sprawled on the ground where Slim had dropped him. "We should put him somewhere more comfortable."

"Naw, he's good where he is. He's gonna be mad as hell when he wakes up anyway, might as well not waste the effort."

"Slim!" Lady said, slightly outraged, but felt her lips widen a bit. How the man kept a light view on the world despite the tragedy was a mystery to her. Did he lack any depth of feelings or was he simply an expert at hiding from the darkness?

"Fidelia." Eustace came to stand by her side. Dirt clung to every inch of him, the shiny brass buttons and cavalry emblems tarnished and cloth ragged. His eyes looked tired, but his jaw held the determined set that always sent a warning. He wasn't about to give up.

Lady let out an exhausted sigh. "Eustace, I'm not going to Denver."

"Fidelia, please listen."

"No." Lady shrugged off Slim's arms and swung around to face the captain. She'd had enough. Everything conspired to bring her to this end and for once she had to make a choice. The locket was gone. The quest for revenge pointless with Mordecai buried beneath the mountain. Not even the promise of gold existed anymore. Now it was time she made a choice on a direction. And if there was one thing she discovered through this entire campaign, it was she had become someone so different from the young, feckless twit that frequented the balls and social events of Boston that she could never return.

She was a woman with no name. It was time she went and discovered what it was. "I know that my father does not accept defeat. But that does not change my mind. You will have to return to him without me. He wants the daughter he once had. Well, I am not that girl. And I think we both know there is no future for us. I don't think you ever really believed we were meant to be married. Did you Eustace?"

"Us? I do not know. I am not convinced it matters. But

Fidelia, I--,"

"No, there is nothing you can say that will win this battle. I am staying in the west. I do not know what I will do. Find happiness I hope. But I belong here, not under my father's hand. Not under any man's hand." She cast a quick look at Slim, and he just smiled wide, his eyes shining with an odd humor. She'd never understand that man. But she'd far rather spend time with an irascible gambler than bow to a proper gentleman and gossip with tittering ladies.

"Lady damn it, I don't want you to come back with me," Eustace said with frustration. She stared at him, open mouthed and taken aback. "I have no interest in a marriage to you and if you do return with me your father will no doubt insist. It is far better that we announce your death. You have left enough wreckage across this territory that such a claim will be easily believed. By society, if not your father. And if he wants to find you, he can very well come looking himself."

"You do not want a marriage between us?"

"Of course not. You are hardly worth the trouble." He made the comment so matter of fact that Lady was not certain she should take offense. It did solve her dilemma rather well. But still, it was a bit insulting. She looked to the ground and heat rose to her cheeks.

A muffled cry brought her attention back to Eustace only to find him lying on the ground holding his nose and Slim shaking his hand and grimacing. "Damn man has a hard-ass face."

Lady's hand flew to cover her mouth as a sharp laugh burst forth before she could quell it. "Slim that was hardly necessary."

"I do believe, my lady, that your gentleman had every

right to strike Captain Wright. He does have a way of saying something insulting." Zhao Jin stepped forward and stood over Eustace, his manner oddly respectful.

Slim clenched his fists and Lady felt equally defensive. This man had pursued Sybil to the very end. Things might have ended very differently if he had not hounded her trail, pushing her to a destiny no one deserved. Lady said, "You should have died in there with the MacHurdyGurdys. You destroyed everything. What right do you have to survive?"

"Perhaps none. But that is not a question that is ever answered, my dear. We've all lost something this day. Don't think that your enemy has anything less to lose than you do. However, not everything was lost." Zhao Jin held up his hand to show two lockets hanging on thin chains, one with an eagle a second with a serpent. "I believe this belongs to you."

Lady held out her hand, her fingers shaking as the cool metal touched her skin. It had been so long. Had it really shined so brightly beneath the sun when she had it in Boston? Perhaps the western sun held a more intense light which made everything seem more brilliant. She'd left everything behind for this little bauble, her home, safety, security. It seemed a little thing to exchange for so much.

She looked down at Eustace, still writhing on the ground in pain and threw the locket on his chest. "Take this to my father please. I am sure he will be happy for its return and may be a little less cross at your incompetence." Lady turned away and put her hands on her hips and glared at Slim. "The last I checked, Miss Blackwood still had my steam wand. I would very much like to have it back."

He threw his head up and laughed. "Darlin, that sounds like a whole lotta fun." Slim bent down and grabbed Juan by the shirt and hauled him onto his shoulders. "I figure the MacHurdyGurdys won't be needin' their cart, so let's get a move on."

They settled Juan in the back of the cart, tucked between boxes of blue bottles. Slim grumbled about devil's piss, but Lady assured him they would dispose of the snake-oil salesman's inventory down the road. She wanted to leave that place behind. She would miss her friend terribly, but if nothing else, she would remember the smile the lovely dancer had on her lips as she stood with her people. It was not a life Lady would choose, but if it was happiness she wished for her friend, then she could not begrudge the woman her choice.

With the mules harnessed, Slim snapped the reins and the cart jolted into motion. Just as they crested a distant ridge, Lady looked back and Zhao Jin bowed his head. An uncomfortable feeling fell into her belly and she was certain it would not be the last time she encountered the dangerous Chinaman. She turned back toward the horizon, ready to take on a new adventure and perhaps find a new name.

Books by Erin Lausten:

Viator series:

Unexpected

Unforeseen

Shadows and Intrigue

Steampunk:

Cibola's Promise

Cibola's Revenge

Other:

Love Uncommon

Discover Erin Lausten titles at

http://erinlausten.com

Find Erin on the Web:

https://www.facebook.com/erinlausten

http://erinlausten.wordpress.com/

https://twitter.com/erinlausten

www.ingramcontent.com/pod-product-compliance
Lightning Source LLC
Chambersburg PA
CBHW050911250626
47155CB00001B/191

* 9 7 8 0 9 9 1 1 2 1 0 2 1 *